A Million Tiny Pieces

More by Nicole Edwards

The Alluring Indulgence Series
Kaleb
Zane
Travis
Holidays with the Walker Brothers
Ethan
Braydon
Sawyer
Brendon

The Club Destiny Series
Conviction
Temptation
Addicted
Seduction
Infatuation
Captivated
Devotion
Perception
Entrusted

The Dead Heat Ranch Series
Boots Optional
Betting on Grace

The Devil's Bend Series
Chasing Dreams
Vanishing Dreams

Writing as Timberlyn Scott
Unhinged
Unraveling
Chaos

A Million Tiny Pieces

Nicole Edwards

SL Independent Publishing, LLC
PO Box 806
Hutto, Texas 78634
www.slipublishing.com

A Million Tiny Pieces is a work of fiction. Names, characters, businesses, places, events and incidents either are the products of the author's imagination or used in a fictitious manner. Any resemblance to actual persons, living or dead, business establishments, events, or locales is entirely coincidental.

Cover Image: © zelfit – 123rf.com; © arsgera – 123rf.com
Cover Design: © Nicole Edwards Limited
Editing: Blue Otter Editing

ISBN: 978-1-939786-39-5

Dedication

To you, the reader.

I recently celebrated two years of writing full time and I have to say, without you, I wouldn't be here. I am truly blessed. Thank you.

Table of Contents

Prologue

End of August

AFTER THE SUDDEN death of his father three months ago, venture capitalist Phoenix Pierce has become the youngest team owner in NHL history. We are here to announce that, with the NHL board of governors' official approval, Phoenix's minority share in the Austin Arrows combined with his father's majority share now puts twenty-nine-year-old Pheonix at the helm of the Arrows organization.

When recently asked whether there would be changes to the team in the upcoming season, Phoenix advised that there had already been plans in the works prior to Sidney Pierce's death. Sid died suddenly from a heart attack back in May.

From what we've learned from Tarik Marx, the public relations spokesperson for the Arrows, Phoenix intends to implement those changes and move forward. He has assured us that the team is healthy and strong and looking forward to a solid year ahead.

Phoenix refused to comment further on the pending lawsuit from real estate mogul Damien Landry. According to our sources, prior to Sid's death, there was a rumor that the team was to be sold to Landry for a reported $280 million. Forbes.com recently valued the Arrows at $205 million, although the team has reported an estimated $10 million loss each year due to its continued decline in rankings.

We were told by a source close to Landry that Sid had backed out of the deal two months prior to his death; however, no documentation has been provided to support Landry's claim. Yet Landry refuses to go away quietly.

As Tarik made his way into the room, Phoenix hit the button on the remote to turn off the television, causing the darkened room to be cloaked in silence.

Dropping onto the arm of the sofa, Tarik forced a smile as he watched his boss stare at the blank TV screen. It was far too early in the morning to be drinking, but since neither of them had gone to sleep yet, it was fitting.

Twisting so that he could face Phoenix, Tarik held up his beer bottle. "You're in full control now. It might be bittersweet, but it's still a win."

"Bittersweet," Phoenix echoed, not bothering to look up from where he was slumped on the sofa as he blindly held up his beer bottle, clanking it with Tarik's. "Bitter-*fucking*-sweet."

»»»»»» ♥ «««««

MIA CANTRELL PROPPED her shoulder against the wall, staring out one of the floor-to-ceiling windows of the high-rise condominium she had recently purchased and moved into as she willed her fluttering heart to settle. Kings of Leon softly crooned through the speakers in her living room but did little to ease the tension that had been building for the last few days.

With her second cup of coffee warming her hands, she watched the sun peek over the Austin skyline laid out before her, trying to get a grip on herself. It would've been decidedly easier if she weren't pondering how her life had gone so wrong.

Wrong? No, wait. She tossed the word around in her mouth for a moment but didn't like the feel. Maybe *wrong* wasn't necessarily the appropriate word.

Touching her lips with the tips of her fingers, Mia realized she was smiling. Now that she thought about it, she was inclined to say that she was actually quite content for the first time in a very long time, even excited about her new lease on life. So maybe it was more accurate to use the word *different* in this case.

Yes … things were now so very *different.*

Moving her hand to her chest, she noticed her heart had finally stopped pounding, although she could still feel the anxious flutter in her tummy.

As soon as she had crawled into bed last night, she had realized how eager she was for this day to start. Naturally, that excitement had carried over into her dreams. Two hours ago, just as Mia had done in grade school when her mother would wake her on the first day of a new school year, she had practically leaped out of bed. But not from her mother's sweet words or her mother's gentle hand nudging her awake. Nope, Mia's alarm clock had belted out a noise — one that should be illegal in at least half the country — that got her moving today. It had had the same effect a fire alarm would have. She had thrown off the covers, shot upright out of her bed before she'd even realized she was awake.

As she'd learned that morning, it was vastly different getting ready these days than it had been for the last few years. When it wasn't necessary to get perfectly coifed, lacquered, and spit-shined, things were considerably easier. After drying her hair, Mia had realized that she didn't need to curl her long blonde locks. And when she went to put on her makeup, she recognized it was not necessary to accentuate her bright blue eyes with tons of eyeliner and mascara, either. She wasn't that girl anymore.

So, instead of spending an extra hour polishing herself to perfection, Mia had pulled her hair back into a ponytail, secured it in place with a brightly colored rubber band, applied a clear gloss to her lips, and pulled on her favorite outfit these days — jeans and an oversized, comfy T-shirt.

What was left was a much younger woman staring back at her, and she happened to like the new image. This new version of herself ... well, she seemed less confined, less restricted.

Significantly more confident.

As far as Mia was concerned, this was exactly where she was meant to be. And in a few minutes, she would be taking the next steps in jump-starting the rest of her life.

Her first day of college.

Chapter One

January

"GOOD MORNING, MR. Pierce," Phoenix's doorman, George, greeted, holding the glass door open to allow him to enter when he strolled up to the building.

Strolled. Right. Because *that* was what he was doing.

Waving him off briefly, Phoenix stopped inside the lobby to catch his breath. Folding himself over, he pressed his hands to his knees and sucked in oxygen as though the world were in short supply. His lungs happened to feel as though it really was.

These days, his hour-long morning runs were getting the best of him. During the particularly brutal form of hell that he'd put himself through today, Phoenix had finally convinced himself that this was another kind of self-punishment that he was allowing to get out of hand.

Not that he planned to do anything about that — he had merely accepted it.

"Good morning, George," Phoenix replied when he could form words and not sound like a vacuum hose stuck to a pillow.

George smiled down at him. "I didn't realize you were back in town, Mr. Pierce. Will you be here for a while?"

"Nope," he answered, the only word he could shove past his constricted lungs. Forcing his tired muscles to return him to his full height, he slapped the air fleetingly, an exhausted form of a wave, and headed toward the elevators that would take him to the penthouse.

"Good morning, Mr. Pierce," Roy, the elderly man who prided himself on manning the front desk, said cheerfully as he punched the up arrow on the wall to call the elevator. "The other elevator's on the fritz again. We've called a repairman, so hopefully it'll be back to normal in a bit."

Phoenix nodded in Roy's direction, still trying to preserve what oxygen he did have. He didn't really care about the status of the elevators, but he wasn't going to tell Roy that.

Instead, he walked in a circle on the gray travertine floor, hands on his hips, chest still rising and falling rapidly, trying to keep his muscles from locking up as he watched the numbers above the elevator doors, waiting for the next car to arrive. It had momentarily paused at seventeen and was down to two before he stopped pacing and stood stone still, hoping like hell his quads weren't going to do some sort of new trick and refuse to stretch enough to walk.

Phoenix dropped his gaze to the floor, allowing his hood to cover most of his face, not wanting to make eye contact with whomever was coming off the elevator. Today was not the day for a complete stranger to want to engage him in a conversation about hockey, something he found himself doing more and more often these days.

14

When the doors opened, the first thing he saw was a pair of running shoes. They were too small to belong to a man, so he allowed his gaze to travel north slowly.

Very slowly.

A pair of trim, jean-clad legs came into view. And as he continued his path upward, moving on to admire the small, curvy hips attached to the impressive legs, he found himself skipping over the oversized sweatshirt until he met a pair of crystal-blue eyes staring back at him. From this distance, those eyes seemed to glow — a brilliant turquoise, so clear, so pure that the color was probably only rivaled by that of the waters of the Caribbean.

"Excuse me," the succulent mouth attached to the beautiful face that held the bright blue eyes said.

Those words had Phoenix's gaze sliding back down to her lips. Perfect pink lips that he noticed were *not* forming a smile.

Well, hell.

Phoenix nodded his head — a nonverbal form of an apology — knowing there was no sense trying to force the words out through his abused lungs. Although now they were oxygen deficient because this woman had taken his breath away, not because he'd run nine miles.

Phoenix couldn't look away as she moved around him, giving him a wide berth, those striking blue eyes tracking his every move as though he might jump on her at the first possible chance.

Oh, jumping on her was definitely on his mind, but not in the way she was probably imagining. Phoenix was suddenly thinking about naked acrobatics, actually. Some slick, sweaty sex that resulted in those blue eyes piercing his as he made her come a hundred different ways, in a thousand different positions.

He realized he was still staring at her, watching the gentle sway of her sweet, heart-shaped ass encased in lucky fucking denim. He wanted to be her fucking jeans at that moment.

The elevator dinged, and Phoenix turned back to see the doors were beginning to close. He shoved his arm in to stop them, waving Roy off, not wanting to wait another five minutes for the damn thing to return. As he backed into the car, he watched the sexy blonde smile at George as they engaged in a short conversation.

He wanted to be George.

Okay, no. He did *not* fucking want to be George.

But Phoenix did have every intention of talking to George a little later. After all, he wanted to know who those blue eyes belonged to. Apparently the doorman knew her well enough to earn a sweet smile before the woman moved closer to the door.

When she stepped out onto the street and out of his line of sight, Phoenix punched in a code that would take him to the penthouse. As the elevator doors closed, effectively blocking any opportunity of seeing the woman who was responsible for kicking his heart rate back up into dangerous territory, he gave in to his exhaustion and allowed the wall to hold him up.

Jesus Christ, he was acting like a fucking teenage boy. He really needed to get a grip.

The elevator ride to the top floor was as painful as waiting for the damn thing on the first floor, and by the time the doors slid open, Phoenix was desperate to get out of the steel box. He stepped into the lavish entry that smelled oddly of cinnamon for reasons unbeknownst to him, and after crossing the vast space that separated his door from the elevator, he punched in another code to gain entry to his condo.

Nudging the door open a fraction of an inch, he glanced back over his shoulder, trying to locate the source of the smell. It had to be his mother's doing — that was the only logical explanation — but for the life of him, Phoenix had no idea what the hell it could be. The only thing he noticed — with the exception of all the Christmas decorations having finally been taken down — was a bowl of pinecones resting on the antique table that sat between the two sets of elevator doors.

Did pinecones smell like cinnamon? Surely not.

Realizing he truly didn't give a shit, Phoenix grabbed the knob and pushed open the front door to his condo.

When he stepped inside, he was breathing regularly and his heart was no longer trying to crack through a rib. He grabbed the stack of mail that was sitting on the table inside the door, the same place his bodyguard/public relations spokesman/assistant, Tarik Marx, put it every day.

The guy had too many fucking job titles, that was all there was to it.

As usual, Phoenix took a moment to flip through the envelopes, not finding any of them especially appealing. Tossing them back on the table, he glanced in the mirror hanging on the wall in front of him.

Damn. No wonder the blue-eyed woman had given him a wide berth as she'd come off the elevator. The black hoodie he wore covered most of his head, and the little bit of his face that was visible looked downright lethal. His black hair fell across his forehead, his green eyes glittered, probably from the pain and suffering of having pushed himself to his limits that morning. Hell, even his nose looked a little more crooked than normal. Scrubbing his hands over his jaw, he realized he needed to shave.

Hopefully, he'd had the decency to smile when she had been standing there, allowing him to eye fuck her first thing in the morning. Knowing him, he hadn't. He didn't smile much these days, mainly because it took too much fucking effort.

"Phoenix, is that you?"

"If it's not, then I may have to question who you let in here, Mother," Phoenix replied, snatching the mail up once more and flipping through it again. Anything to look busy.

His mother made it her job to visit him every morning. She had her own condo in the same building, yet she arrived at some point after Phoenix left for his daily run, and she stuck around for a short time after he got back, longer if he didn't appear to have anything to do. Not that he didn't love his mother, but despite what she thought, he really was busy.

Too busy.

"Don't you get smart with me, young man."

Smiling to himself, Phoenix didn't respond.

His mother must've known he had no retort, because she added, "Tarik should be here any minute."

"Yes, he should. And your point?" he asked, keeping his eyes on the envelopes and making his way through the vast, open area that served as a living room, dining room, and den.

His condo consisted of the entire thirty-sixth floor. Roughly five thousand square feet overlooking downtown Austin in a building he personally owned that housed three hundred and forty additional condominiums. It should've been enough space to keep him from having to run into someone every time he walked through the door, especially since he lived alone, but that never seemed to be the case.

With one eye still on his mail, Phoenix stepped into the commercial-grade kitchen, feeling his mother's eyes track him as he stopped in front of the refrigerator.

Sometimes Phoenix wished Tarik didn't feel the need to go down to the gym every morning while Phoenix went for his morning run. If the guy would come to work first thing, Phoenix would be spared this awkward daily confrontation with his mother. Most of the time, Phoenix was back before Tarik arrived, which meant he was left dealing with his mother alone.

Tossing the less-than-interesting envelopes onto the black granite counter for Tarik to deal with later, Phoenix flipped the hood off his head, opened the refrigerator, and grabbed two single bottles of orange juice. He had learned long ago that drinking out of the carton — although he was the only one drinking from it — was a surefire way to get his mother to ride his ass first thing in the morning.

Tarik's solution: individual bottles.

Phoenix couldn't argue with the man's logic. Wasn't the first time he'd thought Tarik was a genius, either.

As he tipped the first bottle to his lips, Phoenix glanced at his mother. As always, Ellen Pierce was dressed in one of her beloved black silk pantsuits, her short ebony hair, severely cut and board straight, resting on her shoulders. While Phoenix watched her, those observant green eyes, so similar to his own, raked over his face.

"Are you here to stay for a while?" Ellen asked.

Phoenix shook his head. "On the road this week."

His mother didn't respond immediately, simply watched him carefully. Studying him silently.

She was always trying to figure him out. He'd informed her on more than one occasion that it wasn't worth the time or effort. Half the time, he couldn't predict what he would do or say next; no sense in someone else trying to do the same.

In his defense, Phoenix was only unpredictable as long as it didn't have to do with business. When it came to his companies, he was as straightforward as he was shrewd and single-minded. At twenty-nine, he'd built an empire that couldn't be rivaled by many, and he didn't make any apologies for it, either. It hadn't come easy, but it had helped that his father — God rest his soul — had taught him everything he knew before he'd died nine months ago. A fresh wave of grief passed through him as he thought about his father. God, he missed him more with each day that passed.

But he'd had little time to grieve for the man who'd been his mentor and role model. After Sidney Pierce had suffered a heart attack that'd taken his life and stolen the person Phoenix had been closest to in the world, he'd been hard-pressed to move forward, to keep things going in the right direction, to prove to himself — as much as to his father — that he was worthy.

Now that Phoenix was the owner of the Austin Arrows, one of the youngest teams in the NHL, as well as Pierce Industries, a multi-million-dollar venture capitalist firm, he didn't have nearly as much time for erratic, impulsive behavior as he'd once had.

As he figured it, either the job was getting to him or he was getting old.

He refused to believe the latter.

Twisting the lid off the second bottle of juice, Phoenix said, "We'll have dinner next weekend. Will that work?"

The smile that formed on his mother's ageless features brightened her entire face. "I'd like that."

Draining the second bottle of juice, Phoenix tossed both bottles and the lids into the recycle bin, knowing Tarik would have his ass if he didn't. Sometimes he threw them in the trash solely to listen to him bitch and moan.

It was the little things that got Phoenix going in the morning.

"I've got to shower," he informed his mother. "Then I've got a meeting at the office."

Ellen nodded. She of all people knew he wasn't much of a morning person, and standing around waiting for him to spark a conversation before he'd had his first cup of coffee was like waiting for him to find any interest in a woman for more than one night.

It just didn't happen.

Leaving his mother in the living room, Phoenix escaped to his bedroom, locking the door behind him.

WITH HER SUNGLASSES shielding her face, Mia stepped out onto the sidewalk, the blustery January wind slapping her in the face, instantly freezing her nose. As she fought the overwhelming urge to turn around and sneak a peek at the guy she'd passed on her way out of the elevator, she gave a cursory glance around to see if any reporters were lurking nearby. She was happy to see that today must've been a big news day elsewhere, meaning she was alone.

Don't look back. Don't look back. Don't...

Luckily the windows on the building were reflective, and even if she attempted to look inside, it would be futile, so she shrugged off the notion. She reminded herself that she didn't have time for men, especially intimidating ones whose faces she couldn't even see thanks to the hood that had been covering his head.

As she passed the coffee shop next door, she wished she had a few minutes to go in and grab a coffee to go, but she knew she was going to be late if she didn't hurry. With winter break now over, she had learned last week that her professors had a renewed sense of vigor when it came to keeping things on track. She wondered how long that would last. Regardless, she didn't want to be late for class.

As she pulled her hood over her ears and ducked her head, Mia smiled to herself. Oh, how things had changed from a year ago. If all those people could see her now, battling the elements as she walked to school rather than having someone chauffeur her around… She knew that her story had probably been heard before: lonely young wife of a rich and powerful man finds herself kicked off the pedestal she'd once been put on, forced to move back into a regular routine, without the glitz and glamor that had been an integral part of her everyday life … blah, blah, blah.

But that's where her story began to differ.

At least she'd like to think that was the case.

First of all, no longer wed to the insufferable asshole, Mia had shunned her married name and taken back her maiden name. So that made her the *ex*-wife of a rich and powerful man — a crucial piece to the new puzzle that was her life.

Secondly, the glitz still seemed to be following her around, but only if the bright flash of cameras constantly in her face whenever she walked out of her building and on the street could be considered being in the limelight. For whatever reason, they wouldn't leave her alone. *They* being the paparazzi. It seemed there were still some people out to get the juicy dirt on one of the most newsworthy businessmen in the great state of Texas, Damien Landry. Mia's ex-husband.

And they were apparently accomplishing that goal by following her around. Well, except for today, which was a nice change of pace.

How much did you get in the divorce, Mia?

Are you upset that Damien has moved on?

Did you actually catch him in bed with another woman?

Can you tell us about the lawsuit, Mia?

What will you do now, Ms. Cantrell?

She'd heard all the questions a million times over, but every time she answered with the same: "I'm not married to him anymore. Not sure what he's doing."

They didn't listen. But she wasn't surprised.

Whatever floozy was hanging on Damien's arm at this point should have to deal with all of their constant harassment, not her. She'd relinquished that burden when Damien had come home from a business trip reeking of perfume. *Cheap* perfume, at that. Since Mia knew he hadn't taken to wearing it, she had assumed that it belonged to another woman. And truthfully, she knew Damien was not that stupid, which meant he'd wanted her to catch him. From the beginning, Mia had warned him that cheating was a deal breaker for her. He had called her bluff.

He had quickly learned that she wasn't bluffing.

And here she was — officially single as of two months ago, when her divorce was final — crossing one of the busy downtown Austin streets on her way to the University of Texas campus, wondering how she'd ended up, now twenty-four years old, back where she'd started.

Granted, Mia wasn't the same naïve young girl she'd been when she'd first met Damien. No, that twenty-year-old virgin had long since disappeared, in her place a woman who was much smarter, much less gullible.

At least she'd like to think so.

Being married to Damien might've robbed her of her innocence, made her into a woman she hadn't recognized for the last few years, but Mia couldn't blame him for everything. She'd been a willing participant. Right up to the moment she'd told him that she wanted a divorce — nine months ago.

Looking back on it now, Mia realized it hadn't been all that difficult to fall for an attractive, wealthy man like Damien. He was older, some would say far too old for a twenty-year-old girl who, at the time, had still been living at home with her mother while she plotted out the rest of her life. Unfortunately, she hadn't figured out until later — much, much later — how true that really was.

At twenty, Mia hadn't been even remotely old enough to handle being married to a man like Damien. Hell, even now she questioned whether she was mentally strong enough to deal with the emotional upheaval he was known for.

That never stopped her from trying to make it work. The way she saw it, marriage was supposed to be forever. Apparently, she and Damien hadn't been reading from the same book when it came to the sanctity of their wedding vows.

She had met Damien on a Friday night at a restaurant in downtown Austin where Mia had been having a celebratory dinner with some of her closest friends. They'd all been gearing up to start college in the fall after taking a year off to enjoy themselves, something Mia's mother had advised her against. But in her opinion, she'd needed a break. And when she'd met Damien, she'd been ready to grow up, ready to move on to the next phase of her life, school be damned.

At the time she'd started dating Damien, he'd been a young thirty-three, as he'd liked to tell it, thirteen years her senior. He was single, rich, and known for his playboy status. Not to mention, he'd avoided marriage on multiple occasions. Or so he'd proudly informed her.

According to him, he'd been waiting for the right woman. Her.

Rolling her eyes, Mia realized how silly that sounded thinking back on it now. Yes, she'd definitely been naïve and gullible at the time, hanging on every sweet word he'd told her until he'd charmed her right out of her panties two weeks after they'd met.

Although Mia hadn't intended to skip a large portion of young adulthood and move right into marriage, she'd found that Damien was a very persuasive man. He was handsome and charming, and she'd been putty in his hands from the very beginning. The media had made them out to be the perfect couple, and Mia had been too naïve to know what she was getting herself into. She'd been a beautiful blonde trophy — their words, not hers — on the arm of a man who was continuing to prove himself as a power player in the real estate market. At the time, Mia had felt like she was right up there on top of the world with him.

Her mother had warned her, but at the time, Mia had thought she was too overprotective, something Clarice Cantrell had been for most of Mia's life. So, Mia had done what any inexperienced twenty-year-old girl would do when faced with that sort of challenge: she'd ignored her mother's reasoning, insisting that she knew what she was doing.

Yeah, well, it wasn't the first time Mia would have to admit that she'd been wrong.

Unfortunately, her mother had been forced to sit back and watch her. And just as she'd predicted — something she'd later told Mia — Clarice had watched Mia climb, only to see her fall back down to earth, her broken heart in her hands.

However … what Mia's mother didn't understand was that her heart didn't have anything to do with it. Not in the end. Not after having endured all of the hardships living with Damien had brought her. No, what no one else seemed to realize was that Mia's heart had been shattered into a million tiny pieces long before that night.

Her marriage to the enigmatic man had proven to be the opposite of the fairy tale she'd thought it would be. She'd fallen in love with a blond-haired, blue-eyed charmer in the beginning, there was no doubt about that. But by the third year, Mia had watched her life crumble around her, and she'd known it wouldn't be long before she would have no choice but to get out. She'd decided at that time to reclaim her heart, even before she reclaimed her life.

Still, there were tiny fragments of her heart that she feared would never be put back in their original place, no matter how much she despised Damien, no matter how grateful she was to be able to move on.

Thankfully, Mia had planned for the worst, and she'd run fast and hard toward the infinitesimal light at the end of the tunnel in the end.

There had been a prenuptial agreement, but only because Mia had suggested it.

Seriously, the man was worth millions; it should've been Damien who had insisted on the legality. Nope, that'd been her.

She knew that was about the only reasonable thing she'd requested going into the relationship, and that was *after* her mother had broken down and cried. Mia was giving up her college years to be with a man who insisted that he be the one to take care of her, so, according to her mother, she should at least have something in writing to ensure she didn't have to start completely over.

She and Damien had worked out an agreement with the help of his ruthless lawyers so that she would get one million dollars for every birthday she spent married to the man — a mere crumb off the loaf of the Landry fortune — provided the marriage ended amicably. She'd spent three birthdays with him, would've been four had he not come home smelling like cheap perfume two weeks before her twenty-fourth birthday. Even knowing what she was giving up, Mia had left him the very next day with a suitcase packed full of her most beloved items and nothing else.

There had also been a clause that stated she would get an additional ten million if Damien cheated on her. At the time, Mia hadn't considered the fact that she would have to be able to *prove* the latter. Of course, the floozy on his arm these days wasn't admitting to anything, so she and Damien had agreed to disagree. It'd been easier on Mia just to let it all go and walk away. After all, cheating really was a deal breaker as far as she was concerned, and his admission had been enough for her. So, because she'd wanted out, she'd ended the marriage stating irreconcilable differences, and she'd walked away with three million dollars.

From the second the ink was dry on the divorce papers and the funds made it to her bank account, she'd become incredibly frugal with her money, despite her one and only splurge — the condo she now called home. Mia had plans, and that money would help her accomplish her goals and keep her from having to live with her mother until she could get to the point where she was financially stable. It would eventually be gone, and she didn't have any preconceived notions that she would ever make the kind of money that Damien did, nor would she run in the same circles that she had previously, but she was okay with that. She simply wanted to be happy, and for the first time in as long as she could remember, she was.

Which was how Mia had gotten to where she was now, walking up the steps on the UT campus, on her way to her first class of the day. She was probably a little too anxious, especially since she'd been doing this exact same thing for going on five months now, but she couldn't help herself. It'd been a long time since she'd had something like this to look forward to. But that was where she found herself. Looking forward to another day of school.

College.

How it had happened, she didn't know, but she'd been accepted at the University of Texas, and back in August, Mia had taken the necessary steps to move on with the rest of her life. Pursuing her degree in psychology, she was taking control of her destiny, no longer being led around by the nose, flaunted as a trophy, looked at as though she didn't have a brain cell in her head.

Each day seemed like her first day all over again, and she prayed the excitement didn't dwindle.

When Mia had first started school, she hadn't known what to expect because she'd been out of the loop for so long. Spending day and night with high society had left her with a detachment to the norm, which she'd longed to get back. She was glad to say that she had.

Opening the door to the building, Mia smiled to herself. Yep, this was a new day, another chance to keep moving forward, to live in the moment. What the future held, she didn't know. For now, she was going to embrace life. Embrace the woman she was becoming.

Chapter Two

PHOENIX MANAGED TO shave, shower, and dress in the same twenty minutes it took him every day, coming out of his bedroom a different man than when he'd ventured in. Gone were the hoodie, mesh shorts, and running shoes. In their place, a three-piece black Brioni suit, white shirt, Italian loafers, and the Bulgari watch his father had bought him for his last birthday. Today's tie was emerald green because it was the first one he'd touched when he'd hit the button on the ridiculous electric tie rack his mother had given him for Christmas one year.

"Mornin'," Tarik greeted, placing a cup of coffee on the kitchen table with a copy of today's paper as Phoenix made his way down the narrow hall.

Fixing the knot on his tie as he stopped in front of the glass-topped table, Phoenix remembered the question he had wanted to ask Tarik, but he decided to hold off. "Morning," he replied, doing his best to ignore the heated look he could feel coming from Tarik's golden eyes.

In an attempt to avoid his penetrating gaze, Phoenix paid more attention to the newspaper than he cared to while he sipped his coffee, purposely leaving Tarik standing there as he did every single morning.

It didn't matter how much Phoenix tried to ignore him, though, it never worked. First, Phoenix was acutely aware of Tarik's overwhelming presence in every possible way. And secondly, even when he tried to forget that he was there, Tarik made sure he couldn't.

Sparing Tarik a brief glance, Phoenix allowed his eyes to graze over all six foot three inches of the other man in those few seconds. He noted that Tarik was still wearing his workout clothes, the large muscles in his arms flexing as he gripped his cell phone tightly. Tarik's usually stylish hair was unkempt, sweat glistening near his ears, which meant he hadn't bothered to stop by his place to shower yet.

"Something wrong?" Phoenix questioned, turning to face Tarik fully, nodding his head to Tarik's casual wardrobe.

"Not yet. Why?" Tarik smirked.

Phoenix rolled his eyes and turned away. He despised the way Tarik enjoyed pushing his buttons, trying to make him want something he refused to want ever again. Phoenix was no longer in the market for a crazy, casual encounter. He'd had to grow up immensely in the last few years, even more so since his father had passed away nine months ago. Fact was, Phoenix didn't have time to incite the press with his nontraditional lifestyle. He'd made a vow to himself that he would move on, do things the right way going forward.

Which meant he had to make a firm decision regarding which direction he would swing when it came to his sexual desires. Although if he had his way, he wouldn't have to pick. He'd much prefer to have both, but that seemed to be frowned upon by society, and that was why Phoenix had opted to go the female route. No more threesomes, no more experimenting.

Only because it was the lesser of two evils.

"Breakfast?" Tarik asked in that gruff, no-nonsense tone that Phoenix had grown accustomed to over the years. "I can have something delivered in fifteen minutes."

"Not today," Phoenix told him, leaning over the table once more and skimming through the pages in front of him. Anything to keep from having to face Tarik directly.

Tarik had been working for the Austin Arrows as their public relations spokesperson for the last six years. However, Phoenix had known him longer than that. They'd met nearly eight years ago when Phoenix, while still in college, had been working with a local kids' club to establish a hockey program. Tarik had been employed as a security guard for a local firm while volunteering at the club on the side, spearheading the program from the club's side. In order to get the program up and functioning, the two of them had ended up working closely during that time. Over those few months, they'd also become friends.

Turned out that Tarik had a knack for dealing with people, articulating what was needed and why, something he'd shrugged off when Phoenix had tried to talk to him about it. So, when Phoenix's father had been looking for a new PR person a couple of years later, Phoenix had approached Tarik. Reluctant at first, Tarik had finally given in.

It wasn't until nearly a year after Tarik had started working for Sid that Phoenix had realized Tarik wasn't just Sid's PR liaison. Somewhere along the way, Tarik had morphed into Sid's assistant, as well as his head of security — aka his personal bodyguard. Although they'd agreed to publicly call him the head of public relations because it seemed less intimidating — at least according to Phoenix's mother.

When Sid had died, Phoenix hadn't questioned Tarik's contribution to the organization, fully intending to keep him on as public relations, although Tarik had merely transferred his commitments to Phoenix, becoming his assistant/public relations spokesman.

However, something he'd told Tarik from the beginning, Phoenix wasn't keen on having a bodyguard, even though Tarik had insisted on assuming that position along with the others, despite Phoenix's grumbling. Tarik's presence seemed to make Phoenix's mother happy, so he'd kept his arguments to a minimum.

Granted, Tarik's expertise had come in handy for Phoenix once in the last year, coincidentally a few months before Phoenix had taken the reins of the Austin Arrows organization. It didn't have anything to do with running a multi-million-dollar NHL team that had him needing personal security, however. No, regrettably for Phoenix, he'd ended up in bed with the wrong woman — and by wrong, he meant *married*. Unfortunately, he hadn't learned that she was married until after the fact. More accurately, he hadn't learned until *after* the psycho husband had come after him. Literally.

Once things had finally calmed down, a few weeks after the crazy bastard had shown up at the Arrows training facility, where Phoenix had been talking with his father, and pulled a gun on him, threatening his life, Phoenix had joked that Tarik had nothing to do, yet Phoenix's mother insisted that he continue to keep an eye on Phoenix.

Regardless of his duties, there was no doubt about it, Tarik knew Phoenix better than anyone else because they spent roughly ten hours a day working in close proximity to one another, sometimes longer. And when they weren't working, they still tended to hang out because they'd become close over the years.

Phoenix shook off the memories of what had happened between him and Tarik so long ago, refusing to go back there. He'd made his decision; it was high time he gave up on that shit once and for all.

Shoving the paper away, he glanced over at the man who was responsible for managing damn near everything in his life. Which meant he was also responsible for answering any questions Phoenix might have, despite how ludicrous they might sound. As far as Phoenix was concerned, he paid Tarik enough money for him to appreciate every damn word that came out of his mouth.

"You know of any new tenants who've moved into the building recently?" Phoenix probed, bringing his coffee cup to his lips.

"How recently?" Tarik questioned, leaning against the wall that partially separated the dining area from the living room, his feet crossed at the ankles, the bunching of his muscular thighs catching Phoenix's gaze briefly.

"Hell if I know," Phoenix grumbled, forcing his attention from the man's legs and eyeing Tarik's wardrobe selection instead.

As on most days after he strolled in from the gym, Tarik was wearing a black T-shirt that hugged his massive chest, black shorts, and black cross-trainers. Tarik's dark brown hair was short and in a wild state of disarray, more so now that Tarik had raked his hands through it. And the stubble on his face probably hadn't seen a razor in at least two days. In a word, the guy was intimidating.

However, it wouldn't be long before Tarik was dressed similar to Phoenix, an expensive suit covering the hard length of his impressive body. The only difference was that Tarik would likely have his Glock tucked beneath the jacket. Phoenix knew that Tarik was as dangerous as he was efficient.

They got along well.

Tarik stabbed a button on his phone, his eyes scanning the screen. Phoenix waited patiently, knowing he would have the answers he was looking for in less than...

"Mia Cantrell. Divorced. Blonde hair. Blue eyes. Twenty-four years of age. Moved into seventeen-oh-four on August eighteenth. Paid cash for the condo. She's the only one on the deed, and she's currently a full-time student at the University of Texas."

... a minute.

Sometimes it was a little creepy the kind of information Tarik could pull up at a moment's notice. Phoenix often wondered what Tarik would be capable of if he'd been given a week. Shit, Phoenix would probably know the name of this girl's third-grade teacher if that were the case.

"She's the last tenant who moved in here?" Phoenix asked, surprised.

"No, but she's the one you were eyeing in the lobby earlier."

Phoenix flipped Tarik off as he made his way to the kitchen. Damn man always knew everything that was going on, even when he shouldn't.

"Twenty-four, huh?" he asked, meeting Tarik's inquisitive gold eyes as he gripped his coffee cup.

"That's what it says."

"Well, at least I know she's too young for you," Phoenix told him, smirking.

"Fuck off," Tarik said in that dark, gravelly tone that made the ladies go crazy.

"I'd say thirty-eight is probably too old for a twenty-four-year-old," Phoenix said casually, taking another sip of coffee as he looked at Tarik over the rim of his cup.

Tarik laughed. "Good thing I'm only thirty-one, asshole."

Tossing back what was left of his cold coffee, Phoenix grinned. Riling Tarik up first thing in the morning was the highlight of his day. Hell, riling Tarik up at *any* time made for a damn good day.

Well, that was before he'd been graced with seeing crystal-clear blue eyes on the elevator. She was another highlight of Phoenix's day.

Now he had to figure out a way to meet her without looking like some kind of creepy stalker.

»»»»»» ♥ «««««

AMUSED, TARIK WATCHED Phoenix as he made his way across the kitchen, pleased when the other man went to fiddle with the coffee maker.

It was a habit that Phoenix probably didn't even realize he had, making his own coffee whenever they were alone together. Considering in recent months, Tarik had become, for all intents and purposes, Phoenix's assistant — although a rather loose interpretation of one, as far as Tarik was concerned — he should've been the one making the coffee, but he didn't bother to move from where he leaned against the wall.

He figured that preoccupying himself with other things was Phoenix's way of putting a little space between them whenever he felt they were getting too close. Not that they were particularly close right then, but for Phoenix, the fifteen feet that separated them was likely a little too close for comfort.

Tarik let his gaze follow Phoenix as he moved around the kitchen, fidgeting with the single cup coffee maker, then walking to the refrigerator to get... Hmmm. Interesting. Phoenix came back empty-handed and stared at his coffee mug, apparently doing his best not to look at him. Another telling sign that Phoenix was doing whatever was necessary to avoid him.

Like most mornings, Phoenix was pretending to be distracted, although Tarik figured he really was wrapped up in his thoughts, something that happened more often than not these days. Granted, it was generally business that was plaguing Phoenix, worrying about the next meeting, the next issue, the next purchase. The guy spent a ridiculous amount of time worrying about shit that he paid other people to worry about. As a venture capitalist, Phoenix's job was investing money in start-up companies, so Tarik could see how that might be a little stressful. Phoenix took a significant amount of risk with every move he made.

On top of that, Phoenix now managed the day-to-day of an NHL team whose previous losing record had fans hovering on the brink of abandoning ship. Until this year. This year had started off with a bang, the team currently on a winning streak that no one had predicted. It left Phoenix little time to deal with anything other than dealing with the press.

However, this morning, Phoenix's distraction seemed to be a woman, which, quite frankly, surprised the shit out of Tarik. That was very unlike him. So far out of the norm that Tarik had already made a mental note to dig in to who this woman was.

Tarik wouldn't have known except for the fact he'd gone down to the lobby to check on the elevator and had opted to take the stairs at the same time Phoenix had come in the building. Habit had him stopping halfway up to the second floor, keeping his eyes on Phoenix as the other man waited for the elevator. That was when he'd noticed Phoenix's intense reaction to the blonde who'd stepped into the lobby.

Honestly, whoever she was, she was already added to the rare list of women who sparked Phoenix's interest without her being naked. It wouldn't have surprised Tarik to have come back from the gym to find the blonde naked on the couch being plowed into the leather as Phoenix fucked her into oblivion. That was how the man worked. No strings. Rarely any lingering interest.

Never before had Phoenix asked about a tenant in the building, which was the first warning sign. And now, as Phoenix watched the coffee pour into his cup, Tarik figured he was pondering the details Tarik had supplied him with. Another rarity. At least to the point where Phoenix appeared distracted.

Okay, yes, Tarik had to admit as he glanced down at his phone once again, the woman was attractive. He'd seen her on the security cameras several times in the last few months since she'd moved in. Not to mention, a picture of her had been part of the details he'd pulled up from the complex's files. However, there was one thing that Tarik had noticed right away… She wasn't what Tarik would consider the type of woman Phoenix generally went after — appearing far too innocent for the likes of Phoenix.

That didn't mean Tarik couldn't see why the man was interested.

"Why'd you ask about Mia?" Tarik asked, both curious and wanting Phoenix to look at him.

"No reason," Phoenix answered with a shrug, not tearing his gaze from the coffee cup. "I think she was the woman I saw in the lobby this morning. I wanted to know if she was a tenant."

"Right," Tarik retorted sarcastically. "Because you generally inquire about random women in the lobby."

"Shut up," Phoenix bit out, his green eyes coming up to meet Tarik's briefly.

Tarik made sure to capture and hold Phoenix's gaze for a few seconds before releasing it. It was an intimidating factor Tarik used to keep people at arm's length. It worked on most people, generally. Not Phoenix. No, his boss wasn't intimidated by him in the least, and that made for some entertaining times between them, especially since Phoenix reacted to him in other ways. Ways he wasn't even sure Phoenix was aware of.

Tarik seemed to have a slightly different effect on Phoenix, but — except for that one night many months ago — Phoenix pretended otherwise. On the other hand, Phoenix affected Tarik like no one else — man or woman — that he'd ever known, and therein lay the problem.

Phoenix claimed to be straight these days, despite the man's admission to having been intimate with men in the past, to what degree, Phoenix had never elaborated on. Not in full detail, anyway. Then again, Phoenix had been drunk the night he'd rambled on to Tarik about his sexual preferences. Tarik suspected that declaration had been more wishful thinking than truth, though. Sure, Phoenix worshiped women and pretended that nothing had ever happened between the two of them, and because of the latter, Tarik almost believed it. Almost. Phoenix would need to work on hiding his physical reaction a little better if he expected Tarik to believe him entirely, though.

And like Phoenix, Tarik appreciated a beautiful woman and frequently indulged himself when the need arose. But *unlike* Phoenix, Tarik wasn't interested in hiding the other side of himself. From the time he was old enough to know what physical attraction was, Tarik had accepted the fact that he got a hard-on for both men and women.

"Are you ready to head to the office?" Tarik asked, pushing off the wall and walking to the bar that separated the enormous kitchen from the living and dining areas. He adjusted his semi-hard dick as he moved toward the incredibly handsome man who could make him hard purely by looking at him.

"Yeah," Phoenix said, sipping his coffee and watching Tarik. "You?"

"It's not about me, remember?" he responded caustically. "You're the boss. I just do what I'm told."

"Right," Phoenix said with a snort. "You're a lot of damn things, but obedient certainly isn't one of them."

No, obedience definitely wasn't in his repertoire of skills.

"Give me ten minutes to shower and change." Offering Phoenix a smirk, Tarik turned and headed out the front door. He'd need a cold shower before he was ready to face the rest of the day with Phoenix.

Chapter Three

TARIK TOOK THE stairs down to his floor rather than waiting for the elevator. He lived on the thirty-third floor, in a condo significantly smaller than the one Phoenix occupied. Had it not been for Ellen's insistence that Tarik remain close to Phoenix at all times, there would be no way he'd have lived in the same building as his boss. Hell, if Phoenix's mother had her way, Tarik would've lived in the same condo as Phoenix, but that was where Tarik had drawn the line. Working with him day in and day out was one thing; having to suffer living there and always being close to him was more than he could bear.

When he reached his floor, he pulled his key from his pocket and unlocked the door, letting it swing shut behind him as he headed for his bedroom. Flipping on the water in the shower, Tarik pulled off his shirt and walked back to the spare room he used as an office for the days he worked directly from home. Since they were always on the road, the space wasn't used much, but Tarik still appreciated not having to go to the office to get things done.

Grabbing his laptop from the small desk in the corner, he headed back to his room, kicking off his shoes as he walked. Tossing the laptop on the bed, he pushed his shorts and underwear down his hips and stepped out of them on his way to the shower. He was nothing if not efficient, and he knew not to keep Phoenix waiting for too long. Once the man was ready to go, if Tarik wasn't following behind him, he'd be left trying to catch up.

He mentally ran through Phoenix's agenda for the day while he scrubbed his body and his hair. As he washed his face, he considered shaving but then shrugged off the idea. He'd have no choice in a couple of days, or he'd look like a mountain man, but until then, he simply didn't have the energy to do it.

As it was, he wished there was more time in the day to get shit done. If he had his say in the matter, they'd forego the office and work from home until they had to catch a plane later that evening.

Tarik preferred to work out of the condo for many reasons. For one, it was a hell of a lot easier to keep an eye on Phoenix from there, and since that was a large part of his job description, Tarik took it very seriously. And two ... well, Tarik wasn't all that fond of people, to be honest, although, yes, admittedly, he did have a knack for talking to them. He merely preferred the solitude that came from working from home.

With the exception of Phoenix's mother, Ellen, Tarik seldom had to encounter anyone other than Phoenix on the days they handled things from either Phoenix's condo or Tarik's. On occasion, there would be a stray woman that Phoenix would invite up to his penthouse. But aside from hearing the noises coming from the guest bedroom — if he hadn't managed to sneak out in time — Tarik didn't usually have to deal with the woman. Unless, of course, Phoenix was in one of those moods where he would invite Tarik to join them. Another reason Tarik didn't believe Phoenix was entirely immune to him: since the first chance encounter nearly six years ago, Phoenix had been inviting Tarik into his sexual encounters quite often, although he still managed to keep his distance. Tarik sensed that Phoenix trusted him, felt safe including him in the sexual encounters that he wasn't looking to have exploited.

Not many people knew the extent of Phoenix's sexual desires. Threesomes were part of his regular routine or had been until recently. And for the last few years, the only other person Phoenix invited into the bedroom with one of his many conquests was Tarik. Not that he was complaining. A threesome was a threesome. The best of both worlds, as far as Tarik was concerned. However, there were plenty of times he wished that Phoenix would give in one more time to that side of himself he worked so damn hard to deny.

As much as Phoenix wanted to pretend he wasn't interested in threesomes *or men*, Tarik knew better. Well, maybe that last part was only partially true. As far as Tarik knew, Phoenix had never had intercourse with a man. Although they hadn't gone quite that far, what had happened between them that one night nearly eight months ago was proof that Phoenix was interested. It also wasn't all that Tarik wanted from Phoenix. But for now it was enough to keep him hopeful.

Tarik showered and dressed in record time, knowing not to keep Phoenix waiting too long or else his mood would take a turn for the worse. After grabbing the Glock from his bedside table, checking that the safety was on, Tarik tucked it into the waistband of his slacks, letting his jacket cover the piece. Grabbing his laptop, he then ventured into the kitchen and pilfered a power bar.

A second later, like clockwork, his front door opened and Phoenix stepped inside.

"You done primping yet? We've got shit to do."

Tarik laughed as he snatched his key off the bar and headed for the front door. Based on the lack of mug in his hands, Phoenix had already given up on the coffee, which could be a bad thing for everyone if the man didn't get enough caffeine. But he didn't have time to think about that, because Phoenix was already heading out the door, so Tarik fell into step behind him, shutting and locking the front door after they exited.

The elevator, as usual, took its own sweet fucking time getting to his floor, and when it finally arrived, Tarik moved inside ahead of Phoenix, hitting the button for the parking garage after entering a code that would bypass all other floors, even if someone called the elevator. It was one of the safety precautions they rarely used; however, it was one that Tarik had put in place not long after he'd been assigned to watch over Phoenix. It still amused him that the elevator was equipped with passcode overrides, but the damn thing took a decade to get from one floor to another.

Had it not been for the ruckus stirred up by the lawsuit currently pending against Phoenix, Tarik might've been a little less concerned about Phoenix's well-being. Although he didn't take it lightly, Tarik knew the attempt by the jealous husband had been an isolated incident. But the way shit seemed to be going these days, he couldn't be too careful. It was as though everyone wanted a piece of Phoenix at the moment. Hell, it was enough fending off the reporters camping out between the condo, the office, the training facility, as well as the Arrows Center. Yep, Phoenix was making headlines these days, and Tarik had been on guard more often than not these last few months.

"Run down my schedule for me," Phoenix said as they rode the elevator down to the parking garage.

"We're in Montreal on Tuesday, Tampa on Thursday, then back here Friday. You've got a charity ball Friday evening and a home game Saturday night."

Phoenix nodded, his eyes darting toward the numbers on the elevator. "Do I need to prepare anything for the charity event?"

"You're off the hook with this one. No speech for you this time."

"Anything else I should be worried about?" Phoenix asked.

"Not at this time, no." Tarik wasn't about to go into detail about the little things he was in the process of tracking. There was no sense in worrying Phoenix if he didn't have to. It was Tarik's job to ensure that the threats remained as far from Phoenix as possible.

"You coming with me?"

"To the ball?" Tarik questioned, glancing over at his boss. "You want me to?"

Phoenix didn't respond immediately, and Tarik waited, meeting those intense green eyes when they finally slid over to him.

"Yeah. I do."

Releasing the breath he hadn't realized he'd been holding, Tarik nodded. "Then I'll be there."

Chapter Four

"THANK YOU, GEORGE," Mia said to the older man who kindly held the door open for her when she arrived back at her condominium building at five o'clock.

"My pleasure, Ms. Cantrell. And how was class today?"

"Tiring," she admitted honestly. She was exhausted, and the only thing she had done for the majority of the day was sit in one classroom after another and review syllabi and expectations for the new semester's classes. Not exactly how she had anticipated the day going, but at least it was over.

"Do you go back tomorrow?" he inquired, looking as though he was trying to remember what day it was.

Mia stopped inside the door, mainly to get away from the paparazzi who were stalking outside the building, and then turned to face George to avoid being rude. "Nope. Like last semester, I've got Tuesdays off. I think I might sleep in tomorrow."

"Well, then I look forward to seeing you on Wednesday."

She smiled at George and hoisted her bag higher on her arm, thrusting her hands into the front pocket of her hoodie. As she normally did when she walked through the grand lobby of the building she now lived in, Mia admired the decor. It was still new to her, even all these months after she'd moved in, and she hadn't gotten bored with the interior just yet. There were always fresh flowers sitting at the reception desk and on the small tables in the seating areas scattered about. The grand staircase that led to the second floor, with its detailed wrought iron railing, drew her eyes. It seemed more like a fancy hotel lobby than what Mia would've expected in a condominium complex in downtown Austin, but she had learned to expect the unexpected. After all, having been married to Damien, she'd seen what money could buy.

Mia made her way to the elevator doors, pushing the up button and watching it light up. She'd been there long enough to know that taking the stairs would've probably taken less time than waiting for the elevator to arrive. And she lived on the seventeenth floor, so that was a little off-putting.

It would've also been a bit more cumbersome now that she was hefting a few required textbooks, however, still probably faster. She found that somewhat amusing considering how plush the lobby was. They could've spent a little less on fresh flowers and splurged for a set of elevators that were installed in this century at least. As it was, only one of the two usually worked. Based on a paper sign hanging on the other set of doors, it looked as though only one was working now.

As the doors opened, someone walked up beside her, but Mia refused to look over. She noticed the elevator car was empty, so she stepped on, hit the button for the seventeenth floor, and moved back out of the way, not stopping until her back hit the mirrored wall. The man who joined her punched in a code on the control panel, and the penthouse button lit up.

He took a step back and glanced over. Mia was doing her best to avoid his gaze, but something piqued her curiosity enough to have her eyes slowly traveling up his tall — he had to be at least six feet, maybe a couple of inches over — lean, well-dressed form. The suit was a nice touch. Expensive.

She expected to arrive at a middle-aged face, but what she saw when her gaze landed on his exquisitely chiseled features had her eyes immediately darting to the control panel once again.

Come on, elevator. This is ridiculous.

He smelled ridiculous.

Good ridiculous, but still ridiculous.

Damn it.

"Elevator's a little slow," the extremely attractive, much-younger-than-Mia-thought-he-would-be, well-dressed man said in a voice that was rich and dark and way too sexy.

"Dust collects faster," she replied absently, meeting his gaze briefly.

The brilliant smile he gifted her with had her gripping the metal bar that was currently pressing into her back. She swallowed hard and looked away.

Nope. Not going to happen.

Mia was not going to get distracted by a handsome face. Especially not one that belonged to a man whose suit cost more than her mother's mortgage in an area known for its million-dollar homes. Okay, maybe not that much, but perhaps close. She was done with men like that. Give her one like the guy she'd seen in the lobby that morning, wearing shorts and a hoodie, looking like he'd just gotten back from his morning jog. Someone a little less ... expensive. Yeah, she'd willingly take a guy like that. Not one who eyed her like she was next on his long list of playthings that he wanted to play with briefly and then toss out.

No, thank you.

The elevator dinged, and Mia unclenched her hands, forcing herself to relax.

Without saying a word, she stepped off, walking slowly in the hopes that the doors would shut before she reached her door. Last thing she needed was to let some stranger — no matter how well dressed he was — know where she lived.

The doors finally closed, and she made a mad dash for her front door, shoving the key in the lock and letting herself in. Once inside, she even peered out through the security hole to ensure the good-looking, expensive-suit-wearing, penthouse-living man hadn't decided to follow her.

Why would he?

Jeez.

Letting her bag drop to the floor at her feet, Mia glanced down at what she was wearing. Seriously? Why would that guy have any interest in her? She looked like she should be coming home to greet her mother after a long day at school.

High school.

Shaking her head, Mia made her way to the kitchen and straight to the refrigerator. She'd done her grocery shopping on Saturday, but as she stood there, she realized she'd been on a health kick that day. Which reminded her … wasn't one of her resolutions to start going to the gym?

Ignoring the wayward thought, Mia studied the contents of her refrigerator.

Right now, she simply wanted some Ben and Jerry's and a clean spoon. That would suffice for dinner.

Unfortunately, the only thing she had that could possibly curb her sweet tooth would be the frozen Greek yogurt she'd bought. And that, honestly, didn't sound appealing at all.

So, instead of trying to pretend ice cream would materialize if she thought about it hard enough, Mia grabbed an orange from the produce drawer and made her way to the trash can to peel it. That took a lot less time than she thought it would, and the next thing she knew, she was back in front of the freezer, once again looking for ice cream.

It still wasn't there.

She glanced at the clock and then back to the refrigerator.

Hmmm.

There may not be any ice cream hidden behind the frozen Healthy Choice TV dinners, but there was a coffee shop next door. They wouldn't have ice cream, but they would have some sort of coffee concoction that could easily make up for it.

Smiling at her brilliance, Mia grabbed her wallet, the paperback she'd bought at the bookstore conveniently located across the street from the building her last class was in, and her condo key from her bag before heading out. Thankfully, she didn't age much as she waited for the elevator this time. However, she found herself once again sharing the car with an incredibly attractive, albeit quite menacing-looking, man.

This one looked nothing like the guy in the suit she'd seen earlier — except for the fact that he, too, was wearing a suit — although he smelled just as good. How that was possible, she had no idea. With his shaggy dark hair that hung over his forehead and dark shadowed jaw, plus black suit and crisp white shirt, he held an air of danger. When his golden eyes raked over her, starting at her feet and working upward, a shiver raced down her spine, and she fought the urge to outwardly shiver, hoping he didn't notice how affected she was by his perusal.

Lord have mercy, she was doing it again. What was it with this building? It seemed each man she saw was as handsome, if not more so, than the first. And where the hell had they all come from? She'd lived there for nearly five months, and all of a sudden they'd decided to venture out? Doubtful.

Maybe there was a hot guy convention or something. Did they do that sort of thing there?

Doing her best to ignore him and his tantalizing scent, Mia focused on the numbers above the door, counting down in her head as each floor passed. A muted ding signaled the arrival to the first floor, and Mia had to hold on to the bar behind her to keep from bolting as soon as the doors opened.

"Ladies first," the man said kindly, although it sounded more like a growl. A deep, seductive rumble that made her toes curl.

Forcing her feet to move, Mia mumbled a polite thank you as she exited the elevator and made a beeline for the front doors. She could feel his eyes on her, and then she remembered what she was wearing. Definitely not her most flattering outfit.

You're not supposed to care, a little voice in her head said as she walked briskly toward the front doors of the building.

I don't, she mentally replied to the voice.

Yep, keep telling yourself that.

Mia grumbled, realizing she was now arguing with herself.

"Did you say something?"

Looking up, she noticed the tall, sexy stranger from the elevator was standing beside her as George held open the door for them both.

"No, sorry," she muttered softly and then turned, quickly heading away from the guy as fast as she could without looking too conspicuous. She hoped.

With a heavy sigh of relief, she stepped into the small coffee shop, inhaling the heavenly aroma. Mia could've lived in there if they'd let her. Just to wake up to that smell every single day.

The barista behind the counter greeted her with a tired smile, and she ordered quickly, familiar with the drill. She gave her name, handed over her credit card, and then stepped out of the way when the weary woman behind the counter returned it a second later.

While she waited with two other people for her drink to be made, Mia studied the patrons scattered throughout the relatively small space. There was an older man — probably in his sixties — sitting at a table with a laptop in front of him. He looked deep in thought as he stared at the screen, and Mia imagined him to be an author, deeply engrossed in the next best seller he was writing. A dark-haired woman sat in one of the more casual chairs, her legs crossed as she listened intently to the phone that was stuck to her ear, sipping her coffee as she nodded her head. In Mia's mind, the woman was talking to her sister, debating on where they would go for dinner next weekend. Then there was a young woman standing with a guy who Mia assumed was her boyfriend a few feet away, waiting patiently for their drinks.

The man making the coffee called out a name, and the couple moved forward, taking two cups and heading straight for the door. Mia moved closer to the wall, watching them leave hand in hand when she noticed another guy come in. Narrowing her eyes, she tried to get a better look at him in the dimly lit space, which wasn't easy to do with the sun's reflection off the building across the street silhouetting him from behind. As he moved closer, she realized he looked a lot like the guy from that morning in the lobby.

No, wait.

He looked *exactly* like the man from the lobby. He was even wearing the same black hoodie and shorts. Did he not have a job? Then again, maybe he ran twice a day. Since she wasn't much for exercise — hence the need for non-fat frozen Greek yogurt and Healthy Choice meals in her freezer — what did she know about the habits of runners? Hell, she couldn't even convince herself to go to the state-of-the-art gym in her building, opting to hang out in a coffee shop rather than ratchet up her pulse for the good of her heart.

Then again, looking at that guy was doing a damn fine job of raising her blood pressure.

He made his way to the counter, and the girl who had forced a smile at Mia when she had been in that spot a few minutes before beamed back at the man as though she'd recently awoken from a two-hour nap.

"Hey, Coach. What can I get ya?"

Coach? Really? That was his name? Well, it kind of explained the clothes.

Regardless, those two were clearly on a first-name basis, possibly more based on the way the woman caressed him from head to waist with her eyes as he stared back at her.

He rattled off his order, and that dark, seductive voice sounded eerily familiar. Like she'd heard it somewhere before. As she allowed her gaze to rake over him, hoping he didn't turn around and catch her staring, Mia tried to figure out if they'd actually spoken to one another.

No. There was no way. She'd seen him that morning, but he hadn't talked to her, had he?

"Mia!" the barista called as he pushed a plastic cup out onto the counter, tossing a paper-wrapped straw alongside it.

"Thank you," she called out to him, but he'd already moved on to help the next customer, which happened to be the man in the hoodie.

Not thinking, Mia unwrapped the straw and stuck it into the cup before bringing it to her lips. As she turned around to throw the paper in the trash, she practically ran right into Hot Hoodie Guy.

"Sorry," she muttered, stepping around him at the very last second, avoiding a full-body collision by mere centimeters.

Mia dodged looking directly at him, thankful the hood covered most of his head because she hoped it limited his ability to see the evidence of her embarrassment in her heated cheeks. With her head down, she darted toward one of the empty chairs in the corner near the windows at the front. That way she could read her book and watch the people on the street.

And, more importantly, keep her back to Hot Hoodie Guy.

Placing her cup on the small table, she opened her paperback and pretended to read what was on the page. She was actually peering over her shoulder at the hoodie guy, trying to get a better look at his face. He was talking to the man making the coffee, leaning on the counter casually as they spoke. The glass partition that separated the customer side of the counter from where they worked as well as the hood he had over his head were obscuring her view.

Not like it really mattered what he looked like anyway. Mia didn't have time to be admiring anyone, not even from afar. She had too much to focus on. School was keeping her plenty busy.

And on top of that, she didn't want to date anyone, so it didn't really make sense that she should get caught ogling some attractive runner who quite possibly lived in her building. She had a plan. And it definitely didn't consist of a relationship — casual or otherwise — anytime in the near future.

Chapter Five

"I HEAR YA, man," Phoenix told the guy behind the counter, although hearing him was about as far as Phoenix got, which was the same as most days he came into the coffee shop.

The name of the guy making his coffee was Brian, he knew that much. He was married with a kid. Other than that, Phoenix didn't really know him, but every time he came in the coffee shop, which was usually at least twice a day on the days he was in town, Brian greeted him as though they were long-lost friends. Somewhere along the way, they'd given him a nickname — Coach — and though it had stuck, Phoenix had never bothered to correct them on the fact that he technically wasn't a coach. Granted, his driver and a few others had adopted the nickname just to fuck with him, so he'd gotten used to it.

Today, Brian was telling a story about how his son had started kindergarten that year and wasn't all that keen on having to go back now that the holidays were over. Phoenix couldn't relate — he didn't have kids and wasn't around them at all — but he smiled and nodded, tacking on the appropriate encouraging phrase when necessary. He knew how to hold a conversation even when he knew little about the topic; he'd been doing it most of his life.

When Brian passed over the drink he had ordered, Phoenix walked back over to the register, dropping a five-dollar bill into the glass jar labeled *TIPS*. It wasn't that he was feeling overly generous as much as he was trying to get a look at Mia.

Yes, Mia.

He knew her name thanks to the information Tarik had provided him that morning, but now he had another reason to know her name. A reason that was significantly less stalkerish than having someone pull up her personal information without her knowing. Brian had conveniently announced her order as Phoenix had been paying for his own, which meant he now had a suitable excuse. Running into her for the third time in one day seemed almost ... too good to be true.

During their trip up to the seventeenth floor, Phoenix had wondered whether or not she had realized he was the same guy from their run-in in the lobby that morning. He didn't think so, based on the way she was darting looks at him. And that intrigued him for reasons he didn't quite understand. Not that she had given either "him" an approving look, but Phoenix had to wonder why she'd gone out of her way to avoid looking at him both times. Hell, he'd laughed when she'd practically launched herself out of the elevator when they'd finally reached her floor.

Mia.

He had to admit, even her name gave him a hard-on.

Deciding he wasn't ready to allow this opportunity to pass him by, he took his coffee over to the corner she was sitting in and dropped down into one of the chairs behind her. She looked intently focused on the novel in her hand, and he would've believed that she was engrossed in the story, but even he noticed that the thing was upside down. Not that he intended to say anything. She was too damn cute, and he liked the idea that she was possibly trying to avoid him.

Her cell phone rang, and Phoenix sat back, waiting. He still wasn't sure whether he would interrupt her or not, but he was seriously considering it. He'd never been the kind to let an opportunity pass him by.

"Hey," she greeted the caller.

Phoenix immediately liked her voice. Soft and a little raspy. Not the high-pitched, saccharine type he'd heard far too many times.

"Yeah, it was good. Kinda boring."

He wished he could hear what the caller was asking her. He had an overwhelming urge to know what she was talking about.

"No."

Pause.

"Yes."

Pause.

"Tomorrow night? Are you—?"

Pause. (Obviously interrupted by the person on the other end of the line.)

"Hockey? Really? I don't know, Alex..."

Well, hell. Phoenix frowned. *Alex?* Seriously? She was talking to some guy? About hockey? That would be just his fucking luck.

"Got it. Yep, I'm in."

Pause.

"What *about* Friday?"

Pause.

"Aww, crap. I totally forgot about that. Yes, you can pick me up."

Pause.

"Yes," she said, chuckling. "Friday night. It's a date."

Pause.

"Okay. See you tomorrow night."

A strange wave of disappointment flooded him as he watched Mia tuck her phone into the pocket of her sweatshirt. She had a date with *Alex.* Two dates, it sounded like. He found it odd that it bothered him. He'd really have to give that some thought. It wasn't like he knew the girl, so why the hell should he care if she were going out on a date?

Shit.

Getting to his feet, Phoenix grabbed his coffee and headed for the door. As he pushed it open, he glanced back at Mia. She was looking at her book again; this time it was right side up in her hands, and she didn't seem to be paying any attention to him.

Seriously. He was going to have to figure out what the hell his problem was, because he didn't chase women. Ever. He didn't have to. There were too many lining up to spend a night in his bed. And that wasn't ego talking, either. Sometimes it was irritating as fuck because … well, because sometimes it was just irritating.

Maybe he would like the chase; he didn't really know. If and when it ever happened, he'd know.

Stopping at the door, he dared one more look at her. This time, her arctic-blue eyes slowly slid up to meet his. God, she was beautiful. In a sweet, innocent sort of way. He offered a small smile, a barely there tilt of the corner of his lips, and he felt a jolt of heat hit him square in the gut when her cheeks turned a fascinating shade of pink right before her eyes darted back to her book.

As he headed out of the coffee shop, his cell phone chirped, signaling a message. He pulled it from his pocket and glanced at the screen. A text from Tarik.

The blonde girl's cute. Not your type, but cute.

Phoenix smiled and typed a quick response. *Not your type, either. Hands off.*

Not surprisingly, he received one more message before he reached the elevator to take him to the penthouse.

No promises.

»»●««

When Phoenix walked into his condominium a few minutes later, after waiting for the damn elevator for longer than he'd cared to, he was grateful to be alone. Tarik wasn't there, and surprisingly, Phoenix's mother wasn't there to greet him, either.

Maybe that sounded strange, but it was necessary to understand his life to realize why he'd prefer to be met with silence than someone asking him questions about his day. Living alone, it should've been a no-brainer that he would have time to himself, but strangely, it seemed people were always traipsing in and out his door, never offering him a moment's peace.

Case in point, when Phoenix had come home earlier, Tarik had been in Phoenix's home office, his laptop sitting on the desk in front of him and the phone to his ear. It wasn't unusual to find Tarik in his condo at any time of the day. When it came to business, Tarik took his job very seriously. Oddly, Tarik was about the only person Phoenix could tolerate in large doses.

Tarik had greeted him with a gruff look, which, now that he thought about it, really was the guy's one and only expression, but no words. That had lasted all of about a minute before Phoenix had headed for his bedroom, changed out of his suit and back into street clothes — which so happened to be the same as his running clothes, his going-to-the-store clothes, and … hell, they were pretty much the only thing he wore when he didn't have to be somewhere important — then darted back downstairs. Initially, he had gone in search of coffee, but seeing Mia had briefly changed his reason for being there.

Dropping down onto the leather sofa that sat in the center of his living room, facing the wall of windows in a room that he spent little time in — there wasn't a television, therefore he didn't have much use for the room — Phoenix contemplated his little hang-up on the blonde-haired, crystal-blue-eyed woman who lived in his building. She was hot, there was absolutely no doubt about that. But seeing a sexy woman didn't generally spike his pulse the way she did, or send him into some sort of fixation. Clearly this woman had something … something incredibly appealing.

Was it the look of innocence in her blue eyes? Possible.

That or it really was the chase.

He genuinely liked the fact that she'd looked right past him, strange as it sounded. Three times in one day, in fact. Although, again, he really didn't think she'd figured out that he was the same guy she'd seen that morning and again on the elevator. *That* he found interesting as well. Then again, maybe she didn't care.

He grabbed his laptop from the side table and flipped open the lid, leaving his coffee to sit untouched. He pulled up his web browser and typed in Mia's name. Maybe, just maybe, there was something he could find on her. Why, he didn't know, but he figured it was worth a shot.

Two seconds later, he slammed the lid closed.

No. He was not going to go there. If there was something to learn about her on the Internet, he didn't want to know. He'd had enough of those types. If she was worth getting to know, he was going to get to know her on a personal basis, no Internet involved.

Staring out at the Austin skyline as the orange and pink from the setting sun slowly settled into darkness, Phoenix realized he had a problem. This was not how he usually managed things. He didn't get a glimpse of a woman in an elevator and become some slobbering idiot who wanted to know more about her. That was fucking absurd.

Nor did he think about Tarik with that very same woman, both of them naked and writhing in the throes of an intense orgasm. Yet his mind had drifted there more than once that day, the mental images playing like a slide show through his head, one erotic scene after another. Now, as he imagined the two of them, Phoenix superimposed himself into those encounters. He could practically feel the hardwood biting into his knees as he knelt before Tarik, sucking his cock deep into his throat while Mia kissed Tarik, watching everything he was doing while Tarik fingered her pretty little pussy.

Son of a bitch.

Shaking off the thought, Phoenix focused on the buildings outside the window.

What the *fuck* was he doing? He was supposed to be thinking about Mia. *Only* Mia. Not entertaining thoughts of threesomes or … *or* pleasuring Tarik. He'd never fixated on interactions with men before. Well, nothing more than a couple of hand jobs and some rather exquisite blow jobs during a time in his life when he'd been trying to identify some of those lingering desires. Sure, he might've sated some curiosity, and maybe he'd gotten off to gay porn a time or two, but that didn't mean… He wasn't…

Fuck.

He was. He so was.

Tossing the laptop onto the cushion beside him, he grabbed his cell phone. Pulling up his contact list, Phoenix held his finger over the button that would dial the number, one of the few numbers he had that weren't business related. It would take the push of a button, and Phoenix would prove that he preferred women over men any day. He enjoyed women.

Damn it.

He hesitated, staring down at the phone.

"Son of a motherfucking bitch," he growled, backing out of the screen and tossing his phone on the cushion beside his laptop.

Calling any woman other than Mia — which wasn't even a possibility because he didn't have her phone number — wasn't going to do a damn thing to curb the ache that had taken up residence in his balls since that brief run-in that morning. Even if a woman came over and gave him exactly what he needed, he would still go to bed longing for something he couldn't have. And what fucking good would that do him?

An hour of mindless sex with a woman who didn't want anything from him wasn't going to help. It never had before. Even if his dick thought otherwise.

But he needed to do something. Whatever he had to do in order to stop thinking about the woman who'd been on his mind for no other reason than she had captured his interest that morning in an elevator.

Fuck.

Mindlessly, he stared out the window and slid his hand down into his shorts, gripping the steely length of his erection, stroking ever so slowly. His mind drifted back to Mia, to the way she'd looked that morning when she had stepped off the elevator. Those tight jeans that hugged a perfect little heart-shaped ass, the trim legs that would feel like heaven wrapped around his hips while he thrust into her.

Jerking his cock more firmly, Phoenix let his head drop back against the cushions, closing his eyes and imagining those soft pink lips wrapped around the head of his dick while he fucked her mouth, his fingers twining into the silky strands of her blonde hair.

The fantasy morphed into something far more erotic, and Phoenix imagined Tarik behind him, driving his thick cock deep into Phoenix's ass while Mia continued to suck him, her sweet lips caressing the head of his dick.

Oh, God.

»»»»»♥«««««

THE FIRST THING Tarik noticed when he walked into the darkened penthouse was that Phoenix was home. He could see the back of his head as he sat on the couch facing the wall of windows and the illuminated Austin skyline beyond.

Closing the door as quietly as he could, Tarik moved closer. He had come to give Phoenix shit about the blonde woman and then see if he wanted to grab dinner, but he was pulled up short when he heard Phoenix speak.

"Oh, fuck yes," Phoenix said breathlessly.

Tarik narrowed his eyes, moving closer still, trying to see if someone else was there. That was when he realized Phoenix was jacking off on the couch, no one else in the room. That was new. Tarik's dick stood up and took notice immediately, and he was tempted to pull out his cock and stroke it along with Phoenix, but he managed to refrain, mesmerized by the sounds coming from the couch, the soft moans, the low growls.

"Fuck. Oh, yeah. That's good." Phoenix groaned, jacking his cock harder, faster, his head leaned back against the sofa cushions, eyes closed. "Tarik. Mia. Oh, fuck."

Tarik nearly swallowed his own damn tongue when he heard Phoenix say his name. It didn't surprise him that Phoenix had called out for Mia. He was fixated on the pretty little blonde for whatever reason. But for Phoenix to say *his* name... Did that mean...?

Phoenix groaned, followed by, "Oh, fuck. I'm gonna come. Take all of me."

Tarik wished like hell he knew what fantasy was playing out in Phoenix's head right then. Was he thinking about Tarik positioned between his legs, sucking his dick? Or was he thinking about Mia riding his hard cock while Tarik fucked her ass?

It didn't matter. Whatever Phoenix was thinking about included him.

"Coming," Phoenix moaned, his arm stilling, his head rolling side to side on the couch cushion.

Not wanting to interrupt or to let Phoenix know that he'd been watching, Tarik slipped back down the hall to the front door. He exited silently and then headed for the stairs.

Once inside his own condo, Tarik maneuvered through the darkened living room, and without an ounce of finesse, he yanked open his pants, shoving them to his thighs as he plopped onto his couch and took his dick in his hand. Closing his eyes, he pictured Phoenix on his knees, his sweet lips wrapped around the head of his cock, sucking him hard and fast while Mia straddled Tarik's face. He wanted to taste her, to lick her pussy until she was screaming and begging for more.

He had no idea why he'd become infatuated with her after only seeing her once in the elevator, but he had. Maybe it was the idea of Phoenix wanting her; maybe she had some sort of voodoo. Shit, he didn't fucking know, but he couldn't stop thinking about her any more than Phoenix could.

Tarik stroked himself faster, cupping his balls with his free hand, fondling them aggressively while he jacked himself. He didn't stop until the pleasure accosted him and the only thing he could do was come in his fucking hand.

And as he'd suspected, when he opened his eyes, bringing himself back to reality slowly, Tarik was left with an even stronger desire and a still-hard dick.

But at least one good thing had come from tonight… Tarik now knew that Phoenix *did* think about him. No matter what he wanted Tarik to believe.

Chapter Six

"I STILL CAN'T believe you cooked that all by yourself," Mia teased Alex as she helped to remove the dishes from the table.

Alex's husband, Johnathan, shot Mia a knowing look. One that said he had given his wife a hand with the fantastic meal they'd recently devoured.

"Never doubt my abilities," Alex replied readily. "Now, shoo," she told Johnathan. "You've got a game to watch. We'll take care of the dishes."

Johnathan planted a quick kiss on Alex's lips before heading back to the room he'd been in when Mia had arrived a good half hour before.

"Did he just leave the other guys in there while he ate dinner?"

"Yeah," Alex said. "They're used to it. I've offered to cook for them before, but they refuse every time. So I quit asking."

"I guess the game's more important?" Mia carried the last of the plates to the sink, where Alex had flipped on the water and was rinsing the dishes.

"Of course. I think my husband would bypass dinner if he didn't think I'd be upset with him."

"Would you?" Mia asked.

"No. But don't tell him I said that. I like having dinner with him."

Mia laughed as she opened the dishwasher and began loading dishes.

The only thing Mia had walked away with from her divorce from Damien, other than the three mil and her personal effects in one single suitcase, was her friendship with Alexandra Henry, better known as Alex. She had met Alex after Mia and Damien were married. Mia had been attending a charity event, bored out of her skull, when Damien had left her sitting at a table alone so he could converse with everyone else in the room. *Everyone* but her. Alex had joined Mia at the table, and they'd hit it off with shots of Patron. Alex's idea. They'd forged a solid friendship, and over the next few months, and the years that followed, they had become best friends. Alex had even stuck with her during the divorce, proving that their friendship wasn't based on her marriage to Damien. Mia was grateful to Alex for that. At this point in her life, she certainly needed a friend.

Until the last four or five months, they'd usually managed to get together at least once a week for girls' night. Since school had started, Mia had found herself busier than usual between that and trying to keep her mother convinced that she was doing fine now that she was single and living on her own. Not that Clarice believed her, but Mia certainly tried her best to assure her.

Mia missed spending time with Alex, though, even when that time consisted of drinking wine on the living room sofa while men acted like teenage boys in the room beyond.

"His love for hockey really is his only flaw," Alex stated with a giggle as Mia glanced over her shoulder toward the room where Johnathan and a few of his friends had locked themselves in order to watch tonight's Austin Arrows game.

Mia knew absolutely nothing about hockey. Nor did she even care for it. That was probably due to Damien's complete and utter fixation on the sport for the last year. Ever since he'd gotten it in his head that he needed to own a hockey team, one of his many obsessions, things had started to go downhill.

"I hope for your sake that they win tonight," Mia said as a round of boos erupted from the back room. Closing the dishwasher, Mia grabbed a hand towel and wiped her hands.

"Me, too. Things get rather interesting when they win."

Mia didn't need Alex to elaborate to know what she was referring to. It was no secret that Mia's best friend had a very exciting sex life. It wasn't something they had in common, because, of course, Mia had been married to Damien. Not that she knew what interesting sex should be like per se, but she got the sneaking suspicion that it was more than she'd ever experienced with her ex-husband.

"I don't even want to know what that means," Mia said, laughing as she headed into the living room.

"Of course you do," Alex teased. "Sit. I'll be right back."

Mia made herself comfortable on the plush, chocolate-suede sectional that sectioned off the formal living area from the rest of Alex's exquisitely detailed house. Maybe *mansion* would be a better description. The house was two stories, ten bedrooms, twelve bathrooms, and if she recalled correctly, somewhere around twelve thousand square feet. It was ginormous, even more so considering Alex and Johnathan were the only two who lived there aside from Kevin, their live-in house butler.

Alex returned a minute later with two glasses. She set them on the table, flipped on two of the lamps at the ends of the sofa before disappearing again. Mia watched her friend as she moved about.

"I'm so glad you're here," Alex stated when she returned with a bottle of wine, patting Mia's hand before dropping onto the sofa and pouring two glasses and handing Mia one.

Mia took a sip, her eyes following Alex as she once again jumped up and headed toward the kitchen.

"Where're you going?" Mia asked, not bothering to get up and follow her friend. She was too comfortable where she was, and knowing Alex, she wouldn't settle down for at least another five minutes.

"I forgot something. Don't move."

"Don't worry, I won't."

An eruption of shouts and clapping echoed from the back room, and Mia glanced over her shoulder toward the closed double doors in time to see one of them swing open as Johnathan stepped into view. "Where's Alex?"

Mia pointed toward the kitchen as she watched him stalk across the room. He looked so unlike the man she was used to seeing. Although scrubs were a suitable outfit for him, she was used to seeing him dressed in slacks and a tailored shirt that Alex usually picked out for him. Today he was wearing an Austin Arrows sweatshirt and jeans, a baseball cap on backward, making him look a decade younger than he actually was.

"Hey. Who's winning?" she asked.

"The Arrows," he said excitedly as he passed through the living room. "They're on fire this season."

Nodding her head as though she actually knew why that was, Mia watched Johnathan disappear into the kitchen. A second later, Alex returned, laughing as she ran toward Mia.

"That man is insatiable," Alex declared as she retrieved her glass from the table and flopped back down onto the sofa at the opposite end from where Mia was sitting. "So, tell me, how's school?"

"Good," Mia told her friend. "This is the first full week back since winter break, so it's like starting all over again. I don't know what to do with the extra time I have right now."

"Maybe you should relax a little. You've been going nonstop for months now. You deserve a little break. Speaking of break, how was the Colorado trip?"

Alex was referring to Mia's Christmas vacation with her mother, something they'd started a couple of years after her father had died. It was a way for the two of them to get away and spend time together without normal life intruding. "It was ... interesting."

"Uh-oh. What does that mean?"

Mia sipped her wine and then considered her next words carefully. "I think my mother is seeing someone."

Alex's perfectly plucked, dark eyebrows shot skyward, and a huge smile broke across her face. "Really? Is it serious?"

"I don't know. I think she's scared to tell me."

"Did you ask her?"

"Sort of," Mia explained. "I was trying to be nonchalant about it. I don't think she got the hint. That or she didn't want to talk about him."

"What makes you think so?"

"She spent a significant amount of time texting on her phone. And I could tell it wasn't work-related because she was usually smiling like a schoolgirl."

"Are you happy for her?" Alex asked.

Mia heard the concern in her friend's tone. "I am," she said, nodding. "My father died when I was ten, and my mother's been alone since then. I think she deserves to find love again."

Neither of them said anything for a moment. Mia sipped her wine, thinking about how happy her mother had been during their vacation. They'd spent time at a ski lodge, neither of them doing any skiing, but they'd had a good time, anyway. She looked forward to that trip every year, and now she had to wonder whether or not her mother would be inviting someone else to go with them. Even while Mia had been married to Damien, she had gone with her mother each year. Alone. He had refused to go with her, claiming he couldn't be away from things for an entire week. It had been a weak excuse, but Mia had never pushed him.

As though reading where her thoughts had gone, Alex asked, "Have you heard from Damien?" Her expression was guarded, as though she knew Mia didn't want to talk about him, but felt the need to inquire anyway.

"Not a single word," Mia said. "Thank God."

"I'm glad."

"How about you?" Mia asked, glancing toward the kitchen to where Johnathan had yet to return from.

"No. Doesn't surprise me, though. Johnathan never was a big fan of Damien's."

Johnathan traipsed through the living room then with several beers dangling from between his fingers, seemingly oblivious to the fact that they were talking about him. Then again, he knew his wife, and as far as Alex was concerned, nothing was off-limits to talk about on girls' night. Including her own husband.

For the next half hour, Mia chatted with Alex about school, what they'd both done for the holidays, and the hugely successful charity drive at the children's hospital that Alex had recently concluded. The conversation had lulled enough that Mia considered heading home when Johnathan erupted from the room he'd been holed up in, followed by a round of cheers.

"I take it they won?" Alex asked, sparing Johnathan a look.

"They did," he said, a huge grin on his face. "I want to listen to the owner's press conference, and then we're off to bed."

Alex nodded, sending a mischievous look toward Mia.

"That's my cue to go," Mia said, pushing to her feet.

"I'll have Kevin drive you home," Alex said, referring to their butler.

"I can call a cab," Mia told her friend. "No need to have him get out this late."

"Are you kidding? I'm sure he'd be happy to get a few minutes without all the noise. At least when he gets back, it'll be quiet around here."

"Sure it will," Mia teased.

"Well, besides that," Alex confirmed with a sly grin.

»»»»»» ♥ ««««««

"DINNER AND A beer to celebrate?" Phoenix asked Tarik as he passed him on the way to the locker room, where the players had converged a few minutes ago.

"After the press conference," Tarik agreed, reminding him that he had something else to take care of before he could relax for the evening.

Not that relaxing was the first thing on his mind. He was still reeling from the close game that they'd won in the last seconds. His blood still pounded in his veins the same as it always did when he was that close to the action. The only thing that could've been better would've been if he'd been out on the ice with those guys.

Nodding his understanding to Tarik, Phoenix continued down the hall, heading in the direction of the cheers and shouts that erupted on the other side of the heavy wooden door. Making his way inside, Phoenix encountered the rough-and-tumble group celebrating another win.

Bringing his fingers to his lips, Phoenix let out a sharp whistle, wanting to gain their attention quickly. "Hey, guys. I wanted to stop in and congratulate you. Big win tonight. I'm impressed with the stats. You played hard. It was close, but still a W. Can't ask for much more than that."

Several hands came his way, and Phoenix shook them, clapping players on the back, mentioning some of their personal achievements of the night. He'd made a point to talk to the team after every game. Although his coaching staff did a damn fine job of motivating the team, Phoenix felt it was important to remain hands-on as much as he could. It was something his father had prided himself on.

When the players started heading for the showers, Phoenix nodded to the team's head coach as he worked his way back out to the hall, locating Tarik, who was waiting for him.

Camera flashes erupted when Phoenix walked into the room that had been dedicated to the press conference. He was the first from his organization to arrive, but he knew the coaches and a few of the players would be along shortly. Hopefully by then, Phoenix would be on his way to the hotel, and they could handle the rest of the political crap for the night.

"Phoenix! What do you think of the team's performance tonight?"

Questions were lobbed at him right and left, and Phoenix did his best to answer them with a smile. He'd made a decision to be as transparent with the media as he possibly could, something that he hoped would keep him out of the limelight as much as possible. For the most part, it had worked, although he did find himself answering questions he preferred to pass on to others.

"Phoenix! Can you tell us more about the lawsuit with Damien Landry? Rumor is that you're meeting with him next week."

Phoenix pretended not to be surprised by the statement. He dared a glance over at Tarik, who gave a very subtle nod, confirming the rumor. "I won't have anything to say until after that meeting takes place."

"Do you plan to settle with Landry?"

"I have no comment at this time," Phoenix stated. He didn't want to go into the details of the absurd accusation that Damien Landry had heaped on him shortly after Phoenix's father had passed away. According to Landry, Sid Pierce had been negotiating the sale of the team to him, yet no one else was aware of the transaction. No one.

Which made Phoenix believe it was all a bunch of bullshit made up by a man who was looking for attention. Not that he would tell the press that.

"Mr. Pierce will hold another news conference in the future, once he has more details," Tarik interjected before urging Phoenix out of the room.

Phoenix adjusted his suit coat and followed, thanking the press for coming.

A few minutes later, once they were safely ensconced in the limo, Phoenix let out a ragged breath. "I still don't know how my father did this."

"He made it look easy," Tarik confirmed, staring at him as the limo pulled into traffic.

"That he did." Pinning Tarik with a glare, Phoenix followed with, "Why didn't anyone tell me I'm meeting with Landry?"

"Just came up. He's a persistent little fucker," Tarik snarled. "He wants a one-on-one with you."

"Who thought that would be a good idea?" Phoenix questioned.

"Phil."

Phoenix made a mental note to have a conversation with his lawyer. Why he'd want to force Phoenix to talk to Damien Landry, he didn't know. As far as he was concerned, the guy needed to go away. Whatever nonsense he'd conjured up in his head about Sid selling the team to him was exactly that … nonsense. "When's this meeting?"

"Monday."

Phoenix stared out the window as the limo weaved its way through the parking lot.

"There's something else you should know," Tarik said, drawing Phoenix's attention toward him.

Without asking, Phoenix waited for him to continue.

"Mia Cantrell. Your mystery woman from the elevator…"

Phoenix cocked an eyebrow. "What about her?"

"She's Damien's ex-wife."

"Are you shitting me?" Phoenix asked, sitting up straight and staring at Tarik.

"Not at all."

"Motherfucker."

"Exactly. What are the odds that you've got a hard-on for Landry's ex?"

That was a damn good question. Was it a coincidence that she'd crossed Phoenix's path? "How long have they been divorced?"

"Officially only a few months. She asked for the divorce nine months ago."

"Nine months?" Surely that couldn't be a coincidence. That was about the time Landry had brought a lawsuit against him.

"If it's any consolation," Tarik said quietly, "I don't think she has a clue what Landry's up to. According to what I found out, she left him because he cheated on her. She moved in with her mother temporarily and filed for divorce. Once that was done, she bought the condo and started school."

Phoenix nodded. He didn't know what to say to that. He knew it was a damn good reason for him to get the woman out of his head. It didn't matter if he couldn't stop thinking about her. He didn't know her, so there would be no loss on his part if he pretended she didn't exist.

Too bad he didn't want to go that route.

Chapter Seven

FRIDAY NIGHT — ODDLY dubbed date night by Alex — came far faster than Mia thought it would. Since she went to school on Monday, Wednesday, and Thursday, she had been lucky enough to have the entire day to lounge around, which she had.

She'd spent the morning in the coffee shop, studying for a test that was coming up the following week. Then she had walked a few blocks over and gotten a manicure and pedicure, something she'd denied herself for the last few months in an attempt to save money after spending an enormous chunk of change purchasing the condo. Frugal had seriously become her middle name.

When she got back to her building, Mia was quite relaxed and looking forward to spending a night out with Alex and Johnathan. The three of them hadn't been out together since before Mia's divorce, although she'd gone to their place several times, and she generally talked to Alex at least once a day on the phone.

Alex was worried about her, she had said when they'd spoken on the phone earlier that morning. Apparently, Damien had become exaggerated in some of his media claims after last night's hockey game, and for whatever reason, he'd dragged her name into it, something he'd done for a while now. Mia wasn't sure why he'd mentioned her. Based on what Alex had told her, it didn't make any sense. But Damien was Damien, and she figured he was all about gaining attention, something that was relatively easy for him.

Mia had told her friend that there wasn't anything to worry about. Mia was actually happier now than she had been in months, maybe even years, and she really didn't give a shit what Damien had to say about her. On the days she went to school, she focused only on that. On the days she had off, she studied. But no matter what, every day that week had been a better day than those she'd spent married to Damien. At least over the course of the last year of their marriage.

She was quite content with things exactly the way they were now.

Granted, she'd thought about the guy from the coffee shop — Hot Hoodie Guy, aka Coach — every single one of those days, too. The same guy she'd practically run over in the lobby when she'd stepped off the elevator. She refused to think about the other guys who'd caught her attention, hoping that by limiting her options, she'd eventually let go of the fantasies altogether.

Considering she wasn't interested in a relationship, Mia knew that nothing would come of her errant thoughts, so from time to time, she allowed them to run free. Not too much that she'd get carried away, but enough to give her mind a little break from her schoolwork.

Now, as she ran her curling iron through her hair, touching up the few pieces that hung down from the twist she'd fixed on top of her head, Mia watched herself in her bathroom mirror. She certainly wasn't thinking about Hot Hoodie Guy now. She was too busy wondering whether or not she was going to run into Damien tonight.

The date Alex had insisted Mia go on with her and her husband was actually a charity event that had been planned a full year in advance. Mia had RSVP'd her attendance long before she'd asked Damien for a divorce, and when Alex had mentioned it earlier in the week, she'd realized she really did want to go. Just because she'd given up that life didn't mean that she had to give up everything that was important to her. So, Mia had agreed to go with Alex.

And now she was getting ready.

The black, single-shoulder, A-line chiffon gown she was going to wear was lying on her bed, her heels on the floor, and the jewelry that would adorn her ears and neck sitting on the bathroom counter. She'd bought the dress online, having fallen in love with it instantly. It was both sexy and elegant, which was exactly what she was going for. After wearing jeans and sweatshirts all week, Mia was kind of looking forward to dressing up.

She spent more time than usual on her makeup, figuring she'd go all out. She lathered one of her favorite perfumed lotions on her skin and pulled on her dress. The shoes could wait. They'd be killing her feet by the time she made it to the hotel where the function was being held, so she didn't feel the need to torture herself any longer than necessary.

Once she was ready, Mia stood in front of the full-length mirror, studying herself for a bit. She didn't look much different than she had nearly a year ago when she'd attended the last charity function, that time on Damien's arm. She might've gained a couple of pounds since then, although if you asked her mother, Clarice would say that was a good thing. However, Mia had made a resolution for the New Year to start going to the gym, but only so she could afford to add a little fat to her freezer content. Damien had always given her a hard time about not being skinny enough — whatever that meant — and since she hadn't cared to rock the boat, she had found herself doing as she was told, eating bland foods, doing yoga although she detested it, and otherwise making herself miserable to fit into a mold Damien had expected her to fit in.

Needless to say, she felt better these days. Not only because she wasn't twisting herself into a pretzel or on some strict diet of fruits and vegetables, lean meats, and no carbs. It was a combination of things.

Her cell phone rang, ending her self-inspection. Grabbing her shoes, Mia ran to the kitchen, snatching it up from the bar before it went to voice mail.

"Hey," Mia greeted, knowing that the only person who would be calling her was the woman who was coming to pick her up in a few short minutes.

"We'll be there in five. The limo will be out front. Want us to come up?"

"No, that's all right. I'll head down now. See you in a few," Mia told Alex.

After tossing her phone into her clutch alongside her credit card, driver's license, and lip gloss, Mia grabbed her wrap and her shoes and headed for the door. She waited until she was at her front door before slipping the four-and-a-half-inch, strappy silver Manolo Blahniks on her feet and then smoothing her gown with her hands. This would have to do.

Mia locked the door to her condo and made her way to the elevator, pressing the button to call it to her floor. While she fixed the wrap over her bare shoulders, she noticed the only elevator that was working was currently stopped at the penthouse, and she was momentarily tempted to run back into her condo and let it go by.

Or maybe she could take the stairs.

Her eyes darted back and forth between the elevator doors and her front door. She still had time. She spared another glance at the numbers above the door. Crap. It was on eighteen.

No time now.

Maybe, if she were lucky, it would be empty.

The muffled ding echoed in the hallway, signaling the arrival, and Mia held her breath as the doors slowly opened.

Nope. Not empty.

Oh.

Crap.

Just as she'd feared, there in front of her was the same handsome, black-haired, suit-wearing guy from the other day. Only this time he wasn't wearing an expensive suit. He was wearing a freaking tuxedo. Armani, if she wasn't mistaken. And Mia was pretty sure it wasn't a rental.

He wasn't alone, either.

Clearly, one sexy man wasn't enough for the universe's idea of a cruel joke, because standing next to him was Tall, Dark, and Intimidating wearing an equally impressive tuxedo — Calvin Klein, she guessed — and looking far too sexy for his own good. They were both watching her closely, and Mia took a deep breath, willing her feet forward. Apparently they had plans for Friday night, as well.

She had to pay careful attention to walking because she nearly tripped, her eyes trailing over their impressive forms one at a time. One thing she noticed instantly was that they took up a drastic amount of real estate in the small elevator. Both were tall, probably over six feet, and broad. Green Eyes had wide shoulders, a trim waist, and long legs. In a word, he was delicious. He took up a lot of space, but it wasn't only physical. The man exuded confidence like no one she'd ever met. And dressed like that... Mia found it difficult to look away.

Then, of course, there was the other guy. Golden Eyes was even bigger than the other, both in width and height. His torso appeared long, his hips narrow, his feet big. Where the other man had a confident air, this one gave off a no-nonsense vibe. But he looked equally scrumptious in the well-cut tux.

Just clothes, she told herself. Clothes did not make a man. As she had learned the hard way with Damien.

Mia stepped onto the elevator and offered both men a small smile, avoiding their gazes as she turned and faced the elevator doors, clinging to the wrap hugging her shoulders and holding her clutch in front of her. They smelled good. The rich, spicy scent of cologne wafted up her nose, and she inhaled deeply, unable to resist. She wasn't sure what expensive brand it was, or which of them wore it, but she liked it. A lot.

"Guilty, by Gucci," the sexy-voiced, green-eyed man said.

"What?" Mia asked, glancing at him over her shoulder.

"My cologne."

Crap. Was he a mind reader? Or had she said that out loud? God, she hoped not.

She blushed, her face heating as she spared him a sideways look, meeting his glistening green eyes. Mia suddenly felt like a science experiment due to the way he was studying her, the way his penetrating gaze raked over her from head to toe. Slowly.

"You look beautiful," he said, and Mia nearly choked on her tongue.

Somehow she found her manners and thanked him for the compliment before facing the doors once more, doing her best not to look at the numbers counting down on the elevator. She needed it to get to the bottom floor. Stat.

Finally, the car came to a jerky stop, and Mia reached forward to keep from stumbling, but not before strong hands were on her hips. Her entire body went hot instantly as she realized Golden Eyes was touching her.

"Careful," he said in that rough, gravel tone she'd heard the other day.

When the doors opened, Golden Eyes held out his arm as though keeping the doors open. She smiled again and stepped out. Looking back wasn't an option because she definitely didn't want either man to see her interest. She didn't have time for fancy suit-wearing, handsome, green- *or* golden-eyed, penthouse-living strangers.

And maybe if she kept that mantra on repeat in her head, she'd eventually realize how very true it was, because her hormones certainly hadn't gotten with the program. Her skin tingled, her insides churning, and there was an unsettling pulse between her thighs. One that had been dormant for far too long.

Seeing the limousine sitting out front was a relief. It gave her something to focus on. That and the sound of her heels against the travertine floor. Anything to avoid looking back over her shoulder at the men who were still walking relatively close to her. They were apparently both going to the same place she was. The front doors.

George wasn't on duty tonight, but another kind gentleman who Mia had only seen once opened the door for her. After she had passed through, she heard him greet the men behind her. She didn't catch what their names were, doing her best to put as much distance between herself and them as quickly as possible.

Not that she cared what their names were, anyway.

When she stepped outside, the chill of the January evening hit her. There was the scent of rain in the air, and she instinctively looked up, noticing the clouds forming in the already darkening night sky. Maybe it would hold off until after she got home tonight. Then she'd welcome the rain. Maybe they'd even get lucky enough for snow.

Johnathan stood beside the limo door, smiling at her as she approached. He kissed her on the cheek and whispered that she looked stunning. It wasn't lost on her that his compliment in no way reflected that of the stranger's in the elevator. Johnathan's was a platonic, almost brotherly approval, while the green-eyed stranger's voice had held a hint of something else. Something … that Mia was not going to think about tonight.

"Hey," Alex greeted when Mia slid into the seat, moving to the opposite side so that Johnathan could sit by his wife.

"Wow. Love the dress," Mia told Alex, admiring her plum-colored strapless gown that accentuated her full breasts, long, silky black hair, and her light gray eyes.

"This old thing?" Alex teased, looking down at her breasts and adjusting them.

Mia laughed. That was one of the many things she loved about Alex. She wasn't one of those snooty, obnoxious rich bitches that they, unfortunately, had to spend so much time with. Well, technically, Mia no longer had to congregate with them. The thought gave her pause.

This was the first public event that she would attend since Damien and she had split. Which meant she'd probably receive a flurry of pitied glances from those who believed Mia was the one who'd received the boot.

Great.

Why she hadn't thought about that sooner, she didn't know.

"Smile, Mia. We're going to have a good time."

Alex knew her all too well. She knew when Mia got lost in her own head, and more importantly, Alex knew just how to cheer her up.

Mia prayed that Alex was on top of her game tonight, because she had the feeling Alex was going to have to work overtime.

»»»»»» ♥ «««««

"I DON'T THINK she's all that impressed with you," Tarik joked once they were both inside the limo that would take them to the hotel where the charity ball was being held.

"Fuck off," Phoenix bit out, sparing him a brief glance before returning his attention to the scenery outside the car.

Feeling an odd sense of rebellion, Tarik chuckled softly, then, keeping his voice low, he said, "Name the time and place."

The way Phoenix's gaze slid over to him made Tarik's dick twitch.

"In your dreams," Phoenix replied roughly, looking away quickly.

"Every fucking night," Tarik muttered as he continued to watch Phoenix.

For the last few days, Phoenix had been acting strangely, and Tarik didn't think it had anything to do with the fact that he had been giving him a hard time about the blonde, either. After Tarik had shared the news that Mia Cantrell had at one time been married to the asshole in the process of suing Phoenix for a ridiculous amount of money, Phoenix had withdrawn slightly.

But he didn't think that Mia was the sole reason for Phoenix's social retreat.

There were times over the last two days when he'd noticed Phoenix watching him intently, but only when he thought Tarik didn't see. What Phoenix didn't realize was that Tarik noticed everything. He was completely aware of his surroundings at all times. It was a trait that had been ingrained in him from an early age. When you had to be on the lookout for a backhand coming your way at any time, you tended to become more cognizant of the things going on around you.

And he was even more aware when Phoenix was near.

Not to mention, he knew that Phoenix had called out his name when he'd been jacking off the other night, something Tarik wasn't sure he would ever be able to forget for as long as he lived.

"Don't push me tonight," Phoenix warned.

"Or?"

"Or I'll make you assist me in ways you've only dreamed about."

"Ready when you are," Tarik told him gruffly.

There was no denying the fact that Phoenix had a starring role in plenty of Tarik's fantasies, but he happened to believe that he played as many roles in Phoenix's. Only Phoenix wasn't willing to admit it. Yet.

Tarik knew it was only a matter of time before they indulged again. At some point, Phoenix would remember what had happened between them that night so many months ago. The night Phoenix had gotten so drunk he'd stumbled into the condo with some nameless woman on his arm. The night Phoenix's inhibitions had been drowned in a bottle of Jack. The night Tarik had somehow managed to release control for one single night and give in to what he'd known Phoenix secretly wanted.

He was pretty sure that Phoenix probably believed that had all been a dream, but that night had happened, and there was rarely a day that went by when Tarik didn't think about it. It was only a matter of time before he got his hands on Phoenix again, but he'd vowed long ago not to push him. That didn't change the fact that there was a lingering curiosity in Phoenix's gaze, one that grew stronger the more time went by. And one day, Tarik knew that Phoenix was going to give in.

Phoenix glared at him, but again, Tarik saw the interest burning brightly.

Opting to change the subject because the current conversation ultimately wasn't going to go anywhere, Tarik said, "I worked my magic and had some seats rearranged tonight."

Phoenix's eyebrows lifted as he stared at Tarik, evidently waiting for additional details.

"Some dumbass had Mia sitting at Landry's table. I worked it so that she was sitting elsewhere."

"Who the fuck does that shit? Do they live in a fucking cave?" Phoenix snapped.

"Don't know. But if it's any consolation, she'll be sandwiched between you and me tonight."

"That'll likely piss off her boyfriend," Phoenix muttered beneath his breath.

"The guy she's with isn't her boyfriend," Tarik stated, noting the relief that relaxed Phoenix's face.

That was quickly followed by another look. The heat that blazed in Phoenix's green eyes mirrored the fire that ignited inside Tarik at the thought of the sexy blonde literally sandwiched between them. His mind drifted to the fantasies he'd conjured up just that week, the ones that involved a sexy, naked Mia Cantrell riding Tarik's cock while Phoenix fucked her ass. Even now, his dick recalled the memory, pressing firmly against the zipper of his slacks.

"She's off-limits to you," Phoenix informed him, his tone reflecting a hint of possessiveness.

"Like I told you before, no promises." As far as Tarik was concerned, he and Phoenix had an equal opportunity relationship. They gave each other shit all the time, so Tarik had no qualms about pushing Phoenix to the breaking point.

The tension in the car ratcheted up another notch, which only turned Tarik on more. He happened to enjoy Phoenix's wrath, especially when the guy clearly had no idea what it was that he really wanted. There was no doubt in Tarik's mind that Phoenix was interested in Mia Cantrell. Hell, he couldn't even blame him. The woman was smoking hot, something he had purposely downplayed when he'd tormented Phoenix by text over the first few days after they'd met her.

But at the moment, she was merely a pawn in Tarik's game. He didn't intend for her to be a casualty, but he was growing tired of the game he and Phoenix were playing. He was growing frustrated with the casual sexual encounters they both were involved in with other people. One way or another, Tarik was going to push Phoenix to the point he'd either give in or tell Tarik to fuck off. Since he hadn't done the latter in all the years they'd been playing this game, he was inclined to believe they were getting awfully damn close to the giving-in stage.

And Tarik couldn't fucking wait.

Chapter Eight

MIA GAUGED THE length of time from her condo to the hotel by the one glass of champagne that she had. She didn't have time to down two, which meant the ride was too short for her liking. It wasn't nearly long enough to settle the nerves that had started a riot in her belly when she'd shared an elevator with the sexy, penthouse strangers, but it helped.

A little.

That and Alex's incessant chatter about what they should expect from the night. Her friend went over the amount of money the charity was looking to raise, and then she mulled over the list of people who would be in attendance. When she mentioned Damien's name, Mia went stone still.

"Really?" Mia asked.

Johnathan offered a sympathetic expression but said nothing.

Okay, so her hopes that Damien would have something better to do were instantly dashed. Then again, she should've known better. This was Damien Landry, the man who demanded attention wherever he went, the same one who would never miss an opportunity to be the center of attention, and what better opportunity than a black-tie charity ball?

She'd been delusional to think he wouldn't be there, but she'd had her reasons. Maybe because he hadn't been a part of the charity that raised awareness and money for suicide prevention until Mia had shown an intense interest in it. Considering her father had taken his own life, Mia felt a very deep passion for the organization. Every year when they'd attended the event, he'd complained — loudly and to anyone who would listen — about having to go. But she should've figured he would make an appearance. After all, if there was any sort of publicity to be had, Damien would be front and center.

Mia could easily overlook his attendance if he happened to donate the large sum of money he was known to give. After all, that was generally his reason for attending any function, but not because he had an interest in supporting it per se. He wanted to flaunt his money and ensure that everyone knew how much he would give to various organizations. They didn't realize until it was too late that his money normally had strings attached. He wanted publicity. He definitely didn't give out of the goodness of his black heart.

When the limo stopped, the driver made his way around, and Johnathan climbed out first. Alex was next, and Mia followed close behind. They stayed together, Johnathan offering each of them an arm as they made their way through the extravagant hotel lobby and directly to the ballroom where the event was being held. Invitations and coats were taken, and then they were allowed entrance, all three of them greeted by name.

Stepping into the ballroom was like stepping into a fairy tale. The decorations were lavish, and this year's theme appeared to revolve around … ice. Interesting. There were a large number of sculptures backlit by brilliant blue and white lights, set up throughout, all some sort of exotic sea animal chiseled from enormous blocks of, yes, ice.

Large round tables that sat eight were set up in front of a long, narrow stage, where the honorary attendees would make their speeches dedicated to raising awareness and asking for additional donations while dinner was served. Hoping to not have to mingle, Mia excused herself from Alex and went in search of the table where she'd been placed. It took only a minute to locate it, and she was happy to see that Johnathan and Alex would be there as well, but oddly enough, Mia wouldn't be sitting next to them. Being nosy, she quickly skimmed the other place cards on the table, ensuring she wouldn't have to endure a dinner with her ex-husband. Mia knew the event was for charity, but she could only be expected to exert a certain amount of hospitality in one night.

No Damien at their table, which was a bigger relief than she'd thought it would be.

A tuxedo-clad waiter delivered a flute of champagne, which she accepted with a gracious smile. Rather than take her place at the table, Mia wandered close by, admiring the women in their beautiful gowns and the men in their elegant tuxedos, many of whom she recognized from previous functions. Quite a few of those who ran in Damien's circles.

"Mia?"

Hearing her name, Mia turned and came face to face with Charles and Delilah Somerhaus. The older couple looked exactly the same as the last time she'd seen them, at the last charity event she'd attended. Charles was decked out in a tux, and Delilah looked stunning in a navy blue gown that accentuated her narrow waist. Mia was pretty sure that if it weren't for some pretty good plastic surgeons, Delilah wouldn't look to be at least half her age. But she definitely did.

"Oh, honey, it's so good to see you," Delilah greeted, moving in for a quick hug, air-kissing her on each cheek before pulling back.

"It's good to see you, too," Mia said, watching the couple carefully as she took a sip of her champagne, hoping she didn't appear as suspicious as she was. Of all the people in the room, the last two who she would've expected to greet her were the Somerhauses. Although they were pleasant, Mia knew they'd always looked down their narrow, aristocratic noses at her. She wouldn't have doubted if they'd had a party to celebrate her divorce. One of those grand galas where everyone who was anyone was invited and they sipped Cristal out of twenty-four-karat gold-rimmed glasses.

Okay, so they were a little pretentious. Mia had never pretended to like them any more than they'd pretended to like her.

"I'm so sorry to hear that you and Damien parted ways."

Mia fought the urge to laugh, mainly so she didn't snort champagne through her nose. The way Delilah said it was as though they'd had a business arrangement. Instead of calling her on it, Mia said, "It was for the best. How are you? How's Teresa?"

Mia hadn't actually met Delilah and Charles's daughter, Teresa, but she'd heard so much about her she felt as though she knew her personally. Although, based on some of the things she'd heard, she wasn't exactly interested in making her acquaintance.

"Oh, my. You haven't heard?" Delilah asked, appearing stricken as she looked over at her husband and then back.

"Sorry, heard what?" Mia asked, glancing back and forth between the couple.

Of course, Delilah was the one to speak. "She's … uh… well, she recently got engaged. Tonight, in fact."

Mia lifted her eyebrow, waiting to see if the older woman would elaborate. Why did that seem to bother Delilah? When the other woman didn't continue, Mia followed with, "That's wonderful. Tell her I said congratulations."

"We sure will," Delilah stated, casting a nervous glance at Charles once more.

Mia knew there was something they weren't telling her, but the truth was, she really didn't want to know. "Well, it was great seeing you. I've got to…" Not bothering to explain, Mia turned and ventured a little ways past her table, waiting for them to move on to someone else.

Unfortunately, her solitude didn't last long, but at least the company proved to be a little less self-important.

"Mia? Is that you?"

Mia glanced to her left to see Harrison Abbott. "Harrison," she said, smiling. "It is me."

Harrison moved in for a hug, and Mia returned the gesture, holding on to her champagne.

"You look incredible," he said.

"I'd have to say the same to you," she replied.

"Thank you." Harrison glanced around as though looking for someone, and when he met her gaze again, he looked a little confused.

"Something wrong?" she asked, unsure what to expect from him.

Harrison was a former employee of Damien's. The two of them had worked together for years, but they'd had a falling out not long before Mia had moved out. Harrison was an accountant, and he'd been working for Damien for nearly a decade when something had happened and Harrison had gone his separate way. Mia had liked him immensely, finding him to be one of the few down-to-earth types that Damien usually steered clear of. Probably the reason he wasn't employed by Damien any longer.

"Sorry, no. I'm a little surprised to see you here. Are you by yourself?"

He sounded as though the thought was preposterous, so Mia plastered on a smile. "I am. You?"

"No, I'm … uh… my date's around here somewhere."

"How is your wife?" Mia asked kindly.

Harrison's eyes lowered to the floor. "We separated about a year ago."

A year ago? That was around the time Harrison and Damien had had their falling out. "I'm so sorry to hear that."

"Thanks. Things are better now," he said, pasting a smile on his round face, but Mia could see the resentment still lingering in his dark brown eyes.

"Well, I certainly don't want to keep you," she told him, glancing around as though trying to help him locate his date, although she had no idea who he was there with.

"You're really here by yourself?"

Mia smiled, chuckling to herself. "I really am. Is that a problem?"

"No," he said quickly. "No. Sorry. That's not what I meant. It's just…"

Unsure what to say when it was clear Harrison didn't know, either, Mia nodded. "Well, you know, it's for a good cause. I figured I didn't need a date."

Harrison smiled sadly. "Well, I guess I should go mingle. These things make me a little uncomfortable, but like you said, it's for a good cause."

"It was good to see you," Mia said in return, watching him as he departed.

Although she was trying to enjoy herself, a small voice in the back of her mind continued to whisper that it hoped the time would pass by quickly. Sitting at home with a good book sounded so much better than forcing a smile for the rest of the evening or having to endure any more sympathy from the people she'd once considered... What had she considered these people? They weren't exactly friends.

It's for a good cause, Mia reminded the voice.

That didn't help, but at least she had a sound argument.

Maybe she should've been worried that she was arguing with herself, but she really didn't care. For charity or not, Mia still had to worry about running into a man she had hoped to never have to see again. As it was, seeing the people he was close to was more than she could bear. She wanted to jump up and down and tell them that she was fine. Happy, even. But she knew it would be pointless. These people only saw what they wanted to.

By the time Alex found her, fifteen or twenty minutes had passed, along with at least three more couples who wanted to offer their sympathies regarding Mia's failed marriage. Johnathan wasn't with her, but she brought Mia another glass of champagne, which she kindly accepted. Mia wasn't much of a drinker, and three glasses without food was already making her a little light-headed. She didn't care about that, either. She was trying to keep a smile on her face, not wanting anyone to think that she feared running into Damien.

Which she didn't.

Okay, she did.

A little.

"This is nice," Alex said, standing by Mia's side and motioning toward the open dance floor. "Much nicer than the last black-tie event we went to."

"Oh, right." Mia snapped her fingers, trying to remember what event that had been. It hadn't been a charity function, she knew that much, but for the life of her, she couldn't remember what it was. Giving up, Mia asked, "You didn't like the farm theme?" She recalled the odd decor from that event. She had no idea who'd thought it was a good thing to go with an elaborate western theme, but they had.

"They had an actual pig there," Alex said incredulously, chuckling.

"I know. Tacky. But this is beautiful. It reminds me a little of my prom," Mia told her.

"Yeah? I guess I could see that."

Mia had no idea what Alex's prom had been like. In her head, she envisioned a room decorated with diamonds and gold. Alex came from money. Her parents were wealthy, so marrying into it hadn't been much of a change for her. One thing Mia loved about Alex was that her world wasn't centered on it. Aside from the fact that she did volunteer work at local hospitals, rather than being out in the real world trying to make a living, you wouldn't have known that her net worth — not including Johnathan's — was likely hovering around a billion. Maybe more.

Mia had never been intimidated by Alex or her money. Not the way she had been with Damien. Then again, Alex and Damien were polar opposites when it came to the way they presented themselves. The same with Johnathan. He was one of the highly sought after plastic surgeons in the area. Mia often teased him that he should've moved to Beverly Hills because he would've probably had his own television show. He would laugh, then tell her that wasn't what he was about. He wasn't lying, either. That wasn't what he was about. Johnathan spent a significant amount of time working with burn units at children's hospitals, offering his services for free or at a substantial discount.

Mia hadn't been left wanting as a child. Her mother was a well-respected pediatric surgeon, and her father had been a professor at the University of Texas. They'd been well off, but Mia had been raised with the understanding that one made one's own way in life, and one had to make an effort. Nothing was ever simply handed to her. And she respected her mother for instilling her with that value, especially after she'd been thrust into Damien's world.

Granted, not all of the people Mia had associated with over the last few years had been quite as ostentatious as the Somerhauses or nearly as generous as Alex and Johnathan. In fact, most of them were somewhere in the middle, putting forth the effort to be noticed while ensuring that they would get something out of it. Especially Damien.

Yes, Mia recognized that it didn't say much about her that she had been married to the man, or that she had continued to put up with his selfishness throughout the marriage. But she liked to think that she'd turned over a new leaf recently.

"Come on, let's sit," Alex said, nudging her arm.

Mia followed Alex to the table, placing her clutch on the white linen tablecloth that covered it before lowering herself into her chair, adjusting her gown as she did. Johnathan arrived a moment later, kissing Alex sweetly before convincing her to move so that he could take the seat farther from Mia, yet leaving two empty spaces between her and Alex. The change put Johnathan almost directly across the table from Mia. Glancing over at the seats between them, specifically the one closest to Alex, Mia realized there was a busty brunette fine-tuning her cleavage while eye fucking Johnathan as he spoke to Alex. That explained the reason he'd traded places. Mia only hoped Alex didn't claw the woman's eyes out before the last course was served.

It wasn't long before the tables began to fill. The conversation that had been muted due to the size of the room became louder as people began congregating in a much smaller area. When most of the other guests arrived at their table, Mia realized she didn't know any of them, which was another relief. They would be her only source of conversation for the next hour, so she considered herself lucky. If she didn't know them, then hopefully they wouldn't spur discussion of her divorce.

She also hoped she could carry on a conversation long enough to make it through the meal. Then, if the universe was working in her favor tonight, she could sneak out while everyone else enjoyed the rest of their evening.

Just as the waiters were delivering the first course, the chair directly to her right, as well as the one to her left, pulled back, and tuxedo-clad bodies came into view on either side of her. It wasn't until each man was sitting that Mia realized who they were.

The guys from the elevator.

Damn.

Mia turned her attention to the others at the table, hoping to look as though she was part of the conversation they were having. She laughed when Alex did, although she had no idea why Alex was laughing. Alex turned her head, her eyebrows darting down briefly in confusion. Mia simply smiled.

Unfortunately, the waiter didn't realize that Mia was purposely trying to avoid the newest members to their table, and he came to her right side, tapping her on the shoulder as he stood between her and Green Eyes. When she turned to look at him — the waiter, that is — Mia met the piercing gaze of the guy sitting next to her first before she focused her attention on the waiter looming at her side. The waiter motioned to a bottle of red wine in his hand, and Mia nodded. She sat back while he filled her glass, then poured some into the glass of the man sitting next to her.

When the waiter moved to her left side, offering wine to the golden-eyed stranger, she made the mistake of looking that direction. She then noticed that the newcomer was staring at her, a mischievous grin tilting the corners of his full, sexy lips.

Oh, God.

He had a dimple.

A freaking dimple.

In his left cheek.

It somehow softened the overly masculine structure of his handsome face, making him seem a little less ... intimidating. Just a little.

"Mr. Pierce," someone across the table said, which thankfully pulled her attention away from the golden eyes peering back at her.

She took a deep breath, trying to feed her starving lungs, because apparently she'd been holding her breath without realizing it. The universe was clearly out to get her. She couldn't think of any other reason she would've been seated between both of these men.

It could be worse, she thought. At least she wasn't sitting at Damien's table.

Mr. Pierce — better known as Green Eyes — began a conversation with a man two seats over, and Mia watched the exchange, unable to look away. She admired the way he spoke, eloquently answering the constant barrage of questions that was coming his way while pretending not to be bothered. Maybe he wasn't, or maybe he was merely a superb actor. Either way, she should've looked away, but she didn't. Not until he looked back at her, catching her in the act of admiring him. Only then did she glance away, pretending to be watching something across the room.

That didn't last long because the man with the golden eyes cleared his throat before saying, "It's nice to see you again." As he leaned closer to her, Mia got a whiff of his intoxicating scent.

"You, too," she lied. It wasn't nice to see him. Either of them. Quite the opposite, actually. Mia wanted nothing more than to put at least a ballroom between them because she was beginning to do things she'd sworn never to do again. At least not for a long, long time. Like entertaining the idea of reaching out to touch him to see if his chest was as hard as it appeared beneath that fancy tux.

But somehow, both of them had sparked a dry bed of kindling inside her, and she was hard-pressed to keep the flames from turning into a full-blown inferno. Which, in her opinion, was utterly ridiculous. It was ludicrous to find one of them attractive. But both of them… That was just too much.

"Tarik Marx," the guy said softly, holding his hand out toward her. "And you are?"

"Sorry," she said, placing her wineglass on the table and returning the gesture. When his big, warm hand engulfed hers, Mia tried not to focus on the strange tingling sensation that erupted in the tips of her fingers. "Mia Cantrell. Nice to meet you." She hoped she sounded polite and not incredibly eager to hear him speak in that dark, rich voice for a little while longer. She thought she heard the hint of an accent, but she couldn't place it.

Before Tarik said anything more, the man on her other side leaned in, his gruff voice greeting her as well. "It's nice to meet you, Mia."

"You, too, Mr. Pierce," Mia said quickly, jerking her head toward him, hoping she sounded as though she knew who he was. Truth was, she hadn't a clue.

It must've worked, because he merely smiled, not bothering to tell Mia to call him by his first name, or even what it was, which only made sense. He was one of *those* guys. The type who got off on being addressed formally, not caring to make any personal interactions with people he wouldn't likely see again. Damien was like that, which had always driven her crazy.

A crooked smile tipped the edge of his impressive mouth, one sleek, dark eyebrow lifting casually as his eyes locked on hers for one heartbeat, then another. She was the one to finally break the stranglehold he had on her with his eyes. Looking across the table, she swallowed hard and ran her damp palms over the napkin in her lap, hoping neither of them noticed. Only then did she offer him her hand.

After she shook Mr. Pierce's hand, the heavyset guy across the table picked up the conversation again, and the waiters began serving the food. Mia pretended to eat, spending more time moving her food around her plate than actually eating. She wasn't really hungry, and the buzz she'd garnered from the champagne was making it difficult to focus. However, she did find herself feeling a little better.

She heard bits and pieces of all the conversations going on around her. The woman on Tarik's other side — the one who'd been eye-fucking Johnathan earlier — seemed enthralled with him, talking nonstop while the hefty guy on the other side of the table kept Mr. Pierce's attention. Although she could pretty much repeat the conversations verbatim, Mia wasn't included in any of them, which was fine by her. She didn't mind sitting there by herself; it was easier, actually.

Dinner consisted of four courses plus dessert, and by the time everything had been served, she was full. Mostly because she'd practically scarfed down the decadent chocolate mousse that had been offered and two more glasses of wine. Once the plates were cleared and coffee was poured, the lights dimmed, and the guests of honor took the stage. Before the last person was finished talking, Mia considered sneaking away from the table under the guise that she had to use the restroom.

Honestly, she didn't want to be sitting there when the lights came back up. She did not want to have to engage in conversation with either of the strangers from the elevator if at all possible. As it was, her obvious attraction to each of them was beginning to be a thorn in her side.

Mainly because she wasn't supposed to be drawn to anyone. She wasn't supposed to find them even remotely attractive, yet she did.

No, she'd sworn off men altogether. Especially men like them. Men who had money and affluence. Men who wore those damn expensive suits like they were their second skin.

It had to be the alcohol. That was all there was to it, because instead of getting to her feet and running as fast as she could, Mia found herself once again looking into the emerald eyes of the sexy man at her side.

"Care to dance?" Mr. Pierce asked.

Mia heard the question, but she didn't respond. She was having a hard enough time swallowing, much less speaking.

"I'll take that as a yes," he said with a rumbling chuckle as he got to his feet. When he held his hand out to help her up, Mia slid her fingers into his. The electric spark that ignited from the contact went straight to every erogenous zone in her entire body.

Rather than taking that as a sign to go, Mia allowed the handsome man to lead her to the dance floor, where other couples were beginning to assemble. There was a nervous flutter that started tap-dancing in her stomach, and it only intensified when Mia found herself pulled flush against Mr. Pierce. Her senses were instantly heightened, and she noticed the warmth of his hand as it caressed her low back, the smoothness of his large fingers as he took her hand with his free one, the delicious scent of his cologne, the rock-hard plane of his upper body against hers.

Ugghh. She was in so much trouble here.

Even with her four-and-a-half-inch heels, he was quite a bit taller than her. With her shoes, Mia topped out at five foot eight, and he had at least another five or six inches on her, which required her to crane her neck to look at him. Without speaking, Mia danced through one song, but she did everything in her power to keep from looking up at him. When the song ended, she was about to pull away, but then another song began, and Mr. Pierce kept her close.

She momentarily stopped as she heard the music begin. "I know this song," she said, looking up at him and meeting his eyes.

"'Gravity' by A Perfect Circle," he said at the same time she did, a sexy smile pulling up the corners of his mouth.

She knew the song was an odd choice for the event, but something about it pulled her in, kept her eyes locked with his. The beat was somewhat faster than the last song, but their bodies continued to move slowly, sensuously, as though they were one. As the bass thumped, her heartbeat kept a timely beat, her pulse ratcheted up by the way the stranger held her gaze, drawing her in.

And it was then that Mia knew she had to get away from him.

It was that or she was going to give in to the dark side.

Chapter Nine

PHOENIX'S NIGHT HAD gone from mediocre to downright perfection as soon as he'd taken his seat at the table for dinner. Seated directly beside Mia Cantrell, likely the most beautiful, intriguing woman he'd ever laid eyes on but hadn't had the pleasure of talking to, Phoenix had found himself mesmerized by her nearness. He knew he had Tarik to thank for the seating arrangement, but he hadn't had a chance to speak with him since they had assumed their seats at her side.

When Phoenix hadn't been talking to Samuel Evergreen, he'd been stealing glances at Mia, desperately searching for something to say, something to spark some sort of conversation, but she'd continued to evade him although they'd been separated by mere inches.

Admittedly, he had no idea what it was about her that drew him in, but it was something. Something that had gripped him once again in the elevator on his way to the event and hadn't let go, even now as he held her in his arms, moving slowly around the crowded dance floor.

Unfortunately, his euphoria was short-lived when the song they'd both been intrigued by stopped.

"Thank you for the dance," Mia said softly, pulling away from him and taking a step back.

"My pleasure," he said, reaching for her hand again. "I'll escort you back to your seat."

Surprisingly, she didn't argue as she slid her soft hand into his palm. He tucked her arm beneath his, cradling her hand in both of his, which forced her to walk right beside him. As he weaved through the crowd, leading her back to their table, he knew his night was about to take an abrupt turn and not for the better. He could feel it by the way she carried herself, Mia was going to bolt as soon as the opportunity presented itself.

Phoenix was powerless to prevent it.

For now.

He was still shocked that she'd agreed to the dance in the first place. She'd managed to strategically avoid him throughout dinner although he'd been sitting less than a foot from her. Thanks to Samuel and his constant stream of questions, Phoenix hadn't had a chance to talk to anyone else at the table. The coincidence — although Tarik had had a major hand in making the change — of sitting directly beside Mia had been wasted on some technology bigwig who wanted to talk about start-ups. At least he hadn't wanted to talk hockey.

Then again, at least Phoenix hadn't been practically manhandled by a big-breasted brunette who wanted to maul him the way Tarik had. It had served him right, considering Tarik would've had plenty of opportunities to talk to Mia. It couldn't have gone better if Phoenix had planned it.

As soon as the lights came up, Phoenix had expected Mia to haul ass, only to be pleased to find she hadn't. His offer to dance had easily slipped right off the end of his tongue, an attempt to spend a few minutes in her company. He didn't regret it. Whatever it was about this woman, he was captivated by it, intrigued beyond measure.

They stepped over to the table to find several people were still there, including a couple who'd been sitting across the table. Phoenix assumed the man was the infamous Alex, but his original assumption that the man was Mia's date had vanished at Tarik's admission in the limo. He hadn't been able to disguise the relief he'd felt in knowing she didn't have a date.

Releasing her hand as they approached the table, Phoenix turned to face Mia, only to receive another polite thank you. He didn't even get a chance to say anything before she managed to make herself scarce, disappearing into the crowd and leaving him standing there, staring after her.

He had no idea where she had vanished to, but now that people were slowly getting up from the tables, he knew it would be damn near impossible to catch her.

"Alex," the man who'd been sitting across the table said, "I'd like you to meet Samuel Evergreen. Samuel, my wife, Alexandra Henry."

Well, wasn't that fucking awesome, Phoenix thought with a smile.

From the instant Phoenix had stepped out of his building earlier, watching as the well-dressed man had kissed Mia on the cheek before helping her into his limo, Phoenix had been accosted by a strange disappointment. Sure, at first he'd figured the guy was her date — the one she'd been talking to in the coffee shop — but there had been a small kernel of hope remaining, exacerbated because of Tarik's information and for the simple fact that she hadn't had anyone sitting beside her at the table.

And now...

Well, a flood of relief overcame him as Phoenix turned back to look in the direction Mia had gone, lending a partial ear to the conversation taking place beside him. Alex certainly wasn't Mia's boyfriend. Alex wasn't a boy at all. That was good to know.

Very good to know.

Granted, it would be a hell of a lot better if he could locate Mia, but she was currently ... well, she was currently MIA.

He smiled at his own joke.

Phoenix was tempted to ask Alex if she knew where Mia might have gone but reminded himself that he was aiming for less stalkerish. As it was, he was still reeling from the dance, from the way Mia had felt pressed up against him. It'd taken a tremendous amount of willpower to keep from pulling her lips to his. He had an overwhelming urge to kiss her, to thrust his tongue in her mouth and see if she tasted as sweet as he imagined.

For a moment out there on the dance floor, Phoenix had thought she'd been longing for the same thing. The way her blue eyes had glittered, her soft pink lips had parted... She had been entirely kissable at that moment.

But somehow he'd managed to resist the urge.

"Put your tongue back in your mouth."

Phoenix rolled his eyes as he turned and came face-to-face with Tarik.

"Where'd you go?"

"To check on a couple of things," Tarik said, handing Phoenix a bottle of beer before turning to survey the crowd.

"And?"

"All's good. How was the dance?"

Phoenix didn't bother to answer. He knew Tarik was trying to rile him up, had been ever since they'd stepped out of the elevator behind Mia.

"Ah. Okay. She disappeared on you, huh? I knew you'd lose that magic touch at some point."

Phoenix smiled around the lip of his beer bottle. He disliked Tarik almost as much as he liked him. It was an ongoing battle simply to put up with his jabs, but because they'd become good friends over the years, Phoenix had learned to tolerate him. Barely.

"Fuck you. I didn't see *you* dancing with her."

"The night's still young," Tarik countered as he turned toward Phoenix.

When the other man took a step closer, their arms brushing, Phoenix swallowed hard. He tried to ignore the current of electricity that coursed through his veins whenever Tarik dared get close enough, but it was getting harder and harder. Then again, so was his dick. And for the life of him, Phoenix couldn't explain the untimely reaction. He'd already decided what he wanted, or rather, what he *didn't* want. As far as he was concerned, the hedonistic thoughts and fantasies he'd succumbed to recently didn't count. But this... It was beginning to get out of hand.

Tarik leaned in closer still, his breath warm against Phoenix's neck. "But I'm always open to sharing."

"Of course you are," Phoenix said.

Tarik was as open to threesomes as Phoenix was. However, as the line that separated Phoenix's interest in Tarik had begun to blur, he'd put a halt to those encounters. Not to mention, the tabloids were having a field day with their speculation.

Didn't matter that Phoenix had jacked off to thoughts of Tarik and Mia nearly every fucking day for the past week, and his fantasies seemed to be getting more and more intense, more detailed. And unfortunately, they left Phoenix wanting something he wasn't sure he could deal with.

"Phoenix Pierce."

Damn it.

"I'll be back," Tarik rumbled against his ear before making a hasty exit.

Phoenix didn't blame him. He knew he should've escaped out the back door when he'd had the opportunity. The voice coming from behind him was recognizable even before he turned around. He also knew that he didn't *want* to turn around because what she had to say to him would probably only end up pissing him off.

But he figured he might as well face the music. Get it over with. That or he was going to spend the rest of the night avoiding her, and he preferred the cat-and-mouse game he seemed to already be involved in. The one where he was the cat, not the prey.

Pivoting slowly, he came face-to-face with Teresa Somerhaus. "Teresa."

"It's so good to see you," Teresa said in that saccharine tone that made his teeth hurt. When she leaned in, kissing him on each cheek, one at a time, he didn't return the gestures. He wasn't much for kissing.

Well, that wasn't entirely accurate. He was all for kissing, but not this woman. Not anymore.

"How've you been?" Phoenix asked, aiming for polite. Pretending to actually give a shit.

Teresa held up her left arm, wiggling her fingers, and that was when he noticed the huge rock weighing down her hand.

"Nice," he said, thinking nothing of the sort. He had known from the beginning that the woman was out to land her a man with money — she'd outright told him so when they'd first met. Apparently her goal had been achieved.

"Aren't you going to congratulate me?"

"Congratulations," he replied resolutely. He really didn't give a shit that Teresa was now engaged … again. If his count was correct, this would've been fiancé number four; however, she'd never married.

"Thank you. I'd love for you to meet my man, but" — Teresa glanced around the room before she returned her gaze to his — "he's currently talking business. You know how that goes."

Oh, Phoenix certainly knew how to play the game, but he obviously differed from her new man, because he would've never left his date to fend for herself or chat it up with old fuck buddies while he talked business with the stuffy white collars who filled the room. It wasn't who he was. His encounters were usually only one night, but that didn't mean he didn't have a deep respect for women. He was always up front with them about what he wanted and what he *didn't* want, but for the time he was with them, he did make an effort to treat them the way they deserved to be treated, and leaving them alone at an event like this wasn't in his nature.

"So, who's the lucky guy?" he asked, attempting to look relaxed as he let his gaze roam the room, still trying to locate Mia.

"It would've been you, if you'd ever bothered to ask," she said thoughtfully, batting her thick, fake eyelashes as she always did.

And it would've *never* been him, because he would've never asked. Not that Phoenix was opposed to marriage or permanent relationships, but he often found the women he ended up with weren't looking for much more than what his wallet could afford them. Teresa was a prime example. He always figured the day he found a woman who looked past his net worth, he'd be down on one knee in an instant.

As he rapidly approached his thirtieth birthday, he still hadn't found her. Granted, he wasn't going to tell Teresa that.

"Well, congratulations again, Teresa," he said politely, hoping to end the conversation. Phoenix raised his eyebrows, as though peering at someone across the room. "It was great to see you. I need to … uh…" He didn't bother filling her in, because at that point, she wasn't paying much attention to him, anyway; her gaze had drifted to the diamond sparkling on her finger.

"I'm marrying Damien Landry," Teresa blurted before Phoenix could get two steps away.

The admission drew him up short.

Damien Landry. Was she fucking kidding? That man was a first-class asshole. And according to Tarik, the bastard had cheated on his wife…

Mia.

Holy. Shit.

"I wish you both well," Phoenix told Teresa now, a bald-faced lie. He forced his feet to move, wanting to get as far away from the woman as he could. Where most women had hands, Teresa Somerhaus had claws, and she did whatever was necessary to get a good, firm grip on a man's wallet. And that meant that she'd likely been the woman Damien had been cheating on his wife with. Or one of them, anyway.

Phoenix wanted to pound the shit out of the guy.

Moving across the room, Phoenix did another search, hoping to find Mia because... Hell, he didn't even know why he wanted to find her now. Knowing that she'd been the trophy on Damien's arm should've told him more than he cared to know about the woman. So why he wasn't heading in the opposite direction, he didn't know that, either.

According to what he'd read in the tabloids, Landry had tossed his wife aside for a newer version, but now that Phoenix thought about it, Teresa Somerhaus certainly wasn't a newer version of anything. But Teresa had a couple of things going for her: she was wild in the bedroom — maybe that was what Landry was after — and if that wasn't it, her father was loaded.

Shit.

Phoenix still wanted to punch Landry in the face.

Thankfully, that opportunity didn't present itself, but Mia did, and as he watched her glide across the room, her eyes scanning as intently as his had been, Phoenix wondered if she was looking for him. Funny, because he got the impression she was, but her perusal wasn't for the same reason he'd been looking. No, if he had to guess, Mia Cantrell was trying to stay far, far away from him.

Then again, if she'd been burned by Damien Landry, Phoenix couldn't necessarily blame her.

But that didn't mean he was going to step back and let her get away. In fact, it made him want to chase her all the more. There was something about that woman. And he intended to find out what the attraction was, even if he had to spend every waking moment pursuing her.

»»»»»❤«««««

TARIK SAW HER as soon as she rejoined the crowd. He had gone with his gut, figuring she'd escaped to the bathroom to do whatever it was women did when they disappeared in there.

He'd been right.

So, while he'd kept a close eye on Phoenix, he had watched for Mia, and he wasn't disappointed to see that she was moving toward him. She was scanning the room, which was probably why she nearly ran right into him. That or the fact that he stepped right into her path. Either way.

"Mia," he greeted softly, gently gripping her arm when she nearly fell right into him.

"Oh! I'm … sorry," she replied, looking up at him with wide eyes. Beautiful eyes. Guarded eyes.

"Would you care to dance?" he asked, doing his best not to glance down at her glossy lips.

"I … uh … I was just…" She seemed perplexed on how to answer, so he helped make the decision for her.

"Just one," he told her. "Then you can pull a Cinderella and disappear into the night if you wish."

Mia smiled. He'd apparently caught on to her plan.

"Thank you, Mr. Marx."

"Call me Tarik, please."

Taking her hand in his, Tarik tried not to focus on the softness of her skin or the sweet scent of her perfume as they moved through the crowd and over to the dance floor.

The song playing was conveniently slow, and as he pulled her into his arms, noting how well she fit against him, Tarik sent up a silent wish for another slow song to follow. He wasn't sure one dance would be enough for him. She settled against him nicely, her heels making it so he didn't have to lean too far down. With the significant difference in their height, Tarik still had to bend to get his mouth close to her ear, but it wasn't a hardship, by any means.

With her soft body pressed up against him, Tarik whispered against her ear, "Are you having a good time?"

"Surprisingly, yes," she said, laughing softly. "Sorry. That was probably a little too honest."

"I like honest," he told her. "It's one of my favorite qualities in a woman."

"Is that so?"

134

"I didn't say it was top of my list, but not too far off," he teased as he slid his hand down her back, being a perfect gentleman and keeping it above the rounded globes of her delectable ass. Although the desire to pull her completely against him was intense, he managed to keep himself in check. They were in public, after all.

"So what *is* at the top of your list?" she asked.

"Are you sure you want to know?" he replied, leaning in closer, his mouth dangerously close to her ear, his lips barely grazing the outer shell.

Her breath hitched, a sexy sound that made his body harden. He forced back the lascivious thoughts that drifted seamlessly through his mind. No reason to scare her off yet, he told himself.

"Maybe not," she answered, her voice a little shaky.

Nodding his understanding, Tarik held her tightly and moved slowly across the floor. He wondered if Phoenix knew they were dancing. Probably so. Knowing the man, he was keeping tabs on Tarik as much as he was keeping an eye on Mia for this exact reason. Not that Tarik cared. He would've danced with Mia either way, but he liked the idea of Phoenix stewing for a minute. Considering how hot and bothered he'd kept Tarik all week, the man deserved a little payback.

"Are you enjoying yourself tonight?" Mia asked. The question sounded like a form of polite conversation, making Tarik smile.

"I am now," he told her, keeping his voice low. "Have I mentioned how beautiful you look tonight?"

Standing to his full height, Tarik looked down at her, noticing the slight blush on her creamy cheeks, visible even under the dim lights above them.

"Thank you. You look pretty nice yourself."

"This old thing?" he joked, looking down at his chest. "I pulled it out of the back of the closet."

Mia laughed, just as he hoped she would.

"I believe it," she muttered, causing Tarik's brows to furrow.

There was something in her tone. It sounded a lot like distaste, and he wondered where he'd gone wrong.

Repositioning himself so that he wasn't looking down at her, Tarik wrapped his arm more tightly around her, holding her close. He wanted to enjoy this moment for as long as possible. The song would be over soon, he knew, and as he'd seen her do earlier, Mia Cantrell was going to run far and fast.

The song began to fade away, and Tarik leaned close to her ear. "Don't leave. One more song."

Mia's body tensed, and he didn't know if that was a good thing or a bad thing, but when another song began on the heels of the first and she didn't pull away, he exhaled deeply.

The song wasn't even halfway through when Mia pulled back. Tarik immediately glanced down at her, and he noticed she was looking to his left. Slowly peering over, he realized what — or rather who — had caught her attention.

"Mia."

"Damien," she said curtly.

Tarik didn't release her, although he got the impression she wanted him to. Keeping his arm around her, Tarik moved to her side, his eyes pinning Damien in place. Tarik knew more about Damien Landry than he cared to. With the pending lawsuit against Phoenix, Tarik had made it his mission to learn every damn thing there was to learn about the bastard.

"I'm glad you could make it. Nice to see you're making wise choices with how you spend my money."

Mia jerked as though Landry had slapped her, and Tarik couldn't contain the growl that erupted in his chest.

"*My* money," Mia stated through clenched teeth. "And it's nice to see that you're still the same condescending asshole you've always been." Mia looked up at Tarik. "I need to go."

"I'll walk you," Tarik told her, glancing back up to meet Landry's gaze, masking his features but making sure Landry could see the promise of retribution in his eyes. Clearly the guy wasn't too happy that his ex-wife was dancing with another man.

Not that Tarik gave a shit. The guy deserved to feel the pain of losing her. After what he'd done, he deserved a hell of a lot more than that.

Granted, Tarik wasn't going to say as much, because he'd acquired his information by doing quite a bit of digging into Mia's background. He had yet to share all of the details with Phoenix, because he hadn't felt the need to. Yet. Now that he saw the blue flame of hatred that burned in Mia's eyes when she looked at Landry, his worries about her intentions abated. She'd clearly been hurt by this man.

Mia turned abruptly, and Tarik had to walk fast to keep up with her. When she stopped suddenly, he nearly ran her over.

"Thank you for the dance, Mr. Marx. But I really must be going."

With that, Mia turned and walked away, leaving Tarik staring after her.

Tarik, he thought. *Call me Tarik.*

When he lost her in the crowd, Tarik looked over, noticing Phoenix was watching them intently, a concerned look on his face. A simple shrug of his shoulders was the only answer Tarik could give. But knowing Phoenix, he was about to swoop in and try to save the day.

And Tarik planned to be not far behind.

Chapter Ten

IF MIA HADN'T been trying to avoid the sexy, tuxedo-wearing dinner and dance companion she'd had tonight, she probably wouldn't be in the position she found herself in now. Although she'd had every intention of running out before the lights came back up, Mia had found herself in Mr. Pierce's sturdy arms on the dance floor. However, she had taken the opportunity to flee as soon as it presented itself, but, unfortunately, she hadn't been strong enough to keep going. Something had compelled her to return to the ballroom after she'd made a brief pit stop in the restroom.

She should've kept walking, she thought sadly as she made her way through the grand hotel lobby.

The moment she'd seen Mr. Pierce talking to *her*, she'd been distracted. Mia didn't know the name of the woman Mr. Pierce had been talking to because she refused to read the articles, but she knew her from the pictures she'd seen. The ones that had *her* hanging on Damien's arm. She was Damien's floozy. She'd also looked quite chummy with Mr. Pierce, and Mia wouldn't put it past the home wrecker to be doing them both.

The thought still made her stomach twist into a knot. God. How could she be so stupid?

At first, when Mia had seen the two of them standing there talking with their heads so close together, Mia had wanted to scratch the other woman's eyes out, but then she'd remembered she didn't care. She didn't care that this man might be doing her, too, just like Damien was. Mia hadn't staked a claim on Mr. Pierce, and she had absolutely no intention of doing so.

She should've been relieved, but oddly, she wasn't.

Which was how she had ended up in Tarik's strong arms on the dance floor, despite her better judgment. When he had politely asked her to dance, she'd found herself unable to refuse him. It'd been a long time since she'd felt desired by a man, and tonight, there'd been two who had seemingly put her in their sights.

Feeling slightly less off-kilter with his eyes on her, Mia had graciously accepted his offer and had actually enjoyed herself. He was as intense as Phoenix, but there was an underlying easiness about him that had calmed her briefly. Well, sort of. Her attraction to him was fierce, and she found the mere feel of him against her had caused her girl parts to sing.

But then *he* had ruined everything. Damien had officially ruined her entire night.

"Ugghh," Mia groaned as she reached the hotel's front doors, pulling her phone from her clutch and shooting off a quick text to Alex, letting her know that she was finding her own way home. There was no way she could stay.

Regrettably, as she found out when she stepped into the chilly night, that was easier said than done. She had hoped for a taxi, but all she saw for miles was limos. And to top it off, she'd left her wrap inside, so the biting cold wind gnawed painfully at her skin.

"Going somewhere?"

Mia spun around so fast she lost her footing and ended up, once again, in the powerful arms of the handsome Mr. Pierce. Thankfully, she quickly recovered, offering him a courteous smile but not answering his question. She needed to get away from this man. He wasn't good for her health, much like Damien hadn't been good for her. It seemed she was having some sort of crazy reaction to him, much to her dismay. No matter how much she tried to convince herself that he would be her downfall should she give him even a minute of her time, Mia couldn't seem to stop thinking about him.

Which was why she needed to go home. Now.

Turning away from him, she continued to study the line of cars out front, wishing a taxi would miraculously appear any minute and save her from herself.

"Can I give you a ride home?" he asked, his voice sounding from behind her.

"No, thank you," Mia replied kindly. "I wouldn't want you to leave your date."

"My date?" he asked, sounding confused.

Great. He was better than she'd thought.

"The woman you were with? The two of you looked as though you know each other well," she told him over her shoulder, not bothering to look at him. Unfortunately, as soon as the words were out of her mouth, she realized how she sounded. Was she really jealous?

A slight pause preceded his next words, which were spoken softly, as though he were speaking to a wounded animal. "Excuse me?"

Mia rolled her eyes, but luckily her back was to him, so he didn't see her less-than-graceful response to his avoidance of the conversation. It was an immature reaction, but thanks to the champagne and her brief run-in with Damien, she wasn't feeling all that mature at the moment. "I'll just get a cab."

"Good luck with that," he stated, but his tone was clipped, not nearly as soothing as it had been.

"I think I can manage," she said, feeling her own frustration rising, which, sadly, did little to warm her.

"Mia? If it's any consolation, I'm not here with anyone," he told her. "And I'm certainly not here with Teresa Somerhaus. She's here with her fiancé, Damien Landry."

"Teresa Somerhaus?" Mia spun around to face him. She knew her mouth was hanging open, but she couldn't help it. Damien was engaged to Teresa Somerhaus? *That* was Teresa Somerhaus?

Well, at least that explained why Charles and Delilah had appeared so uncomfortable when they'd shared their daughter's news.

"Do you know her?" he asked, his eyes locked with hers as he shrugged out of his jacket.

Mia ignored the question, not sure how to answer, or whether she even wanted to.

Silence lingered between them for a moment before Mr. Pierce said, "Let me give you a ride back to your condo. You aren't going to get a cab unless you call for one."

When he settled his jacket around her shoulders, Mia dropped her head in defeat. He was right. There weren't any cabs at the moment, because the event was still in full swing, which meant either she'd have to do as he said and call, or wait for Alex and likely endure a lengthy conversation with this man. Those were her choices, and the lesser of the two evils only slightly leaned toward accepting his offer of a ride home. At least with the latter, she could keep her distance, and she wouldn't take a chance of possibly having to dance again. With him or with Tarik.

She wasn't sure she'd survive another dance with either of them.

Sighing, Mia resigned herself to the inevitable, pulling his jacket around her. "Yes, thank you," she finally said, looking up and meeting his gaze once again. "If you're leaving now, I'd appreciate a ride back to my condo."

The smile that tilted his firm lips had her insides tingling, so she immediately looked away, hating that he'd won this round.

Not a game, Mia. You're not interested, remember?

She ignored that annoying little voice in her head, mainly because it was right. She wasn't interested, no matter what her libido thought. An image of a hoodie-wearing hottie named Coach flashed in her mind, making it only slightly easier to ignore the handsome man standing beside her. She'd had her fair share of heartache at the hands of a man like him. One whose contents of his closet cost more than she'd make in a decade. This guy was no exception.

He was the enemy, and she would do well to remember that.

Two minutes later, a sleek black limo was pulling around, and only when Mia allowed Mr. Pierce to help her toward the car did she realize Tarik had once again joined them.

He gave her a seductive half smile, which was sexy but still intimidating. Although he was as nicely dressed as Mr. Pierce, there was something about him. Now that she thought about it, the guy looked like some sort of ... bodyguard. Who the hell was Mr. Pierce, anyway?

Then again, he could very well be ... what? A date?

Oh, Lord. That thought set off a whole slew of mental images of these two men in her head. Naked, hard, sweaty bodies, lip-locked, embracing one another while they...

A shiver raced along her spine, and she forced her gaze away from Tarik.

Yeah, okay, she was seriously going to have to stop reading those books, because she was getting way too carried away.

She didn't bother to ask any of the questions running roughshod in her head, not really wanting to know any information. If she could get back to her condo with minimal conversation with these guys, she'd be better off.

Once inside the limo, Mia moved toward the opposite door, leaving plenty of space between her and… Tarik joined her, but he quickly repositioned to the seat across from her while Mr. Pierce climbed in last.

"What's your first name?" she asked him as he settled into the seat beside her. Referring to him as Mr. Pierce made him sound like one of her professors, and that was a little creepy.

"Phoenix," he answered easily.

Phoenix. Lovely name. Now she wished she hadn't asked. She didn't want to know that he had a sexy name. The less she found out about him, the better. As it was, Mia knew he was someone important — he garnered attention from other affluent people, he lived in the penthouse of her building, and his wardrobe consisted of expensive suits and immaculate tuxedos.

Oh, and he smelled incredible.

Even with the pep talk about keeping her distance, Mia found herself blurting out another question, directing it to Phoenix as soon as the limo was in motion. "What is it that you do?"

"A little of everything," he told her simply. "Basically, I lend money to start-ups."

Great. Another reason to despise him. With every new thing she learned, he was more and more like Damien. Granted, that should've made it easier for her to resist him.

"And you?" she asked, looking over at Tarik.

"Public relations."

"Really? I pegged you for security."

Tarik didn't respond, but his smirk, and the dimple that formed in his smooth cheek, said it all. He might be in public relations, but that wasn't all he did. She would bet her life on that.

"What about you, Mia?" Phoenix asked.

"Me what?" Mia did her best not to fidget in her seat as both men watched her.

"What is it that you do?"

"I'm a college student for now." The admission made her feel slightly childish. "Better late than never, huh?" she added, feeling a little self-conscious about the fact that she was twenty-four and only now starting her secondary education.

"Better late than never," Phoenix echoed. "How long have you lived in my building?"

Mia studied him momentarily. The way he said "my building" set off warning bells. He wasn't merely referring to it as the place he lived, he meant that…

"You *own* the building?" The words got away from her before she could stop them.

"I own quite a few buildings," he said with a wicked gleam in his eyes.

"Good to know," she mumbled, glancing away to look out the window. "And I've only lived there for a few months."

"Like it so far?" he questioned.

Mia turned her head and met his gaze as she said, "It's all right. The elevator leaves something to be desired."

Surprisingly, they both laughed, which eased some of her tension.

"I'd have to agree with you there," Tarik commented. "I've been on him for years to get them fixed."

"Do you live there, too?"

Tarik nodded, but he didn't elaborate, so Mia didn't question further.

Knowing they would be back at her — no wait, *Phoenix's* — condominium building very soon, Mia decided to ask a random question. One that she hoped would make them believe she was uninterested, although she knew that wasn't the case, no matter how much she wished it were. "Since you own the building," she began, looking at Phoenix, "you probably know most of the people in it."

"Some of them, why?"

"There's this guy," she said hesitantly, unable to look him in the eye as she spoke. "I haven't actually met him, but I saw him in the lobby and again in the coffee shop next door. I think I'd like to ... you know ... meet him." Hoping she didn't sound as silly as she thought she did, Mia dropped her gaze, studying her hands folded in her lap.

"You're gonna have to give me more to go on," Phoenix stated, sounding slightly amused.

Mia looked up then, his eyes meeting hers and holding.

147

"He's a runner, I believe. The day I saw him, he was wearing a hoodie and running shorts," she said, feeling incredibly stupid for bringing this up but knowing she had no choice but to see it through.

"That describes quite a few men in the building," he replied. "What else do you know about him?"

"Not much. I heard someone call him Coach." The car stopped before Mia could say anything more, leaving her feeling a little strange about where she'd been going with the conversation. Luckily for her, the driver was out and around to the door before either man asked her anything more.

She took Phoenix's hand and allowed him to help her from the car, Tarik following right behind them. To her dismay, Phoenix didn't release her hand once she was on her feet. Instead, he turned to speak to the driver.

"Anything else tonight, Coach?"

Mia knew her mouth was hanging open — something she seemed to be doing a lot of this evening. She also knew she had turned beet red, but she couldn't do anything about it. This guy … was *that* guy?

No way.

She was praying for a strange coincidence, but she knew the name wasn't all that common.

Oh, God.

When Coach … er … Phoenix turned around to face her once more, Mia saw the mischief in his glimmering green gaze at the same time she heard Tarik's gruff chuckle. They'd known all along that she was talking about him.

"I'll walk you in," Phoenix said confidently.

She wanted to refuse him but couldn't. Mostly because she couldn't get words to form at all.

And now she only had one more question, one that he wouldn't possibly be able to answer.

Why was this happening to her?

Chapter Eleven

PHOENIX FOUND THE fact that Mia was speechless a little amusing. However, he did try to hide his reaction as he led her through the lobby and to the elevators, which, according to Mia, left something to be desired about the building. That statement had cemented his interest in the woman.

Not only was she incredibly beautiful, she was also straightforward and blunt. Characteristics he found quite appealing. Most women told him what they thought he wanted to hear, certainly not what was on their mind the way Mia had. It was refreshing, to say the least.

"So, this guy you're looking for … the one you'd like to meet…" Phoenix began when the doors to the elevator opened, unable to hide his grin.

"Shut up," she said softly, stepping in as he put his hand on the small of her back.

He chuckled as he turned and hit the button for her floor, Tarik moving in to stand behind her.

"Why didn't you tell me you were the same guy?" she asked as the elevator slowly began its ascent.

"How was I supposed to know you were interested in meeting me?" Phoenix asked, trying to avoid staring at her sweet lips.

Tarik laughed but otherwise continued to remain silent. Thank God for small favors.

"I'm *not* interested," Mia said adamantly, glaring at them both.

Phoenix knew she was lying through her teeth, but he didn't call her on it. For whatever reason, Mia was trying to throw him off. She'd purposely led him to believe she had an interest in another man, but now that she'd found out he was that same guy, she was back to being as standoffish as she had been before the conversation had started.

The elevator finally reached her floor, and when the doors opened, Phoenix signaled for her to precede him, following behind her. As he stepped out of the elevator, he turned to Tarik. "I've got this. I'll see you tomorrow."

Tarik nodded, his smirk reflecting his amusement. "It was a pleasure to meet you, Mia."

Mia turned back to Tarik. "You, too," she said, her tone terse. Clearly she was flustered.

When the elevator doors closed, Phoenix urged her forward, following her as she made her way down the hall.

"You don't need to walk me to my door," Mia said, digging in her purse.

"It's what a gentleman does," he told her.

"And you're a gentleman?" she asked, incredulity ringing in her tone.

"Have I done something to make you think otherwise?" he asked as she inserted her key into her front door.

"Well, you could've stopped me before I made a complete fool of myself. That would've been a good start."

Phoenix laughed. "Would it have made a difference?"

Not at all surprisingly, Mia didn't answer his question, and Phoenix knew she was going to send him on his way as soon as she stepped inside. What she didn't know was that he didn't want to come inside. Not yet, anyway. He was enjoying this little game they were playing. More than he'd thought he would, and leaving her alone tonight would give her time to think about him.

"Thanks for the ride home," Mia said, turning to face him but not looking him in the eye as she spoke.

Phoenix took a step closer, reaching out and placing his finger beneath her chin. Her skin was so damn silky and smooth, and he was desperate to find out if her lips were just as soft.

But not tonight.

"You're very welcome, Mia," he replied when her brilliant blue eyes met his. "I look forward to seeing you again. Have a good night."

And with that, Phoenix lowered his hand and made his way back to the elevator. He punched the call button, then slipped his hands in his pockets as he glanced back at Mia's door. She was still standing there staring after him. He wondered if she had something else she wanted to say, but he didn't probe her. If nothing else, Mia was incredibly cautious. Then again, she'd been married to Damien Landry, so she had every right to be.

As far as he was concerned, they had all the time in the world, at this point. And he fully intended to show her how much she could trust him. Starting tonight.

"Good night," he said again before stepping in the elevator, hearing the click of her deadbolt before the doors closed and he was sealed inside the steel box once more. Entering his code, Phoenix hit the button for the penthouse and waited.

Once he was inside his condo, he shed his jacket and made his way to the highboy that held a decanter of Glenlivet. Pouring two fingers into a glass, he headed to the floor-to-ceiling windows and looked out at the Austin skyline bathed in darkness. The clouds had moved in earlier, and he could see lightning in the distance. They'd be getting a storm soon, which was quite fitting for his night.

Sipping his drink and admiring the view, Phoenix thought back to seeing her at the charity ball.

He remembered watching her dance with Tarik, a sight in and of itself. Two of the most … stunning — maybe that was the right word — people he'd ever met, pressed up against one another. Watching them move together as one, it'd been both erotic and sensual. Phoenix hadn't been able to tear his eyes away from them.

He was curious about Mia. More so than he'd been about any woman, possibly ever. And it wasn't only a need to know what she would feel like naked and writhing beneath him while he drove his cock deep inside her, either. Although there was that. He could practically see her stretched out on his black silk sheets, her silky blonde hair spread around her as he slowly slid into her.

His dick hardened at the mental image. And he didn't miss the fact that he'd pictured her in his bed, a place he'd never taken any woman he'd brought to his place. That was what he had a guest room for. Although he had some rather lascivious thoughts running through his head, Phoenix couldn't actually picture Mia in that other room. No, he could picture her sprawled out damn near anywhere else, but not there. Not where he took women he wanted to fuck for the night and send home before he went to bed.

Why that was, he didn't know, but Phoenix decided not to question it. For now, he had something to look forward to. Pursuing Mia was going to be interesting; he knew that for a fact.

»»»»»♥«««««

TARIK LEANED HIS shoulder against Phoenix's living room wall, crossed his ankles, and watched Phoenix as he stood staring out the window that overlooked the impressive Austin skyline. He didn't make a move to join him, wanting to give Phoenix a little time to digest everything that had happened that night. As it was, he was actually surprised to see him back so early, figuring he'd surely talk his way into Mia's condo for a little while.

As for why he'd come up rather than locking himself in his condo for the night, he wasn't quite sure. Part of him felt as though they'd left something unspoken between them tonight. Something that Tarik felt needed to be said. What the words were, he wasn't sure about that, either.

Not that Tarik thought they'd made great strides, with one another or with Mia, but he got the sense that Phoenix was spending a significant amount of time thinking about things that weren't business-related. And that both intrigued and worried Tarik, which was why he'd returned to the penthouse rather than going back to his place, where he belonged.

After the night they'd just had, he could understand Phoenix's infatuation with Mia. Hell, Tarik would go so far as to say that he was having some rather interesting thoughts about her himself. She was a far cry from any woman either of them had taken an interest in as of late, that was for sure. Maybe that was part of her appeal. She was sexy and sweet, smart and witty. But above all else, she seemed genuine, if not a little flighty. From what he could tell, she wasn't trying to play games, and Tarik didn't get the feeling that she gave a shit about Phoenix's money.

However, he did get the impression she was nursing a broken heart, even if she didn't want anyone to notice.

But as much as Tarik thought about Mia, as intrigued as he was about her, and as eager as he was to get his hands on her, he still couldn't stop thinking about Phoenix. He wanted to eliminate the vast amount of physical and emotional distance between them, take Phoenix in his arms, and force him to face whatever this was between them.

It wasn't purely physical; there was something else there. Something with a steady pulse that continued to spark between them. For whatever reason, Phoenix was fighting it. And in the same regard, Tarik wasn't pursuing him the way he should. Not if he expected to gain ground, that is.

After all this time, after all the feelings he'd developed for Phoenix, the truth was, he was scared shitless to let their friendship fall apart. Sure, he worked for the man, but there was more to it than that. Which was probably the reason that every time he was around the man, the words he wanted to say eluded him. Like now.

Just when Tarik was going to call it a night and head out the door and back to his condo, Phoenix turned around, their eyes meeting across the open living room.

"I heard you breathing," Phoenix said softly.

"I tend to do that from time to time."

"If you're here to ensure I didn't slip into Mia's and have my wicked way with her, well, now you know."

"That's not why I'm here," Tarik stated.

"Then why *are* you here?" Phoenix asked, his piercing gaze raking Tarik from head to toe, kicking off shock waves of lust raging in Tarik's veins.

Tarik shrugged. He'd been asking himself the same question.

"No matter how hard you try, you're not going to figure this out," Phoenix said, his voice pitched low.

"Figure what out?" Tarik asked, not moving from his spot as he watched Phoenix move toward the glass decanter, refilling his glass.

"Me. This. Whatever you think I want from you."

Tarik studied Phoenix for a moment before he pushed off the wall and joined him on the other side of the room. He came to a stop directly in front of Phoenix. "Whatever *I* think you want?"

Phoenix's gaze slowly rose until he was looking directly into Tarik's eyes. Moments before Phoenix spoke, Tarik saw the honesty flooding his features, knew the words weren't going to be easy for Phoenix.

"I don't know what it is about her, but for the first time in my life, this doesn't feel like a game to me. I don't know what this strange attraction is between you and me" — Phoenix motioned between them with his glass — "but I'm not willing to risk what might come of this thing with Mia."

Tarik knew what he was about to do could have disastrous repercussions, but he couldn't help himself. Taking a step closer, eliminating the gap between them, he reached for Phoenix's glass. Setting it on the glass-topped table beside them, he inched another step forward until they were practically chest to chest. Phoenix didn't move.

"Does this feel like a game to you?" Tarik asked, keeping his voice low and even before he leaned forward and pressed his mouth to Phoenix's. When the other man didn't pull away, Tarik slid his hands up and gripped Phoenix's hips, pulling him forward as he thrust his tongue past Phoenix's lips.

He tried to hide his surprise when Phoenix grabbed him, his powerful arms sliding behind him, pulling him even closer as he crushed their lips together, Phoenix's tongue forcefully pushing against his, an urgent, heated battle igniting instantly. Within seconds, the heat consumed them both, the kiss turning into a conflagration of energy and desperate need as they devoured one another. Tarik took what he'd sought for the last eight years from that kiss, his lust coming to a rapid boil, threatening to burn him alive.

Tarik had waited a lifetime for this kiss, or so it felt. He'd thought about it, dreamed about it, willed it to happen, but none of those fantasies equaled this. Not even close.

When Phoenix's hands slid into Tarik's hair, pulling hard enough to send shards of pleasure-pain firing down his spine, he thought for a second he was going to detonate. But then it was over as fast as it had started. Still, Phoenix didn't move away. Not far, anyway. Just enough that Tarik was forced to release him.

The confusion that flared in Phoenix's eyes made Tarik feel like shit, but the frustration had built to a crescendo, and for the first time in years, he had to know whether or not there was a possibility of something between them. Something more. Something … real.

"It doesn't feel like a game to me," Tarik growled. "It's never been a fucking game. That night that you've conveniently blocked out, that was fucking real, Phoenix. Goddamn real."

The memory of that night came flooding back as Tarik waited for Phoenix to respond:

"You just gonna sit there and stare? Or you wanna join in, too?" the woman asked, her shrill voice grating against Tarik's ears like nails on a chalkboard.

Her name escaped him, or maybe Phoenix hadn't even bothered to introduce them, Tarik wasn't really sure. What he was sure of was the blatant making out the two of them were doing on the couch only a few feet away.

Tarik knew he should've gone back to his condo, given the couple some privacy, but he'd been there when they'd come traipsing in a few minutes ago. He'd been waiting for Phoenix, making sure he made it home safely. Both Phoenix and the woman were drunk, he could tell that much. But that wasn't surprising. Phoenix had been drowning his emotions in liquor and pussy for nearly a month now, his way of dealing with his grief over losing his father, Tarik figured.

"You're kinda cute," the woman said, peering over at him as she straddled Phoenix's lap, her short red skirt hiked up to her hips while Phoenix slipped his fingers between her thighs. "I wouldn't mind if you came over here."

Tarik didn't move a muscle, merely watched. The suggestion was quite tempting, but not for reasons the woman probably thought. No, if Tarik had his way, he'd be on his knees, and his lips would be wrapped around Phoenix's cock, making him moan his name as he came down Tarik's throat.

"I've heard rumors about your wicked ways," the woman told Phoenix. "I've heard you like to do erotic things, crazy things."

"And?" Phoenix asked, not bothering to deny the accusation.

"You know what would be really hot?" the woman asked, her hands sliding through Phoenix's disheveled hair as she ran her lips over Phoenix's stubbled jaw.

"What's that?" Phoenix slurred, his half-lidded eyes focused between the woman's thighs.

"It'd be hot to see the two of you make out."

Tarik watched as Phoenix's eyes slowly roamed up the woman's body, over her impressive tits, and then met her eyes.

"You wanna see me make out with him?" Phoenix asked, the words garbled, thanks to his intoxicated state. He didn't sound bothered by the idea, which surprised Tarik.

"Yeah." The woman giggled uncontrollably and then turned her attention to Tarik once more. "Come over here, handsome. I wanna see you kiss him."

Once again, Tarik knew he should've gotten up and headed home, but that wasn't what happened. No, when his body rose from the chair, he moved toward Phoenix rather than away from him. He lowered himself to the sofa beside the pair, his eyes never straying from Phoenix's face.

When he was seated, the woman gave them both a hand, palming the backs of their heads and urging them closer. It seemed like a juvenile thing to do, but Tarik wasn't complaining. He'd wanted this for so damn long.

"Kiss him," the woman whispered loudly in Phoenix's ear. "And then, I wanna see him suck your dick."

At that admission, Tarik's cock thickened, pulsing behind the zipper of his jeans, a blaze of heat rocking him. He feared that Phoenix would be able to hear the erratic pounding of his heart if he listened closely.

Phoenix leaned in, whether on his own or because the woman was still encouraging him, but it no longer mattered when Tarik's mouth met Phoenix's. In fact, everything else disappeared except for the warmth of Phoenix's lips, the taste of bourbon, and the insistent thrust of Phoenix's tongue against his own.

A rumble erupted in Tarik's chest as he reached for Phoenix, pulling him closer, sliding his hands into Phoenix's hair as he kissed him back, holding him, never wanting to let him go.

"Holy shit, that's hot. Two hot guys kissing. Oh, yeah."

Tarik ignored her and her overuse of the word hot, *sliding his tongue against Phoenix's, searching his mouth, melding their lips together as the soft, silky strands of Phoenix's hair slipped through his fingers.*

They broke apart when the loss of air became too much, but Tarik didn't want the kiss to end. He hadn't gotten his fill yet. He feared he might never get enough.

Tarik locked his gaze with Phoenix's, and what he saw there encouraged him. He could've done without the woman being there, but at the moment, Tarik was going to take what he could get.

"You wanna suck his dick?" the woman asked, giggling once more, another discordant sound that made Tarik want to shove his fingers in his ears and burst his own eardrums.

Tarik didn't know who she was talking to, but he nodded his head anyway. When Phoenix reached down and unbuttoned his jeans, Tarik's breath lodged in his throat.

"What are you waiting for?" Phoenix asked, tossing the woman to the side as he lifted his hips and pushed his jeans down to his thighs, his impressive erection jutting up from between his legs.

The woman wrapped her hand around Phoenix's cock, eliciting a hiss from him while Tarik wished he were the one touching him.

"Get on your knees," the woman commanded gleefully, chortling yet again.

Tarik slid to the floor and maneuvered between Phoenix's legs, forcing Phoenix's jeans to his ankles, still watching him, his eyes never releasing Phoenix's gaze.

"Now put your mouth on him," the woman stated, her words running together from the alcohol that was flooding her system.

"Is this what you want?" Tarik asked Phoenix.

Phoenix didn't hesitate before he said, "Yeah. For a long damn time, it's what I've wanted."

Tarik nodded, understanding. They'd been doing the same dance for some time, but Phoenix had never admitted anything remotely close to that in all the time Tarik had known him, although he'd suspected.

"Put your mouth on my cock," Phoenix instructed firmly, leaning forward and cupping the back of Tarik's head, pulling him down.

Using both hands, Tarik circled Phoenix's dick at the base, sliding up slowly, then back down, stroking him easily as he relished the smooth length of him against his palm, admired the way the thick head darkened even more. His mouth watered to taste him, to suck him deep, to make Phoenix beg him to finish what he was about to start.

He waited until Phoenix pulled his head toward him once more before opening his mouth and taking Phoenix's cock between his lips, skimming his tongue over the swollen head, circling it before sliding all the way down his shaft and taking him deep into his mouth.

"*Sonuvabitch.*"

"*Does it feel good?*" the woman asked, her voice barely registering as Tarik focused all his energy on sucking Phoenix's dick, pleasuring him in ways he'd only fantasized about.

"*Fuck yes,*" Phoenix agreed. "*So fucking good.*"

"*That's hot,*" the woman muttered.

"*Finger yourself,*" Phoenix instructed her. "*Make yourself come while he sucks my dick.*"

Tarik continued to lave Phoenix with his tongue while he used one hand to firmly grip the base of Phoenix's shaft, the other sliding down to fondle his balls.

"*So fucking good,*" Phoenix groaned. "*Don't stop sucking me. Take me deeper. All the way. Fuck.*"

Phoenix's rambling only spurred him on, made him wish they were both naked so he could toss Phoenix onto the black leather and slide his dick into his ass, fucking him until neither of them knew their own names.

"*Oh, God,*" the woman moaned. "*I'm gonna come.*"

Tarik ignored her, sliding his tongue down the underside of Phoenix's cock and then sucking his balls into his mouth, teasing them, rolling them as he stroked Phoenix's hard length with his hand.

"*Fuck yes,*" Phoenix groaned.

"*Come in his mouth,*" the woman encouraged.

"*I plan on it,*" Phoenix said, his eyes meeting Tarik's when he looked up. "*It's too good.*"

"*Do you like watching him?*" the woman asked.

"*Yeah,*" Phoenix said on an exhale. "*Suck me harder, Tarik. Make me come in your mouth.*"

"Do you wanna fuck him?" the woman asked.

Tarik's eyes darted up to Phoenix's face, wondering how he would answer that question.

"No," Phoenix said hoarsely. "I want him to fuck me."

Tarik released Phoenix's balls and slid one hand into the front of his sweatpants, stroking his own cock while he sucked Phoenix harder, closing his eyes and imagining himself buried to the hilt in Phoenix's tight ass. He couldn't control the moan that escaped.

"Fucking shit," Phoenix cried out. "I'm gonna come, Tarik. Motherfucking hell. I'm gonna come in your mouth."

Tarik continued to jack both of their cocks, increasing the speed of his hands as well as his mouth as he sucked Phoenix deeper, until Phoenix's entire body stilled, his hips thrusting up as he came with a roar. Tarik let himself go, coming in his own fucking hand as he swallowed every drop from Phoenix. All while praying like hell that Phoenix would remember what had happened in the morning.

Now, as he stared back at Phoenix, he wondered what the other man remembered when his memories cast images of that night. Had the alcohol obliterated it all, or did Phoenix remember as clearly as Tarik did?

"I didn't block it out," Phoenix admitted roughly, taking a step back and bumping into the glass table. "I relive that fucking night over and over again. It was just as fucking real to me. Don't pretend to know how I feel."

"That's the problem — I'm not pretending," Tarik barked. "I don't have a fucking clue what you want. I don't know whether I should let it go or take you hard and fast against the fucking wall."

Phoenix's eyes widened, his throat working as he swallowed hard. "Why now? Because I want this woman? Why the hell do you have to fucking complicate things *now*?"

Tarik didn't know how to answer that question. And he feared that Phoenix was right. There was something about Phoenix's interest in Mia Cantrell that felt different than any of the other women Phoenix had brought home. And for the first time, Tarik feared losing that possibility of something with Phoenix that had always been just out of his reach.

He had no idea what to say, so he backed off, putting more distance between them before turning to head to the door. Just when he thought the night was going to end on a shitty note, Phoenix called out to him.

"I don't know what this is, either." Phoenix's tone lacked the frustration it'd had moments before. "But to answer your question, yeah, it feels just as fucking real to me."

Tarik turned and looked at Phoenix.

"That doesn't mean I'm gonna do anything about it."

Swallowing past the lump that was quickly forming in his throat, Tarik nodded and turned away. He had nothing else to say. That kiss had said it all.

But the one thing he hoped Phoenix realized … Tarik's patience was quickly wearing thin.

Chapter Twelve

WHEN THE ELEVATOR delivered Mia to the first floor early Monday morning, she gave the lobby a quick once-over before stepping off.

Deeming it safe because she didn't see Phoenix or Tarik anywhere, she made a beeline for the front doors. Strangely, she would rather deal with the paparazzi than their knowing smiles and flirtatious gazes this morning. As it was, she'd spent all weekend locked in her condo, refusing to leave because she didn't want to chance running into either of them.

Granted, she'd also spent both days thinking about them more than she should have. Even when she had tried to get in some last-minute studying, she'd found her thoughts drifting to Friday night. Each time they did, she'd blushed to the roots of her hair as she'd recalled what had happened in the limo. How could she have not known that Phoenix was the same guy she'd seen before?

"Good morning, Ms. Cantrell," George greeted her as she approached the front doors.

"Good morning, George," she said in return.

"I hope you brought an umbrella this morning," he told her as he pushed open the door.

Mia pulled her small, handheld umbrella from her purse, showing him that, yes, she had thought ahead before leaving her condo. Technically, she'd had to go back to her condo to get her umbrella because she'd forgotten it. She'd also forgotten her coat, her school books, *and* her purse, but she wasn't going to mention any of those things to George. He probably didn't care that she'd been so caught up in thoughts of running into Phoenix and Tarik that the only thing she had remembered was her key.

"Have a good day, Ms. Cantrell," George said when Mia stepped outside. She instinctively looked up at the sky, scanning for raindrops. There weren't any, which made her feel better. She didn't mind a little rain, but she preferred not to arrive at school looking like a drowned rat first thing in the morning.

As she began walking, Mia felt eyes on her, and she figured the reporters were lurking somewhere, but she pretended not to notice, keeping her eyes down and her feet moving toward the college campus. It wasn't until she came to the corner that she got the distinct feeling that she was being followed. It was a first for her. She'd been lucky that, so far, the paparazzi hadn't been overly persistent in their need for information and had generally let her be once she left the building.

Fearing her luck had run out, she began moving faster, glancing over her shoulder. It was because of her distracted state that she didn't notice the man coming toward her until she nearly ran right into him.

"Mia? Everything all right?"

168

Mia turned back around and looked up into those familiar green eyes. The ones she'd been avoiding all weekend. "Yeah," she said quickly, breathlessly, once more glancing over her shoulder.

She noticed Phoenix was studying their surroundings as well.

"Someone following you?"

"I don't think so," she said, but then opted to go for the truth. "Maybe. I kinda felt like someone was watching me."

"Where're you headed?"

For the first time since he'd walked up, Mia gave him a once-over, noticing he was wearing a hoodie and shorts, although his head was uncovered unlike the other times she'd seen him in the lobby of her building and at the coffee shop. Had he bothered to keep his head visible either of those times, she wouldn't have been left to feel like a complete idiot a couple of nights ago.

Shaking off the thought, she met his gaze. "School," she told him, pointing in the direction of the campus.

"Let me get my driver," he said. "He'll take you."

"No, that's okay. I'd much rather walk." Not to mention, she would much rather get as far away from him as she could. The guy rocked a tuxedo like no man she'd ever seen, but there was something distinctly sexy about the outfit he was wearing now, the way his hair was slick with sweat, a fine sheen coating his handsome face, and she had no idea why that was.

"Then I'll walk with you."

Mia met his eyes again. "No. That's not necessary. Really." She didn't want him walking her. That would mean she'd actually have to talk to him, and she didn't want to do that. Mostly because she *did* want to do that and she knew she shouldn't.

When his hand touched her arm, Mia fought the tremor that threatened to wrack her entire body. She liked the way his hand felt on her arm. Too much.

"Two choices, Mia. Let my driver take you, or I'm walking you. Your choice."

"I'm sure you're busy," she retorted, doing her best to appear unaffected as his thumb casually grazed her forearm back and forth. She wasn't even sure he was aware he was doing it, but she sure as hell was. Hyperaware was the state she was currently in, and it had nothing to do with someone following her and everything to do with this sexy, sweaty man standing in front of her.

"I've got time," Phoenix informed her, and Mia realized that arguing with him was going to get her nowhere. At this rate, she was going to be late for class if she didn't hurry.

Rather than saying anything more, Mia simply nodded, then started walking, and Phoenix fell into step beside her. They continued for a few minutes in silence. Of course, Phoenix was the one to spark the conversation, because Mia would've managed to go the entire way without saying a single word. It was enough just to breathe while walking next to him.

"What time are your classes over today?"

"I'll be there until four thirty," she answered easily. Too easily.

"Why don't I meet you at the same place I leave you then? I'll walk you back."

"Don't you have a job?" Mia asked, feeling stupid as soon as the words left her mouth. She knew he had a job. He'd told her so.

Phoenix merely grinned as he said, "I've got a job. But I can adjust my schedule to accommodate."

The charm that oozed from his pores set off warning flares in Mia's head. Damien had been that way, too. Always saying the right things, doing the right things. But in the end, she had learned how little she'd meant to him. She didn't have any interest in repeating history, but she didn't say anything.

What was she going to say? *You remind me of my ex-husband?* Even Mia knew that sounded absurd. Especially since he didn't remind her anything of Damien. Not in the least.

Sighing, Mia gave in. She wanted to get to school, get the day over with, and then snuggle up with a pint of ice cream. Maybe then she'd be able to relax.

Twenty minutes later, Mia stopped at the steps that led to the building where her first class was. Turning to look at Phoenix, she offered her thanks.

"You're welcome. I'll see you this afternoon."

"Okay." She glanced over her shoulder at the building before meeting his beautiful green gaze once more. "I'll see you this afternoon."

The smile that tilted the corners of Phoenix's mouth had her insides breaking out in song — a silent song, but a song nonetheless.

Forcing herself to turn around and walk away, Mia fought the urge to look back at him. She hugged her bag closer to her body and made a beeline for the doors, just as she felt the telling plop of water on her head as it began to rain. She could feel Phoenix's eyes on her, and that giddy feeling stirred in her belly.

There was no way she was getting away from this man. Not even if she wanted to.

Which, she was quickly realizing, she didn't.

»»»»»» ♥ «««««

AFTER PHOENIX WATCHED Mia go inside the building, he remained where he was for a moment, studying his surroundings until he felt raindrops on his head. Shit. Just what he needed.

He still didn't bother to move as he looked at the people milling about, moving toward the building, some heading in the opposite direction down the sidewalk. Was someone watching her?

Something had spooked her, he just didn't know what. Or who. As much as he wanted to find out, he knew he had to get back to his condo or Tarik would be calling out a search party soon. He was also hoping to avoid the downpour that the weatherman had predicted. In order to prevent his bodyguard having an unnecessary panic attack, he pulled his cell phone from his pocket and dialed Tarik's number.

"Where the fuck are you?" Tarik asked by way of greeting.

"On my way back," Phoenix answered. "And good fucking morning to you, too."

"Did you need something? Or were you simply calling to fuck with my mood?"

"You've got cameras outside the building, right?" Phoenix asked, launching into the reason he called.

"Yeah," Tarik stated, and Phoenix heard the clacking of a keyboard. Tarik was nothing if not efficient, which meant he was already pulling up the cameras before Phoenix even had to tell him the reason he was calling. "How far back do you need me to go?"

"Half an hour ago," Phoenix instructed as he walked across the street, back in the direction he'd come from. The rain was beginning to come down harder, the wind picking up, and a rumble of thunder in the distance told him the storm was headed their way.

"Got it. What am I looking for?"

"Right at the point I come around the corner in front of the building. Go back a minute or two from there. See anyone around that looks suspicious?"

Tarik was silent for a moment, but when he came back, the information Phoenix was hoping to get wasn't forthcoming. "Nothing, man. Does it have something to do with Mia?"

"I think so," Phoenix answered. "She was spooked, but I didn't see anyone around."

"Probably reporters," Tarik said. "They're lurking outside more and more these days. Now that Landry's engaged, they're probably hoping to get some dirt on him."

"Maybe. I'd think she'd be used to the reporters."

"I'll go back to an hour ago and watch to see if I see anyone. I'll let you know. Did you escort her to school?"

Phoenix purposely ignored Tarik's question. It was obvious, as far as Phoenix was concerned. Not to mention, he wasn't sure how to explain this protective feeling he had toward Mia. Hell, he didn't even understand it himself. "I'll be back in a minute," he said instead, ending the call.

He wasn't sure what he'd expected Tarik to find on those cameras, but he was disappointed that nothing had come up. He found it peculiar that Mia would've been spooked by nothing.

Shaking off the thought, he ran through his list of things he needed to do. After he showered and got ready for work, he would have to go into the office for a little while. There was a meeting he couldn't avoid, and he was anxious to get it over with as soon as possible. From the instant he'd learned about the damn thing, he'd been dreading it, but now he was actually looking forward to it. Phoenix couldn't help but think that fate had played a little part in his stalling tactic this time.

But now he knew exactly what he had to do. And he was more than happy to do it.

Two hours later, Phoenix had made it into the office, checked his emails, had two cups of coffee, and was heading to the only meeting he had on his calendar for the day. A rare occurrence, but one he wasn't going to question.

"Mr. Pierce."

As Phoenix entered the executive boardroom that was generally reserved for larger meetings than this one, he lifted his head and met the crude blue eyes of the man he'd purposely been avoiding. "Landry."

Tarik followed closely but moved to stand against the wall behind Phoenix, pretending to be invisible as usual.

When Damien held out his hand, Phoenix ignored it before pulling out the seat across from him and meeting his gaze. "Lay off the niceties, Damien. We both know why you're here."

"So, I take it you've been updated on the most recent developments?" Damien asked, pulling his hand back and extending a belittling grin, his eyes darting up to Tarik and then back.

"I know just enough to be dangerous. But still not enough to be worried." Phoenix unbuttoned his suit coat before lowering himself into the chair across from Landry.

Damien's smile faltered slightly before widening, and Phoenix hated the man even more now than he had before. Not only was Damien a cheat and a liar, he was a first-rate asshole to boot.

"You don't think you should be a little worried that your father backed out of a deal that's going to cost you millions?" Damien questioned, looking far too cocky for a man who wasn't going to get the answer he was hoping for.

"Considering that never happened, I'm not the least bit worried," Phoenix stated, leaning back in his chair, steepling his hands and resting them on his stomach. Two could play this game.

Damien didn't say anything, merely studied Phoenix momentarily.

Phoenix had never actually met Damien Landry before today. He'd known of the man, but then again, Damien was a well-known businessman — it would've been hard not to know who he was. For the most part, Phoenix did his best to steer clear of guys like Damien. Arrogant, greedy assholes who thought they'd accomplished something others couldn't possibly.

They didn't run in the same circles, didn't have any mutual friends. Actually, the only reason Phoenix had had any interaction with Landry was thanks to his father's previous discussions with him. Back when Phoenix's father had been alive, a month or so before he'd passed, to be exact, the old man had mentioned Landry's interest in buying the Austin Arrows, much to Phoenix's dismay. However, Sid had never intended to sell the team, so where Landry had come up with the absurd idea that Sid had backed out of a deal, Phoenix didn't know.

If he had to guess, Sid Pierce had entertained the notion because that was the way he did business. He listened to what people had to say. Always said it was good business, that it made people trust you. Based on what Phoenix knew of Damien, the guy had likely misconstrued Sid's attention to the idea as something more than it was.

But Phoenix didn't plan to play that game with Landry. Although he could be as shrewd as the next guy when it came to the high stakes of his company, Phoenix had always put people first. When he did something, he always weighed the good with the bad. It was clear that Damien Landry didn't work that way. He was a greedy, selfish bastard who had only his own best interests at heart.

"I'm sorry if somehow you mistook my father's kindness for something more than it was, Landry, but I assure you he had no intention of selling the team."

Landry's blond eyebrows shot up into his hairline, his forehead wrinkling with the move. Apparently Phoenix had surprised him with that response. Of course, Damien was the type to think that everyone would bow to him when it came down to it.

He was about to learn a lesson that Phoenix hoped the guy would never forget.

"I think you need to give this the attention it deserves," Damien said quickly. "Sid and I had an agreement. He backed out of the deal, and I have every intention of recouping my losses here. What I stood to gain from taking on the team far outweighs any amount you could settle for."

"That's a little overdramatic, even for you, Landry. Regardless, I have no intention of settling," Phoenix replied confidently, making sure to show absolutely no emotion. "In case you forgot, my father was a very smart businessman. If you had proof of your claim, you'd have presented it by now."

"Oh, I've got proof. I think we can handle this civilly. I'm merely giving you another chance to consider my offer."

"See, I've always said *you* should avoid that. The thinking part. It'll only get you in trouble," Phoenix countered, his frustration with Landry's snobbish responses beginning to get the best of him.

"I could make you a very rich man," Landry said through gritted teeth, clearly unhappy with Phoenix's retort. "The publicity alone from this lawsuit is going to benefit you."

"Money's not the most important thing to me, Landry," Phoenix informed the other man, clenching his teeth as he finally grew tired of the conversation.

"It should be."

Phoenix leaned forward, resting his forearms on the table. "Is that why you're engaged to one of the biggest gold diggers in Texas?"

Not surprisingly, Damien didn't jump to defend his fiancée. Then again, this was the same guy who'd cheated on his wife.

"Teresa comes from money," Damien said quietly, his lips a hard, thin line. "The relationship will be good for both of us."

"I know Teresa well. We go way back," Phoenix said, purposely insinuating how well he knew her with the inflection in his tone. "And you're correct, she does come from a very wealthy family. But in case you haven't verified her net worth prior to putting that rock on her hand, you might want to know that her father is the one with the money. Not her."

"At least her father is a sensible businessman," Damien returned, the hostility in the man's tone making Phoenix feel only slightly better.

And while he mentally celebrated the small win — pissing Landry off didn't bother him in the least — he pretended to consider the statement. Teresa's father couldn't be too sensible if he were willingly backing his daughter's impending nuptials to one of the biggest assholes Phoenix had ever had the displeasure to meet.

"Last I recall, you were already married," Phoenix stated, once more resuming his casual stance, leaning back in his chair.

"Divorced." Damien's response was almost instant, as though the guy knew he had to be on the defensive.

"I'm sorry to hear that," Phoenix said, pretending to actually give a shit.

"I'm not. Mia didn't have what it took to support a man like me."

Phoenix chuckled, glancing down at his hands, imagining them wrapped around Landry's thick neck. "A man like you."

"She was too soft. Too..."

A growl sounded from behind Phoenix, but he didn't turn around. He knew that was Tarik's way of informing him he wasn't happy with the conversation.

"*Too* what?" Phoenix inquired, wanting Landry to explain himself.

His heart rate had spiked from the hatred that began sizzling in his veins. He might not know much about Mia, but he knew that she deserved someone a hell of a lot better than Landry.

"You should know," Damien smarted off, looking up at Tarik. "The two of you looked kinda cozy the other night. Not that it matters. She got what she wanted," Damien said, obviously not planning to finish his earlier statement as he met Phoenix's gaze again.

"Which was?"

"Money."

"Is that right?" Phoenix said, biting his tongue to keep from saying something he shouldn't.

"She walked away with three million. Now she can get the education she never bothered to get. She'll make some blue collar worker a nice wife one day." Damien nodded toward Tarik as he said the words.

"According to what I read, she should've received another ten mil for your infidelity," Tarik stated.

"That was never proven."

"Of course it wasn't," Tarik muttered.

Phoenix growled, the sound radiating from his chest before he even realized it. "We're through here," he told Landry.

Damien pushed to his feet, his eyes still locked with Phoenix's. "Is this about Mia? Is your lackey over here trying to get in her panties? Trust me, it just takes a little money to get her to spread 'em. I doubt *he*" — Damien nodded toward Tarik again — "makes nearly enough to satisfy her."

Another growl emanated from behind Phoenix, and he knew that a shit storm was about to rain down.

"We're. Done," Phoenix snapped as he leaned forward.

"You're making a mistake, Phoenix."

"I don't think I am. But if that's the case, it won't be the first time."

"See, that's where you and I differ," Damien said through gritted teeth. "Every single thing *I* do, I do for a reason. I don't make mistakes."

Phoenix grinned defiantly. "You already have, Damien. You already have."

Damien glared at him for a second longer but then turned and walked out, leaving Phoenix to himself.

"That's not the only way we differ, you bastard," Phoenix muttered to himself.

»»»»»» ♥ «««««

TARIK WAS TEMPTED to follow Landry out into the parking lot and beat his ass into a slimy pulp. The bastard irritated the fuck out of him solely by breathing, but then he'd gone and made the mistake of talking shit about Mia. The possessive instinct that had overwhelmed him damn near had him doing something he'd likely regret later.

Somehow he managed to maintain his composure. But it wasn't easy.

"Ten million? Really?" Phoenix asked when he got to his feet, the lethal tone he'd used with Landry no longer present in his voice. Phoenix casually slid his hands into his pockets as he moved toward the door. Tarik fell into step behind him.

"The prenup had a fidelity clause. Of course, Landry's lawyers made it damn near impossible for Mia to win that one."

"So she just let it go?"

"From what I can tell, yes. She got a mil for every birthday she spent with him. She asked for a divorce a couple of weeks before year four."

"Well, that proves she wasn't in it for the money."

"Honestly, I don't know what the fuck she saw in him," Tarik stated fiercely.

"You and me both," Phoenix agreed as they stepped out of the conference room and back in the direction of Phoenix's office. "I'll be ready to head out in a few."

Tarik nodded and then went to his office to get his laptop. He couldn't stop thinking about Damien's comment. Could the asshole really be that stupid? Did he honestly believe the bullshit he'd spewed about Mia? Or was that his ego talking? After all, she'd up and left him for cheating. Tarik wasn't sure that Phoenix had ever dated a woman who would've cared as long as she was sitting in the lap of luxury while he dipped his wick in someone else's pool.

It made him like Mia all the more, and he realized he already liked her quite a bit. So much so that he'd been a little disappointed that he hadn't been able to see her over the weekend. At one point, he had considered stopping by her condo to talk to her but had thought better of it. First of all, Phoenix had warned him away from her — not that he had any intention of following direction for the simple fact that he enjoyed the hell out of getting Phoenix riled up. And second, Tarik had spent most of the weekend trying to figure out how to deal with the situation with Phoenix, doing a little more research on Mia Cantrell while he was at it.

He still didn't have an answer for how to handle Phoenix, but he did understand Mia quite a bit more now.

From what he'd read, Mia had been barely twenty when she'd said her vows to Landry. From the pictures he'd pulled up, she had looked like a woman in love. Damien, on the other hand, had looked like a man who'd acquired something he'd longed to get his hands on. Knowing Phoenix as well as he did, Tarik understood the emotion behind an acquisition, but he also knew how quickly the elation faded when all was said and done.

Based on the stories he'd found, through the years, Mia had stood by Damien's side, flaunted as a trophy, talked about as though she lacked a single brain cell — by the press *and* by Landry. He'd noticed a change in Mia through the progression of pictures over time — her smile and the light in her eyes had dimmed over time. Yet Tarik had been surprised to find that there weren't any stories from Mia's point of view after she'd asked for a divorce. She had never gone to the press, never tried to fight for the money that was due her. It said a lot about the woman they'd both found themselves taken with.

"You ready?"

Tarik looked up to see Phoenix standing in the doorway. He hadn't even realized he'd sat down at his desk until that moment. The thought bothered him. He wasn't supposed to sit down. The whole PR/assistant thing was more of a way to stay close to Phoenix without hovering, something that had irritated Phoenix in the beginning. Not that Tarik minded the details of his job. They didn't bother him one bit. Talking hockey was more a hobby than a job. And Phoenix had never made him feel as though he had to do anything for him. Tarik did them because he wanted to. His real job was to protect Phoenix. And he was clearly failing.

"I'm ready," Tarik said as he grabbed his laptop and pulled the key to the Escalade from his pocket. "Where to?"

"Let's grab lunch and then stop by the training center. We'll be meeting Mia at UT around four thirty when her classes are over."

Tarik didn't respond, merely lifted his eyebrow at the news. It wasn't his place to argue with Phoenix.

Nor did he want to.

Chapter Thirteen

MIA WAS NERVOUS as she exited the building on her way to the spot where she'd left Phoenix that morning. It wasn't because of what had happened or the possibility that someone had been following her that had her on edge, either. No, her nerves had been slowly ratcheting up one notch at a time for the last hour as she'd counted down the minutes before she would see Phoenix again.

It could've also been due to the information she'd immersed herself in during the day. And no, she wasn't referring to schoolwork.

If someone were to ask her to explain anything her professors had discussed in any of her classes, she would've been at a total loss. For the better part of the day, she'd been daydreaming, lost in her own thoughts. She felt like a schoolgirl anxiously hoping she would get a glimpse of the boy she was crushing on as she passed him in the hall, never mind the fact that she was, technically, in school. When she wasn't doing that, she was researching.

As she walked across the campus, she rapidly glanced from one face to another until she saw him. Luckily, her feet continued to move her forward, because her chest had tightened and her belly fluttered at the mere sight of him standing there exactly where she'd left him that morning. She wasn't the only one who had noticed him, either. Then again, there weren't many men on the planet who drew attention the way Phoenix Pierce did. And of course, it didn't hurt that he was wearing a suit and looked like he'd stepped out of GQ magazine.

"Mia," he greeted when she approached.

The way he said her name, his tone low and authoritative, had the army of butterflies desperately trying to escape her stomach.

"Hey," she said, still admiring him when he took her bag from her arm, hefting it on his shoulder.

"I hope you don't mind, but I brought the car."

"I don't mind." Hell, she didn't know what she was even saying, but she decided to go with it because he seemed to be okay with her answer.

When they approached the sleek black Escalade, she realized the driver was none other than the sexy, intimidating Tarik Marx. She wasn't sure she should've been surprised. He was, after all, Phoenix's right-hand man — as she'd learned via her Internet research. Since Phoenix was none other than the owner of Austin's very own NHL team and Tarik was responsible for public relations, it seemed fitting that the two of them were always together. It didn't hurt that she'd read hints that Tarik was also Phoenix's bodyguard, although that had never been publicly stated by Phoenix or Tarik. However, she remembered the knowing gleam in Tarik's eyes when she had mentioned it.

Still, knowing all that she did now, she ignored the myriad of questions she had for both of them as she smiled at Tarik. His golden eyes traveled over her briefly as though he was sizing her up to determine whether or not she was a threat.

That or he wanted to eat her for dinner.

The thought sent a tremor of awareness snaking down her spine.

She could've assured him she wasn't a threat — not to Phoenix and certainly not to him — but she didn't. She merely thanked him when he opened the door for her. Phoenix climbed in behind her, and the door closed, sealing them inside.

Alone.

At least until Tarik made his way around and into the front seat.

More butterflies began a flurry of activity inside her belly. Her thoughts drifted to the information she'd pulled up online. The *interesting* stuff. Not the articles that went on and on about hockey and the Arrows organization, or even those that talked about Phoenix's other company. No, Mia was thinking about the stories that had alluded to the two of them involved in certain sexual encounters. Things that Mia hadn't thought really happened. Well, except for in the erotic novels she had stumbled upon a few short months ago.

"How was your day?" Phoenix asked, his tone friendly but loud enough to catch her off guard, causing her to jump.

"Sorry." Smiling through her nervousness, Mia added, "Good." Looking over at him again, she tried her best to ignore the intimidating man glancing back at her in the rearview mirror, all while avoiding the curiosity regarding what these two actually did behind closed doors.

She could feel her cheeks heat when she saw that Phoenix was looking at her, as well. She wasn't sure why she was so nervous, but the more she'd thought about him that day, the more anxious she'd been to see him. Adding Tarik to the mix didn't make it any easier.

There had even been a point in the day — a brief half hour between classes when she had grabbed food in the cafeteria — that she had pondered the idea of actually seeing where things might lead with this man. Well, more accurately, her thoughts had bordered on the lascivious until she'd had no choice but to toss her food in the trash and sneak off to the restroom to run cold water over her wrists in an attempt to cool herself off.

Absurd, she knew, but she hadn't been able to shake the thought. And as the day had passed, she'd secretly wished that he would make a move. What kind of move, she didn't know, but she felt significantly more educated after reading the information she'd found about him online.

"Are you hungry?" he asked.

Glancing down at her jeans and sweatshirt, Mia realized that she wasn't dressed to go anywhere with him. By comparison, she looked as though he had picked her up at a homeless shelter, and that certainly wouldn't do for going out in public with him dressed like that, so she answered with, "No, I'm good."

"You sure? I could change. There's a fantastic Japanese restaurant around the corner."

Mia met his green gaze and hesitated. She wanted to say yes, but she didn't know how.

When Phoenix smiled, she knew he had figured her out.

"All right. We'll drop your stuff off, I'll go to my place and change, and I'll meet you in the lobby in ... say ... twenty minutes."

"Okay," she said instantly. His smile grew even wider, and Mia's insides lit up like a bonfire.

Half an hour later, Mia stepped off the elevator back in the lobby and came face-to-face with Phoenix. She had to admit, she was a little disappointed to see that he was alone. Part of her had hoped that Tarik would accompany them tonight, but she shoved the thought away. She was getting too carried away with herself.

Phoenix looked incredibly handsome, which didn't help all that much in pulling her mind out of the gutter. He had abandoned the suit in lieu of a pair of distressed jeans and a forest-green polo coupled with a sexy brown leather jacket. Mia felt her mouth begin to water. She'd seen him in his running gear, she'd seen him in immaculate suits, and she'd even seen him in a tuxedo, but this… She'd never seen him look as good as he did right then. Casual. Sexy.

"We'll walk, if you don't mind," Phoenix said, coming to stand directly in front of her.

"Sounds good to me." Kicking out her foot, Mia showed him that she hadn't changed out of her athletic shoes. She'd considered putting on something nicer but then refused. It was one thing for her to give in to the pleasure of his company; it was something else to put forth more effort than she should simply to get his attention.

Phoenix placed his hand on the small of her back and urged her toward the door. When they stepped outside, the lingering January chill filled her lungs and made Mia long for spring. As much as she loved this time of year, she was ready to be rid of the blustering winds and the biting chill in the air. There was still the possibility of snow — something she would love to see — between now and spring, but even with that chance, she longed for warmer temperatures.

By the time they reached the restaurant, Mia was shivering and her fingers were numb. She tried to pretend not to be cold as she smiled at Phoenix.

The hostess greeted Phoenix by name, which wasn't all that surprising. Considering he lived around the corner and had rattled off the place as his first suggestion, it wasn't shocking that he frequented the establishment enough for them to know him. The woman gathered two menus and then led them through the restaurant to a small table in the back.

Once they were seated, the pleasant hostess left them alone for a few minutes, and Mia took the time to study the menu.

"What do you suggest?" she asked Phoenix, primarily to make conversation. When she looked up at him, she saw that he was watching her, his hands resting over the closed menu, a mischievous gleam in his eyes, only highlighted by the flicker of candlelight from the table.

"Do you like sushi?"

"Yes," she replied, holding his gaze.

"Then I say we load up on it."

"I'm game if you are," she said softly, her mind drifting to other things she'd be willing to load up on. Namely him.

As though the waiter had been listening in, he appeared at their side, a pad of paper and pen at the ready. Mia allowed Phoenix to order for her, and he didn't hesitate, rattling off what sounded like half the menu.

"Tell me about you," Phoenix suggested when they were alone once again.

"What do you want to know?"

"Did you grow up here?"

"In Austin, yes," she admitted. "My mother lives in Circle C. She's a pediatric surgeon."

"And your father?"

"He was a professor at UT. He died when I was ten," Mia told him sadly.

"I'm sorry to hear that. Health problems?"

Mia's eyes dropped to the table. "No, he committed suicide. He was diagnosed with bipolar disorder in his early twenties. He battled with long bouts of severe depression his entire life."

"Which explains why you're an advocate for suicide prevention," he stated. There wasn't an ounce of judgment in his tone. "My reason for supporting is similar, although the person I lost wasn't a family member. He was a player."

Mia nodded, saddened by the thought.

"My father passed away nine months ago," he stated. "I don't think it's easy to lose someone you're close to at any age. For any reason."

"No, it's not." All her memories of her father were good ones, and she could spend hours going through the photo albums she had of them when she was younger. It was still difficult to talk about him, though, but only because she missed him terribly. She didn't hold it against him that he'd felt life had become unbearable enough that he had taken his own life, but she wished she'd have been able to do something to prevent it. "What about you? Are you from here?" she asked, changing the subject.

"Born and raised. I went to UT, got my MBA from McCombs School of Business."

"And you own a hockey team?"

She'd apparently surprised him with that information, because his eyebrows rose slightly as he said, "Among other things."

"Pierce Industries?" Mia asked.

His smirk said he caught what she'd said. "So you did a little investigating, did you?"

"Just a little," she answered, her face heating.

She'd actually spent her entire first class period devouring every bit of information she could pull up in the Google search engine. There was enough detail on the Internet on Phoenix to write a book. In the hockey world, he was a celebrity. On the business side, he'd taken the world by storm, making millions by investing in some well-known companies long before they were well-known.

It wasn't until her second class that she had encountered some of the most *interesting* articles about him.

"What else did you find out?"

She opted to go with the safe things she'd learned. "Your father bought the expansion team nearly a decade ago."

"Correct," Phoenix confirmed. "I think he did it more for me. His father was a venture capitalist, made millions investing in people with ideas that he knew would make them both rich."

"Sort of like *Shark Tank*?" she asked, referring to the television show she'd watched a time or two.

Phoenix's smile lit up his entire face. "Exactly. My father followed suit, taking over when my grandfather passed away. I don't think it was ever really his thing, although he was certainly good at making a buck. Since I was such a hockey fanatic as a kid, I think he bought into my passion."

"But hockey wasn't your first love?" she asked, enjoying his enthusiasm.

"It warred with my analytical side, I think. I didn't dream of being a hockey star. I wanted to be like my grandfather. Investing in other people's dreams and seeing them through does something for me."

Mia could understand that. Especially when he explained it with so much light in his eyes.

"What else did you learn?" he asked after the waiter brought their drinks.

"At twenty-nine, you were named one of Austin's most eligible bachelors. And just a couple of months ago, you were called one of the sexiest businessmen in Texas. Hmmm... What else did I read? Oh. You've never been married, have lived in the building you also own for the last seven years."

She wasn't about to tell him that she'd read a story about a threesome he'd been involved in, one that had included him and Tarik in a precarious situation. Obviously the woman who'd told the story had either been looking for her fifteen minutes of fame because she'd been involved with the infamous playboys — as they'd been called — or she was after the money. Mia wasn't sure.

"Impressive. And what will I find if I Google you?"

Smiling, Mia said, "Are you trying to tell me you haven't Googled me yet?"

"Maybe. Maybe not. But even if I have, I'd much rather hear your version of things. So, what's the most newsworthy thing about Mia Cantrell?"

Mia looked down at the table. She could easily answer that question, but she wasn't sure she wanted to. There were so many articles written, some before and during her marriage to Damien, but quite a bit afterward. Mostly afterward. It seemed that the media didn't have any issues reporting on mere speculation, and some of the things they'd said about her didn't paint her in a very flattering light.

But that wasn't the worst of it. Mia had stumbled across an article that mentioned Damien and Phoenix together, so of course, she'd been curious. As it turned out, Damien was currently suing Phoenix. Mia had no idea what was going on, nor did she want to get in the middle of that, but she couldn't help but think Phoenix would believe otherwise if she brought it up.

"Just say pass," Phoenix said softly, reaching out and touching her hand, the warmth of his touch sending a zing of pleasure coursing down her arm. "If you don't want to answer, I won't press you."

"No, it's…" Mia briefly glanced around to see who else might be in hearing distance. She was happy to see they were alone at the back of the restaurant. "I'm divorced. The man I was married to is in the public eye. And as you know, since you've got experience with the media, they can be brutal. There're plenty of stories about me, some not so nice."

"Trust me, I'm sure you've read some not-so-pleasant things about me," he offered. "I don't believe everything I read, so we're good."

Mia nodded, giving him a small smile. She really hoped he meant that, because, should he decide to look up information on her if he hadn't already, he'd see that she'd been called a gold digger, a whore, and plenty more colorful words. It didn't matter that she'd never once said anything negative about Damien publicly; they still attacked her. As did Damien. There wasn't anything to substantiate the fodder, but she'd learned there was nothing she could do to stop the press, either. They were relentless when they wanted a story.

"I'm sure by tomorrow morning, there will be pictures of you and me floating out in cyberspace," Phoenix said.

Mia blushed. After reading what she had, she wasn't sure she wanted to know what they would speculate on. The one thing she was grateful for, although she'd initially been disappointed, was that Tarik hadn't come along. Who knew what those rumors might be.

"I wouldn't doubt it," she told him. "I can't seem to escape the paparazzi. They've camped out in front of the building a time or two." Although now that she knew who Phoenix was, she had to wonder whether they were really there to catch a glimpse of him. That made more sense. "Things seem to have escalated somewhat, and I'm pretty sure that's because my ex recently got engaged. Why they think I'd have anything to say about that, I don't know."

That was another thing Mia had had to endure during her Internet search. She'd been both angry and relieved at the same time. Considering Teresa Somerhaus was the new woman in Damien's life, Mia was angry all over again at the fact that Damien had cheated with her, but relieved at the same time because she'd seen Phoenix talking to her at the charity ball. If Teresa was marrying Damien, then that meant she would have to keep her claws off Phoenix. At least she hoped.

"I'm sorry to hear that," Phoenix said, his eyes seemingly searching hers.

"I'm not," she stated affirmatively. "I don't care what he does or who he does it with. I wish they'd leave me out of it entirely. Now that he's making news with someone else, I'm relieved. Maybe they'll leave me alone."

"I can't promise that'll be the case once someone sees the two of us together," Phoenix told her, his hand still resting on hers. "I've been known to incite the press to write some rather thought-provoking things."

Mia wanted to ask him to elaborate, but she held back the words. She wasn't sure she was ready to hear the details. She'd read enough; hearing about it would likely make her ears catch fire.

It was another tick mark in the con column on Mia's list of reasons she'd started for staying away from Phoenix. The pro column seemed to be lust driven; the con column was riddled with all the things she'd learned from being with Damien.

But she'd told herself that she wasn't going to let her fears drive her anymore. Simply wanting to get to know this man didn't mean she had to get involved with him.

Now if her hormones would only listen to reason, she might stand half a chance.

Chapter Fourteen

PHOENIX HAD ENJOYED the evening far more than he'd thought possible. Especially considering sex hadn't been on the agenda. It was new for him, something he didn't often do. Getting to know a woman past what she felt like beneath him wasn't high on his list of priorities these days.

With Mia, he found that taking her to bed wasn't the *only* thing on his mind. He couldn't deny the fact that he'd had some salacious thoughts about her, because … well, because, hell, he'd pictured her naked plenty of times throughout dinner. He'd thought about what it would be like to lay her on the table, right there in the restaurant, and devour her, licking her from her sexy little nose all the way down to her toes. Slowly.

More than that, though, he'd enjoyed the conversation. She was extremely easy to talk to. There hadn't been a single giggle that had escaped her, which he found to be one of the things he liked most about her. She was incredibly smart and articulate, and never once had she just nodded her head and agreed with what he'd said.

And now, as they walked back to their building, Phoenix had pinpointed the highlight of the evening. As they had exited the restaurant, when he had reached for her hand, Mia hadn't balked at sliding her silky smooth fingers in his. He was torn between wanting to hold her hand for the rest of the evening and wanting to pull her into his arms so he could feel her soft body against his.

Not that he would do the latter, because he knew Mia would run. Fast and far. Which would ultimately undermine all the progress they'd made tonight. As it was, he was happy that she'd agreed to dinner, and he hoped when he asked her out again, she'd be equally willing.

When they made it into the elevator, Phoenix knew that the night was ending for them, much as it had on Friday. However, unlike then, he didn't want to simply walk away. Not that he was ready to invite her to his place or try and coax his way into hers. No, he knew with a woman like Mia, he would have to take things slow.

He could do slow.

It might kill him, but he could do slow.

His thoughts immediately drifted to Tarik. More specifically, the kiss they'd shared. Whatever was going on between him and Tarik had redefined the word slow in his book. It'd taken nearly two years for them to progress to that kiss. Not counting that night so long ago, the one that had confirmed for Phoenix just how much he wanted the man. But Phoenix had been able to attribute that to the overabundance of alcohol he'd consumed that night. Didn't matter that he would've done it stone-cold sober.

What was worse, Phoenix was so fucking confused between his apparent infatuation with Mia and his desire for Tarik that he wasn't even sure what he was doing.

"Thank you for dinner. And for walking me to school. Oh, and for the ride home," Mia rambled as they made their way to her front door, pulling him out of his thoughts.

"You're welcome. Thank you for accompanying me. I had a great time."

After she retrieved her keys from her purse, Mia looked up at him. She was standing so close he could smell the sweet strawberry scent of her shampoo, see the silver flecks in her crystal-blue eyes, hear her slightly irregular breathing.

So she felt it, too?

Phoenix reached out and slid the back of his finger along her smooth cheek, his eyes locked with hers. Seconds passed, and neither of them moved, seemingly stuck there in that single moment of time, nothing else in the world existing except the two of them.

Phoenix tried. He tried really fucking hard to avoid the temptation, but the longer they stood there, the greater the pull to her seemed to get, until he found himself saying, "I'm going to kiss you, Mia."

When she didn't argue or try to move away, Phoenix took one step closer, his body coming into contact with hers. His dick hardened instantly as he cupped her face with both hands, noticing the way her glossy pink lips parted ever so slightly.

God, she was so fucking sweet.

Leaning in, Phoenix brushed his lips against hers lightly. He felt the warmth of her breath against his mouth, heard the hitch in her breathing, which only spurred him forward. Angling her head a hair to the right, Phoenix pressed his lips to hers more firmly, sliding his tongue along the seam until her hands came up and fisted in his shirt. It was then that the fragile grip he had on his control slipped, then threatened to snap, but he managed to hang on to it. Barely.

Sliding his tongue into her mouth, past her lips, gently stroking her tongue, he was overwhelmed by sensation. Something so powerful he felt the aftershocks clear down to his toes. When he was met with a sweet, fervent resistance, her tongue gliding over his, her mouth opening for him, Phoenix took control, delving deeper, pulling her closer, cupping her face more firmly. And when she moaned into his mouth, Phoenix knew he had to stop or he was going to do something he would easily regret.

Mia Cantrell was not a one-night woman. As much as he wanted to tell himself he could sweet-talk her out of her clothes and into bed, Phoenix didn't want that. Well, not *only* that. He wanted more than one night with her, which meant he had to slow down, had to get a secure grip on his self-control.

"You're so damn sweet, Mia," he mumbled against her lips as he pulled back, keeping his mouth only a breath away. "I could get lost in you if I let myself."

He hadn't meant to say the words; they'd just come out. For the first time in his adult life, he hadn't been saying them in an attempt to get her naked, but the way Mia's eyes widened told him he'd gone a little too far.

She took a step back, her hand coming to rest against her lips, but she still didn't say anything. Her eyes traveled over his face slowly, as though she was trying to figure him out. He could've told her that it wasn't possible, but he got the strange feeling she might be able to see deeper than anyone before her, so he kept his thoughts to himself.

"Good night, Mia," he whispered, keeping his eyes locked with hers.

"Good night," she murmured as she took another step away from him, her back touching her door. She turned, inserted the key, and then escaped inside before he could convince his legs to move. Once she was safely on the other side, Phoenix exhaled and turned away slowly.

And when he got into the elevator to go up to his floor, Phoenix knew without a doubt that life as he knew it had taken a significant turn.

He just wasn't sure what to do about that, even if he could acknowledge it.

»»»»»»♥«««««

TARIK HEARD THE front door when it closed, and he fought the urge to get up off his couch. There was only one person who would stop by his condo, only one person who would merely walk in without bothering to knock first.

Phoenix. The one person Tarik didn't want to see at the moment.

As it was, for the last two hours, he hadn't moved from where he reclined on the couch. After taking a shower and changing into sweats, fighting off the thoughts of Phoenix and Mia together, Tarik hadn't been in the mood to do anything other than sit down and mindlessly stare at the television. He hadn't even bothered to turn the damn thing on.

And now that Phoenix was there, Tarik had to wonder what had happened at dinner. Evidently Phoenix hadn't convinced Mia to go back to his place. So, the only positive thing was that the two of them weren't about to get down and dirty in Phoenix's guest room. Or on the couch. Tarik knew Phoenix didn't take women to his bed. When Tarik had asked him about it once, Phoenix had told him that until he found someone worthy of more than one night, his bed was off-limits.

It made sense. More sense than it should, probably.

Tarik wanted to be invited to Phoenix's bed. Almost more than he wanted his next breath.

A throat cleared, followed by Phoenix's deep voice. "You awake?"

Tarik sighed but didn't move. For half a second, he debated whether or not he should pretend to be asleep. At least that way he wouldn't have to see Phoenix, wouldn't have to hear about his date with Mia. Wouldn't have to deal with the jealousy that threatened to rip him to pieces at the thought of the two of them together. Without him.

"Yeah," he said instead, opening his eyes but not bothering to get up.

Phoenix moved into view, propping himself up against the living room wall as he stared down at Tarik.

Tarik let his eyes rake over Phoenix momentarily, taking in the way his jeans stretched nicely over his thick thighs and the shirt he wore accentuated his impressive chest. When he met Phoenix's gaze, he held it. "Where's Mia?"

"I took her home."

Tarik did his best not to read into that. Phoenix hadn't been gone long enough for the two of them to have gotten naked. Not *nearly* long enough.

"Need something?" Tarik asked.

Phoenix didn't answer him; his eyes merely continued to roam over Tarik leisurely. When his perusal caused anger to slice through him, Tarik knew he had to send him on his way. He was in no mood to put up with Phoenix's strange moods or his confusion. As it was, he felt a little beaten down by it.

"I'm gonna call it a night," Tarik said slowly, trying to mask his irritation. "Did you *need* something?"

And just like that, Phoenix stood up straight, shook his head as though he'd had a moment of clarity, and he turned to walk out. Tarik was off the couch and following him down the short hallway that led to the front door. "Hold up!"

Phoenix stopped abruptly, spinning around to face Tarik. Bumping into him was an accident but not entirely unwarranted. Face-to-face with Phoenix, Tarik was about to ask what his problem was, but Phoenix managed to steal the words right out of his mouth when he reached for him, grabbing his hips and yanking him forward, their bodies slamming together at the same time their lips collided.

Tarik groaned as Phoenix's hands slid upward, stroking the bare skin of his sides. Tarik reached for Phoenix, pushing his hands through his hair and pulling his head back, controlling the kiss. The desire that had been pulsing between them intensified right there against the wall in the darkened hallway.

When Phoenix bit his bottom lip, thrusting his hips forward, their erections grinding together, Tarik wasn't sure he was going to be able to stop. He was shirtless, and Phoenix's hands were roaming over him, the warmth of his touch igniting every nerve ending.

"Tarik," Phoenix growled as he pushed him, causing him to stumble, his back slamming into the opposite wall as Phoenix pursued him, their mouths never breaking completely apart. "What the fuck *is* this? Why can't I stop thinking about you?"

Tarik didn't know how to answer that question. At least not for Phoenix. He knew what this was for him. It was every fucking thing he'd wanted for as long as he could remember. Phoenix's hands, his mouth, all of it focused on him.

"Don't think too much," Tarik said when they came up for air, their foreheads pressed together.

"I can't *stop* thinking," Phoenix bit out. "I'm so fucking confused."

"Well, I'm not." No, Tarik knew exactly what he wanted. This man. Every single glorious inch of him.

Their lips brushed against one another as Phoenix continued to speak. "I want her. And I want you, too. How can you not be confused? It makes no damn sense."

"It makes perfect sense," Tarik whispered.

"It's not like the other times," Phoenix said. "One night won't be enough. Not with her."

"Why only one night?" Tarik asked, licking Phoenix's bottom lip. "Why does it have to be all or nothing?"

Phoenix didn't answer, his lips melded to Tarik's, their tongues searching. Some of the intensity faded, but the passion still lingered. Phoenix's hands traveled over Tarik's bare chest, his thumbs brushing over his nipples, eliciting a sharp inhale. He wanted Phoenix to put his mouth there. To bite his nipples, to send shards of pleasure mixed with an erotic pain straight through him.

Knowing the moment wouldn't last forever, Tarik palmed Phoenix's head, urging him down. Phoenix didn't fight him, his lips trailing down his jaw, his neck, his collarbone. As though the other man knew exactly what he needed, Phoenix's mouth left a trail of blazing hot kisses across his chest and right to his nipple. He licked a circle around it, then clipped him with his teeth. Tarik thrust his hips forward, needing friction on his dick.

"Fuck yes. Bite me, Phoenix," Tarik demanded.

Phoenix did, nipping him harder, then chasing the pain away with his tongue.

While Phoenix continued to drive him out of his mind, Tarik reached between them and rubbed his palm against Phoenix's cock, his jeans limiting his ability to touch him skin to skin.

Then Phoenix's mouth was on his once more, one hand coming up to grip his hair, holding his head still. "I've dreamed about this, Tarik." Phoenix's words came out in a harsh whisper, the desperation in his tone making Tarik's dick pulse and throb.

Phoenix slid his other hand into Tarik's sweatpants, gripping his cock firmly, stroking slowly.

"Fucking hell," Tarik muttered.

"I've thought about what it would be like to put your dick in my mouth. To suck you until you come down my throat."

Tarik didn't say anything. He couldn't. The pleasure was too much. The way Phoenix's firm grip wrapped around his cock, every muscle in his body was strung tight.

"I've never done that before," Phoenix admitted. "I've had men blow me, but I've never returned the favor."

Tarik opened his eyes and met Phoenix's hard gaze, his honesty like a brutal slap to the face. He'd never...? Tarik knew, based on what Phoenix had told him, that he hadn't had intercourse with a man, but he'd never...? *Holy fuck.*

"I want to feel what it's like for you to fuck my mouth. I want your hands in my hair, holding me still while you drive your dick down my throat." The rough, aroused tone of Phoenix's voice made Tarik's cock jump in Phoenix's hand.

His thoughts were all over the map, but Tarik couldn't produce words. For all the time he'd known Phoenix, he'd never known the man to relinquish control. But what he was telling him now was exactly the opposite. Had he been waiting all this time for Tarik to take the control from him?

As tempting as that was, Tarik needed Phoenix to give himself to him first. As Phoenix had said before, one night would never be enough. Never.

"What about Mia?" Tarik asked.

"I want her just as much. I've fantasized about my cock sliding into her warm, slick heat while you fuck my ass."

Tarik's breath got stuck in his throat. Phoenix's hand was still stroking Tarik's dick, faster now. He wasn't going to last much longer, he knew that much. If Phoenix didn't stop, he was going to come in his fucking hand.

"I've imagined her sucking your dick while I'm fucking her from behind. Sliding my cock into her warm, wet pussy."

Tarik understood everything Phoenix was saying — he'd had the same fantasies. But he knew what the problem was. Mia was too sweet for that. No matter how many times he tried to envision it, they were simply fantasies. When he attempted to match it to what little he knew of the woman, it never worked. She was too innocent to give herself over to two men.

He had to wonder whether Phoenix realized that, too. Was that why he was finally giving in?

Suddenly Phoenix's breath was no longer on his mouth; his hand disappeared from inside his sweats. Tarik tried to take a deep breath, ready to accept that this wasn't going to happen, but then Phoenix dropped to his knees, yanking Tarik's sweats down his legs.

"Oh, God," Tarik groaned, dropping his head against the wall when Phoenix engulfed his dick, taking him all the way in his mouth. He resisted the urge to fist his hands in the man's hair. He could so easily do it, so effortlessly take control, but he needed Phoenix to finish what he'd started. And not because Tarik forced him to. Because Phoenix wanted to.

Looking down the length of his body, Tarik watched as his cock disappeared inside Phoenix's mouth, the way his lips wrapped around him, stretching tight.

"That's it," Tarik encouraged, his hands balled at his sides. "Take all of me, Phoenix. Suck my dick. Damn, that's good."

Phoenix laved his dick with his tongue, using only his mouth to pleasure him.

"I'm gonna come down your throat," Tarik told him. "I want to watch you take all of me."

Phoenix groaned, the vibration sending shockwaves of pleasure straight to Tarik's balls. He wasn't going to last, not while he watched the one man he'd wanted for so damn long on his knees sucking his dick with so much eagerness. It was more than he could bear.

"Faster," he instructed. "Take me deeper. Oh, fuck, Phoenix. I'm gonna come."

No sooner did the words leave his mouth than Tarik exploded, his dick pulsing, spurting into Phoenix's throat as he sucked him dry.

Any other time that he'd had his dick sucked, Tarik would've been satisfied. He would've been able to breathe easier for just a little while. But as he helped Phoenix to his feet, pulling him in for another kiss, tasting himself in Phoenix's mouth, Tarik knew that this wasn't going to be easy. Nothing about Phoenix Pierce was easy. It didn't matter that he'd finally given in to something they'd both wanted for a long damn time.

There was still someone else. Someone they both couldn't stop thinking about.

Chapter Fifteen

THE WEEK FLEW by without incident, something Mia was incredibly grateful for. The reporters had all but disappeared. Mia wasn't sure if that was a fluke, but she didn't question it, grateful not to have to endure overly pushy people who wanted their questions answered regardless of what it was they were asking. Whoever might've been following her — if her imagination hadn't merely been playing tricks on her — hadn't been back, either. Then again, Phoenix had insisted that his driver take her to school and pick her up on Wednesday and Thursday. He'd said he would've done it, but he was out of town on business.

Initially, when Phoenix had informed her that he and Tarik would be gone for a couple of days, she'd been disappointed but made sure she didn't show it. The last thing she wanted was to appear needy, although she'd somehow developed a bit of a crush on both men, despite her frequent denial.

In fact, her curiosity had been the reason she'd made an attempt to speak with Phoenix's driver, whose name she had learned was Gus, on Wednesday morning when he'd taken her to school.

"Do you drive many women to school these days?" she asked, keeping her tone light, despite how much she wanted to know the answer to that question.

"Never," he answered straightforwardly. "Well, no one other than Ellen from time to time, but I doubt she's the type of woman you're referring to."

The glint in his perceptive brown eyes told her he'd definitely understood her inquiry.

"Sorry," she said absently. "I don't mean to be nosy."

The older man gifted her with a knowing smile, and Mia fidgeted slightly. "Ms. Cantrell, I can tell you that you're in good hands with Mr. Pierce and Mr. Marx. They're good people. I started out working for the elder Mr. Pierce, which means I've known Coach for most of his life."

Mia's cheeks burned at the memory of how she'd learned who Coach really was.

"Phoenix and Tarik are close, huh?" she asked, glancing out the window at the passing scenery.

"Very. Probably closer than they even realize."

Mia had attempted to decipher Gus's last statement after he'd dropped her at school. She'd noticed they were closer than a mere employer/employee relationship. A lot closer. And that realization had only led to a myriad of questions pummeling her brain.

She had tried to convince herself that she was only interested in Phoenix, but there was something about Tarik that had her curious. And nervous. Truth was, Tarik *made* her nervous. Not because she feared him, but he did intimidate her. Whether it was his size or the look of sheer determination etched on his chiseled features, she didn't know. However, her anxiety had been abated yesterday when he'd surprised her.

"Hello?" Mia greeted the caller, not recognizing the number.

"Mia? It's Tarik."

Mia's heart leaped into her throat when she recognized his voice. "Hi."

"Meet me for lunch," came his next request.

"Today?"

"Yes," he said with a gruff chuckle.

"Okay." The answer came out far easier than she'd anticipated. "My next class isn't until two."

"I'll pick you up in five minutes."

Fifteen minutes later, Tarik was leading her to a table in the back of a small café not far from campus. They were handed menus and then left alone while the waitress scurried about, helping the other people already seated.

"I thought you and Phoenix were out of town," she said after scanning the menu quickly and deciding on what she wanted.

"We got back this morning."

"Where's Phoenix?" she asked, hoping she didn't sound as though she wasn't happy to be there with him.

"Home. He had a conference call. I thought I'd take advantage and get you alone for a bit."

Mia's heart skipped a beat — maybe two — as she stared into his golden eyes. The guy really was incredibly handsome. His hair was darker than Phoenix's, his skin a little lighter, not quite as bronzed as Phoenix's. She wasn't sure why she was making a comparison between the two, but as she stared back at him, she saw so many differences, and not only in their appearance. Enough that Mia was even more intrigued by him right then than she had been before.

When Tarik had called her cell phone and asked her to lunch on Thursday, Mia had nearly swallowed her tongue, but somehow she had accepted. She'd felt a little guilty, as though she were cheating on Phoenix, but she had reminded herself that she and Phoenix were only friends. That kiss — although mind-blowing — couldn't happen again. Without a doubt, Mia knew she wouldn't survive another relationship with a man like Phoenix.

Unfortunately, after that incredibly comfortable lunch where she and Tarik had talked about everything from where he was born to what classes she was taking at school, Mia had been even more confused than before. She'd given in to the idea that she was physically attracted to Phoenix and enjoyed his company immensely. But she'd had a very similar reaction to Tarik.

And that was the main reason Alex was on her way over. Mia needed a sounding board, and she hadn't had a chance to talk to Alex. So much had happened since the night of the charity ball.

But the waiting was over, because she was about to get a chance to chew Alex's ear off, and she hoped her friend was ready.

As far as she was concerned, there was nothing better than a bottle of wine shared between friends on a Friday night. She'd take that over going out to clubs any day of the week. Uncorking the wine, Mia took the bottle to the living room and set it on the small wooden coffee table along with the two glasses she'd placed there earlier. The music was playing softly, an upbeat playlist that Mia had been listening to for the better part of the afternoon in anticipation of her friend's arrival.

The doorbell chimed, and Mia smiled as she skipped to the door, flinging it open and coming face-to-face with a cheerful Alex.

"Girl, you're lucky you invited me over, because I was getting ready to crash your condo," Alex said as she walked in, hugging Mia briefly before looking around. "Holy shit. This place looks fantastic."

"Thanks. You wouldn't believe what bargains you can find online if you search long enough." Mia smiled to herself as she thought about the other things she'd uncovered when she'd been searching the Internet over the last few weeks.

"I love it."

Alex hadn't been to the condo since the day Mia had moved in. As was usually the case, Alex's schedule was tight, and their girls' nights generally had to be planned well in advance just so Mia could see her. Granted, back when Mia had been with Damien, they'd crossed paths more frequently at various functions, but now that Mia had reverted to a commoner, those encounters were less frequent. The blame certainly couldn't be laid at Alex's feet, though, and Mia felt a twinge of guilt for not spending more time with her closest friend.

"Sit," Mia suggested as she motioned toward the sofa. "I've got wine."

Alex walked toward the couch, still looking around the condo as she did. "I really like this, Mia. It seems so … you."

"As opposed to?"

"That prison Damien calls a home," Alex said bluntly. "I never liked the fact that you weren't able to put your stamp on it. This is cozy and fun."

"Thanks. It definitely suits me."

Alex dropped to the sofa after kicking off her flats, then curled her feet up underneath her. "So tell me about school. How's the new semester going? What you thought it would be?"

"I don't know that I had any expectations," Mia admitted as she poured the wine into one of the glasses, then handed it off to her friend. "Quite frankly, it's boring. But I love it."

"I'm glad you decided to go. I'm so proud of how in control of your life you are."

Mia laughed as she took the other glass once she filled it. "I wouldn't say I'm necessarily in control. These days I feel anything but."

"Spill," Alex said, her eyes meeting Mia's when she lowered herself to the other end of the sofa, pulling her legs up so she could face her friend.

"I'm not sure there's anything to spill," Mia said, gauging her friend's reaction but unable to hide her grin.

Just as she'd suspected, Alex smirked, a knowing smile that told Mia far more than she wanted to know. Alex had always been able to read Mia like a book. "Well, let's see if I can figure it out. You know I wanted to be a private investigator in my past life."

Mia chuckled. She did know that. Alex prided herself on being a super sleuth, attempting to solve every mystery she came up against.

"I'll rewind back to the charity ball. If I recall correctly, you were sandwiched in between two incredibly sexy men. I also have it on good authority that the seating arrangement wasn't an accident."

"*What?*" Mia leaned forward, holding her wine away from her body to keep from spilling it on her shirt. "What do you mean it wasn't an accident?"

"You know I'm friends with a member of the board. She told me that someone specifically requested — at the very last minute, mind you — a change to the table arrangement."

"Are you serious? Why?"

"Well, at first I thought it was because someone smarter than the person who put the seating chart together realized they'd put you at a table with Damien."

Mia frowned. She hadn't known that.

"But from what I remember, the two men who were flanking you couldn't seem to take their eyes off you."

"That's not true," Mia said defensively.

Alex chuckled and sipped her wine. "Oh, honey, trust me. I had the perfect view. The way Phoenix Pierce was looking at you … I thought a couple of times you might go up in flames."

Mia looked down at her hands, her face heating from her embarrassment.

"And the other guy… Crap. What's his name? He's the PR guy for the Austin Arrows."

"Tarik Marx," Mia said quickly, realizing a second too late that she'd fallen right into Alex's trap.

"That's exactly what I thought. So, of course, me being the overprotective friend that I am, I did a little investigating of my own."

"I take it you've figured it all out?" Mia teased, hating that Alex knew her so well.

"I guess you haven't seen the tabloids, huh?"

Mia shook her head. She'd purposely been avoiding recent events on the online gossip sites, and she did her best never to read the magazines at the grocery store. After her research spree, she'd found enough information to keep her busy for a lifetime without having to delve into things that had happened in the last few days.

"Let's just say you've looked pretty happy in the pictures they've snapped of you over the last couple of weeks. But what's with them walking you to school?"

Mia leaned forward and poured more wine into her glass. "It was only one day. On the Monday after the charity ball, when I left for school, I swear someone was following me. They'd never done that before, so it kinda freaked me out. I ran into Phoenix — literally — around the corner, and he insisted on walking me to school. He insisted that his driver took me the other days."

"Are you sure it was nothing?" There was concern in Alex's stern tone.

"I never saw anyone, so I figured I was being paranoid. If there was someone, I'm sure it was a reporter, anyway."

"Never assume, Mia," Alex said gravely. "You're a single woman now, and that's a widely known fact. You need to be careful. There are some serious nut jobs out there."

Mia waved her off. "I'm careful, I promise. And Phoenix and Tarik aren't letting me go far without one of them with me."

"So, tell me more about them. By the way, I think it's incredibly hot that you've got two guys catering to your every whim."

"It's not like that," Mia stated cautiously. "We're just … friends."

"Yeah? So why're you blushing?"

Mia didn't say anything, but she couldn't wipe the smile off her face.

"Did you kiss them?"

"What?" Mia exclaimed. "No! Well, not *both* of them. No."

"Which one?" Alex's curiosity caused her to lean forward, her eyes fixed on Mia's face.

"Phoenix."

"How was he?"

"Oh, God, Alex, it was … incredible. I've never in my life been kissed like that." As soon as the words were out of her mouth, Mia realized how she sounded.

Alex giggled, her grin splitting her face from ear to ear. "I know you're probably expecting me to give you a hard time. And I would, except I'm so happy to see you smiling."

"It's been a while, huh?" Mia looked down at her lap again. Truth was, there for a while, she hadn't been sure she'd ever smile again. When Damien had cheated on her, she'd stood tall and done what needed to be done, but her heart had been ultimately broken.

"Too long. So what about Tarik? You didn't kiss him?"

Mia laughed. "Why in the world would I kiss two guys?"

"I don't know. Maybe to see which one is the better kisser. That'd be why I'd do it."

"Oh, my goodness, Alex. Are you serious?"

"As a heart attack."

"Do you think that's really okay?" Mia asked, her voice soft.

"Why wouldn't it be?" Alex questioned excitedly. "You're not married. Good grief, woman. You need to live a little."

"I've never dated two guys at one time. Not that I'm doing that now," Mia tacked on.

"Well, it sure looks like it to me. So, they're walking you to school. They both danced with you at the charity ball. According to the tabloids, you were seen at dinner with Phoenix, then yesterday having lunch with Tarik. What else have you done, you little minx?"

"It's much more innocent than I'm sure they made it sound. I don't see them much. Really. They're out of town most of the time."

"Away games," Alex said. "By the way, Johnathan is a little jealous. He wants to know when you're inviting us to dinner with Phoenix."

Mia laughed. "I'm sure he is. I don't know that *I'll* be having dinner with Phoenix."

"So why don't you ask him out? Or, hell, ask 'em both."

Mia couldn't believe her friend was suggesting she do such a thing. It felt like a betrayal even though she had her suspicions that they would be all for it.

"Oh, come on," Alex stated. "They know about each other, right?"

"Well, yeah. But..." Mia wasn't even sure what her argument was going to be. "Can I ask you a question?"

"Of course."

"Are…" Mia paused to take a swig of her wine, tempted to down the rest of the glass just so she could get the question out. "Are threesomes really that common?"

Surprisingly, Alex didn't laugh in her face, which was what Mia thought would happen. Instead, she smiled. "More common than you think."

"Have you ever…?"

"No," Alex answered immediately. "Johnathan is far too possessive for that. And I can guarantee you that I'm never letting another woman touch my man."

"So is it a bad thing if a man wants to share a woman with another man?"

"No. To each his own, Mia. And yes, I know where you're going with this. I've seen the stories about Phoenix. I'm nosy like that, which is the only reason I even bother to read that crap."

Mia knew her friend was quite fond of the gossip magazines. They used to sit for hours and make fun of the stories, and the people, that they read about.

"Do you think there's something going on between them?" Alex questioned, surprising Mia with the direction she'd taken the conversation, although it was something she'd wondered herself.

Mia frowned. "What do you mean?"

Alex held out her empty glass, and Mia moved to refill it, anxious to hear what Alex was getting at. She wasn't disappointed. Well, she was and she wasn't. It was all in how she took what Alex said next.

"Phoenix is a very newsworthy guy. He's been known for his bedroom's revolving door over the years. But I also recall a story about—"

"Him and Tarik together," Mia said, completing Alex's sentence. "I read that, too. Seeing them together, sure, it seems like there might be some … chemistry there."

"But they clearly like women, too."

"I think so. Hell, I don't know," Mia said, exasperated. She laughed, a hysterical sound that announced her discomfort with the conversation, although she'd been the one who wanted to talk about this. "I really don't know how any of that stuff works. I thought that was just something they did in porn. Or erotic books. I had no idea that normal people did that stuff."

"Normal people?" Alex asked, laughing. "There are all kinds of kinks out there, Mia."

"Well, I didn't know that," she said a little sensitively. "Remember, I was a virgin when I met Damien."

"Oh, right. The sweet little innocent virgin."

"Shut up," Mia huffed, still giggling. "I don't understand why they might be interested in me if they're actually lovers."

"Ever heard the term bisexual?"

"Of course I have." Mia pondered that for a second, following with, "Oh."

"Exactly. And it's really not as uncommon as you think."

"Really? Well, there was this one story…" Mia thought back to the story she'd read about Tarik and Phoenix together.

"Clearly I'm falling behind on my reading. What story?"

"Apparently Phoenix took home some chick, and according to her, things got a little freaky. Something about his bodyguard going down on him." Mia worried her lip for a moment, thinking about that as she recalled the article. The mental image that she came up with had her feeling the need to fan herself. It wasn't a bad feeling, which surprised her. She'd never been into that. Then again, with Damien, she hadn't really been into anything. When it had come to their sexual encounters, she'd been generally left lacking, although he'd tried to turn it around and blame her most of the time. These days, she was at the mercy of the books she read. Well, those and her trusty vibrator.

"Earth to Mia. You're still blushing."

Mia focused on Alex's face, the mental image dissipating. "So, you really think they're bisexual?" she asked, her curiosity unmistakably piqued.

"You know them better than I do. What do *you* think?"

"I don't know them that well," Mia admitted.

"Well, honey, if I were you" — Alex's smile widened as she held up her glass for a toast — "it's time you get to know them better. Just go for it. I mean, hell, what do you have to lose?"

Her heart.

That was what she had to lose. But she didn't bother to tell Alex that. She was her best friend; she already knew how Mia's heart worked.

Chapter Sixteen

A week and a half later

MIA COULDN'T BLAME the annoying beep of her alarm clock for waking her before the sun was up. It hadn't even gone off when she found herself lying in bed, staring up at the ceiling, her mind replaying the dream she'd been woken from.

She almost wondered whether or not it had only been a dream — it had seemed so real. So much so that she really wished she hadn't woken, so she could see where it might lead. In all her life, she'd never experienced anything like what had happened in her sleepy brain.

Apparently she'd been thinking too much about the whole threesome, ménage, bisexual stuff. She'd actually spent the better part of the weekend doing even more research because it fascinated her. Why, she had no freaking clue. The idea of two men sharing one woman… Well, it seemed… The only fitting word would be hot. Yes, it was *hot.*

Touching her lips with the tips of her fingers, she smiled at the memory of her dream. Her entire being had been affected by what had happened. In her dream, she'd been in her kitchen, and Phoenix and Tarik had both been there. It had started out innocent, the three of them simply talking, but it had quickly escalated into something significantly ... hotter, for lack of a better word. Phoenix had kissed her, overwhelming her with his scent, his touch, the way his lips moved over hers — very similar to the way it had been when he'd kissed her for real. But then Tarik had pressed up against her back. She'd felt the warmth of his lips on her neck, his calloused hands along the skin of her stomach as he touched her, pulling her against him while they both proceeded to pleasure her beyond anything she'd ever known before.

Turning her head now, she looked at the blue numbers on the clock. She should be asleep. She didn't have school on Tuesdays, which meant she had the opportunity to sleep in, yet no matter how hard she tried, she couldn't keep her eyes closed. That dream... It'd felt so real. And part of her was scared to give herself over to it once again, fearful that she'd want something she knew she wasn't equipped to handle.

Maybe she should go to the gym. She'd put it off since she'd moved in, always coming up with one excuse or another, but it all boiled down to, she didn't want to put forth the effort. But maybe it would help to get her mind out of the gutter and back where it needed to be. She was supposed to be focused on herself, on her education, not dreaming about wicked sexual encounters with not one but two men.

A *Million* Tiny Pieces

A rumble of thunder echoed outside her bedroom window, and Mia turned her head to the opposite side. The pitter patter of raindrops against the glass was soothing, but not enough to lure her back to sleep, so she did the only logical thing she could come up with. She kicked off the blankets and forced her legs over the edge of the bed. When her feet hit the floor, she stood and went to the bathroom.

Ten minutes later, she was dressed in her workout clothes — the ones she'd had to take the tags off of when she'd pulled them from the back of her closet. Feeling determined, she practically skipped into her kitchen.

Pulling the carton of orange juice, along with an apple, a mango, and the leafy kale from the refrigerator, Mia realized she was humming. Retrieving a banana from the holder on the counter and the small jar of protein powder she'd picked up last week, she headed for the cabinet. Pulling out a glass, she hefted her items over to the sink and set everything on the cutting board. She smiled. She'd always wanted to make a smoothie, and she'd heard that they were good for her, so why not?

That could be considered living in the moment, couldn't it?

It only took her a few minutes to prepare the fruit and to get the juicer set up. Once that was done, she tossed everything inside, adding two scoops of protein powder and some orange juice, then set her glass in the designated spot and hit the power button.

"Yuck." The kale caused it to turn green instantly, looking not at all appetizing.

Figuring she had come too far to turn back now, Mia flipped off the switch when it was finished and picked up the glass. She swirled the nasty-looking liquid around as she studied it.

"Now or never," she said aloud.

Smiling to herself, Mia tipped the glass to her lips and took a drink, nearly spewing the juice through her nose when it proved to taste as disgusting as it looked. Her nostrils flared as the aftertaste lingered in her mouth. Lunging for the open carton of orange juice still sitting on the counter, she took a swig.

Okay, so maybe health drinks weren't her thing. She probably looked ridiculous. Did people really drink that stuff?

Staring down at the green liquid, she scrunched up her nose at the memory of the taste. She was procrastinating; she knew that much. That was what she did. Especially when she was about to go do something she dreaded, like exercise.

Figuring she would never get it done if she didn't just go, she grabbed her iPod, her headphones, and her house key before venturing out into the hall. Waiting for the elevator was an exercise in futility, and she was half tempted to go back to her condo rather than wait. But finally, it arrived on her floor, blessedly empty.

She hit the button for the second floor and waited, watching the countdown of numbers above the doors. When they finally opened, Mia stepped out into a plush entry that rivaled the lobby on the first floor, with its dark hardwood floors and soothing taupe walls with bright white, modern trim. There was even a vase of fresh flowers on a small table beside the keypad. Mia moved in that direction and punched in the four-digit code she'd selected when she had moved in. There was a click when the lock on the glass doors disengaged, allowing her entry. She walked in to find there were two people there, one older man on a treadmill and another guy in the corner with the free weights, his back to her so she couldn't see his face. Neither of them were paying her any attention.

Mia didn't really have a preference when it came to cardio equipment, usually favoring *no* equipment to any of the fancy machines in front of her. But she was there for a reason, so she opted to go with the treadmill because it seemed the least complicated to figure out.

It only took her a few minutes to hit the correct buttons, and then finally the machine came to life, and she began to walk. Well, stroll was more like it. Compared to the older guy running full out, she looked like a slacker, so she upped the numbers until she was moving at a brisk pace, but that was where she drew the line. She could easily do this for a little while.

Somehow she managed to put her headphones in and not fall on her ass, so she kept going. It wasn't long before she realized the older guy had left, and she was alone in the gym with the man still working with the weights. She kept glancing over at him, trying to get a look at his face, but he was well hidden in an alcove lined with varying sizes of weights. Not wanting to get caught staring, Mia focused on the TV in front of her, the one attached to the machine. How did people watch these things? She felt as though she might get seasick trying to keep her eyes focused on the people talking on the screen. She considered stopping, because not wanting to get sick was a viable excuse if she'd ever heard one, but noticed only fifteen minutes had passed. Then again, that was fifteen more minutes than she'd gotten yesterday. And it wasn't like anyone would know.

She was about to hit the stop button when she noticed movement in the mirror in front of her. She looked up into the reflective glass to see...

Oh, crap.

Phoenix was walking toward her, his head down, his headphones in his ears. She didn't think he realized she was there until he got on one of the treadmills several machines down. Without preamble, he hit the buttons, and his machine started up.

Trying desperately not to stare, Mia knew she was failing miserably. And when Phoenix's eyes met hers in the mirror, she knew her first attempt at working out might very well be her last.

To her surprise, Phoenix abruptly turned off the machine he was on and stepped down, then headed toward her. He climbed onto the one beside her, but his attention wasn't on the machine.

Pulling her headphones from her ears, she forced a smile when she noticed he was still staring at her.

"Good morning," he greeted.

"Hi," she said, realizing she was breathless and she'd only been going … three miles an hour. God, she really was a slacker. But Phoenix didn't know that, so maybe he would think that her rapid pulse and lack of oxygen was related to the exercise and not to the fact that she was once again thinking about that kiss they'd previously shared, or the dream that kiss had clearly morphed into. "I didn't know you came here," she blurted out when she couldn't think of anything else to say.

"I usually don't. I prefer to run outside since it was the one thing I had to fight Tarik on and actually won. He prefers to keep an eye on me, as you very well know. But" — Phoenix nodded his head toward the windows — "it's raining too hard."

Now why hadn't she thought about that? Thanks to the weather, he was forced inside to work out. If she'd known that, she would've stayed in bed.

Then again, maybe not. Maybe this was her subconscience's way of making sure she saw him.

"Oh," she said by way of response — articulate she was not, but she blamed the treadmill — glancing over her shoulder to look out the window only to notice that Tarik was standing behind her. She squeaked in surprise, grabbing for the rails on the treadmill to keep from going down head-first. Phoenix reached over and stabbed the emergency stop button, saving her from an embarrassing incident. Well, *more* embarrassing.

"Mornin'," Tarik greeted in that rough tone she'd gotten so familiar with.

"Good morning," she whispered, looking back and forth between the two men. They were both standing on the treadmills on each side of her, sandwiching her between them.

Her heart began a rapid thump against her ribs, and she briefly wondered whether or not they could hear it.

"I didn't know you worked out here," Mia told Tarik, realizing it was the same thing she'd said to Phoenix.

"Every day," Tarik answered, leaning back against the rail of the treadmill and crossing his massive arms over his enormous chest.

Someone seriously needed to turn on the air conditioner.

"I usually don't come here," she said, realizing they probably already knew that, but she couldn't stop herself from nervously rambling. Neither man said anything. Clearly they were already aware of her lack of exercise.

"No classes today?" Phoenix asked casually, mirroring Tarik's stance by leaning against the rail on the other treadmill, his body facing her.

"Nope," she said, looking straight ahead at the small TV screen, doing her best to appear unaffected by their nearness. It wasn't nearly as easy as she'd thought it would be. "I suppose you both have to work?"

"Depends," Phoenix answered with a mischievous grin.

"On?" Mia asked, knowing full well she should ignore him, but she couldn't.

"On whether or not you want to do something today."

"Like? It's raining," she said, stating the obvious. "So that eliminates anything outdoors."

Okay, so evidently this working out thing was affecting her brain. Maybe it *was* the lack of oxygen that was making her ask stupid things. She should not be encouraging this man. Especially not after the dream she'd had … the one that, in her opinion, had depicted what her future would hold if she did.

"There are plenty of things to do indoors," Tarik stated, and Mia felt her face flame.

Phoenix chuckled, his eyes pinning her in place when he followed with, "Get your mind out of the gutter, little girl. He wasn't talking about that."

Mia's face felt like it was on fire, and she couldn't take any more. Grabbing her condo key from the small ledge on the machine, she turned away from them both, unable to hide her embarrassment, nor could she keep from laughing.

The next thing she knew, Phoenix's warm hands were on her bare shoulders, turning her to face him. When she looked up into those glittering green eyes, she had expected to see heat, but what she hadn't expected to see was the amount of pure, unadulterated, unprohibited desire reflecting back at her.

No man had ever looked at her the way Phoenix was looking at her now.

Except...

Oh, God. Mia's heart kicked into high gear as she looked up into Tarik's golden eyes as he stood beside Phoenix, looking down at her as though he was waiting for her to say something.

"What do you say? Want to have some indoor fun? And seriously, I'm talking about something away from your place. And mine."

Mia swallowed hard and found herself nodding. "Don't you need to finish your workout?" She looked at Tarik and then Phoenix.

"I'm done," Tarik told her, his eyes lingering on her lips.

"I'm good," Phoenix said quickly. "How long will it take you to get ready?"

Glancing down at her iPod, she noted the time. "An hour?"

Phoenix smirked at her. "Just out of curiosity, do you measure in regular time? Or do you use football minutes?"

Mia laughed, understanding what he meant. "When I say an hour, I'll be ready in an hour," she said lightly. "Not an hour and a half. I promise."

"Then we'll be at your door in an hour. Wear something casual."

"We?" she asked, surprised.

"Yes, 'we,'" Tarik said. "It's time the three of us do something together."

Her mind once again barreled right into the gutter, and the thoughts she had weren't related to anything they could possibly do outdoors. Her face flamed once again, and she fought the urge to fan herself as she said, "Okay," in an incredibly shaky voice.

And just like that, Mia found herself giving in to something she wasn't sure she could handle. As she walked out of the gym to the elevator, alone, she realized one very important thing.

She didn't think she was capable of telling these men no.

Ever.

Chapter Seventeen

PHOENIX PURPOSELY ALLOWED Mia to leave before him. As much as he wanted to be around her, he didn't quite trust himself to be alone in an elevator with her and Tarik. Not just yet. Not after all the scenarios he'd played over and over in his head for the past couple of weeks. He'd been so busy that he hadn't had time to do much of anything except work. That hadn't stopped his brain from working double time. He had used the work excuse to keep his distance from Tarik, as well, but he knew he wasn't going to be able to keep away from him for too much longer, either.

Hell, had he known Mia and Tarik would be in the gym that morning, he wasn't sure he would have come. He would've preferred to battle the elements outside than to have to face them, knowing that he couldn't touch them the way he'd been envisioning for the last fucking month. As it was, he was having a damn hard time keeping his hands to himself.

And he was pretty sure they both knew that.

Not that he was going to let that keep him from seeing Mia today. He was glad to see that things hadn't fizzled out between them even though quite a bit of time had passed since he'd done anything more than walk her to school. They seemed to still be making progress, and he damn sure wasn't going into a downhill slide because he couldn't seem to control himself when he was around her.

He'd seen the heat generating in her blue eyes when she'd noticed him, the same heat that had flowed like lava when she had realized Tarik was there, as well. He got the strange suspicion that she wanted to see where this might lead as much as they did, although she probably had no idea what that entailed.

Mia had some hurdles to overcome; even he realized that. She'd recently gone through a divorce, and she hadn't been all that keen on giving him the time of day a few weeks ago. Hence, the reason he had managed to put some space between them. He wanted Mia to have time to think, to ensure that she knew what she was getting herself into. Granted, he hadn't expected her to figure it out quite so quickly, but the way she'd been looking at him and Tarik, Phoenix had to believe she was at least entertaining the same things they were.

Not that he should've been entertaining those ideas. He was supposed to be transforming his life, bypassing those desires that would ultimately get him in the hot seat where the press was concerned.

Too bad he couldn't bring himself to care.

At this point, he only wanted to spend some time with both of them, something that didn't involve work. Even if it meant they would all have their clothes on the entire time.

After another session with his hand last night, when he had fought the urge to go to Tarik's condo, to indulge in him the way he'd fantasized about more often than not over the course of the last month, Phoenix had been left still aching for something more, but he knew that they would both be so worth the wait. He had to believe that, because he'd finally resigned himself to seeing where things went ... with both of them. Together.

That was, if Mia agreed.

He'd felt her passion in the way she had kissed him, how pliant she'd become, how easily she'd given herself completely to him, and he wondered what she'd be like pressed between him and Tarik, naked and writhing...

The blood once again rushed from his brain to his dick, and Phoenix wished like hell there was a way to alleviate the throb, but in the same sense, he wanted it there as a reminder of what was to come. Pun intended.

Phoenix followed Tarik out of the workout room without either of them saying a word. They got to the elevator, and Phoenix managed to push the button, still completely silent. He wondered if Tarik was thinking the same things he was.

When he stepped into the elevator, Phoenix prayed that his mother wasn't upstairs waiting for him.

"I'm gonna take a shower," Tarik imparted, stabbing the button for his floor before entering the code for the penthouse.

"Me, too."

The way Tarik's eyes darkened told Phoenix he had indeed been thinking the same thing. As tempted as he was to pull Tarik into his shower and lose himself for a little while, he knew they didn't have time. He would not keep Mia waiting.

"What are your plans for today? I take it you want me to clear your entire schedule." Tarik leaned against the elevator wall and crossed his arms over his chest, staring back at Phoenix.

"Clear it completely. I'll be done in a few." Unsure how long he'd be able to resist Tarik, Phoenix knew he needed to get away from him.

"Don't touch yourself while you're in there," Tarik said, his eyes focused on Phoenix's face, his voice low, commanding.

An insistent throb started in Phoenix's cock, causing it to thicken. "And if I do?" he countered.

"Don't. It's not an option." Tarik's no-nonsense tone did something strange to Phoenix, leaving him feeling a little more desperate than he had been five minutes ago. And he didn't know what the hell to do about that.

"Meet me upstairs when you're done," he told Tarik when the elevator stopped on the thirty-third floor, needing to maintain some semblance of control.

As always, once Phoenix reached his condo, his routine only took him twenty minutes — and he had managed to keep from jacking off, although he had wanted to do it merely to defy Tarik — and when he emerged from his bedroom wearing jeans and a T-shirt, Tarik was already there, looking at him with that same heat flaring in his eyes.

"Get me a list of things to do indoors," Phoenix told him, ignoring the urge to slam Tarik against the wall and have his wicked way with the man. It was getting so much harder to resist. Ever since he'd given in to the desire and done to Tarik what he'd never done to another man, Phoenix had wanted more. But he wanted Mia, and since he didn't think it would sit well with her that he was spending his time fucking someone else — man or woman — he'd had to refrain.

"Things? Like what? Active things? Or are you wanting movies and shit?"

"Yes. Physically active stuff," Phoenix replied, noticing Tarik had put Phoenix's coffee mug on the bar behind him. "And movies for later tonight, just in case. At that place in the Domain." Phoenix retrieved the cup and headed for the living room, taking a minute to stare out the window. The Austin skyline was layered with dark clouds, and rain was coming down in sheets, making it difficult to make out the cars passing on the street far below.

The sound of Tarik's fingers flying over the keyboard and the gentle hum of the heater were the only sounds in the room, but the noise in Phoenix's head managed to drown them both out. He'd slept like shit for the past few weeks with all of the jumbled thoughts he was having. First, there was the stupid fucking lawsuit, which, after he'd clearly told Damien Landry to drop it, he wasn't giving up. Phoenix had received an update on the situation from his lawyers yesterday, but there was nothing really to tell. They were riding it out, waiting for Landry to make the next move.

And of course, there was the emotional whirlwind he was on. It wasn't normal for him to get involved with anyone for longer than a one-night stand, so this thing with Tarik was weighing on his mind heavily. On top of that, he couldn't get Mia out of his head, which only doubled the confusion.

He hoped like hell that today he could get some clarity on the direction he was supposed to go from here, because he was beginning to get irritated with the complications. It didn't matter that he was the one making things exceedingly difficult.

"Hellooo?"

"Shit," Phoenix mumbled under his breath as he sipped his coffee and turned to face his mother. "Good morning."

"Why are you here?"

Phoenix smiled. "Because I live here?"

"You know what I mean," she said, her green eyes pinning him in place.

"I'm taking the day off," he told her. He knew his lack of explanation was only going to invite more questions, but he left it at that.

Ellen glanced over at the kitchen table and looked at Tarik, who merely shrugged his shoulders without looking up from the computer. Sometimes Phoenix wondered if the guy had eyes in the back of his head, because he rarely looked up but always knew where everyone was and what they were doing.

"Where are you going?"

"Out," Phoenix said, walking across the room toward the kitchen for more coffee.

"What are you going to be doing?" Ellen asked.

Phoenix sighed. "I've got a date, Mother. Nothing serious. No reason for you to run out and buy a copy of *Wedding Bliss* or whatever the hell those magazines are. It's just a date." It was more than a date, but he definitely wasn't going to tell his mother that. As it was, she was going to jump all over this. Phoenix didn't hide the fact that he had an active social life, and sex was usually intermixed in there, but he rarely ever went out on an official date. He would extend an invitation to a woman for something business-related, or a charity event, but he didn't usually go out with a woman for the sake of going out with her.

"Who is she?" Ellen asked. Phoenix could tell she was trying to hide her excitement.

"No one you know. But I promise, if things ever get to the point you need to know her, I'll introduce you." Phoenix downed half of his coffee and then dumped the rest in the sink before making his way over to Tarik. "I need that stuff now."

"I'll bring it with me when I meet you at the car," Tarik stated flatly, his eyes still locked on the computer screen.

"You really don't have to go with us," Phoenix mentioned, although he secretly prayed Tarik didn't change his mind.

Tarik peered up at him, and what Phoenix saw in his hard, glistening gold gaze had him closing his mouth instantly, although the alpha, always-in-control side of him wanted to tell him to take a flying fucking leap. No matter what Tarik thought, Phoenix did hold the reins.

"I'm going with you," Tarik informed him. "I'll meet you in the garage. How much time do we have?"

"We're supposed to pick her up in" — Phoenix looked at his watch — "eight minutes. Fuck."

"See you downstairs."

Realizing he was going to be late, something he refused to do, Phoenix snatched his cell phone from the bar and headed out, hollering a quick good-bye to his mother as he passed through the entryway.

The elevator moved like molasses in winter, which left Phoenix knocking on Mia's door with one minute to spare.

He heard the deadbolt disengage before she pulled the door open.

"Hey," he greeted, letting his eyes trail over her approvingly. She was wearing another pair of those sexy-as-fuck blue jeans, sneakers, and a fitted turquoise-and-black long-sleeve shirt that hugged her beautiful breasts as well as set off her eyes. He was used to seeing her in oversized sweatshirts these days — not counting the workout clothes that had damn near stopped his heart — so the formfitting top had his blood taking an immediate detour to his dick.

"I'll only be a minute. Come in," she said, taking a step back.

Phoenix kept his eyes on hers, noticing the slight uncertainty in her expression.

"Where's Tarik?"

"He's coming." Phoenix hid his smile. He liked the fact that she wanted Tarik there. As much as he wanted her all to himself, he couldn't deny the fact that sharing her with Tarik was probably the single hottest thing he'd ever thought about. And he couldn't fucking wait to make that happen.

He thrust his hands into his pockets to keep from reaching for her. She looked so damn cute and far too innocent at that moment. Not to mention, she made his dick harder with each passing second.

After the front door closed, Mia disappeared across the room and around the corner, leaving Phoenix standing in the small entry alone. Unable to help himself, he walked until he could see the spacious living room in front of him and a section of the kitchen off to the right.

Her home resembled her in ways he hadn't expected. The beige sofa and oversized chair, which sat facing the wall of windows overlooking downtown Austin, appeared soft and comfortable. There were a couple of brightly colored throw pillows set perfectly on each end and a throw blanket hanging over the back. Phoenix realized there wasn't a television in the room, but he noticed an impressive sound system on one of the two floor-to-ceiling, dark wood bookshelves that flanked the fireplace. On the mantle were a couple of pictures and a vase of white flowers. He immediately moved toward the pictures, trying to get a glimpse into Mia's life through the images.

"That's me and my dad when I was eight," she said as she approached.

Phoenix picked up the silver frame and held it closer as he studied the pair in the picture. It was an older man and a young girl, both laughing as they threw red and gold leaves from a huge pile at one another. Placing the picture back where he'd found it, Phoenix picked up the other one. "And this? This must be you and your mother."

Mia looked so much like her mother, Phoenix was sure they were mistaken for sisters from time to time. They both had long blonde hair, bright blue eyes, and porcelain skin.

"Yes," Mia agreed.

Turning to Mia after setting the second photo back in place, Phoenix smiled. "You have a nice place."

"Thank you. I'm still working on the decorations, taking things slow."

"You've got more in your place than I have in mine," he told her.

Mia didn't respond to that, but she did ask if he was ready to go.

Two minutes later, after he'd assisted her with her coat, they were making their way to the elevator. Phoenix couldn't resist any longer, taking her hand in his and pulling her closer when they stepped inside. An older couple was watching them carefully as they joined them. Never one to miss an opportunity, Phoenix stepped behind Mia and pulled her flush against him, her back to his chest as the elevator began to make its slow descent to the first floor.

When the doors opened, Phoenix gave a polite smile to the other couple as they stepped off. He then held on to Mia to keep her close. Bending down so that his mouth was to her ear, he whispered that they were going down to the parking garage. The tremor that shook her small body made Phoenix's cock harden instantly. He was grateful that the elevator didn't take too long, because he found his control slipping with every minute he was with Mia.

And to think, the day was just beginning.

Chapter Eighteen

"WHERE ARE WE going?" Mia asked, trying to mask the tremor in her voice after she and Phoenix had climbed into the backseat of the Escalade.

From the moment Phoenix had taken her hand, she'd been completely overwhelmed by him. His touch was like an electric charge that warmed her, brought to life things inside of her she hadn't realized had gone into hibernation.

And he smelled…

God, she was pretty sure it was a sin for a man to smell that good. She had no idea what it was — cologne, body wash, aftershave, or his own natural scent — but whatever it was, if a retailer hadn't bottled it and started making money on it, they were definitely missing out.

"I thought we'd begin by…" Phoenix paused as he glanced down at his phone.

Mia followed his gaze and noticed he was reading something. She saw the word *skydiving* and decided to look closer. "Is that a list of…?" She leaned in closer to see that it was indeed a list of what appeared to be things to do, sent from … Tarik.

Looking up, Mia caught Tarik's golden gaze in the rearview mirror. "You looked these up for him?" she asked directly, smiling.

She couldn't see his mouth, but his eyes crinkled just enough for her to know he was smiling back at her. "I did."

"Is this the sort of thing you usually do? Doesn't seem quite fitting for a bodyguard."

Tarik's gruff chuckle was enough of an answer, so Mia turned her head and met Phoenix's liquid green eyes. "You couldn't figure out where to go on your own?" As she watched the embarrassed expression flitter over his features, she fought the urge to laugh.

"That's what I pay him for," Phoenix said, a guilty glint in his eyes.

"Well, *Tarik*," Mia said, pulling her eyes away from Phoenix, "where do *you* suggest we go?"

"I provide facts; Phoenix makes the decisions," Tarik said, the growl in his voice lending a hint of danger to the guy.

"Not today he doesn't," Mia replied, looking at Phoenix again. "But since you seem so interested in the list, where have you decided to take us?" she asked, smiling.

"I thought we'd start out slow," he answered as Tarik pulled out of the parking garage and onto the street. The rain immediately started pounding on the roof of the SUV, making it difficult to hear.

"And what does that mean?"

"Have you been to an indoor skydiving place?"

Mia choked. "Indoor *what*?"

"Skydiving."

"No, I can't say that I have," she replied, wondering if he was serious. She hadn't even heard of such a thing.

"It's simple. They put you in a wind tunnel. The air is blowing from beneath you, which lifts you off the ground. Essentially, it allows you to see what it's like to be suspended in midair. Not quite the same thing, but still quite a rush."

"Oh," Mia smirked. "Is that all?"

"Do you think you can handle it?" Phoenix inquired, the dare in his tone like a blinding light.

"I can handle whatever you can dish out," she said confidently, swallowing hard and hoping he didn't notice.

"Then that's where we'll go first."

"First? Where else are we going?"

"I've got a list," Phoenix said as he held up his phone. "It'll be a full day."

"When do I get to pick where we go?"

"Why don't we take turns?" Tarik stated, more a command although he had phrased it as a question, his eyes peering back at her in the mirror.

"We can do that," Mia said, looking over at Phoenix again. "You think you can handle that?"

"I can handle whatever you can dish out," he said, repeating her exact words, although his sexy tone made her think of hot, sweaty sex, which had her face heating rapidly.

When he leaned in closer, goose bumps broke out on Mia's arms. She hoped he didn't realize how much he affected her.

He obviously did if his next words were anything to go by. "You're competitive, are you?"

His mouth was against her ear, his breath hot against her cheek, his voice so low she could hardly hear him over the rain on the roof. Rather than say anything, Mia nodded, keeping her eyes focused on the buildings passing outside the window.

"Good. So am I. Want to put a wager on today?" he asked.

"What did you have in mind?" she asked as softly as she could.

"If I win, you have to come back to my condo for the night."

"And what happens then?"

"That's completely up to you. Your call."

Mia considered that for a moment and then surprised the hell out of herself when she nodded. "Fine. And if *I* win?" She didn't plan to lose.

"That's up to you."

"Okay. And what about Tarik? What if he wins?" She looked toward the front once again.

"Then you have to come back to the condo for the night," Tarik said smoothly.

"Are y'all ganging up on me?" The instant the words were out of her mouth, Mia wanted to crawl into the floorboard and hide.

Their only answer was a simultaneous gruff chuckle.

Oh, crap. She'd set herself up for that one, and she could feel her body temperature rise several degrees.

"So what'll it be?" Phoenix's words were still so low Mia barely heard them.

Turning her head a little so that her mouth was closer to his ear, Mia decided to return the favor, ignoring her rioting nerves. "I'll let you know when I win."

Phoenix laughed, a deep, sexy rumble that had her insides quivering. "When? Not if?"

"Exactly." Mia had no idea what he had in mind, and she knew it had been a really long time since she'd done anything physical like this — and the treadmill certainly didn't count — but she definitely wasn't about to turn down the dare. She wasn't built that way.

"I like your confidence," he whispered. When his lips brushed against the sensitive skin beneath her ear, Mia nearly came up off the seat. If it weren't for his hand coming to rest on her thigh, she might have. "In fact, I like a lot of things about you," he continued, his lips trailing the shell of her ear as the warmth of his hand penetrated her leg. "Like the way your hair smells like strawberries." Phoenix pressed his lips against her neck. "And the way your pulse quickens when I kiss you here."

She fully expected him to say something inherently sexual following that, so when he left the statement at that, her body tingled with anticipation.

"Five minutes," Tarik informed them, causing Mia to pull back abruptly, realizing that he was sneaking glances at them while he drove.

Oddly, the idea of Tarik watching them made her thighs tremble and her insides spasm with anticipation. She was losing her mind. That was all there was to it.

Phoenix evidently didn't care that they had an audience of one, because he continued to nuzzle her neck, his warm breath making goose bumps break out along her arms. She tried to ignore him even though she knew it was futile. Phoenix Pierce wasn't an easy man to ignore. Ever.

Thankfully, they arrived at the skydiving place a few minutes later. It wasn't until Tarik parked the SUV in a spot close to the building that Phoenix opened the door and climbed out. Mia noticed the sudden loss of his body heat, which left her feeling weirdly deserted although he was still close, still holding her hand as he helped her from the Escalade.

"Better hurry, little girl," Tarik said as he came to stand outside the door. "Wouldn't want you to get wet."

Mia heard the double entendre, but she did her best to ignore it, giving Tarik a knowing smile as she did, hurrying toward the door as the rain continued to pound down relentlessly.

"Have either of you done this before?" she asked them as they made their way inside, instantly greeted kindly by an energetic young man.

"A few times, yes," Phoenix admitted, pulling her close to his side as they moved to the check-in desk at the front, Tarik walking incredibly close behind her. Another chill danced along her spine, and this one had nothing to do with it being cold outside.

Mia watched Phoenix's interaction with the pretty woman behind the counter, noticed the way the girl eyed him and Tarik excitedly, likely wondering which one of them was available.

Neither, an insistent voice in her head announced.

Oh, brother. She was in big trouble.

A few minutes later, they were instructed to head up a set of stairs to the second floor. Once there, Mia realized there was a group of children, probably around nine or ten, who were talking and laughing as they watched someone who was already in the wind tunnel where they'd be flying.

Moving to the glass so she could see better, Mia focused on the older man hovering in midair. He looked as though this was possibly his first time. An instructor was accompanying him inside the wind tunnel, helping him to maintain the correct posture to remain airborne. It looked interesting, not like anything she'd ever done before, and Mia found the excitement was infusing her as well.

"You wanna go first?" Tarik asked, stepping up behind her and placing his hands on her shoulders, his broad chest against her shoulder blades while Phoenix came to stand at her side.

She glanced over at Phoenix to gauge his reaction. He didn't seem to care that Tarik was touching her so intimately. In fact, she was pretty sure that was a flame she saw burning in his heated gaze.

Surprisingly, Mia was comfortable with Tarik's touch, and despite her lingering trepidation, she welcomed it. Something about him made her feel safe. More than it should have, she knew, but she wasn't going to think about that today. Today she was going to enjoy her time with them, see where things went. Alex had told her to go for it, so here she was.

It was time she let herself go. This was the time she was supposed to be finding herself, figuring out who she really was. And this seemed like a damn good starting point.

"I'll let one of you go first," she told him, her eyes still glued to the man in the tube. "How long do we get to fly?"

"There aren't many people here this morning, so you'll get a few minutes," Phoenix informed her. "If you want to go again, I'm sure I can work something out."

Nodding her understanding, Mia continued to watch until another employee approached, letting them know he was ready to assist them into their flying gear. Minutes later, Mia had shed her jacket, pulled her hair on top of her head, put on a purple jumpsuit, goggles, and a helmet. Phoenix and Tarik both did the same, only their jumpsuits were blue and they looked far sexier in their outfits than she did in hers. She tried not to stare as she admired the two of them, hoping they wouldn't notice.

The sinful grin on Tarik's face told her he noticed, all right.

Forcing her attention away from him, she followed the employee into a room adjacent to the wind tunnel and sat on a bench that he directed her to. Phoenix took a seat on one side, while Tarik moved to her other side. They watched as the last of the kids in the group climbed in, a little girl who was laughing uncontrollably as the man helped her to get her feet out from beneath her.

Butterflies took flight in Mia's stomach as anticipation fizzed in her veins. She'd never been the adventurous type before, and as she sat patiently waiting her turn, she had to wonder why that was. Granted, catching air in a tunnel was a far cry from actually jumping out of a plane, but still, Mia found her heart rate skyrocketing.

Once the little girl exited, the man motioned for Phoenix as he stepped out of the tube, leaving it empty. Phoenix offered Mia a smile as he got to his feet and, without preamble, launched himself into the tube, surprising her with his agility. Yeah, there was no way this was his first time. She found herself laughing at his antics, enjoying the way he'd clearly mastered this as much as he mastered everything else.

"So, he really has done this before," she said to Tarik while her eyes continued to follow Phoenix.

"A time or two, yes."

"Has he jumped out of an airplane before?"

"Yes."

"And you? Is this something you enjoy doing?"

"It is," he said, his voice rather loud so she could hear him over the wind noise.

When Phoenix's time was up, Mia got a little nervous, but the instructor managed to calm her down as he helped her into the tunnel and into position.

Within seconds, she was flying.

The feeling was strange yet exhilarating. A weightlessness she'd never known before. She tried to stay focused, realizing she was grinning so much that her cheeks hurt as the wind blasted her, keeping her off the ground. She couldn't hear anything except for the roar of the wind and her own heartbeat. Her laughter was drowned out, a mere echo in her head, but she loved every single second of it. And when it was over, Mia couldn't stop smiling.

She wasn't sure she would *ever* stop smiling.

Chapter Nineteen

PHOENIX NEVER TOOK his eyes off Mia the entire time she was airborne. She was so beautiful, even with most of her face covered by her goggles and the helmet over her head. Her smile... Phoenix would have to admit that her smile was the most radiant thing he'd ever seen. He was drawn to her in every way, and when she laughed, he laughed.

Of course, watching Tarik master the wind was an erotic sight all its own. The man moved so easily, so effortlessly that Phoenix found himself admiring every move, every nuance of his facial expressions. The guy was physical perfection.

"He's good at this," Mia said as they watched Tarik take his turn.

Yes, he definitely was. He was good at a lot of things, Phoenix thought to himself.

It wasn't long before those few minutes were up and they were exiting to the main waiting area where they'd originally been sent.

"So, how was it?" Tarik asked Mia when he met up with them.

"Incredible," she said breathlessly. "Is it really like jumping out of a plane?"

"Not exactly." Phoenix glanced down at her as he studied her. "Why? You interested?"

"Maybe one day," she told him, her eyes locking with his. "You never know what you might enjoy until you try it."

The underlying meaning of those words hit Phoenix like a twenty-ton hammer. Based on the way she held his gaze, he knew what she was getting at. He wasn't sure he was going to make it through the rest of the day if she kept that up.

The young man who'd helped them to suit up showed them where they needed to go next. Once they had removed the flight suit and other equipment, Phoenix led Mia and Tarik back down the stairs, where they were greeted by the girl who'd signed them up initially. A few minutes later, Tarik took Mia's hand and led them toward the main doors. Feeling incredibly bold, Phoenix decided to take her other hand, walking alongside them. When Mia didn't flinch or bother to look around to see if anyone noticed, he smiled.

Yes, this was definitely working out better than he had planned.

"So, who's the winner?" Tarik asked as he helped Mia into the SUV after they'd made a run for it in the parking lot. The rain hadn't let up yet, proof in that he was getting drenched just standing there.

"That's a tough one," she told him, glancing over at Phoenix briefly. "I'm gonna have to say Phoenix."

"I agree," Tarik said, grinning from ear to ear as his eyes met Phoenix's.

They were standing so close, the rain coming down heavily, and Phoenix could feel the heat of Tarik's body, smell spearmint on his breath. Neither of them moved for a long moment. A foreign sensation simmered inside him, urging him to take the plunge, to lean in and kiss Tarik right there. The knowing look on Tarik's face, the cocky, crooked grin was the only thing that stopped him.

Yes, he was going to give in, even he knew that much. But for now, Phoenix was going to make Tarik work for it.

Tarik turned away, and Phoenix inhaled deeply as he jumped into the car, brushing the water from his hair and his coat.

"It's your turn to pick a place to go," Phoenix told Mia when Tarik darted around to the driver's side.

She was examining him cautiously, but she didn't seem put off by the moment he'd shared with Tarik. Phoenix had absolutely no idea how she would react if and when he told her that he was as interested in Tarik as he was in her. He wasn't sure he was ready for that reaction. If she rejected him, he wasn't sure he'd survive it.

"Do you play laser tag?" she inquired sweetly, still gazing up at him as he tried to dispel more of the water from his hair.

"I know how, yes."

"You?" she asked, looking to the front toward Tarik, who had jumped into the driver's seat and was doing the same thing. His shirt was plastered to his back — the guy had a passionate dislike for coats, so he'd gone without one, as usual — and Phoenix did his best not to stare at him as he got situated in the front seat, flipping the heater on high.

"I've played."

"Are you good at it?" She was eyeing Tarik intently as she waited for him to answer, and Phoenix fought the urge to draw her attention back to him and kiss her.

"I can hold my own."

"And you? Do you excel at that, too?" Mia asked Phoenix, turning back to him once again.

"You'll have to find out," he stated, putting his thumb on her chin, curling his finger beneath.

He couldn't resist the desire to kiss her, so he leaned in and pressed his lips to hers. When her small hands came up and rested on his chest, Phoenix leaned in closer, enjoying the warmth of her touch, the sweetness of her lips, the fruity scent of her shampoo. The woman affected him in more ways than one, and he didn't think he'd ever been quite so aware of another person in his entire life. Except maybe Tarik.

The kiss was slow and gentle, a languid melding of lips, an unhurried mingling of tongues.

"So, laser tag then?" Tarik called from the front seat, and Phoenix was forced to release Mia's lips.

"Sounds like a plan," Phoenix responded before returning his mouth to hers.

Pulling her closer, he slipped his hand behind her neck, cupping her head and tilting it slightly for a better angle. The leisurely slide of tongue against tongue didn't last long, and the next thing Phoenix knew, he was kissing her hard, driving his tongue into her mouth, desperately wishing they had a little more room because his hands itched to touch her. He wanted to pull her onto his lap so he could feel her warmth against his entire body.

"You haven't won yet," she said softly when they broke for air.

Tarik laughed before backing out of the parking space. If Phoenix had to guess, the other man had been watching. The idea had Phoenix's cock hardening even more.

Mia was smiling, a glimmer of mischief flashing in her brilliant blue eyes.

Hell, he wasn't even keeping score, but he wasn't going to let her know that. At the moment, getting to spend the day with her made him the automatic winner. If they made it back to his condo tonight … he couldn't promise he'd be able to control himself. "If you say so," he replied.

"I definitely say so. We'll talk more after laser tag."

Phoenix laughed, he couldn't help himself. And then he kissed her again, pulling her as close as he could, crushing his mouth to hers and tasting her energy, her excitement.

Half an hour later, Tarik pulled the Escalade into the parking lot of a place dedicated to laser tag according to the sign out front. Phoenix had only played once or twice in his life, and he looked forward to this time. Mainly because he was thinking about the hidden corners within the place where he could crush his body to Mia's and make her beg for mercy.

The three of them made their way inside, the rain having let up significantly, which made it easier all around. Tarik put his arm around Mia's shoulders and held her close against him. It was obvious to Phoenix that he was trying to see how far she was willing to go. Phoenix wasn't complaining, but he damn sure didn't want to push her too far too fast. As it was, this unconventional date had likely taken her by surprise, no matter how well she seemed to be handling it.

"Scared?" Mia teased him as Phoenix held the door open for her.

You have no idea, he thought to himself. "Not a chance," he said out loud.

Tarik took the lead, heading to the counter and paying for the three of them. The guy informed them that the place was completely empty and said for them to have a good time.

Phoenix assured him that a good time was certainly on the agenda.

Once they'd donned their gear and made their way into a small arena, Mia seemed itching to go. He gave Tarik a knowing look, and the three of them wasted no time splitting up and heading in different directions.

265

Phoenix made sure to stay out of sight as he worked his way through the multi-level arena. He was purposely guiding Mia toward Tarik, and Tarik was doing the same. A good fifteen minutes had passed before they managed to sneak up on her. Phoenix tapped her shoulder gently and took a step back. Mia squealed and then spun around, shooting him and hitting the target on his vest dead center. A luminous smile lit up her face, but then Tarik returned fire, hitting her and leaving him the only one not hit. Since they had to wait out the timer that made their guns useless, there was no one to get back at Tarik.

But that really wasn't the point.

Crowding Mia against the rocky wall after placing both of their guns on a ledge, Phoenix tipped her chin up so that he could press his mouth to hers. She didn't hesitate, kissing him back as she grabbed for his shirt on his sides, gripping and pulling him. The vests were obtrusive, but Phoenix ignored them, cupping her face and exploring her mouth with his tongue.

Phoenix felt Tarik move in, obviously refusing to be left out again. When Phoenix pulled back, Tarik quietly watched them both. Initially, Phoenix thought Tarik was going to kiss Mia, and he didn't blame the man, but that wasn't what happened.

Tarik's hand came up and slid behind Phoenix's head, pulling him in as their lips touched. Instinct had him tensing, ready to fend Tarik off, but the gentle press of his lips had him surrendering briefly. His thoughts were temporarily obliterated by the demanding slide of Tarik's tongue against his own. He knew Mia was standing there, still sandwiched between him and the wall, and that thought cleared out the haze of lust that had momentarily overwhelmed him. Pulling back abruptly, he looked down at Mia.

She was smiling, her cheeks flushed.

He wanted to ask her if she was okay, but he wasn't sure that was the right thing to say. Thankfully, she didn't give him time to say anything at all when she said, "This isn't over yet. You know that, right?"

"Not by a long shot, love," Tarik whispered.

Mia laughed. "That isn't what I meant, and you know it."

Tarik offered Mia his crooked smile and then glanced over at Phoenix.

"Time's almost up. You two might want to get ready to lose." And with that, he disappeared around the outcropping of fake stone.

"He's not gonna win this one," Mia declared, grabbing her gun and smiling up at him. She went up on her toes and pressed her lips to Phoenix's fleetingly before turning and disappearing in the same direction.

He started to follow but stopped as he grabbed the laser gun once more and pressed his back against the wall. He'd join them in a few.

Right now, Phoenix needed a couple of minutes.
Hell, he needed a hell of a lot more than that.

»»»»»» ♥ «««««

NEARLY AN HOUR and a half later, Tarik pulled the Escalade into the parking lot of an oversized amusement center. The clouds had passed through, leaving clear blue sky and sunshine overhead, although the temperatures were hovering slightly above freezing. He'd made a judgment call after they'd left the laser tag place because their options had increased without the rain to limit them to staying inside. This was more of a one-stop shop that would keep him from having to drive all over town.

"By the time we leave here, we'll definitely know who the winner is," Mia informed them as they climbed out, joining Tarik as he met them.

"Right now, it looks like we're in the lead," Tarik told her.

"The day's not over yet," she challenged.

Taking her hand in his, Tarik led her inside while Phoenix did the same as he had back at the indoor skydiving place, taking her other hand in his as though the three of them together was the most natural thing in the world. And maybe it was. Maybe that was what the elation was that Tarik felt. He had them both with him, and he wasn't sure he'd ever been happier than he was right at that moment.

His thoughts drifted back to that kiss he'd shared with Phoenix. The one that had clearly taken the man by surprise. Tarik's shock had come when Phoenix hadn't tried to push him away. Multiply that by two when he'd pulled back to see Mia staring up at them, her blue eyes glowing with interest, a satisfied smile tipping her lips.

Yeah, she hadn't been turned off by two men kissing. Quite the opposite, actually.

Which was a damn good thing, because Tarik intended for a lot more of that later in the day.

After Phoenix bought the tickets and they passed through the turnstile, he pulled Mia to him. Tarik stood close and watched the pair.

"One more kiss for good luck," Phoenix whispered against her lips.

Mia didn't seem to mind Phoenix's need to taste her, and had it not been for the kids running through the place, Tarik figured Phoenix could've easily gotten lost in her for longer than a minute. But then she pulled away, smiling up at him.

When he released her, Tarik stunned them both, pulling Mia in close to him as he stared down at her. "It's my turn," he said but didn't move in closer. "Does that worry you, Mia?"

"Should it?" she asked enthusiastically, her eyes locked with his.

"No," Tarik offered and then leaned down, pressing his lips to hers. Probably due to their surroundings, neither of them deepened the kiss, but when Tarik pulled back, he noticed the intensity in Mia's gaze as she watched him.

"Let the games begin," Mia said happily, although a little breathlessly.

Little did she know, but they already had.

Yeah, she was certainly hoping for more, and that thought had Tarik discreetly adjusting himself before taking her hand once again.

For a first kiss, Tarik had to admit that he'd felt the spark from that brief touch of her lips clear down to his feet. It'd been far too short for his liking, but it was as though there was a promise of what was to come that hung between them when he'd pulled away from Mia. Back at the last place, when he'd kissed Phoenix, he had considered kissing Mia first but had held back. More because he had wanted to see her reaction to him and Phoenix together; he had wanted to make sure she understood what direction this was going.

Quite frankly, he was a little shocked that she hadn't freaked out. But then she'd nearly knocked him sideways when she hadn't balked at the idea of kissing him in a building full of people moments after she'd kissed Phoenix just now. Why that was, he didn't know. He *wanted* to know, he just didn't. There'd been plenty of willing women who'd gladly climbed between him and Phoenix over the years, but admittedly none of them were like Mia.

He was beginning to question his first impression of her. Based on the way she'd held his hand and then allowed him to kiss her, he wasn't so sure she was as pure as he'd initially thought. Then again, maybe she was simply caught up in the excitement. He knew he was. His adrenaline was still flowing, his competitive spirit alive and well as they made their way to the rock climbing section of the building.

This was a one-stop shop of all the activities they could possibly want, and by the end of the day, there would be a winner. And unexpectedly, he didn't care who it was, because Tarik got the distinct feeling that it wasn't really going to matter, anyway. If things worked out the way he hoped they would, the three of them would be back at the penthouse engaging in something else that produced a significant amount of adrenaline.

But for now, he only had to survive the rest of the day.

And more importantly, resist the urge to press Mia up against the wall and kiss her the way he really wanted to kiss her.

Chapter Twenty

BY THE TIME they left the adventure park, Mia was exhausted. She hadn't laughed that hard in years. Her cheeks hurt from grinning, her stomach muscles were sore from laughing, yet the euphoric feeling that filled her couldn't be dampened by a little exhaustion.

Tarik and Phoenix were probably the two most competitive people she'd ever met. They had attempted to sabotage one another — good naturedly, of course — throughout the day. On top of that, the heated looks they'd sent one another — and her — had kept Mia in a state of arousal she'd been hard-pressed to fight.

"Hungry?" Phoenix asked as they made their way through the doors and out into the parking lot. The sun was still high overhead, even at five thirty, and the temperatures were holding steady, however not dreadfully cold. But even that didn't put a damper on her mood.

She was once again holding hands with both men, something that felt surprisingly natural, although it should've freaked her out. They'd both done it most of the day, taking her hand, pulling her close, stealing a kiss here and there... She'd felt a little off-kilter, but never had she felt better.

It was all about living in the moment.

She'd spent so many years trying to figure out how to fix everything that was broken, working on changing the past, walking on eggshells to keep from upsetting the unnatural balance of her stormy life. Now she was learning that wasn't even possible. Live for today, that was her new motto. Try new things.

Well, she was definitely checking that one off her bucket list.

Why she wasn't panicking, or worried what others thought about her, she truly didn't know. Tomorrow there would probably be pictures in the tabloids of their outing, and she might have to worry about it then, but for now, she really didn't give a shit.

She was having too much fun.

"What did you have in mind?" she asked Phoenix once they were in the SUV and pulling out of the parking lot. Surprising them both, Mia had climbed into the front seat with Tarik, laughing at Phoenix as he pretended to pout in the back.

"Food," he told her smoothly, his eyes raking over her face and landing on her lips as she glanced at him over her shoulder.

For a moment, Mia got the impression he wasn't interested in food at all. Although her stomach was rumbling, she was inclined to think she might get her fill if they did go back to his place right then.

Not a good idea, she reminded herself.

As much as she liked him, as easy as he was to be around, Mia still worried about the repercussions of being with a man like Phoenix. She'd learned over the course of the day that he wasn't anything like Damien, but those warning flags were still flying high and proud every time she thought about where this was headed.

Tarik, on the other hand, was a little more her taste. He wasn't high profile, although he wasn't low-key, either. But like Phoenix, he made her feel things she hadn't expected to ever feel again. Things that she'd stopped feeling long before her marriage was over. Like that flutter in her belly when they looked at her. Or the tingle in her core when either of them pulled her close. It was a heady feeling that she was beginning to crave like a drug.

"Before we decide on dinner, we need to figure out who the winner of the day is," Tarik mentioned, reaching over and taking Mia's hand in his as he maneuvered onto the highway, heading south toward downtown.

"I think I did," she said quickly, laughing. There was no way she was the winner for the day, but she figured it was worth a shot.

"Not a chance, little girl," Phoenix retorted. "I'd say I'm the winner."

"Like hell," Tarik added.

"If you think *you're* the winner, why did you even ask?" Mia questioned, linking her fingers with his while the heater blasted on her face, warming her considerably.

"Because I wanted to hear you say it."

274

"Okay, fine. I think you're the winner," she told him, glancing over her shoulder at Phoenix once more. "Don't you think?"

"I'm good with that," he answered, grinning.

Of course he was. It didn't matter, because if either of them won, she had agreed to go back to Phoenix's condo.

"Does that mean I get to pick the restaurant?" Tarik asked.

"If that'll make you happy." Mia didn't really care who picked, as long as they got to eat sometime soon. She was starving.

"I know this excellent Mexican place. You up for that?"

Mia looked over at him and smiled. "Sure."

The conversation continued, mostly Phoenix and Tarik arguing affably about who the winner actually was until they were pulling into the crowded parking lot to the restaurant. Mia realized immediately that they weren't too far from her condo. A mile maybe.

Once they parked, Phoenix rushed to help her and then placed his arm around her shoulders and pulled her against him, purposely keeping her from Tarik while he apparently claimed ownership. The fact that they were both fighting — albeit friendly — over her made her feel good.

"Do you two do this often?" Mia questioned when the waiter brought a basket of chips and several bowls of salsa to the table, along with three glasses of water.

"Eat dinner?" Tarik asked sardonically, his eyebrows shooting into his hairline. "It's a daily occurrence for me, honestly."

Mia gave an unladylike snort and then laughed at herself while the two of them smiled. "That's not what I meant. Do you do these types of things often? The laser tag, rock climbing, bowling?"

"Quite a bit, yes," Phoenix told her.

He had crowded her into the booth, stealing the spot beside her and forcing Tarik to sit on the other side. Not that Tarik seemed at all bothered. In fact, he'd planted his huge booted foot between her feet beneath the table. She found she liked that he wanted to touch her.

"It's a good way to relax," Tarik added.

"I'm not sure I'd call today relaxing," Mia told them as she reached for a chip. "Fun, yes. Relaxing, not so much."

"So you had a good time?" Tarik asked.

"The best," she answered truthfully. "I don't think I've laughed that much in years."

The waiter came to take their orders, and all three of them, without looking at the menu, ordered fajitas. When they were once again left alone, Mia continued asking questions, delving into something that had her curious. "So, I've got a question. I … uh…" She felt her face flame as the sentence drifted through her head but didn't come out of her mouth.

Tarik smirked, that crooked grin that made Mia's insides turn to mush. "Spit it out, little girl."

That was not the first time that one of them had called her "little girl," and she felt a frisson of pleasure course through her at the term. It didn't sound at all condescending when they said it, and she found she liked that they'd given her a sort of nickname.

"It's true that the two of you are bisexual?"

Okay, so maybe she should've waited until Phoenix wasn't drinking his water. When he started choking, Tarik roared with laughter, and Mia fought the urge to giggle as she patted Phoenix's back. They'd drawn the attention of several people sitting around them, but Tarik merely waved them off, assuring them that Phoenix wasn't going to die.

"That's not what I expected you to ask," Phoenix finally said, his voice strained as though he were gasping for air. Which, technically, he probably was.

"I didn't know any other way to word it."

Phoenix drank more water, clearing his throat as he stared over at her, his eyes wide in disbelief.

"What? I read it in the tabloids, so it's not like it's not public knowledge."

"It's never been substantiated," Tarik said, reaching for more chips.

"Well, it kinda was today," she told him.

"No one saw that kiss but the three of us," Phoenix mumbled.

"That's what you think," Tarik stated. "There're video cameras in those places."

Phoenix's eyes widened.

"Okay, I think it's safe to say it's true," Mia said, placing her hand on Phoenix's arm. "Did you not want people to know?"

"I don't know what's true," Phoenix said softly, looking down at his hands resting on the table.

"Oh." She thought... But they'd... That kiss had kind of said it all, as far as she was concerned.

"He's in denial," Tarik muttered, peering up at Phoenix as he said the words.

Phoenix's only answer was to glare at Tarik.

Tarik looked at her and asked, "Did it bother you?"

Mia shook her head, fearing she wouldn't be able to get the words out. It hadn't bothered her. Not the way he was thinking. She'd been a little surprised, a lot aroused, but not entirely taken aback since she had read the articles that claimed they'd been together.

"I've never..."

When Phoenix didn't continue, Tarik filled in for him. "He's never been with a man."

Mia read the underlying meaning. Phoenix had never had sex with a man. Interesting.

"But you're attracted to them?" she asked.

"How'd this become an interrogation?" Phoenix asked, his tone clipped.

"Sorry, I just… Forget I asked." Mia reached for her water, wishing like hell the waiter would bring the food and the margaritas. She needed something to do with her mouth and her hands because clearly Phoenix wasn't interested in talking about himself, and after the day they'd shared, she had nothing but questions.

"Look," Phoenix said, placing his hand on her leg. "I'm sorry. And to answer your question, I've been attracted to men before. But I've never … given in."

"Until Tarik."

"I don't consider a kiss as giving in," Phoenix rebutted.

"He's stubborn," Tarik inserted, looking at Phoenix, a silent conversation taking place between them.

Mia noticed the longing in Tarik's golden gaze. She hadn't seen it before now, but it was clear. Tarik wanted Phoenix. Hell, she'd go so far as to say he was probably in love with the man. But Phoenix was obviously not there yet.

Luckily, as though he knew the tension had grown too thick for them to continue, the waiter interrupted, bringing their food and drinks. For the next few minutes, the three of them ate without speaking. An uncomfortable silence settled between them. By the time Tarik was preparing his third fajita and Phoenix was finishing his second, Mia couldn't take it anymore.

"Can one of you explain something to me?" Mia asked, pushing her plate away and pulling her margarita closer. "And I promise, I'm not going ask about your sexual preferences."

Tarik grinned, but Phoenix still looked a little worried.

"What do you want us to explain?" Phoenix asked, looking over at her sideways.

"Is he" — she nodded toward Tarik — "really your bodyguard?"

"Technically, yes. Or he seems to think so. His real job's handling public relations for the Arrows. He needs something more to do besides stand around and look pretty."

Mia grinned as she looked across the table. Tarik was definitely handsome; he was also extremely intimidating, but he certainly was not pretty. "How long have you worked for him?"

"Six years for the Arrows," Tarik explained.

"As a bodyguard?"

Phoenix didn't hesitate with his answer, and Mia realized she'd stumbled onto a much safer subject. "He started out as PR working for my father. Somewhere along the way, he became his pseudo-bodyguard, and he's remained in both roles after the incident a year ago. Nothing serious, but my mother didn't seem to care how small it was. She was worried, and by having him there, I think it puts her mind at ease somewhat."

"Nothing serious?" Tarik snorted. "He had a crazy husband threatening to shoot off his balls and feed them to him."

"Oh." The thought of Phoenix sleeping with married women made her gut tighten. She'd been on the receiving end of a cheating spouse, and she absolutely didn't condone it.

"It sounds worse than it is," Phoenix said, lowering his voice and speaking directly to her. "Honest to God, Mia, I had no idea she was married. Not until the guy threatened my life. That's not who I am."

"He's telling the truth, Mia," Tarik imparted as he leaned over the table, reaching for her hand. Obviously the two of them must've noticed how the news bothered her. "She never told him."

Mia nodded, wrapping her head around it. For a moment, she wondered if Damien had told the women he slept with that he was married. Then she remembered that he was in the public eye, so most likely they'd already known, anyway.

Not that she cared.

Not anymore.

"Well, I think it was smart for you to have someone to watch your back," Mia told Phoenix. "Damien never hired a bodyguard. He insisted that he was man enough to take on any threat."

"He's also a fucking idiot," Phoenix stated under his breath, his tone reflecting his apparent dislike for her ex-husband.

"Sorry, I didn't mean to bring him up," she told him, looking down at the table.

Phoenix took her hand, and she peered back up at him. "Landry's part of your past, Mia. I don't expect you to be able to talk about yourself without his name coming up. Do I like the guy? No. But that's for personal reasons."

"So you know him?" she asked, trepidation churning in her gut. She knew Damien was suing Phoenix, but he'd never brought it up, so she hadn't, either. Mostly out of fear that he wouldn't want anything to do with her. The first time they'd gone to dinner, Phoenix had seemed oblivious to anything to do with Damien, yet she knew that wasn't the case.

Phoenix released her hand and leaned back when the waiter delivered another round of margaritas and started taking empty plates from the table. "I know him. I'm actually surprised that you hadn't heard of *me*. Landry claims that my father backed out of a deal to sell the Arrows, right before he passed away. He's suing me for a ridiculous amount of money to compensate for his time."

"He wanted to buy your team?" Mia asked, trying to think back to previous conversations she'd overheard when she was married to Damien. She hadn't usually been privy to his business because he'd believed that she wasn't smart enough to understand, and quite frankly, Mia had never corrected him. "I knew he'd become obsessed with hockey, but I didn't know he was looking to go that far."

"So he claims. It's all hearsay at this point, because my father's not here to defend himself," Phoenix said, his tone reassuring.

"So what happens now? With the lawsuit?"

Phoenix met her gaze and leaned forward, resting his forearms on the table and clasping his hands together. She looked over at Tarik, then back to Phoenix. She knew that whatever he was about to say wasn't going to make her happy. At least not if his expression was anything to go by.

"I met with him a few weeks ago and informed him that he needs to go away. I'm not interested in him or anything he has to say."

"A few weeks ago?" Mia couldn't believe what she was hearing. If Phoenix had spoken to Damien a few weeks ago, the chances of him making the connection to her had to be rather great. The guy was smart, there was no denying that. She had to wonder why he hadn't said anything. "Before or after you and I went to dinner?"

"Before."

"Why did you act like you had no idea who he was?" she asked, exasperated. She should've known. He was a liar, like Damien.

"That's not entirely true," he stated cautiously. "You asked if I'd looked into your history. I told you that I would prefer to hear the details straight from you. There's a big damn difference there. He's your *ex*-husband, Mia. I didn't think that was relevant."

"So you knew exactly who I was when you had that meeting with Damien?"

"Yes," he admitted.

"And when you manipulated the seating chart at the charity ball?" She didn't know for a fact that he was responsible, but based on what Alex had told her, she figured it was safe to assume.

Phoenix looked at Tarik before nodding his head.

When Phoenix's gaze lowered to the table once more, she knew that was guilt. He'd pretended not to know who she was. So the big question was… "Why? Why did you pretend?"

"I didn't pretend," he said defensively, looking up at Tarik and then back to her. "I wanted to get to know *you*. I don't give a shit about Landry or the fact that you were married to him. That's your past, and it doesn't mean anything unless you want it to, Mia. Last I checked, you weren't party to the lawsuit, so I didn't think it mattered."

Mia didn't know what to say to that. She was angry and hurt, and for whatever reason, all the millions of tiny pieces of her shattered heart were rattling around in her chest, aching all over again. Although for an entirely different reason now. Damien had been blatant with his adultery. He'd purposely ended their marriage by making it obvious that he'd cheated, and he hadn't tried to hide anything. But Phoenix... He clearly wasn't being honest with her. He was pretending.

And that hurt more than it should have.

"I'd like to go home now," she told him abruptly.

Phoenix nodded his head in understanding and moved out of the booth to allow her to get up. When she stood, stopping to look at Tarik briefly, she couldn't resist asking him the same question. "Did you know about this?"

Tarik met her gaze head on. "I know everything that goes on with Phoenix, Mia."

Nodding her understanding while the band around her heart tightened even more, Mia tried to calm herself. She was so angry she felt tears threatening, and the absolute last thing she would do was let another man see her cry. She'd done enough of that with Damien.

Turning on her heel, Mia snagged her coat and headed for the front doors. Phoenix and Tarik followed right behind her.

Mia continued walking until she was outside while Phoenix stopped and talked with the hostess.

She was tempted to start walking home, but her condo was several blocks away, and she wasn't comfortable walking alone that far from home. Especially as the sun was beginning to set behind the buildings, and the shadows were slowly filling in. So she waited, trying her best not to let the anger get the best of her. She found it strange that she felt betrayed by Phoenix in ways she'd never felt by Damien. It wasn't like she knew him all that well. They'd been on a couple of dates, they'd talked and kissed, but other than that…

God, she felt so pathetic standing there feeling as though someone else had purposely trashed her heart for reasons unbeknownst to her. She was a lightweight when it came to relationships, that was clear. Why couldn't she be stronger? More resilient? Wasn't she starting over? Taking control of her own life? Living in the moment?

Shouldn't she be the one with armor encasing her emotions?

Unfortunately, she didn't have answers to any of those questions.

Instead, she was worried that Phoenix was playing her.

Mia took a deep breath, let it out.

Hadn't she kept that information from him as well?

She hated the thought that they'd started this off with secrets between them, but that was exactly what had happened. Mia was doing her best to sever her life from Damien's. She didn't want any part of him or anything he did.

But why hadn't Phoenix mentioned that he'd met with Damien? Was he using her? He'd already said that Damien's beef had been with his father, not him. And it wasn't like Phoenix could use her against Damien, anyway. Her ex-husband had initiated the downfall of their marriage; she seriously doubted he actually cared.

Mia sighed, looking up at the sky as it turned a fascinating shade of dark blue, mixed with pink and purple. She really needed to get a grip.

This wasn't a relationship. If anything, it might lead to something casual, but Mia wasn't looking for anything more.

When Phoenix and Tarik joined her outside a second later, she turned to face them. And the music. She'd overreacted.

"I'm sorry for my reaction," she told Phoenix sternly, feeling both embarrassed and annoyed at her initial response. "I have trust issues, as you can imagine. I think I got a little ahead of myself. You and I … we're … we're friends, and I shouldn't have reacted like that."

To her surprise, Phoenix moved closer, his eyes locked with hers, his mouth a firm, thin line. He cupped her face and stared down at her, the look on his face reflecting what appeared to be … irritation.

Not at all what she'd expected.

"We're more than friends, Mia. At least that's what I'm hoping for," he said, his voice low, authoritative. "If you want friendship, I can offer you that, but I'm looking for more. I can assure you, I didn't withhold information to hurt you. That's not the way I do things. From this point forward, I'll be open with you about what I know."

Mia was lost in his emerald-green gaze. She heard his words, but it wasn't what he said that had her mesmerized, it was the intensity reflected there. He wasn't playing her as she'd assumed. How she knew that, she wasn't sure, but she knew that much.

Not that it made her feel any better. She'd felt used by Damien and then tossed out like yesterday's garbage. She wasn't looking for that again. Ever. But she didn't know how to do this, didn't know how to venture forward without the fear strangling her. Casual sex wasn't her thing. She'd only been with one man in her life, and he'd betrayed her.

"Do you want to go back inside and have dessert?" he asked, his hands sliding down to her shoulders and then running down her arms.

Mia glanced through the window of the restaurant and noticed the hostess and another man staring out at them. "No. I don't."

"What about a movie?" Phoenix asked. "That was next on my agenda."

Mia was too tired to sit in a darkened theater and watch a movie. "No. I think I'd rather go home."

"Why don't we go back to my place then? I'm sure I've got something there for dessert."

Before she could object, Phoenix linked his fingers with hers. The warmth of his touch calmed her further.

"Just dessert, Mia. That's all. What happens from there is your call."

Despite knowing better, Mia found herself agreeing.

Chapter Twenty-One

THE NIGHT HAD taken a decidedly unexpected twist, but somehow Phoenix had managed to salvage it.

He hoped.

After the little blowup in the restaurant, he had been practically holding his breath, waiting for Mia to decide to call it a night after all. Things had taken a strange turn ever since they'd sat down for dinner, starting with Mia's unexpected question about bisexuality. She'd taken him completely by surprise, something that was usually relatively difficult to do.

It wasn't until the elevator made it past her floor that he exhaled, more relieved than he'd expected to be. It wasn't a regular occurrence for Phoenix to have to put so much effort into a woman. Not that he considered this effort, but he admittedly was used to women coming to him, not the opposite. He definitely liked the turn of events as far as Mia was concerned, but he hadn't realized until now just how much emotion went into the chase.

Or how easy it would be to damage something so fragile.

When the elevator doors opened on his floor, Phoenix allowed Mia and Tarik to precede him. He kept his gaze on Mia, watching as she looked around while Tarik unlocked the front door and then waited for them to join him.

"Cinnamon-scented pinecones, huh?" she asked, a small smile curling the corners of her mouth. "A little late in the season, don't you think?"

"I knew that's where that smell was coming from."

Mia chuckled. "I take it they weren't your idea?"

Phoenix looked at Tarik.

"Don't look at me. I didn't do that. Your mother thought it was a good way to spruce things up out here. You should've seen the Christmas tree that she put up."

"Does she live close?" Mia asked as they stepped into Phoenix's penthouse.

"In this building." Phoenix closed the front door and locked it behind them. "When my father passed away, she sold their house. I think the idea of being closer to me worked for her, since she likes to make surprise visits from time to time," he explained when Mia glanced at the front door and then back to him.

"It's nice that you get to see her all the time." Mia turned away from him as she shrugged out of her coat and looked around the spacious room. "My mother works a lot. I get that she's dedicated to her patients, but sometimes it would be nice if she would drop by to see me unexpectedly."

Tarik glanced his way as Mia turned toward the living room, moving farther away from them.

Phoenix wondered what she thought as she took it all in. His place felt more sterile than hers did. He didn't have any pillows on the black leather sectional that sat facing the wall of windows. The chrome and glass end tables didn't hold vases of flowers, and the black-and-white rug on the hardwood floors didn't have a splash of color. But it suited him.

"Ellen drops by every day to check on her little boy," Tarik told her as he led Mia into the living room.

"What about your parents?" she asked Tarik.

"My father's in…" Tarik glanced toward the windows. "He's in prison."

"Oh," Mia said, her eyes never straying from Tarik's face. "And your mother?"

Phoenix could tell she was hesitant about asking that question, but he knew that Tarik was even more hesitant to answer. The man didn't make a habit of talking about himself. To anyone.

"My father's in prison for killing my mother," Tarik said tersely, moving away from them.

Shit.

Phoenix knew Tarik hated talking about his parents. Then again, when most people asked personal questions, Tarik found a way to shrug them off, saying as little as possible. Phoenix was surprised he hadn't done the same now. It was proof of how much he liked Mia.

"This is nice," Mia said, discernably working to change the subject. "What? No television?"

"Not in this room, which is why I spend little time here," Phoenix told her, taking off his coat and laying it on the back of the sofa before thrusting his hands into the pockets of his jeans as he casually moved closer.

"See, I'd be spending all my time here," she explained, looking out the windows at the Austin skyline. "I prefer music and reading to television, anyway."

"I don't read unless I have to. Music is for working out. And television, although rare thanks to my schedule, is one way I manage to relax."

"When you're not playing hooky from work, I take it you're working." Mia's sexy smile was like a punch to the gut, and Phoenix wanted to pull her to him — actually, he wanted to pull her on top of him while he was sprawled out on the couch naked — but he managed to abstain.

"I do," he said, sparing one more glance in Tarik's direction before turning toward the kitchen. "I have no idea what we've got for dessert, but I'm sure I can find something. Worst case, we'll order out and have it delivered."

"I'm sure there's something to scrounge," Mia commented.

"Phoenix doesn't cook," Tarik said, his voice coming from directly behind him.

"Me? You don't cook, either," he retorted as he stepped into the kitchen, Mia right behind him.

"I like to cook," she told them. "It doesn't happen often, because cooking for one is a waste of time, so I eat TV dinners mostly. And for dessert, I usually binge on ice cream or Oreos. Sometimes both."

"We tend to order out." Phoenix had a damn hard time not looking at her lips, not thinking about what she tasted like, how her smooth skin felt beneath his hands.

He didn't even realize their conversation had come to a jarring halt until Mia looked away, her cheeks turning pink. Phoenix was standing directly in front of her, Tarik flanking her back.

Knowing that resisting her was pointless, Phoenix gave in and crowded her against Tarik, meeting the other man's eyes above her head briefly before cupping her face and forcing her to look at him.

"I'm sorry about earlier," Phoenix whispered. "I had a great time today. It probably ranked up there with the best days of my life, actually. I didn't mean to ruin it."

"You didn't," she said softly, her eyes sliding down to his mouth.

"I did. But I intend to make it up to you. My culinary skills suck, but I'll do my best."

He had fully intended to lighten the mood, but apparently his words had the opposite effect, and the next thing he knew, Mia's hands were sliding up to his face, her soft, cool fingers brushing against the day's worth of stubble on his cheeks moments before she pulled his head down.

"I was thinking about something else for dessert," she whispered, her breath fanning over his lips.

He should've resisted, should've stolen a quick kiss to sate him temporarily, but the hunger had built to a crescendo, and Phoenix found himself lifting Mia, then turning and setting her on the counter before settling between her thighs, his mouth on hers. The heat of Tarik's body moved behind him, his chest pressing against Phoenix's back, and suddenly he was overwhelmed by the sensation of being sandwiched between the two of them.

They'd never done anything like this. Well, nothing beyond that one time, but that had been a fluke. This... This was intentional. Generally, when they were with a woman, it was for her pleasure mostly. Tarik never focused his attention elsewhere. Then again, until recently, Phoenix hadn't actually given him permission to.

But now...

Phoenix's heart began a rapid, erratic beat in his chest as Tarik moved closer behind him, his hands gripping Phoenix's hips while Phoenix's lips continued to move against Mia's. He allowed her to lead briefly, her tongue thrusting into his mouth, and he met her with a blinding passion, licking, tasting, exploring. He slowly slid his hands beneath her shirt, feeling the smooth skin of her abdomen. He did his best to keep things as innocent as he could, but that didn't last nearly as long as he'd intended, especially when her hands slipped beneath his shirt, searching at the same time Tarik's did.

"Oh, hell," Phoenix moaned, pulling his mouth from Mia's as the two of them continued to touch him.

He wasn't sure what he would see when he opened his eyes, but the look on Mia's face was one of encouragement, not revulsion. When the silk of her fingers disappeared, he realized that was because she had placed her hands over Tarik's, guiding him.

"Mia." He wanted to warn her, to let her know he was close to the breaking point, but he couldn't get the words out. He wasn't sure she even realized what she was doing to him, to them. Phoenix had been holding back, resisting Tarik for so long, it was natural. But right then, with Tarik's hands on his stomach, the tips of his fingers sliding into the waistband of his jeans, Phoenix wasn't sure he could stop this if Mia wanted him to.

He'd met this woman a little over a month ago, and he felt as though he'd known her forever. Her skin felt familiar, her taste conjured memories he knew didn't exist, her sweet moans had his dick pulsing as though it knew how exquisite this was going to be. Yet he didn't know her. Not yet.

But he did know Tarik, and the emotions that churned through him where the other man was concerned were far greater than he could even admit to. He wanted him with a passion that defied logic, one that defied reason. Wrong or right, he didn't care anymore, because he couldn't hold back any longer. The last thing he wanted to do was scare Mia away, but he owed this to himself, to Tarik. They had to have a chance to see where this went.

But not yet.

When her hands once again touched his skin, gliding higher beneath his shirt, Phoenix pulled back to look at her, letting her explore, although it went against everything in him. He was always in control, never conceding, especially when it came to sex, but here he was, offering himself up to her and Tarik at the same time.

"Shirt off," she whispered, forcing the cotton higher. Tarik did the work for him, lifting his shirt until Phoenix was forced to pull his hands from beneath Mia's shirt so he could remove it, but he put them back as quickly as possible, relishing the smoothness of her skin.

"Fuck," he growled when Mia's mouth went to his chest, Tarik's lips pressing against his shoulder, their tongues trailing over him slowly. When Mia clipped his nipple with her teeth, he thought for sure he was going to come right there in his fucking jeans.

"Mia," he warned again. "Please tell me you understand what's happening here."

Mia looked up at him, her eyes hooded, the heat reflected there a sure sign of her passion, but Phoenix still needed to hear her say the words. This wasn't only the two of them.

"I understand," she whispered back, her eyes sliding up to Tarik. "I understand more than I thought I would."

Phoenix swallowed hard and closed his eyes as she continued her exploration with her hands and mouth.

"Relax," Tarik said softly against his ear. "It's all about you right now."

That was something he'd said to a countless number of women, but never had anyone said it to him. He felt a sense of helpless pleasure, a yearning he'd never known before. And truth be told, it scared him. He didn't want Mia to do something that she would regret. Didn't want her rethinking this once they got so far into it that they lost themselves in the moment.

Phoenix closed his eyes as she explored him with her mouth and her hands. He gripped her hips forcefully, keeping himself as still as he could while he wanted nothing more than to strip her bare and devour her right there on his kitchen counter. He didn't know how long he managed to hold himself back — it could've been seconds, possibly minutes — but finally that little thread that held him together snapped, and Phoenix reached behind him and grabbed Tarik's neck, holding him to him.

"I don't want this to backfire," Phoenix mumbled. "God help me, I want this more than my next breath."

"Relax," Mia said, repeating Tarik's instruction from moments ago. "We all know what we're doing."

He wasn't so sure that was the case, but he was losing himself, losing his ability to maintain control, to worry about how Mia would handle this when she realized what Phoenix wanted from Tarik, and more importantly…

What they both wanted from her.

Chapter Twenty-Two

MIA HAD NEVER been known for her spontaneity. In fact, that was something Damien had always ridiculed her for, telling her she needed to loosen up more. Little had he known, but until she'd met him, Mia had been much more impulsive, much less uptight. An overbearing, controlling man had changed her into someone she hadn't recognized.

Well, she wasn't sure there was anything more spontaneous than this right here.

From the moment they'd stepped into Phoenix's condominium, the flicker of awareness that had ignited in her core earlier in the day had flared to life once again. She wasn't sure whether her unnatural reaction to these two men was due to the adrenaline high from the day, whether she was still reeling from Tarik's admission about his parents, or it was simply her physical attraction to them. Either way, she was fully invested in and quite intrigued by what was happening.

Based on the way Phoenix was watching her, she knew he thought she was going to panic and run. A couple of weeks ago, she probably would have — there was no doubt about that. But she'd been enlightened in recent days, understanding that there were certain lifestyles she hadn't known truly existed, and quite frankly, this just felt … right. It satisfied a curiosity that had built inside her, growing stronger every day, every minute she spent with both of these men.

Mia sat up straight, her legs dangling over the edge of the counter, Phoenix's hard body standing between her thighs, Tarik behind him. She watched Phoenix and Tarik for a moment, trying to make sure she really was okay with this situation. It felt right, but that very well could've been her hormones on the fritz. After all, it'd been a very, very, *very* long time since she'd had an orgasm that wasn't self-induced.

A damn long time.

When Tarik reached around and cupped Phoenix's chin, tilting his head back and then leaning over Phoenix's shoulder to press their lips together, Mia's insides tingled. It felt like a live wire had been released inside her, causing her arousal to flare hot and bright.

They were kissing.

And it might've been the single hottest thing she'd ever seen in her entire life. The way Tarik continued to take charge, careful to ease Phoenix into it as though he knew the man was on the verge of running — something she was curious about, too — was sexy as hell. She'd thought Phoenix would be the aggressor, but that clearly wasn't what was happening in front of her.

In fact, Phoenix seemed to be melting into Tarik, giving himself over completely.

Reaching forward, Mia ran her hands up Phoenix's chest once more, a surge of feminine power flooding her when his muscles tightened, the hard ridges of his abs flexing deliciously, his hands coming up to grip her wrists. He clearly wasn't interested in relinquishing all control.

"Legs around me," Phoenix commanded when his mouth left Tarik's. When she complied, he kept his eyes locked with hers as he braced his hands on her ass, hefted her up, and then carried her out of the kitchen and through the living room, going straight for…

"Is this your room?" she asked as they stepped into an enormous bedroom. The room was dark but for a single lamp on the bedside table and the glow of the Austin skyline out the floor-to-ceiling windows that lined two entire walls.

"Yeah," he said hoarsely as he lowered her to the gigantic king-sized bed.

"Mia, tell me you want this," he said as he kneeled on the bed between her spread thighs, his warm hands traveling up her legs, causing chills to burst along her skin beneath her jeans.

It was the moment of truth, but Mia didn't even need to question what she wanted.

"Come here," she said. "Both of you."

Tarik joined them on the bed, moving up to lay on his side facing her while Phoenix lowered himself to the bed on her other side. She was nervous, there was no denying that fact, and the longer they stared at her, the more time she had to think about what was happening. She wasn't having second thoughts, but she didn't want to give the illusion that she knew what she was doing. This was new for her. Exciting but still unfamiliar.

She didn't want to think, didn't want to try to figure out how this would work. Didn't want to spend a moment worried about the future, about what tomorrow would bring. There would be plenty of time for that.

Just not right then.

Right then, she wanted to feel Tarik's mouth on hers, to get the full experience of his kiss. She'd been aching for it nearly all day. She slid her hand behind Tarik's head, pulling him closer until their lips met.

His lips were firm, insistent yet gentle. As she allowed her tongue to slide against his, her body trembled, the taste of him overwhelming her. His kiss was different from Phoenix's. He was more dominant, and that sent her blood pressure soaring. Tightening her grip on his hair, Mia held on, fearing she was going to lose herself to this man too easily.

Then again, maybe she already had.

His hand slid beneath her shirt, the rough skin of his fingers trailing softly against her belly. He didn't move fast, didn't attempt to move higher, merely brushed his hands over her flesh while his tongue slid against hers.

Mia's rational judgment had been clouded by lust, that was all there was to it. And, holy smokes, did it feel good.

For the first time in a long time, she felt … desired. In ways she'd never felt before.

Times two.

She itched to touch and be touched. She wanted nothing more than to explore every single inch of these incredible men. Nothing else mattered. Not the argument they'd had earlier, not the hurt feelings she'd battled, not the wary thoughts that had been looming over her all day long.

No. None of that mattered right at this moment.

The reverberating rumble that sounded from Phoenix's chest as he pressed up against her side had her insides tingling, and when his mouth slid to her neck, she knew this was a moment she would never — for as long as she lived — forget.

»»»»»» ♥ «««««

TARIK FEARED HE was about to wake up from the most incredible dream he'd ever had. He was tempted to pinch himself to prove that this was real. That the smooth, silky feel of Mia's skin against his palm wasn't just a figment of his overstimulated imagination. That Phoenix truly had given in to them right there in the kitchen, despite the fact that he was clearly worried that Mia was going to freak out because Tarik was touching him.

It had been a gamble to touch Phoenix in the first place, he knew. But he hadn't been able to help himself. His theory had been that if Mia couldn't handle it, she wasn't the right woman. Phoenix may have believed otherwise, but Tarik had taken the decision from him.

After all the months that he'd yearned for Phoenix, praying the man would come to terms with whatever he was fighting where Tarik was concerned, he hadn't wanted to give up the ground that they'd gained in recent weeks.

His surprise had come when he had peered over Phoenix's shoulder to see Mia watching him. The arousal flooding her crystal-blue gaze had been so potent Tarik had nearly been knocked off his feet. The gamble had paid off, and here they were, the three of them on Phoenix's bed, a place no other woman — or man — had ever been.

Hence, the reason he thought he was dreaming.

Except Mia's lips were too perfect, her hands too smooth, her skin too soft. There was no way this wasn't real. And the growl that escaped Phoenix was certainly real.

Pulling his mouth from Mia's, he watched as she turned her head to meet Phoenix's, the two of them melding their lips together in a sensual dance that had Tarik's dick throbbing painfully. He knew he had to rein it in, to keep from losing control, because this was the moment he'd been waiting so long for. He wanted to give Mia as much pleasure as possible and, at the same time, show Phoenix what he'd been missing all this time.

While Mia and Phoenix kissed, Tarik slid his hand up Mia's torso, pushing her shirt higher, revealing a simple yet incredibly sexy white lace bra. He could see her dusky pink nipples through the sheer material, and he longed to wrap his lips around them, tease them into hard points. Apparently Phoenix had the same intention, because he pulled back, and Tarik felt his gaze on him. Tarik reached for the front clasp of Mia's bra while meeting her gaze, waiting for her approval. A slight nod of her head was all she gave him, and with deft fingers, he released the clasp, and the cups fell away, revealing the succulent creamy mounds.

She bowed her back when Tarik cupped one breast, leaning down and blowing lightly against her nipple. Phoenix didn't move, he just watched, and Tarik had never wanted an audience more than he did right then. He wanted to pleasure Mia while Phoenix paid close attention, letting his anticipation grow, his eagerness for them both to multiply. Tarik traced her areola with his tongue, softly making circles over her skin.

"Tarik," Mia moaned, and the way she said his name had him wanting to thrust into her, to possess her, to claim her.

But he didn't do any of that. Not yet.

For now, he needed to savor her, the salty taste of her skin, the sweet scent of her arousal, the soft feel of her fingers as they twined in his hair, urging him closer to her breast.

"More," she pleaded softly.

Giving her what she asked for, Tarik sucked her nipple into his mouth, teasing the tip with his tongue. When Phoenix leaned down and did the same to her other breast, Mia cried out in ecstasy.

He wondered how long it'd been since she'd been with a man, but he wasn't going to ask. All that mattered was that she was there with them.

Fingers gripped the back of his head, sending a thrilling shard of pain shooting down his spine. Mia was so damn responsive, pleading for more.

Releasing her nipple from his mouth, Tarik lifted her shirt, and Phoenix pulled back, realizing what he was trying to do. He managed to free her from her shirt and bra, but he didn't move to unbutton her jeans. Not just yet.

Phoenix had other plans, though, because he climbed off the bed and removed her shoes and socks, leaving her clad in only the denim that encased her hips and her sexy, trim legs. Tarik longed to see her naked. He wanted to lick her from head to toe, and he didn't even care which end he started from, because she was his dessert tonight.

"You okay?" Tarik asked softly, brushing his lips against hers.

"Better than okay," she answered breathlessly, her hands cupping his face and pulling him toward her.

She backed up her words when she thrust her tongue into his mouth, luring him in. When he met her halfway and then forced his tongue into her mouth, she wrapped her lips around his tongue and sucked, sending a bolt of lightning shooting straight to his balls. He imagined her mouth on him, sucking his cock into the molten hot recesses of her mouth.

Tarik felt a firm grip on his ankles and realized that Phoenix was attempting to remove Tarik's boots. Since he was lying on his side, leaning over Mia, the position was a little awkward. Wanting to encourage Phoenix to finish what he'd started, Tarik reached for Mia, pulling her until she was on top of him, straddling his hips.

She was looking down at him, a smile on her lips and hunger in her gaze.

"Lean forward," he told her as he pulled her hips forward, easing her body upward. When she complied, he lifted his head and trailed his tongue over her nipple once again. When she realized what he was going to do, she pressed more insistently against his mouth. He laved her nipple, sucked her breast, nipped her skin gently while Phoenix managed to remove his boots. Mia was moaning by the time Phoenix joined them on the bed once more.

When Phoenix straddled Tarik, his thighs on each side of Tarik's, the hard ridge of his cock grinding against Tarik's, it was evident what he was doing. He leaned over Mia, his hands resting on either side of Tarik's head, nearly crushing her between them. Tarik didn't stop teasing her nipples, loving the way she moaned his name, begging him for more.

"Do you like that?" Phoenix asked her. "His mouth on you? Licking you?"

"Yes," she said on a breathless moan.

"Think about what it'll feel like when our tongues are on your pussy, teasing your clit, thrusting inside you. Do you want that, Mia?"

"Oh, God."

One of Phoenix's hands disappeared from beside Tarik's head, and he realized that Phoenix was holding Mia up. Tarik kneaded her breasts with his hands, pinching her nipples ever so slightly, then a little harder as she continued to moan.

"You're sensitive," Phoenix said.

"Yes."

"Can you come from Tarik teasing your nipples?"

Tarik heard the challenge, and he pulled her nipple into his mouth, sucking firmly while pinching the other between his thumb and forefinger. He alternated, dividing his attention between both of her luscious breasts until she was grinding down on him. His cock was rock hard, a steel rod rubbing against his jeans, pressed firmly against Phoenix's hard length. He wished they had no barrier between them. The idea of his cock sliding against Phoenix's, skin to skin, made his body burn hotter.

"That's it, Mia," Phoenix encouraged. "Let go, baby."

Tarik used his teeth to worry her nipple, pinching her more firmly with his fingers until she cried out again, her body stiffening, her climax thundering through her.

It was the sexiest fucking thing he'd ever seen.

»»»»»»♥«««««««

WATCHING MIA COME from Tarik teasing her nipples was better than any fantasy he'd ever had. The way she gave herself over to the pleasure, moaning and crying out in ecstasy… It had taken a tremendous amount of willpower to remain where he was, but somehow Phoenix managed.

His bare chest was pressed up against her warm, smooth back, the sweet scent of her overwhelming his senses while he watched Tarik take pleasure in giving her pleasure.

But they weren't through with her yet. Not by a long shot.

Tarik eased her back to the bed, but Phoenix remained where he was, still straddling Tarik's legs.

When the other man's eyes met his, Phoenix grinned knowingly. This was what they'd been dancing around for years. What Phoenix had tried to convince himself he didn't want. Had it not been for Tarik's daring move in the kitchen, he wasn't sure he would've given in. Not like this, anyway.

But here they were, and Mia was completely on board, something he honestly hadn't expected. Glancing over at her, he met her hooded gaze. She was watching him, a sexy smirk teasing the corner of her kiss-swollen lips.

"Touch him," she whispered, easing onto her side and reaching for the hem of Tarik's shirt. Within seconds, Tarik had removed it, relaxing back on the bed as he continued to watch Phoenix intently.

Memories of the night Phoenix had given Tarik a blow job in the hallway flooded his mind, and he licked his lips, eager to taste him once more. Since that night, he'd kept his distance from Tarik, worried that Tarik wanted more than Phoenix could handle. With each passing day, he had expected the desire to fade, but that hadn't been the case. If anything, it had intensified tenfold. He wanted Tarik, every single inch of him.

Sliding his hands over the rigid contours of Tarik's sculpted abs, Phoenix took his time touching him, noting the differences between Tarik and Mia. Tarik's skin was more rigid and firm, the muscle beneath hard as steel. Mia's skin was soft, her rounded curves a significant contrast to the hard planes and angles of Tarik's body.

"Touch me," Tarik urged, a hint of desperation in his gruff voice.

"Trust me, I plan to." All in due time.

Sliding the backs of his fingers down Tarik's sides, Phoenix eased his fingertips beneath the denim and then skimmed them toward the button on Tarik's jeans. He pulled the button free and then slowly lowered the zipper as he continued to watch every expression that moved across Tarik's handsome, chiseled features.

Phoenix felt Mia's gaze as it slid over him, then down to Tarik. She seemed as enthralled as Tarik, and that spurred Phoenix on. This was the moment of truth. Either Mia was going to go all in or she was going to walk away. He prayed it wasn't the latter, but if he had to guess, other than possibly watching porn, she'd never been part of something this erotic.

It helped immensely that she was eager.

Phoenix went up on his knees, silently encouraging Tarik to lift his hips. The man did one better. He lifted his ass off the bed and pushed his jeans and boxers down to his thighs.

Mia climbed off the bed, and Phoenix's heart skipped a beat, a sliver of panic racing through his bloodstream until he saw that she was merely removing Tarik's jeans, pulling them down his legs and leaving them in a heap on the floor.

Tarik was completely naked and laid out before them. A feast for the eyes with the hard lines of his muscular body. Phoenix's mouth watered as he trailed his gaze down Tarik's chest, past his rippling abs, and stopping on the thick, heavy erection protruding from between his legs.

Mia returned to the bed, this time kneeling beside Phoenix. He glanced over at her briefly and then did a double take when he realized she'd shed her jeans as well.

"Holy fuck," he growled as he took her in. The generous swell of her breasts tipped with dusky pink nipples, the gentle dip of her waist, the slight flare of her hips, and the… *Lord have mercy*. Her pussy was bare; the skin appeared just as soft and smooth as the rest of her.

She was, in a word … "Beautiful." A soft pink tinged her cheeks when he said the word aloud.

She leaned over and placed a kiss to Phoenix's bicep, her hand sliding down his forearm to his hand, where she linked their fingers together, her hand covering his. As she had earlier with Tarik, she guided Phoenix's hand.

When his fingers encountered the hot, smooth skin of Tarik's long, thick cock, he slid his eyes to Tarik's. He was watching them, his eyes glued to their hands as Phoenix began to stroke him, Tarik's heavy, throbbing cock filling Phoenix's palm.

Mia eased closer to Phoenix's side, one hand sliding over his back while they both focused on Tarik.

Tarik hissed in a breath, drawing Phoenix's eyes up to his once again.

"It's too much," Tarik groaned.

"Not nearly enough," Phoenix replied as he teased the swollen tip. "We're just getting started."

Phoenix gripped Tarik's cock more firmly, slowing the motion of their hands, swiping his thumb over the engorged head, wiping the bead of pre-cum that had formed there.

When he paused completely, Mia leaned around Phoenix and slid her tongue over the head of Tarik's cock.

"Shit." Tarik's hips lunged upward, nearly knocking Phoenix off of him. "Oh, God, Mia. Don't stop. Please don't stop."

Phoenix crawled off Tarik's legs and settled on the bed beside them while Mia took control, her small hand wrapping around the base of Tarik's cock while she hesitantly sucked and licked the head of his cock, her eyes on him.

"That's it, baby," Tarik encouraged. "Just like that. Wrap your lips around my dick. Tease the head. Fuck yeah."

While Mia explored, Phoenix removed the rest of his clothes and returned to the bed, this time behind Mia. Tarik had slid his hands into her silky blonde hair, gently guiding her as she took him into her mouth. Her soft, subtle moans made Phoenix's skin tingle.

Kneeling behind her, Phoenix spread his knees and once again molded himself against her back, his cock sliding against the crack of her ass, his hand slipping around her and then down between her legs.

"Are you wet, Mia?" he whispered in her ear, his lips brushing the outer shell.

She didn't respond, but her answering moan when he drew the tip of his finger through her slick folds was all he needed.

"Mia, oh, God, baby. Your mouth is so good. I can't take much more," Tarik growled.

Phoenix knew Tarik wouldn't want to come yet, and he didn't blame him one bit.

With more self-control than Phoenix would've had, Tarik succeeded in pulling his cock from her lush mouth, and with more ease than a big man like Tarik should possess, he managed to maneuver them so that Mia was on her back. Tarik slid off the bed and stood on the floor between her legs. Stroking himself slowly, Phoenix watched as Tarik took control, something he did so smoothly, so effortlessly, Phoenix hardly realized he'd given over his own control to him.

With a firm grip on her ankles, Tarik pulled her closer to the edge of the bed, in a perfect position so Tarik could lean down and press his lips to her smooth, hairless pussy, which he did, eliciting a startled cry from Mia's lips. Phoenix dropped to the bed beside her, pressed up against her side, and kissed her. Hard.

She reached for him, holding him to her as their tongues dueled, his hand groping her breast while she moaned into his mouth. He explored her mouth while he ground his cock against her hip, the friction making his breath stutter in his chest. He pulled away when her soft hand curled around his dick. He was hovering on the brink, unsure whether or not he would be able to hold out much longer. Her urgent yet gentle touch was more than he could bear, pushing him closer and closer to release, something he refused to do until he was inside her.

Pulling out of her grip, Phoenix rested on his forearm and turned his attention to Tarik, who was eating Mia's pussy like a starving man, his tongue flicking over her clit, his fingers slipping inside her and retreating slowly.

"Tarik. Yes. Please. More," Mia begged.

Tarik continued his sensual assault on her pussy while Phoenix watched. He was desperate to get his mouth on her, but at the moment, he was strung so tight he feared he might break if he even moved.

Then Tarik pulled his fingers from inside Mia and reached for him, gripping his dick firmly, his fingers wet with Mia's juices. Phoenix tried not to focus on how fucking good it felt as Tarik stroked him while he continued to lick Mia, her hips thrusting up against his face.

"Tarik!" Mia's scream shattered the otherwise silence of the room as her orgasm gripped her. Phoenix slammed his mouth to hers once more, inhaling her cries as she came in his arms, fighting the urge to give in to the exquisite sensation of Tarik's hand still firmly stroking his dick.

Chapter Twenty-Three

IN ALL HER life, Mia had never had an orgasm like the one that had just ripped through her. She hadn't even known it was possible, and she wasn't sure whether she was merely a sad, sad case or if she'd just been with the wrong man. Whatever the reason, her body had taken flight, soaring higher and higher while Tarik teased her clit and thrust his fingers inside of her. When he'd curled them, touching a spot deep inside her, she'd been unable to control the torrent of sensation that rocketed through her until she shattered into a million tiny pieces.

She was boneless, nearly too exhausted to move, yet there was an ache between her thighs that yearned to be soothed. She wasn't sure she could orgasm again, but she knew without a doubt that she needed one of them inside her.

"Phoenix," she whispered, sliding her hand over his cheek as she stared into his turbulent green eyes. "I need to feel one of you. Inside me."

She saw his Adam's apple move in his throat as he swallowed hard, a glimmer of pure fire adding to the intensity of his gaze.

The next thing she knew, he was off the bed and moving across the room to a large armoire. He returned with a strip of condoms, and after tearing one off, he tossed the rest onto the bed beside Tarik.

"Put it on me," Phoenix instructed Tarik, the commanding tone in his voice returning after having been absent since they'd started this.

Mia watched as Tarik did as instructed, opening the package and then rolling the latex over Phoenix's long, hard length, but not before Tarik leaned in and melded his lips to Phoenix's, kissing him with a passion Mia could practically feel.

Once Tarik got his fill, he released Phoenix and took a step back.

Without another word, Phoenix joined Mia on the bed once again, positioning himself between her thighs before leaning over and pressing his lips to hers. And just like that, the electricity began to spark beneath her skin, like an adrenaline shot that targeted every single nerve ending. Her body hummed to life, and she wrapped one leg around Phoenix's hip, urging him closer, wanting to feel him, needing to be filled by one of them.

He continued to plunder her mouth as he guided himself to her entrance. He teased her briefly, the head of his cock sliding up and down her slit. She continued to grind against him, silently begging him to enter her, to give her what she needed. And then he lined up once again and pressed forward, the head of his cock breaching her entrance. The flash of pain that sparked surprised her, and she pulled back, staring up at him as she sucked in air, trying to ignore the pain.

It'd been a really long time, and he was much bigger than… He was big, that was the gist of it. She worried momentarily that she wouldn't be able to take him.

"I'll go slow, baby," he said softly, leaning down and kissing the corner of her mouth. "I'll be easy."

The bed shifted near her head, and she glanced over to see Tarik crawling toward her.

"Put your hand on my cock, Mia. I want to feel you touch me while Phoenix fucks you."

His words sent a blinding frisson of heat through her, making her pussy spasm around Phoenix's thick cock slowly sliding deeper. She knew Tarik was trying to distract her, and as her body relaxed, she realized it had worked.

"Your hand's so damn soft," Tarik said, his voice a rough whisper.

When Phoenix pushed up onto his knees, resting his hands on her bent legs, she watched them both. Her sexual experience was extremely limited, and this was something she hadn't even imagined in her wildest, most erotic dreams, but she couldn't look away. Two men, hovering over her, it was … the hottest thing she could imagine, and she wanted more of them. Both.

"Phoenix," she pleaded. "Fuck me, please."

"Slow, Mia. I don't want to hurt you."

He was big, but the pain had subsided, and her body was ready for him, aching for him. She didn't want to wait any longer.

"Put your mouth on me, Mia," Tarik instructed, leaning over her and obstructing her view of Phoenix.

Not that she needed to see him, because he continued to fill her, obliterating her thoughts. Closing her eyes, she guided Tarik's rigid cock into her mouth, sucking him slowly as he began to fuck her mouth. He didn't push far, but he managed to control the pace, something she was grateful for because when Phoenix settled inside her completely, she lost control of her body, giving herself over to the pleasure as he began to retreat before thrusting into her again. Just as he'd promised, he started out slow but increased his pace, fucking her so thoroughly he awakened nerve endings she wasn't even aware she had.

Tarik increased his pace as Phoenix did. Mia had to concentrate to keep from biting him as she moaned from the sheer ecstasy of Phoenix pounding into her.

"Fuck, Mia, it's too good," Tarik growled.

Nicole Edwards

When Tarik pulled back, she thought she'd done something wrong, but then Phoenix fell atop her, his forearm resting beside her face, his hand cupping the crown of her head, his mouth hovering inches from hers. As he stared into her eyes, his pelvis began a slow, sensual grind against hers. Moments later, he was pushing in incredibly deep and then withdrawing, slamming into her over and over. He locked his gaze with hers and whispered for her to come. Only then did she give herself over to the sensations, knowing she wouldn't be able to last forever although she never wanted him to stop. It felt too good.

"Phoenix," she cried out as an electrical current of sensation erupted in her core, barreling outward through her arms, legs, fingers, toes. The only sounds she heard were her rapid breaths, Phoenix's sexy grunts, and the roar of her own blood in her ears. "Phoenix!"

"Fuck, yes, Mia. Come on my cock," Phoenix ground out, his voice rough. "I'm coming, baby. Come for me. Fuck."

She shattered once more, brilliant sparkles of light flashing behind her closed eyelids, her inner muscles clenching around Phoenix's cock still buried inside her, a delicious tingle lingering in her core. Seconds passed, maybe minutes, but she didn't open her eyes, relishing the most exquisite pleasure she'd ever known. Wishing it didn't have to end.

Mia was coming down from her high when she finally opened her eyes, watching as Tarik slid his hands into Phoenix's dark hair and thrust his cock between his lips.

"Suck me, Phoenix. I wanna come in your mouth. Oh, fuck, yes. So good."

Mia's pussy clenched, a sweet aftershock reverberating through her as she watched Tarik fuck Phoenix's mouth. Phoenix groaned at the same time Tarik did. Unable to help herself, Mia leaned over and placed her hand on Tarik's hard, muscular thigh, feeling the power in him as he endured the pleasure Phoenix offered him. He took her hand without looking at her, linking their fingers and holding it closer to his side as he tensed once again.

"Stroke me," Tarik ordered. "Tighten your fist. Harder. Ahh, yeah. Like that." Tarik's body went rigid, his hips driving forward, burying himself in Phoenix's mouth while Phoenix's hand continued to stroke Tarik's shaft. Animalistic groans erupted in the room moments before Tarik cried out one final time. "I'm coming. Oh, God, yes! Phoenix. Fuck. Suck me dry."

And despite her exhaustion, another orgasm ripped through her when Phoenix slammed into her one final time.

»»»»»» ♥ «««««

TARIK WASN'T SURPRISED when Mia drifted off shortly after they finished. He had lifted her off the bed so that Phoenix could pull back the blankets and then lowered her onto one of the pillows. She hadn't said a word, simply turned on her side and curled up with her hands beneath her face. Once again, she looked as sweet and innocent as he had originally pegged her for. But he'd seen a wildcat beneath that sweetness, an erotic woman whose inner desires hadn't been tapped yet.

There would be plenty of time for that, he knew.

"I'm going to take a shower," Phoenix said, not looking directly at Tarik as he padded naked across the room and escaped into the attached bathroom.

Tarik waited until he heard the water come on. He pulled the blankets up over Mia, leaned down, and brushed a kiss against her forehead. "We'll be right back."

She stirred a little, murmured something he didn't understand, but she didn't open her eyes.

Without knocking, Tarik entered the bathroom to find Phoenix standing in the shower, his head resting against the tile as he stood beneath the spray. The steam billowed up and over the clear glass enclosure, making the chocolate-brown slate tiles shine with moisture.

Not trying to be silent, Tarik joined Phoenix in the shower and stepped up behind him, wrapping his arms around Phoenix and holding him before the other man had a chance to protest or push him away. The hot water pounded down on his face, but Tarik didn't move, not wanting to let go of Phoenix.

Neither of them said anything for several minutes, and it wasn't until Phoenix moved, placing his hand on Tarik's arm, squeezing gently, that he released the breath he'd been holding. Things were going to be all right. He knew they would be.

Phoenix wasn't an easy man to read, and Tarik had feared he was going to retreat, try to push Tarik away. Things were heating up between them, and there was no turning back. At least not where he was concerned.

Pressing his lips to Phoenix's shoulder, he started slow, his arms still wrapped tightly around him as he kissed across the tense muscles of his back, up his neck until Phoenix's head lifted and he turned slightly, giving Tarik better access.

Tarik's cock hardened, and he couldn't resist pressing his hips against Phoenix, his dick sliding along the crease of his ass as he closed his eyes, a silent thank you going out to whoever was responsible for giving him this moment. He wanted more than anything to bury himself inside Phoenix, to claim him in ways he'd never been claimed before. It was too soon, he knew that much, but he still wanted it more than anything.

Phoenix must've realized, because he turned in Tarik's arms, placing his hands on his chest and forcing him backward until Tarik was the one pressed against the rough tiled wall.

"Don't think I don't want this, because I do," Phoenix whispered, pinning him with his hard gaze.

Tarik nodded his understanding, reaching for Phoenix, but he was stopped when Phoenix reached for both of his hands, twining their fingers together and then lifting Tarik's arms above his head, forcefully pinning him there.

"I know you're used to being in control," Phoenix said, his voice deep and even. "I'm not sure I can give it up. Not completely."

Tarik wanted to assure him that he could, but he didn't. Phoenix was a control freak. They constantly battled over it in their day-to-day life, so Tarik hadn't expected that this would be any different. But he knew when the time came, Phoenix would relinquish his control, would give himself over to Tarik. It was merely a matter of time.

"Kiss me," Tarik commanded, letting Phoenix know he was willing to compromise, hence the way he was being pinned to the wall, but ensuring he knew that Tarik was still in control.

Phoenix leaned in and brushed his lips against Tarik's. Just enough to make Tarik want more of him.

"Fucking kiss me," Tarik ordered, straining his arms to take control of the situation.

Phoenix tightened his grip, keeping him pinned to the wall as he crushed his mouth to Tarik's. The brutal assault was so fucking thrilling Tarik was tempted to believe he could come from that kiss alone. He ground his hips forward, sliding his still-hard dick against Phoenix's, pulling a delicious moan from the other man.

"I want you," Tarik told Phoenix when Phoenix pulled away. "I want to turn you around, make you put your hands on the wall while I slide my cock deep in your ass." He kept his tone low and even as he continued, "I want to own you, Phoenix. I want to fuck you until you scream my name. Until you know who can make you lose control. Me. Only me."

Phoenix's eyes widened, and Tarik recognized, even though he was the one restrained against the wall, that he'd won this round. Phoenix wanted it as much as Tarik did.

"But I can wait," Tarik added softly, needing to reassure Phoenix that they had time. "I've waited this long. I can wait a little while longer. But just know this." He leaned forward as far as he could, resting his forehead against Phoenix's. "I will take you; I will own you. Don't try to fool yourself into believing otherwise."

Phoenix shifted Tarik's arms so that he was holding his wrists with one hand, the other sliding down between them. The rough hand that gripped his cock made him suck in a breath. The pain was exquisite. Phoenix began jacking him urgently, roughly, exactly the way Tarik needed it.

"Fuck," Tarik groaned as his cock hardened completely.

"You like that?" Phoenix ground out through clenched teeth, his mouth only a whisper away from Tarik's. "You like when I take control? I know you do. Don't deny it. What would you do if I turned you around and buried my cock in your ass, Tarik? Would you let me take you? Let me fuck you hard?"

"God, yes," he groaned. "Any way you want." The admission was easy. He'd wanted Phoenix for too long. His ass clenched, the need building as Phoenix continued to stroke him harder, faster until Tarik's eyes closed and the pleasure nearly overwhelmed him.

"Open your eyes," Phoenix demanded.

Tarik forced his eyes open, meeting Phoenix's determined gaze.

"Look at me when I make you come."

Tarik nodded, unable to do anything more as the pleasure gripped him.

"I want to watch you come."

Phoenix's grip on Tarik's wrists tightened; the slice of pain was the extra push he needed. "Fuck," he groaned. "I'm coming."

His cock pulsed as he came, but Phoenix didn't release him. Phoenix kept a firm grip on his softening dick, and the other on his wrists as he pressed his lips to Tarik's.

"Give me time, Tarik. That's all I ask. Just a little time."

Tarik nodded. He wanted to tell Phoenix he would give him forever just to know that he would eventually have him. But he didn't say the words, unable to admit that much. He wanted Phoenix to know, but he feared what might happen if Phoenix panicked. And he would panic if Tarik told him exactly how he felt.

Yeah, there was absolutely no doubt in his mind that Phoenix would retreat if Tarik admitted that what he felt for Phoenix was the closest thing to love he'd ever known.

But this, right here, right now, was so worth it.
So fucking worth it.

»»»»»» ♥ «««««

SLEEP ELUDED HIM. No matter how hard he tried, Phoenix couldn't get his mind to shut down. Lying in his bed with Mia curled up against his side, Tarik on the opposite side of the bed, he was more content than he'd been in a long time, but he couldn't get his thoughts to settle.

The room was silent except for the gentle hum of the heater and Mia's soft, even breaths. Tarik was quiet, and Phoenix wondered whether he was awake, but he didn't want to ask. He didn't want to talk.

It'd been a whirlwind of a day, both emotional and physical, and Phoenix felt wrung out, depleted. Yet he wouldn't have traded it for the world.

He thought back to Mia's admission that she had trust issues. He'd known that from the first moment he'd asked her to dance. When he'd found out about Landry, it all made sense. But tonight, when she'd come back to the penthouse, there hadn't been any mistrust there. There was an odd sensation in his chest when he thought about how the two of them had taken over, guiding him into a situation he'd been avoiding for so long he hadn't even known how to make it happen.

And then Tarik... The man didn't push him, but Phoenix could sense his urgency, the need to grab hold of whatever this was and tighten his grip, do something that would keep them from drifting apart when they had seemingly made so much progress. Phoenix couldn't explain it, but that alone gave him a security he hadn't thought he'd needed.

Having always been the one in control, it was strange and comforting at the same time to know that there were two people willing to catch him if he fell. Not that he planned to, he was too sturdy for that, but he wasn't invincible.

"Quit thinking." The deep rumble of Tarik's voice made him smile in the darkness, but he didn't respond.

Mia's hand slid over Phoenix's stomach, and his body tensed. Her soft touch stirred him to life, but he knew she wasn't awake. If she were, there still wasn't anything he could do, because he knew she would be sore tomorrow. He'd known the instant he'd burrowed inside her that she hadn't been with anyone in a long time. Her pussy had gripped him like a velvet vice, so fucking tight, so fucking perfect.

He groaned softly, and he felt the mattress move as Tarik shifted onto his side. Another hand came to rest on his stomach, this one much bigger than Mia's. Just like her touch, Tarik's soothed him. More than he'd expected. Laying his hand atop theirs, Phoenix forced his eyes closed, wishing for sleep.

He had no idea how much time passed, but he finally succumbed, for the first time in forever, sleeping so deeply he didn't even dream.

A *Million* Tiny Pieces

Chapter Twenty-Four

"ANOTHER WIN! GO Arrows!"

Phoenix heard the crowd cheering as the limo pulled out of the parking lot of the Arrows Center. The Saturday night home game had gone off without a hitch, thanks to some quick thinking by his team. They'd been spectacular, proving to everyone what they were made of. If they kept up this pace, they would make the playoffs for the first time in six years.

"It was a good game," Mia said, pulling Phoenix's attention back into the car.

He'd issued the invitation for her to go to the game with them that morning. Her agreement had ignited something inside him, something that still burned bright and hot.

"Did you enjoy it?" Tarik asked

"I don't know much about hockey, but yeah. I had a good time," Mia told Tarik. "I didn't know it was that … exciting."

"It can be," Tarik stated as he leaned forward and pressed a button that raised the partition separating the back of the limo from the driver.

Phoenix watched Mia's eyes widen as she glanced back and forth between them. "What are you doing?"

"Giving us a little privacy," Tarik said easily.

"Why would you do that?" she asked, a knowing smile forming on her lips.

Phoenix reached for her, pulling her onto his lap without giving her a chance to realize what he was doing. Once she was settled over him, straddling his hips as he faced her, Tarik joined them, moving into the seat directly beside Phoenix.

Gripping the back of Mia's head, Phoenix pulled her mouth to his, thrusting his tongue past her lips. He was still riding the adrenaline high from the game and from being close to the two of them for the last couple of hours. The trip back to the condo wasn't a long one, but he couldn't wait.

He didn't want to wait.

Phoenix felt Tarik's hand as it eased between his body and Mia's, sliding down to reach between her legs. As he pressed his hand there, Phoenix couldn't resist the urge to grind his cock against Tarik's fingers, wishing like fuck they weren't in the back of a limousine. He wanted them both naked, spread out before him so he could feast on them.

Mia moaned into his mouth before pulling away. "Oh, God," she whispered softly. "Oh, God, that feels good."

Phoenix reached for the button on her jeans, knowing they wouldn't have much time.

"What are you doing?" she asked, wriggling over him as he flipped the button free and lowered the zipper.

"Tarik's gonna make you come. And then we're gonna go to my penthouse, and I'm gonna make you come again. With my mouth."

Without preamble, Tarik dropped to his knees on the floor, his chest pressing against Mia's back, his arms coming around her so he could slide his hand inside her jeans.

Phoenix glanced down between their bodies, watching as Tarik's tanned fingers disappeared into her silky red panties.

Mia leaned back against Tarik, giving Phoenix a better view as Tarik began teasing her.

"Oh, God, yes," Mia cried out.

Phoenix ground his hand against the hard ridge of his cock as he watched the erotic sight.

"Come for us, Mia," Phoenix urged as Tarik's hand moved faster. "Come all over his fingers."

"You're so wet, baby," Tarik muttered. "That's it. You like when I play with your clit?"

"Yes. Oh, God, yes."

Knowing he wouldn't find relief in the next few minutes, Phoenix rested his hands on Mia's thighs, keeping his eyes glued to the spot between her legs where Tarik's hand was hidden in her jeans. He wanted her to come. He wanted to hear her scream.

"Tarik!" Mia cried out. "Oh, God. I'm … coming!"

A few minutes later, after Phoenix had righted her clothes and then pulled her against him, the limo arrived at the condos. The doorman opened the door, and Phoenix hustled Mia out, keeping her close while Tarik offered their thanks to the driver before joining them in the lobby.

Once in the elevator, Mia pulled away from Phoenix, turning her intent gaze on him and making him smile. So they'd worked her up good, had they?

"What are you doing?" he asked when she reached for his belt.

"Just playing," she said softly.

Phoenix gripped her wrist before she could do any more. As much as he wanted to have his wicked way with her in the elevator, there were cameras, and he didn't figure she would be too happy about that.

Luckily, they were in his penthouse within minutes, and he was more than ready to give her free rein. Which she took, surprising them both when she reached for a belt loop and pulled them both toward the sofa.

"Not in the bedroom?" Phoenix asked.

"No time for that," Mia said, a mischievous gleam in her eyes.

"Won't hear me arguing," Tarik said as he did the work for Mia, shrugging out of his suit jacket before quickly shedding the rest of his clothes.

Figuring he would be left behind if he didn't get with the program, Phoenix followed suit, stripping down to nothing in less than a minute and then watching her.

"Now sit," Mia instructed, nodding toward the sofa as her eyes raked over them both.

Phoenix lowered himself to the cushion, gripping his rigid cock, Tarik moving to sit beside him, the hair on Tarik's leg rubbing against him, making him achingly aware of their nearness.

Mia glanced behind her and then took a seat on the coffee table, apparently deeming it stable enough to hold her.

She leaned forward, taking one of Tarik's hands and one of his, crossing them, and carefully placing them on each other's cocks.

Phoenix hissed in a breath when Tarik's rough fingers grazed the sensitive skin of his dick.

"Stroke each other," she commanded.

Phoenix's eyes moved up to meet hers. He studied her for a moment, wondering who had taken over Mia's sweet, innocent body. Sure, she'd given in to them the other night, but this...

It was a pleasant surprise was what it was.

Doing as she asked, Phoenix wrapped his hand around Tarik's thick cock and began stroking slowly as Tarik did the same. He was torn between watching Mia, watching Tarik's hand as it pleasured him, and watching his own hand as he tugged the hard length of Tarik's erection.

"Strip," Tarik ordered, apparently talking to Mia since she was the only one still dressed.

She didn't balk at the command, simply stood and began stripping.

Slowly.

So fucking slowly.

Phoenix was no longer confused about what he wanted to pay attention to. She was the only thing he could see as she peeled off the Arrows jersey he'd bought her when they'd arrived at the game, tossing it to the side before unhooking the silky red bra that matched the panties he'd gotten a glimpse of earlier. Once she was topless, Mia kicked off her shoes and then shimmied out of her jeans as she eyed them both, her gaze looming over their laps where they continued to stroke one another.

"Is that better?" she asked sweetly.

"Panties, too," Tarik commanded.

When Mia hooked her fingers into her panties and slid them down her smooth legs, Phoenix's jaw damn near hit the floor.

"Sit," Phoenix stated sternly, nodding to the coffee table.

Mia primly lowered herself once again.

"Spread your legs apart," he insisted when she tried to keep them closed.

A pretty blush crept up her neck and infused her cheeks as she sat there. He might've been willing to let her lead, but she should've known she wasn't going to remain in control.

"Let's play a game," Mia said, her eyes meeting Phoenix's.

"A game?" he asked, trying to hide the intense interest that overcame him.

"Yes. Ever heard of Simon Says?" she questioned.

Tarik chuckled, but his hand tightened around Phoenix's cock, making Phoenix suck in a breath, the pleasure-pain nearly too much.

"I've heard of it. Remind me how to play," Phoenix said through clenched teeth.

"In my version, we give each other things to do by prefacing it with Simon says. Two of us will play at a time. If you don't say Simon says, then the other person isn't supposed to do the command. But instead of saying Simon says stop, we'll use time limits."

"What does the loser have to do?" Tarik asked, amusement reflected in his tone.

"Whatever the person who isn't playing wants them to."

"I'm in," Tarik said quickly.

Phoenix wrapped his free hand around Tarik's wrist, effectively stilling him. If he kept that up, there wouldn't be a need for any games. He'd be done.

Tarik pulled his hand back at the same time Phoenix did.

"What about you?" Mia asked. "You up for it?"

Phoenix glanced down at his cock. "Baby, I'm up for anything right now."

Mia blushed again.

"Who goes first?"

"I do," she said confidently. "After all, it was my idea."

It might've been her idea, but Phoenix wasn't about to tell her that there was no way she could win. No matter how much she wanted to.

The stakes were just way too high.

»»»»»» ❤ ««««««

MIA HAD ABSOLUTELY no idea what had come over her. What she'd been thinking when she'd suggested they play Simon Says, of all things, she didn't know. But it sounded like fun. Especially since they were all three naked and she was having too much fun watching them.

This way, she'd get more time to admire them and have less time to spend thinking about being naked. And maybe a chance to boss them around for a change. She didn't have the grand illusion that she would win, but she knew she could have some fun with them in the process.

"Simon says, you have to kiss him for ten seconds," she told Phoenix.

Phoenix's eyes darkened, but he didn't balk at the request. He simply turned his head, leaned over, and pulled Tarik's mouth to his. Ten seconds wasn't nearly long enough, but Mia knew things would get out of hand if she allowed too much time.

When they broke apart, she smiled.

"Okay," she said, thinking about her next command as she watched them carefully. "Simon says, for fifteen seconds, you have to suck his…" She felt foolish when she couldn't get the word out. She'd never been one for vulgar talk. The first word that came to her mind was penis, but now that she thought about it, that didn't sound nearly as sexy.

"You have to finish the instruction, or I can't do it."

Mia felt her face flame as she swallowed hard. "You have to suck his…" Taking a deep breath, Mia spit out the next word, "Cock. For fifteen seconds."

With a smirk, Phoenix leaned over and placed his lips around Tarik's cock, giving her the perfect view of what he was doing. Her body ignited, and she had the sudden urge to touch herself. She managed to keep her fingers curled firmly around the edge of the thick glass tabletop instead.

Tarik moaned at the same time Phoenix pulled back. When Tarik's hand slipped into Phoenix's hair and he pulled him back down, Mia laughed. "Nuh-uh. Time's up."

Tarik met her eyes, and she could see the disappointment there. "Now, you have to kiss him again for ten more seconds."

Phoenix moved back up, his lips landing on Tarik's. "You lose," she said triumphantly, trying not to sound as breathless as she felt. "I didn't say Simon says."

There was a glimmer in Phoenix's eyes, and Mia had to wonder whether or not he'd done that on purpose. And now Tarik got to tell Phoenix what to do.

"Do I have to put a time limit on it?" Tarik asked, his grin widening, that sexy dimple forming on his smooth cheek. She loved that he'd shaved. He didn't do it daily, and there was usually at least two days' worth of dark stubble lining his jaw, but tonight it was smooth.

"No," she said softly, trying not to fidget as she waited.

"Then Simon says Phoenix has to lick your pussy. Until I say stop."

A flash of blazing heat streaked over her skin. Mia wouldn't be surprised if she was sweating.

"Lie back on the table," Phoenix instructed as he dropped to his knees on the rug that covered the hardwood.

Mia eased back on the glass table, praying it was strong enough to hold her.

"It's strong enough. I promise," Phoenix said, as though he could read her mind. "Now spread your legs. Let me see your pretty pussy."

With her feet on the floor, Mia spread her legs as she stared at the ceiling. She tried to focus on her breathing, but that wasn't working, especially when she felt Phoenix's warm breath caress her most intimate place.

"Very nice," Tarik crooned.

Mia's blood pressure soared, and she felt her skin heat another degree or two.

But her embarrassment was obliterated when Phoenix's tongue grazed her slit. Her fingers tightened on the glass, where she continued to hold on for dear life.

She withstood the pleasure as Phoenix's tongue did magical things to her, making her body hum and pulse as he licked and sucked, occasionally driving his tongue into her. She needed more, but she refused to beg.

"Time's up," Tarik finally called, his voice rough and dark. It sounded as though he was just as affected as she was, although she knew that wasn't possible.

When Phoenix's mouth left her, Mia groaned. "He didn't say Simon says."

"Well, in that case…" Phoenix moved forward again, but Tarik stopped him. "Nope. Now it's my turn to give the instruction next," Tarik stated.

"You just did," Phoenix informed him.

"That was just the punishment for not doing things right."

"I damn sure wouldn't call that punishment," Phoenix declared.

Phoenix helped her to sit up, and her body swayed, the pleasure still coursing through her veins.

"Simon says," Tarik began in that gruff voice that set electrical charges pulsing in her core, "you have to finger your pussy for ten seconds."

Mia had known this was coming. She'd known they weren't going to let her off easy, but still, it was harder than she'd thought. Trying not to focus on them watching her, she slipped her hand between her legs, spreading her thighs wider as she grazed her clit with her finger. A moan escaped her, and her eyes darted up to meet Tarik's determined gaze. Out of the corner of her eye, she noticed Phoenix was stroking himself, and she let her gaze drop to his lap as she teased her clit with her finger, slowly. She didn't apply too much pressure, knowing she would go off like a rocket. Phoenix's tongue had driven her crazy, and she was only seconds away from detonating.

"Time's up."

Mia's hand moved away quickly, but Tarik surprised her when he reached for her wrist, lifting her hand and then sucking her fingers into his mouth. Her breath caught in her throat as his eyes locked with hers.

"Now you have to suck his cock for ten seconds."

Mia's brain wasn't functioning correctly, but she forced the lust-induced haze away, replaying his words in her head. That was when it dawned on her. "You didn't say Simon says."

The corner of Tarik's mouth lifted, and she knew he'd done that on purpose.

"I guess I get to play again," Phoenix said as he sat up. He turned his attention to Tarik this time, and Mia felt a flood of relief mingled with a slight bit of disappointment. As much as she'd wanted to play the game, she was ready to quit.

Because she was ready to get on with it.

Chapter Twenty-Five

TARIK WAS DOING his best not to lose the fragile grip he had on his control. Watching these two while playing this erotic twist on a game he'd played as a kid was pushing his limits.

Now it was Phoenix's turn, and he wasn't sure he was going to last much longer.

"Simon says on your knees." Phoenix's command was laced with a hard edge, proof that he was nearing the breaking point as well.

Tarik got to his knees.

"Simon says come here," Phoenix ordered, pointing to the empty space between his legs.

Tarik eased between Phoenix's splayed thighs.

"You," Phoenix said to Mia, "come sit right here. On my lap."

Mia took her own sweet time getting up and doing as Phoenix instructed, but the next thing Tarik knew, he was staring at Mia's glistening pussy and Phoenix's rigid cock jutting up between her thighs as she took a seat on Phoenix's lap, facing Tarik. If Phoenix repositioned them, Phoenix could easily slide up into her wet cunt. Tarik suddenly wished he would. Keeping his thoughts to himself, he waited for instruction as he forced his gaze up to meet Phoenix's.

This game was as good as over, even he knew that much.

"Simon says suck my cock."

Tarik leaned forward and wrapped his lips around the engorged head of Phoenix's cock, inhaling the musky scent of Mia's pussy splayed out in front of him. It was a temptation he was hard-pressed to resist. He wanted to lick her at the same time, to devour them both. Somehow he managed to remain focused, pleasuring Phoenix with his mouth.

"Put your hands in his hair," Phoenix instructed Mia.

Her small fingers curled into his hair, pulling him gently toward her.

Phoenix groaned as Tarik took him to the back of his throat before sliding his mouth off him once more. He repeated the motion, sucking him hard.

"Fuck," Phoenix growled. "Lick her pussy."

"You didn't say Simon says," Mia whispered.

"Fuck Simon," Phoenix belted out. "It's all about us now."

Tarik chuckled but did as instructed, releasing Phoenix's hard cock from his mouth and diving into Mia's pink folds, lapping at her. Gently at first. The hunger quickly took over, and he found her clit, flicking it with his tongue, using his hands to push her legs wider as he devoured her.

Mia's piercing moan made his cock throb. She tasted so fucking good.

"Stop," Phoenix commanded.

The instant Tarik pulled back, Phoenix's fingers slipped down between her thighs, and he drove two of them into her pussy, fucking her hard and fast. Tarik placed his hands on her knees, keeping her legs spread wide so he could watch the action.

Phoenix wasn't gentle as he fingered her. When he pushed three fingers inside her, Tarik glanced up at her face. Mia's eyes closed, and her head fell back against Phoenix's shoulder as a shudder wracked her small body.

"Oh, God! Phoenix! Oh … God!" Mia screamed, her muscles tightening as she came.

"I told you I was gonna make you come when we got up here," Phoenix told her as she relaxed against him. He took his cock in his hand and looked at Tarik. Without a word, Tarik wrapped his fist around the base of Phoenix's cock while he took him in his mouth once again.

"Fuck, that's good," Phoenix groaned as Tarik continued to suck him. "Don't make me come yet."

Tarik wasn't sure he could make that promise. His only goal was to send Phoenix over the edge.

Unfortunately, Phoenix had other plans, because several seconds later, he forced Tarik to release him before managing to ease out from under Mia.

"Suck me, Mia," Phoenix stated as he situated himself into the corner of the sofa. "I want your mouth on me while Tarik fucks you."

Tarik's body went rigid, harder than it had been at the thought of sliding his dick into Mia's sweet, wet pussy.

"Condoms are in the bedroom."

Getting to his feet, Tarik headed to Phoenix's bedroom. When he returned, Mia was on her knees on the black leather, settled between Phoenix's thighs, her sweet ass up in the air. He sucked in a breath as he ripped open the foil packet and then sheathed himself with the rubber.

Unable to wait, he knelt on the sofa behind her, using his fingers to spread her open as he guided his cock against her slick entrance.

Phoenix's hand twined in Mia's hair, pulling her head up as Tarik pushed into her slowly.

"I want to watch your face while Tarik fucks you."

Phoenix shifted and repositioned himself, easing down onto his back beneath Mia, holding her while Tarik was overcome with the most incredible pleasure, her pussy clasping his dick as he eased into her.

"So tight," he growled, holding her hips as he pushed deeper. "So fucking tight."

Mia moaned, pushing her hips back against him, and Tarik didn't hold back. He pulled out, leaving only the head of his cock cradled in her moist heat before he plunged inside once more.

Phoenix began speaking softly to Mia while Tarik continued to fuck her, keeping a steady pace. Sweat formed on his forehead as he fought the urge to fuck her hard, to come inside her. A storm of sensation crashed over him, rocking him from head to toe as he plummeted into her warm depths.

"You want him to come, Mia? You want him to fuck you hard?"

"Yes," she pleaded. "Fuck me, Tarik. Come inside me."

Tarik's control snapped, and he began ramming into her, his fingers digging into the flesh of her hips as he focused on the pure pleasure that practically ripped him to shreds.

"Mia. Baby, I'm gonna come." Tarik's body tensed, but he fought his release, trying to ignore the overwhelming sensation that shot up from his balls, making his dick pulse and throb, not wanting to let go until she did.

He slammed into her once, twice, three times before Mia's cry ripped through the room, and he drilled her once more, coming in a rush that tipped his world on its fucking axis.

»»»»»» ♥ «««««««

PHOENIX HADN'T COME yet, and his balls were aching with the need for release. He'd purposely held off, wanting to bring both of them to orgasm first. But now it was his turn. He fought his selfish side momentarily as he crooked his finger at Tarik. When the man walked closer, Phoenix reached for his softening cock, still sheathed in a condom. He wasn't done yet.

Reaching for Tarik's hips, Phoenix urged him closer to the sofa until Tarik's knees hit the cushion. Phoenix lifted his head and teased the head of Tarik's cock with his tongue before sucking him into his mouth, savoring the taste of Mia that coated the latex. He didn't let up until Tarik's cock was hard and pulsing once again.

Easing Mia off his prone body, Phoenix climbed to his feet, his hand resuming the motion his mouth had just ceased, stroking Tarik slowly, wanting to keep him hard.

He leaned in against Tarik's ear and whispered, "Get rid of the condom and then stroke yourself. I'll be right back, and then I'm going to bury my cock in your ass and fuck you until you beg me to let you come again."

Tarik's eyes flared and his dick twitched in Phoenix's hand, a sign that the man was eagerly anticipating Phoenix's plan.

Slipping into the bedroom, Phoenix grabbed a condom and lube before returning. He found Mia lying in the spot he'd left moments ago while Tarik fucked her mouth slow and easy. The erotic sight had his breath stuttering in his chest. He wasn't sure he would ever get enough of these two. Ever.

With desperate fingers, Phoenix managed to roll the condom on and slather on a generous amount of lube, the friction from his hand driving him higher even with the reduced sensation from the condom. He was on the precipice, so close to exploding it was a wonder he could even think clearly. But he wanted to be inside Tarik when he came. He'd thought about this moment for so long, and the time had finally come.

"Kneel on the sofa. I want Mia to be able to watch your face while I fuck you." Phoenix chanced a glance in Mia's direction, seeing the flush on her face, the arousal still brightening her eyes. There was no fear that she'd abandon them now. She wanted this as much as they did; he could sense it.

Mia reluctantly released Tarik from her mouth before scooting down to give Tarik room to kneel on the sofa, leaving a spot for Phoenix to get behind him.

Phoenix coated his fingers with lube and then eased one into Tarik's puckered hole while he watched the pair kiss, Mia's moans mingled with Tarik's, and Phoenix's anxiety ratcheted up a notch. He needed to be inside Tarik.

He thrust two fingers into Tarik, fucking him slowly, scissoring his fingers to work him open, but he couldn't wait any longer. While Mia and Tarik continued to kiss, Phoenix worked his cock into Tarik's ass. He'd never done this before — not with a man — and the pleasure blinded him as he forced himself past the natural resistance of Tarik's body.

"Fuck," Phoenix growled, stilling as the heat of Tarik's body consumed him.

"Oh, yes," Tarik hissed, breaking his mouth free of Mia's.

She leaned back, her eyes meeting Phoenix's briefly. He knew what she would see. He was barely hanging on; his balls had already drawn up against his body; the telltale tingle at the base of his spine was a warning. He was going to come.

"I need to fuck you," he warned Tarik. "Hard."

Tarik braced himself and then rammed back against Phoenix's hips, forcing him to the hilt.

"Fuck." Grabbing Tarik's hips, Phoenix pulled out and then slammed back in, lights dancing behind his closed eyelids as the sensation ripped through him. Hot, tight. So fucking tight.

Tarik's ass clenched around him, making him bite his lip to keep from crying out as he began to thrust into him, over and over until he couldn't hang on any longer. He couldn't even bring himself to care if Tarik came, the pleasure was so intense, so mind-numbing; the only thing he could focus on was the release that was building in strength.

"Tarik. Oh, fuck, Tarik." Phoenix was pleading, needing something, someone to ground him as he let himself go, fucking Tarik hard, slamming his hips forward, burying his cock in Tarik's tight fucking ass. Faster, harder. Everything became a blur as his orgasm became a living, breathing thing, tearing through him, shooting up through his dick. "Fuck, yes. I'm coming."

Tarik's body jerked as Phoenix slammed into him, and that's when Phoenix realized Tarik was coming, too, all over Mia's beautiful tits.

Ignoring his protesting muscles, Phoenix managed to get Mia and Tarik into the shower with him, none of them wasting time as they washed up and then crawled into bed. Still reeling from all that had happened since the second they'd stepped into his condo, Phoenix curled himself around Mia while Tarik pressed up against her other side.

He was exhausted, but once again, his mind wouldn't shut down. Tarik didn't seem to have a problem, his breaths evening out shortly after his head hit the pillow.

"You okay?" Mia whispered in the dark, her head resting on Phoenix's chest.

"Better than okay," he informed her.

"Me, too."

The relief he felt from her admission surprised him. As ready as he'd been for tonight to happen, there had still been something niggling in his brain when it came to Mia watching them. Phoenix knew there was no denying what he felt for Tarik. He'd done it for so long, and he couldn't keep up the pretenses. He was attracted to the man in ways he'd never been attracted to anyone else, women included. It was different than what he felt for Mia even.

"I was worried how you would react," he admitted truthfully, unsure why he felt like talking but unable to stop himself.

"To what? You and Tarik together?"

"Yeah. I've… I've never been with a man before."

"I wasn't," she said. "Worried, that is. I might not know how this works exactly, but it just feels … right. Like it's supposed to be this way, you know?"

He did know. More than she would ever understand. His life had revolved around this type of lifestyle to an extent. He'd never questioned it until he had decided it was time to move on. But as he'd learned tonight, there was no moving on for him. He'd be denying a part of himself.

Kissing her forehead, Phoenix pulled her closer and then rested his hand on Tarik's chest. He had them both with him, and for the first time in his life, he felt as though things were finally moving in the right direction.

Chapter Twenty-Six

"THAT'S BULLSHIT AND you know it," Phoenix snapped into the phone, pacing the floor of his living room.

It was Saturday morning, and the last fucking person he should've been on the phone with was his lawyer, but sure as shit, as soon as he'd stepped out of the shower after his run, his cell phone had rung, and he'd made the mistake of answering it.

Phoenix was just glad his mother had already come and gone. He damn sure didn't need her overhearing this conversation and asking more questions. Or worse, pressing him for answers he didn't have.

"This is serious, Phoenix. I don't know what he's pulling, but Landry's lawyer claims he has documentation that proves your father agreed to move forward with the sale. He's claiming now that your father changed his mind after the papers were signed."

"*What?*" Phoenix stopped pacing, his heart slamming against his ribs. "What the fuck are you talking about? Landry claimed my father *backed out* on the deal."

Truth was, until now, Phoenix had thought Landry had been referring to a verbal agreement. Although not binding, it was possible for Landry to pursue damages from a promise. Made his case weaker, but stranger things had happened.

"Originally, yes. According to his lawyers, they've found paperwork to reflect otherwise. They claim that Sid agreed to sell the Arrows for two hundred eight million, and they've got your father's signature."

"You and I both know that's impossible. My father would've told me. I've always been a minority owner. And it wouldn't matter anyway. My father's dead," Phoenix replied, keeping his tone calm despite the temptation to throw the phone through the plate glass window. "He can't buy if I'm not willing to sell."

"I agree, Phoenix. Ownership didn't transfer. I'm still obligated to pass on this information. Landry wants to meet on Monday. I have yet to see any physical proof of their claim, but I'm doing my best."

"Fuck him," Phoenix retorted. "We'll meet on my timetable. And not until they produce something tangible. I'm not wasting my breath on that asshole."

"I'll let them know Monday won't work for you," Phil said, sounding every bit the professional Phoenix knew him to be. The man had been handling everything for his father, and now him, for nearly two decades. Even before his father had purchased the NHL team.

Phoenix thrust his hand through his hair, turning when he heard the front door open and close. As soon as he met Tarik's gaze across the room, the other man knew something was up. He moved toward him slowly, his dark eyebrows lifted in question, his body tense as though he expected to take down a threat.

For the first time, Phoenix wondered how much of Tarik's protectiveness was due to the job and how much was personal. More accurately, he wondered how long Tarik had been personally invested in the job where Phoenix was concerned. There was no doubt that he was, but Phoenix didn't know how long Tarik had wanted something more. Not that it mattered either way; Phoenix needed him, needed to know that he was there for him. It was a relief to know that his support surpassed anything that was business-related.

"I'll talk to you on Monday, Phil. Thanks for the call. And for now, tell Landry's lawyer we need proof."

"Will do," Phil answered. "Talk to you on Monday."

Phoenix disconnected the call and gripped his phone hard. He contemplated throwing it against the wall but managed to suck in a deep breath before he allowed his anger to get the best of him.

Flopping onto the couch, he sighed heavily, every muscle in his body strung tight.

"What's going on?" Tarik asked, lowering himself to the chair opposite him, his elbows resting on his splayed knees as he stared back at Phoenix.

"Damien Landry is a fucking psychopath."

"That's not news," Tarik said, his eyes searching Phoenix's as though there might be something to discern from the frustration he knew was flickering on his face.

"That was Phil," Phoenix said, exhaling sharply.

"I got that part," Tarik said. "What'd he want? Must've been important for him to call on a Saturday."

"Landry has concocted some bullshit story claiming my father agreed to sell him the team. Even claims there's paperwork."

Tarik laughed, the sound reflecting the same disbelief Phoenix had had when he'd heard the news. "You're kidding, right?"

"I wish I were. Landry wants to meet with me on Monday. I told Phil that was a no-go."

Tarik pushed to his feet and moved to the window, his hands on his narrow hips. Phoenix stared after him, admiring the way he looked after a hard workout, sweat glistening on his skin, every muscle defined and rigid. He was a masterpiece, and that wasn't the first time Phoenix had admitted that to himself.

The guy was taller than Phoenix by an inch, six foot three inches of solid muscle. He was bulkier, his muscles honed from weights, while Phoenix kept his routine mostly contained to his daily run. Phoenix wasn't interested in bulking up, and he'd been content to maintain the well-toned muscle he had, but he certainly admired Tarik's hard body.

"We've got another problem," Tarik said, still facing away from him.

"What's that?" Phoenix asked, figuring nothing could be as bad as the news Phil had laid on him already.

"You made the tabloids once again."

Phoenix dropped his head back against the cushion and closed his eyes. "Why do they even give a fuck what I do? I'm not a goddamn celebrity. What I do should not be newsworthy."

"Oh, but you are," Tarik explained gruffly. "And since you own a team that's racing toward the playoffs — their words — they want to know what you're doing. And how you're doing it."

Phoenix heard what he said, but he still didn't understand why they gave a shit. The media bullshit should be reserved for world events, not entertainment.

He would give anything to start the day over. As it was, he had been hoping they could spend the day with Mia since he hadn't seen her for nearly a week, since last Sunday when the three of them had woken up in his bed. She'd slipped out quietly after kissing them both and promising to come back. Phoenix had managed to convince her to let his driver take her to school during the week since he'd been out of town. They hadn't gotten back until late last night, and he'd opted to wait until today to see her. According to the phone conversations he'd had with her during the week, she'd been busy with schoolwork, and since Phoenix had been too busy to argue, he'd let it slide, giving her a little space in the process.

"What do they say?" he asked, not really wanting to know.

"It makes more sense now," Tarik said, turning to face him and then nodding his head toward Phoenix's cell phone sitting on the couch. "The article claims that you sabotaged Landry's marriage, seducing his wife when you found out your father was selling the team without your knowledge. He claims that he met Teresa when she came to inform him about the affair you were having with Mia. One thing led to another, she consoled him. It's all bullshit."

Fuck. Phoenix knew where this was going, but he asked anyway. "Are you fucking kidding me?"

"I wish I were. But it gets worse. You know how they get when they want a story. They make up all sorts of bullshit."

Phoenix knew Tarik was stalling. "What. Is. It?"

"They've got pictures of the three of us from last week. They claim that you've set your sights on Mia and have informed Landry that you won't back off until he drops the lawsuit. Landry gave a sob story about how he loves Mia and how he knows you're using her to hide other things. Of course, that's stirred up the rumors of…"

Tarik didn't need to finish his sentence; Phoenix knew where he was going. At one point, they'd claimed he was bisexual; another time, they'd claimed he was gay. Both times it had caused Phoenix's mother to ask questions, but other than having to deal with her hope that he would one day settle down — according to her, she'd be happy either way — it had all just been a pain in the ass.

"Motherfucker." Phoenix leaned forward, placing his elbows on his knees and dropping his head in his hands.

He couldn't fucking believe this shit.

Mia was skittish enough — as soon as she got wind of this, she was going to be livid. She'd admitted to trust issues, and clearly Landry was playing on that.

"I need to go talk to her," Phoenix stated.

Tarik nodded. "Let me shower, and we'll go down there together. Maybe we can do damage control before it's too late."

Phoenix watched as Tarik walked across the living room and then disappeared out the front door. Since last weekend, when the three of them had slept in his bed, Tarik hadn't been back. He'd been giving Phoenix space. Space Phoenix had initially asked for but wasn't really sure he even wanted anymore.

Getting to his feet, he headed to the kitchen for coffee. If nothing else, maybe caffeine would help him think a little better. He certainly had plenty to think *about*, but mainly he was worried about Mia and how she was going to react when she read that fucking article.

»»»»»»♥«««««

MIA WAS SITTING on the couch reading when her cell phone rang. Butterflies fluttered in her stomach as she lurched for the phone, hoping it was Phoenix or Tarik. They'd told her they would be back yesterday, but she hadn't heard from them yet.

When she checked the screen, she saw that it was Alex.

"Hey," she greeted happily.

"What are you doing?" Alex asked, the lack of usual cheer in her tone causing Mia to pause.

"Sitting here. Reading. Why?" Mia asked, placing her Kindle on the cushion and pushing her blanket off her legs.

"Do you have your tablet?" Alex asked.

"I can get it. Why, Alex? What's going on?"

"I take it you haven't been watching the news?"

"No." Mia's worry was building as she walked to her room and grabbed her tablet from her nightstand, powering it on.

"Do a search on your name."

Mia entered her name into the search bar and hit enter. A list came up. She began skimming the titles of the articles and the dates. Pulling up the most recent, Mia lowered herself onto the couch as she began to read.

"This is bullshit," Mia whispered as she continued reading, disbelief swamping her.

We recently had the opportunity to talk to Damien Landry, the Austin real estate developer who claims that Phoenix Pierce's father, Sidney, had agreed to sell the majority share of the Austin Arrows to him prior to his death. According to Landry, his life is in shambles because of the mishap. Not only did Sid Pierce pull back on the deal, but from what we've learned, Phoenix Pierce has moved in on Landry's now ex-wife.

Landry's former wife, Mia Cantrell, filed for divorce after three years of marriage with claims of irreconcilable differences around the time that Landry claims Sidney reneged on the deal.

"I knew something was wrong, but she wouldn't talk to me. I tried to get her to open up, but Mia insisted it was over. I was away on business when she moved out," Landry told us when asked about the reason for the divorce.

Sources tell us that Phoenix has been courting Mia for some time now, and the pair seem to be getting closer. Although we have to question just what he's up to when we look closely at some of these pictures.

Mia looked at the images included in the article. There were some from the night she'd gone to dinner with Phoenix, a few from their adventure date, including one of her holding hands with both Tarik and Phoenix, and even one from when she and Phoenix had been talking after their argument at the Mexican restaurant.

"Oh, my God. Why is he doing this?" Mia asked.

"Because he's an asshole," Alex retorted.

Mia glanced at her phone, remembering that she was on a call.

"I wanted to warn you, Mia. Don't believe a damn thing you read there."

"How can I? He claims I moved out when he was away on business. He *cheated* on me, Alex. He came home smelling like some other woman's perfume."

"I know, honey. Don't let this get you too worked up."

Too late for that. Mia was fuming with anger. She turned her attention back to the article to finish reading.

Landry has informed us that he's been in communication with Pierce after offering to settle their disagreement civilly. "*I attempted to talk to Mr. Pierce. After I explained my case, he informed me that I could speak with his lawyers. When I asked about Mia, he told me that until I dropped the lawsuit, he wasn't going to stop pursuing her. I'm torn. I love her, but this entire thing has made a shambles of my life.*"

Mia's heart thrummed painfully against her ribs. She knew Phoenix wouldn't have said that. Would he? No. He wouldn't. She wasn't going to start doubting him now. She knew better. This was all Damien's doing. Just another heaping pile of lies to make him look good.

"Ugghhh."

"Take a deep breath. Do you want me to come over?"

"No. I'm good," Mia told Alex now. "I need some time to think."

"Well, if you need me, you know where I am."

"Thanks, Alex."

"Sure thing, honey. Oh, and I'm sure your mother's going to get wind of this. You might want to call her before she does."

Mia flopped back against the cushions, tossing her tablet beside her. Alex was right. This was just the beginning. "It'll be easier if I go see her."

"I agree," Alex concurred. "While you're out, if you want to stop by, we'll be here."

"Okay. Maybe I will. But you're gonna want to have the wine ready," Mia warned.

"Already done."

Chapter Twenty-Seven

TARIK HURRIED THROUGH his shower, not wanting to leave Phoenix alone for too long. He could tell the guy was strung tight, and he worried what the recourse might be when he decided to turn that anger on Damien Landry. Not that it didn't belong there, because it did, but Tarik had been witness to Phoenix's meltdowns a time or two. They weren't pretty.

It wasn't that Phoenix wasn't familiar with this type of underhanded bullshit. It happened more often than people believed, sometimes as a way to get a little publicity — which was what he suspected Landry was up to. There were always frivolous lawsuits popping up for whatever reason, and Tarik had seen Phoenix deal with them on multiple occasions over the last several years. Because Phoenix's company dealt with various things, including lending money to start-ups, acquiring others that weren't able to keep afloat, as well as dabbling in real estate — buying *and* selling — there were plenty of things that people used against him. Phoenix had even ventured into property management on occasion, and Tarik had seen some crazy shit on that side of things. This was merely one of the many.

However, Tarik knew that there were other things on Phoenix's mind. Since the last night that they'd stayed with Phoenix a week ago, the other man hadn't been the same. If he had to guess, Phoenix was dealing with feelings he wasn't familiar with. And Tarik wasn't going to believe that Phoenix's feelings were only for Mia, either. What was transpiring between him and Phoenix was real and powerful. So potent he felt a breakdown coming. And it wasn't going to be him breaking down.

No, Phoenix was on a downward spiral, and he was going to explode any time now. Possibly in the next few minutes, and Tarik damn sure wasn't going to be in the shower when that happened.

Shutting off the water, Tarik grabbed a towel and roughly ran it over his hair, then his body before fixing it around his waist.

When he stepped into his bedroom to grab clothes, he stopped short.

There, sitting on his bed, was Phoenix.

Green eyes slowly drifted up until they met his, holding. Tarik was frozen in place momentarily. What he read in that steady gaze nearly leveled him. There was a request there, something he couldn't misconstrue even if he wanted to.

Which he sure as fuck didn't.

"I called Mia. She said she was on her way to see her mother." Phoenix's gaze lowered briefly. "So I came here."

Tarik didn't move, unwilling to break the spell. He understood exactly what Phoenix was telling him. He needed someone, and with Mia not home, Tarik was it.

He briefly wondered whether he should feel like second place, but he couldn't. He'd wanted to see Mia as much as Phoenix, possibly more. If she wasn't home, then there wasn't anything either of them could do about it.

Rather than tell Phoenix any of that, he stood there, stone still as he waited for what came next. Phoenix had to make the first move. There was no way Tarik would be the first, not with something this crucial, something that would ultimately change the dynamic of their friendship forever.

Phoenix pushed to his feet slowly, his gaze like a heated caress as it raked down him an inch at a time. Tarik didn't bother to ask Phoenix if he was okay; he could see in his eyes that he was still strung tight, the equivalent of a rubber band being pulled to the point it was going to snap, and the repercussions were going to be painful.

Which meant there was only one reason he was there.

When Phoenix approached, Tarik didn't move, didn't hardly breathe. Big, warm fingers came up to trail a path from his navel up to his neck and then back down. Phoenix never stopped looking him in the eye, and Tarik found himself lost in his gaze, desperately wanting this to go where he thought it was headed but scared shitless to say anything that might fuck that up.

"I'm tired of thinking," Phoenix admitted softly, his eyes dipping down to Tarik's lips briefly.

"Then don't," Tarik stated firmly.

"That's why I'm here." The uncertainty he heard in Phoenix's tone and saw on his face surprised Tarik briefly. It was not something he was used to seeing in the other man's eyes. Determination, purpose, tenacity, yes. This ambiguity, no.

"Do you know what you're doing to me?" Tarik asked as Phoenix's hands continued to roam slowly over his bare chest, down to his stomach once more. Up and down, the movement was slow and reverent. Almost as though Phoenix was looking for some assurance that Tarik wanted this.

"Yes, I do," Phoenix answered. "The same thing you're doing to me."

Tarik doubted that, but he didn't say as much. The depth for which Tarik cared for Phoenix had been dug over a period of years, not weeks or days. Those feelings weren't new to him. Nor did they shock him with their intensity anymore.

However, what he wanted from Phoenix was likely going to blow the other man's mind.

"I want all of you, Phoenix. Every single piece."

Phoenix nodded, but Tarik still wasn't convinced he knew exactly what he meant.

"Right here, right now. This is between us. I don't want anyone else in the room." Tarik knew he didn't need to explain himself. Phoenix understood precisely what he was getting at. No issues, no problems. Nothing and no one was welcome this first time. The first time Tarik would bury himself in Phoenix, lose himself in the pleasure of the other man's body.

Holy fuck.

"Just us," Phoenix confirmed.

"Take off your shirt," Tarik commanded, letting his eyes trail down Phoenix's body, noting how his muscles bunched and flexed with every little movement. He was tense, and it had nothing, and possibly everything, to do with what was about to happen.

Phoenix complied easily, pulling his shirt over his head and dropping it on the floor.

Tarik was tempted to tell Phoenix to strip so he could see all of him, but he held back. He wanted to touch him, to taste him, and he couldn't wait any longer.

Closing the gap between them, Tarik grazed Phoenix's hard cock behind the zipper of his jeans with the backs of his fingers as he moved his hand upward, trailing up his stomach similar to the way Phoenix had done to him moments ago. He veered off and circled Phoenix's nipple with a fingertip, allowing his other hand to mimic the first, flicking each nipple firmly.

Phoenix's eyes lowered, fluttered, his mouth opening slightly.

When he let his eyes close completely, Tarik tweaked both nipples. "Open your eyes. I want them on me at all times."

Those thunderous green eyes once again opened, and there was a hint of defiance backlighting them, but to Phoenix's credit, he didn't say a word.

As a reward, Tarik leaned down and lashed Phoenix's nipple with his tongue, then used his teeth to nip him.

A harsh inhale was the only response, so Tarik moved to the other, teasing Phoenix briefly. Sliding his hands around to Phoenix's back, he moved up as he stood. Angling his head slightly, Tarik pressed his lips to Phoenix's as he dug his fingers into the tense muscles of Phoenix's back, pulling him closer, their bare chests touching, warmth transferring between them.

He tried to keep the kiss slow and easy, but it quickly morphed into something hotter, stronger, significantly more powerful. It was as though the energy that was thrumming inside Phoenix was redistributed to Tarik. He was infused with it, an urgency making his cock thicken, straining against the cotton towel.

Pulling back because he wasn't interested in ending this before it even got started, Tarik ordered Phoenix to remove the rest of his clothes. When he did, Tarik directed him to the bed with an upward tilt of his chin.

"On your stomach," Tarik commanded as he moved to the dresser to retrieve a condom and lube.

When he turned back, Phoenix was on his stomach, his cheek flat on the bed, his eyes tracking Tarik as he moved toward him. Dropping the items onto the bed so that Phoenix could see them clearly, Tarik released the towel, allowing it to fall to the floor.

He had every intention of massaging Phoenix's back, trying to loosen him up a bit, but as he lay there, his mouth proved to be too much of a temptation. One he couldn't bypass just yet.

"Move closer to the edge," he told Phoenix. "Take me in your mouth."

Phoenix scooted closer, remaining on his stomach as instructed, his mouth within inches of Tarik's cock. Sweeping the head across Phoenix's lips, he waited until he opened before dipping the tip inside.

The mere brush of Phoenix's tongue over the swollen head made Tarik's hips jerk forward. "Open those lips for me, Phoenix. Swallow me."

Phoenix's mouth opened wider as he sucked Tarik's cock into his mouth. Shallow at first, but within seconds he was laving Tarik's dick, tormenting him with the rough swipe of his tongue as he circled the head, teasing the underside, driving him toward the edge with a blinding intensity that took Tarik entirely by surprise.

"Turn over," Tarik instructed as he thought of a better position, needing a moment to regain his composure. "Hang your head over the side."

Phoenix moved easily, and when he was situated, Tarik looked down at the sexy man sprawled sideways across his bed. His tanned, hard body stood out against the black comforter. Tarik wouldn't have minded looking at him like that all fucking day.

"Suck my dick and don't stop until I tell you."

Propping one knee on the bed beside Phoenix's head, Tarik leaned over Phoenix, guiding his cock into Phoenix's scorching mouth. He didn't hesitate before he took Phoenix's cock in his mouth, sucking the head between his lips, teasing the tip with the flat of his tongue. Phoenix rewarded him with an urgent thrust of his hips and a rough growl that Tarik could feel vibrating beneath him.

He knew the only way he'd survive this was to focus on Phoenix and not on the way Phoenix swallowed him, sucking him forcefully while wrapping his hand around the base of Tarik's cock. It was too good. Needing to drive out some of the arresting satisfaction or risk coming too soon, Tarik focused his attention on returning the pleasure, wrapping his lips around Phoenix's thick cock, pulling him into his mouth, releasing him slowly, bobbing up and down.

It didn't matter how much he tried to focus, the blazing warmth of Phoenix's mouth was too much to ignore, causing Tarik to push up on his hands, releasing Phoenix's cock from his mouth with a pop and then pulling his own dick out of the sweet mouth that had given him enough pleasure to make his head swim.

"Back on your stomach," he commanded, crawling up on the bed when Phoenix flipped over.

"No one told me I should've stretched before I came in here. This is a fucking workout," Phoenix joked, rolling back onto his stomach.

Tarik smiled. "I was going to give you a massage, but if you'd prefer we skip that part, I'm game."

"I'm good," Phoenix muttered when he got situated.

Straddling Phoenix's hips, Tarik began kneading the muscles of Phoenix's shoulders, digging deep, trying to drive out some of the tension. He continued to massage deeply, moving from one muscle group to the next until he was at the tight muscles of Phoenix's lower back. The rough groans that had accompanied the massage made Tarik's dick throb. He eased down Phoenix's body slowly, sliding down his legs, and now his cock was nudging between Phoenix's firm ass cheeks, right where he wanted to be.

"Tarik," Phoenix growled, pushing his hips back.

"Not yet," Tarik told him none too gently.

"Fuck," Phoenix muttered. "I need to feel you."

The jagged need in Phoenix's voice was almost enough to have Tarik rushing, but he knew better. He wanted to savor every minute of this. His first time inside Phoenix... Phoenix's first time taking a man inside of him. It wasn't something Tarik wanted to hurry through.

Ignoring Phoenix's pleas, Tarik stretched forward and settled himself atop Phoenix, holding most of his weight above him as he found Phoenix's mouth, kissing him roughly. The angle was a little tricky, but when their tongues met, Phoenix lifted his head, giving Tarik better access as he searched, tasted, savored.

Tarik indulged in the warmth of Phoenix's mouth, relishing the hint of mint and coffee. When he pulled back for air, he continued by trailing his mouth along Phoenix's neck, then planting kisses across his broad back, down the divot between the muscles along his spine, enjoying Phoenix's groans, the way he lifted his hips, begging for more. Sliding down his body, Tarik once again straddled Phoenix's lower legs, kneading Phoenix's taut ass cheeks roughly, dipping his finger between them until Phoenix's breaths were coming sharp and desperate. He grabbed the lube, squeezed a generous amount on Phoenix's asshole before inserting the tip of his finger.

"Fuck. Oh, hell. Tarik, it's too much."

Tarik didn't even respond, just continued to rim Phoenix's tight hole with one finger, dipping it in to the second knuckle, teasing him, tormenting him, driving him higher, making him more desperate. He wanted Phoenix to be delirious with need. He pushed his finger in farther, deeper.

"Tarik." The way Phoenix said his name was a warning. When Phoenix reached beneath his prone body to stroke his own cock, Tarik gripped his arm, stopping him.

"Not yet," Tarik bit out. "I'll say when you can come."

"Damn it," Phoenix growled. "I can't take any more."

"What do you want?" Tarik asked, sliding his finger deep into Phoenix's puckered hole again. "Tell me."

"I want you to fuck me."

"How? Do you want me to sink my dick into your ass? Take you slow and easy?"

Fuck. The thought of Phoenix's ass clenching around his thick cock made the damn thing pulse and throb.

"I don't give a fuck," Phoenix groaned, his body bucking restlessly. "Just fuck me."

Reaching for the bottle of lube, Tarik managed to squeeze more onto his fingers, coating them liberally before replacing one finger with two. Inserting the digits slowly, he encouraged Phoenix to relax as he eased inside him once more.

He continued to fuck his ass with two fingers, adding a third when Phoenix was gripping the comforter and thrusting back against him, once more begging. By the time he had begun an even, rhythmic pace, Phoenix had relaxed somewhat, his breaths soughing in and out of his lungs, still mumbling for Tarik to fuck him.

"Turn over," Tarik commanded, retrieving the condom and sliding it over his dick before adding a generous amount of lube and stroking himself. "I want to see your face when I take you this first time."

Phoenix flipped over, spreading his legs around Tarik's thighs, his wild eyes glued to his the entire time.

Pushing Phoenix's knees back, forcing them closer to Phoenix's chest, Tarik instructed Phoenix to hold them there. He was spread open for him, his rock-hard cock resting on his stomach, his balls tight, an inviting sight that had Tarik nearly gasping for breath, anxious to thrust into him, to claim him, to take him for the first fucking time.

It was nearly too much to think about.

Once more, he began to finger Phoenix's ass while he stroked himself slowly, watching every expression that crossed Phoenix's handsome face as he did.

"Damn it, Tarik," Phoenix snapped, his head going back, his body straining as Tarik worked his fingers inside, massaging Phoenix's prostate, bringing him higher. "Fuck. Oh, holy … *fuuuck*. What the hell are you doing to me? It feels too… Oh, shit. Oh, shit. Don't make me come yet, Tarik!" Phoenix gripped his cock tightly, banding his fingers around the shaft, clearly trying to hold back.

Tarik slowed his movements and then pulled his fingers from Phoenix's ass before leaning over him and guiding the head of his dick to Phoenix's tight entrance.

Their eyes locked, held as Tarik slowly pressed forward.

"So tight." Sweat was beading on his brow as he fought the natural resistance of Phoenix's body, trying to get past the tight ring of muscles. "Relax for me, Phoenix. Stroke your cock." Tarik sucked in a breath. "Oh, fuck, you're tight."

Phoenix kept his hand between his legs, gripping his dick while Tarik slid in another inch. Phoenix hissed, pain flashing across his face. Tarik didn't stop, although still attempting to take things slow despite the overwhelming need to sheath himself in Phoenix's tight ass. He didn't want to hurt Phoenix, but knowing that the pleasure Phoenix would find was looming in the near future, just as soon as Tarik was buried inside him, kept him inching in deeper.

Phoenix's body continued to stretch around him, the oversensitive head of Tarik's dick breaching the ring of muscles.

"Oh, fuck," Phoenix moaned as Tarik pushed in more.

"Am I hurting you?"

"No. Yes. *No.* Oh, hell, it's… It's different. I feel… Fuck. Just don't stop. I want to feel you inside me."

Tarik grinned but then gritted his teeth when Phoenix's ass tightened around him. "Relax," Tarik ground out. "Once I'm inside you, I'll fuck you just the way you need."

"What are you waiting for?" Phoenix asked, his voice strained.

"I don't want to hurt you," he said softly, leaning forward and placing his arms on each side of Phoenix's head, bending him nearly in half as he pushed in deeper.

Unable to resist, Tarik leaned down and kissed him. This time he did keep the kiss slow and easy, their tongues sliding together as Tarik seated himself inside Phoenix fully. He circled his hips, grinding against Phoenix, going deeper until Phoenix was moaning, his hands sliding over Tarik's back, holding him in place.

Pulling back slightly, Tarik locked his gaze with Phoenix's once more. "You don't know how long I've wanted this. To be buried to the hilt inside you."

Phoenix didn't respond with words, simply held him tighter, trying to force him deeper.

Pushing up onto his hands, Tarik lifted his hips, withdrawing slowly before sliding back in, watching every expression on Phoenix's too handsome face, waiting until Phoenix relaxed once more.

And then he began to thrust into him. He maintained a steady pace until his balls drew up tight to his body, and he knew there was no way in hell he was going to last. He wanted to make this as good for Phoenix as he could, but it was overwhelming. He'd wanted this for so damn long.

"Tarik," Phoenix pleaded, pulling Tarik's head down, biting his bottom lip. "Fuck me. Hard. Make me come."

Tarik crushed his mouth to Phoenix's and began to drive into him hard and fast until he was hammering into Phoenix over and over, pounding him into the mattress with every punishing thrust.

Coming up for air, Tarik stared down into Phoenix's face, watching the moment he'd dreamed about for so fucking long.

"Oh, fuck, Tarik! Oh, fuck. I'm gonna come. Fuck."

Tarik held out until he felt the warmth of Phoenix's cum hitting his stomach, his chest. Then and only then did he come, his cock pulsing in time with his heartbeat.

Chapter Twenty-Eight

PHOENIX DIDN'T WANT to move from where he was. If he could, he'd stay for the rest of the day, right there in Tarik's bed. He was pleasantly sated, yet the hunger for Tarik still pulsed beneath the surface of his skin. It was a different type of need, though. One that had him wanting to claim Tarik the same way he'd been claimed a few minutes before. Something more primal than the first time Phoenix had fucked Tarik.

"Hey," Tarik grumbled as he rolled onto his side to face Phoenix. "What's the plan for the rest of the day?"

Phoenix was grateful that Tarik wasn't going to make this weird. As much as he'd enjoyed what had happened between them, as much as he craved doing it again, he didn't want to dwell on it.

At least not right now.

"We need to talk to Mia."

"Yeah," Tarik agreed as he rolled onto his back and sighed, "I was hoping that shit would go away on its own."

Phoenix knew what Tarik was feeling. The fact that someone was trying to use Mia as a pawn in this game was far too convenient, something that definitely suited Landry's intentions. He was out to hurt anyone he could, and it pissed Phoenix off that Landry had put Mia in his crosshairs. It was one thing for him to go after Phoenix, something entirely different to involve an innocent woman.

Before he'd come down to Tarik's condo, before he'd even tried to call Mia, Phoenix had given in and read the article. It was all bullshit, every last word, but he knew Mia well enough to know she'd be hurt by the accusation, although she had attempted to play it off when he'd eluded to it on the phone. She hadn't seemed interesting in talking about it, so he had let it go. If they were lucky, she wouldn't buy into it, but she'd still be hurt, and Phoenix damn sure wasn't going to allow that to happen.

"I'm gonna take another shower," Phoenix said, still making no effort to move. "Then we'll figure out what we want to do. Maybe grab some lunch, wait until she gets home, and go talk to her."

"Great plan," Tarik stated, also not moving.

After another minute, Phoenix laughed, forcing himself to crawl over Tarik. Before he hurdled him completely, he was pulled back down, and Tarik's greedy mouth found his. Phoenix gave in to the kiss as easily as he'd given in to the man earlier.

"I'm not much for conversation afterward," Tarik whispered, his breath fanning Phoenix's lips. "But I want you to know that I fully intend to do that again in the very near future."

Phoenix smiled down at him, a foreign sensation filling his chest. It was the same sensation he got when he was with Mia. "What if I'm not willing to give up control next time?"

"More power to you, boss. Just be ready to do what needs to be done."

"I think I've proven my abilities to do that already." Laughing, Phoenix pushed away and got to his feet. As he dressed, he stared down at Tarik, still lying prone on the bed, gloriously naked, semi-aroused again. It wouldn't take much to give in again, but Phoenix needed to work through all this shit in his head. They had to do damage control before it was too late.

Half an hour later, Phoenix was showered and dressed in another pair of jeans and a maroon polo and heading toward the kitchen. Tarik had apparently finished before him and was sitting at his table with his laptop open, his hair wet. Feeling an odd sense of intimacy, Phoenix walked right over to Tarik, leaned over his shoulder to see what he was looking at on the computer screen. "Anything new?"

"I called Mia to check on her."

Phoenix cocked an eyebrow. "And?"

"Same as when you called. She said she needed to go talk to her mother about the article."

Phoenix stood tall, watching Tarik's face intently. "She okay?"

"Seems to be. Said she read it but didn't elaborate much."

"Shit." Phoenix thrust his hand through his hair.

"She's not buying it," Tarik explained, although the words didn't help Phoenix feel any better. He wanted to see her. Talk to her himself. Make sure she really was all right.

"So what now?"

"Let's grab something to eat," Tarik said, getting to his feet.

Tarik closed the gap between them and surprised Phoenix when he kissed him.

"Food, huh?" Phoenix asked when he felt something inside him release. Tarik's ability to calm him wasn't surprising. Not after all that had transpired between them over the last few weeks.

"Yep. And then we'll figure out what the next step is."

With a nod, Phoenix figured what the hell. He couldn't fix the world at the moment.

Didn't mean he wasn't going to come up with a plan to make it right. But first, he had to eat.

»»»»»» ♥ ««««««

MIA SAT AT her mother's kitchen table, her hand wrapped around a coffee mug while she watched Clarice Cantrell read the article that Mia had seen that morning.

"This is…" Clarice's ice-blue eyes came up to meet Mia's.

"I know. It's ridiculous, Mom."

"Well, yes. That's a given. Not unexpected, because this is Damien we're talking about here," Clarice said, her eyes lowering to the screen once more.

It was no secret that her mother didn't like Damien. The feeling had always been mutual, but Mia suspected that was because Damien thought everyone should like him. Mia had always been caught in the middle.

Not anymore.

"What I want to know is what you're doing with this man," Clarice said, raising the screen to show her the picture of her and Phoenix where they'd been captured at the Mexican restaurant. It looked incredibly intimate, the way Phoenix was cupping her face, his expression serious as he stared down at her. She was surprised her mother had focused on that image and not the one of her holding hands with *two* men. Not that she was going to bring it up.

"His name's Phoenix, Mom," Mia told her, taking a sip of her coffee.

"And you're only friends, right?" The disbelief in her mother's tone told her she was going to have an argument on her hands if she tried to go that route.

Mia smiled. Her mother knew her so well. Or she thought she did, anyway. "It might be a little more than friends," Mia admitted.

Clarice's eyes widened. "Mia, please don't tell me you're gonna get caught up in this lifestyle again."

Setting her coffee cup on the table a little harder than she should have, Mia took a deep breath. "Mom, I'm twenty-four years old. Keep that in mind before you grill me on what I'm doing in my personal life."

"Yes, well, twenty-four or not, you're still my daughter. I had to sit back and watch Damien ruin your life."

"He didn't ruin it," Mia said defensively. "Not entirely." No, he'd merely shattered her heart, but that was all behind her now. "Regardless, I've grown up since then. Learned my lesson."

Clarice cocked a perfectly plucked eyebrow before glancing down at the screen once more. "What if there is some truth to this? What if this Phoenix guy actually did set this all in motion?"

"Mom, seriously!" Mia exclaimed. "This is Damien we're talking about. The man doesn't know how to tell the truth."

"Maybe so, but listen to me for a minute. What if this Phoenix really is using you?"

"He's not," she assured her.

"And how do you know?"

Mia wasn't about to tell her mother the details of what had transpired between her and Phoenix, or her and Tarik. She knew better. Clarice, ever the overprotective mother, would only hear what she wanted to, anyway. No matter how frustrated her mother made her, Mia knew it was only out of love that her mother worried.

"He's not," Mia said, keeping her tone calm. "We're just … dating. It's not serious."

Her mother's eyes raked over her face, and Mia wondered whether or not she could tell she was lying. It was serious. Maybe not for Phoenix. Maybe not for Tarik. But for Mia, it was as serious as it could get. It was the sole reason she'd stayed away from them for an entire week, trying to put some distance there so she could think.

She'd been down the disastrous marriage road already. She had no intentions of doing that again. The problem was, she felt herself falling for both of them. Hard. And the worst part about it was she knew, without a doubt, that she would not survive another round of heartache. Not at their hands.

"Mia, I can't help but feel we've had this conversation before. I only want you to be careful," her mother said soothingly.

"I will. I promise." Needing to change the subject, Mia turned the question on her mother. "Now when are you going to tell me about your new boyfriend?"

Clarice's face went white, and she got up from the table, heading toward the coffeepot. Mia watched her carefully, trying to keep from smiling. Her mother clearly didn't like when the tables were turned and she was the one in the hot seat.

"I… What are you talking about? I don't have a boyfriend."

"Liar, liar, pants on fire," Mia offered with a grin.

She didn't know for a fact that her mother was seeing someone, but she had a good idea. After their holiday vacation, she had been pretty positive her mother was seeing someone but didn't want her to know. The way she responded now only cemented that suspicion.

"I'm not lying," Clarice declared, but Mia noticed she still wasn't looking at her.

"Mom, seriously. It's okay."

Her mother turned around, holding her coffee cup in her hands as she peered across the kitchen at Mia. Her blue eyes reflected her doubt as she asked, "Is it?"

Mia returned her cup to the table and got up, crossing the room to stand in front of her mother. "Of course it is. Why wouldn't it be?"

"Your father…" Clarice began.

"Has been gone a long time, Mom. He wouldn't want you to spend the rest of your life alone. You know that."

Her mother's watery gaze lifted to hers. "He's a nice guy. I really think you'll like him."

Mia smiled, her heart warming at the thought of her mother finding someone who made her happy. It was all anyone ever wanted. The fact that Clarice had spent the last fourteen years mourning the loss of the man she'd loved with her whole heart told Mia just how deeply her mother's love went.

"Come. Sit. You can tell me all about him, starting with his name."

Chapter Twenty-Nine

"WHERE ARE YOU?" Phoenix asked the caller on the other end of the line.

Tarik pulled the Escalade into the condominiums parking garage, wondering who was important enough for him to pick up the phone at this point in the day.

"Are you coming home?"

Easing into the parking spot that was reserved for Phoenix, Tarik left the SUV running. Something told him his evening wasn't going to end yet. As it was, they'd spent the better part of the afternoon fucking around to pass the time, both of them anxiously waiting to hear from Mia and disappointed that they hadn't.

"Can we come pick you up?"

Tarik glanced over at Phoenix, who was now looking at him intently. Okay, so maybe they had heard from her. Phoenix wouldn't have made the offer to just anyone.

"Okay. Text me the address. We'll be there in a few."

When Phoenix stabbed the end button on his phone, Tarik had already put the pieces of the puzzle together. "Mia?"

"Yeah. She's at her friend Alex's house."

Putting the gear shift in reverse, Tarik backed out of the spot and aimed the SUV for the exit. No reason to stall; he'd heard Phoenix's end of the call. Less than a minute later, Phoenix had entered the address into his phone's navigation, giving Tarik instructions on which direction to head, and they were on their way.

"She sound okay?" Tarik asked, glancing over at Phoenix as he drove.

"Yeah. A little intoxicated, but yeah." The smile in Phoenix's tone made Tarik feel better.

Ever since Mia had informed him that she was going to her mother's, he'd been worried. Part of him had suspected she was blowing them off. He knew throughout their afternoon that Phoenix had been on a nervous edge as well, but he had tried his best not to show it. Tarik knew him better than that. Phoenix's relief was evident now as they headed toward the answers to the millions of questions they'd had throughout the day.

Fifteen minutes later, Tarik drove past the security gate of the upper-crust neighborhood after entering a code that Mia provided them in a text and followed the directions to the address she had given them.

When they pulled into the circular drive, the porch lights were on as well as the landscape lighting that accentuated the well-maintained lawn. The neighborhood reminded Tarik a lot of the one Sid had lived in. Each house bigger than the next, every yard looked as though someone spent eight hours a day manually clipping each blade of grass so that everything was neat and tidy.

Once parked, Tarik exited the Escalade and led the way to the front door, hitting the button for the bell and taking a step back.

They were greeted by the same man who'd taken Mia to the charity ball, Johnathan Henry.

"John," he greeted, announcing his name as he held out his hand and took a step back, allowing them entry into the house. "Nice to meet you."

Tarik and Phoenix both returned the gesture, introducing themselves.

"She's a little intoxicated," Johnathan said as he closed the door behind them and then led the way through the lavish entry, down a few steps into another expansive room, and then on a trek through what had to be half the house before they found Mia sitting on a chocolate-brown sectional sofa in another sunken room, looking up at them with a glowing smile on her face.

Only then did the choke chain that had pierced his heart earlier that day let loose.

"Hi." Mia's smile widened, her eyes glassy from the alcohol. "Sit. Stay a while. Johnathan's a big fan. He loves the Austin Arrows. Won't stop talking about them," Mia slurred.

Tarik shot a glance at Johnathan to find the man shaking his head. Clearly he'd been dealing with Mia's inebriated state for a while now.

"Can I get you something to drink? Wine? Beer?"

"A beer would be good," Phoenix stated as he headed across the room to join Mia on the sofa.

"You?" Johnathan asked him.

"Nothing for me. Thanks." Tarik wanted all his faculties about him tonight.

Johnathan disappeared in the opposite direction.

"You okay?" Phoenix asked Mia when he lowered himself down beside her.

Tarik worked his way around the coffee table and joined them, sitting on Mia's other side.

"I am now," she said sweetly, looking up at Phoenix with wide, hopeful eyes before sliding her gaze to Tarik.

"Hey." A bright, cheerful voice sounded from behind him, and Tarik twisted to see the woman from the charity ball coming to join them, a bottle of wine in her hands. "So glad you could make it. She's been missing you."

Tarik wondered for a moment which one of them she was talking to. Had Mia told her friend that she was sleeping with both of them? That they were sleeping with one another?

"Alexandra Henry, but my friends call me Alex," she greeted formally when she approached, holding out a dainty hand. Tarik shook her hand, surprised at how firm her grip was. No limp wrist for this one.

"Tarik," he stated before she reached over and shook Phoenix's hand.

"Well, I can tell you that your girl's in a mood tonight."

Tarik met Alex's silver gaze, realizing she was looking at him now. What *had* Mia told her?

Johnathan returned with two beers, and after handing one over to Phoenix, he joined his wife on the sofa.

"You have a very beautiful house," Phoenix said, apparently trying to start a conversation. "What is it that you do?"

"He's a plastic surgeon," Alex said proudly.

"And you?" Phoenix questioned Alex.

"Oh, you know, I do a little of this, a little of that. Mostly I volunteer my time with local hospitals and charities."

Tarik glanced down at Mia. She looked as though she was going to fall asleep. She had curled up between them both, one hand on each of their legs, her wine forgotten on the table.

"The team's been doing well this year," Johnathan prompted, his attention focused on Phoenix.

"Not too bad," Phoenix said with a smirk.

"I'm sorry about your father," Johnathan said kindly. "I'd actually had the pleasure of meeting him a time or two."

Phoenix nodded. Tarik had no idea what people were supposed to say to condolences of that nature. Luckily, Phoenix didn't have an issue with carrying a conversation with anyone, and he proved it, morphing into the topic of hockey.

Twenty minutes passed and Mia's eyes had closed.

"She's had a rough day," Alex said softly when the conversation hit a lull. "She went to see her mother."

"Is that a good thing or a bad thing?" Phoenix queried.

"You'll have to ask her," Alex said, smiling.

Tarik decided he liked Alex and Johnathan. They obviously cared about Mia.

"Well, we better head home. I think she's out for the night."

Alex got to her feet at the same time Tarik did. Phoenix managed to wake Mia enough to get her to walk to the door, although Tarik would've had no problem carrying her.

"Thanks for coming. She's been talking about the two of you all night," Alex told him, surprising him with the revelation. "She's my best friend. We talk about everything. But don't worry, what hits my ears from her mouth stays right here." Alex thumped her temple lightly. "Just take care of her, would you? I don't know what's in store for the three of you, but keep in mind" — Alex leaned in closer and lowered her voice — "she's fragile underneath it all." Stepping back and smiling brightly, she added, "But don't tell her I said that. She'll kick my ass."

Tarik laughed and then accepted an awkward hug from Alex and another handshake from Johnathan. He assisted Mia out to the Escalade while Phoenix stopped to talk to them. A few minutes later, they were back on the road, heading home, and the vice that had gripped his chest had officially been annihilated.

»»»»»» ❤ «««««

"DON'T GO," MIA said after Phoenix followed her into her condo. He'd planned to get her settled in bed so she could sleep off the wine, but clearly she had other plans.

"Are you sure?" he asked, glancing back at Tarik, who had followed them inside. Honestly, he'd thought she was down for the count, having slept the entire drive back in Phoenix's arms.

"I'm sure." She smiled. "I missed you both. I don't want you to go yet."

Phoenix wondered just how much she'd had to drink and how much the wine would affect her emotional state. He liked the idea of her missing them, but he hadn't expected her to come out and say it.

"Do you want something to drink?" she asked, her gaze darting down the hall toward the kitchen.

"No, thanks. What about you?" Phoenix asked. "Do you want something?"

"Yes," she said, her sleepy eyes drooping, her throaty voice lowering another octave.

His body hardened instantly when he realized she wasn't talking about anything they could get in the kitchen.

She took his hand and Tarik's, then led them into the living room.

"Sit," she commanded.

His mind instantly drifted back to their game of naked Simon Says. As intriguing as that had been, Phoenix wasn't in the mood for games tonight. He'd spent the entire day wondering if Mia would even speak to him again. He wasn't about to waste the time he had with her giving instructions.

Not tonight, anyway.

But he did sit as she requested. He kept his hand linked with hers and pulled her toward him. She tumbled into his lap, and he took control of the moment. Lowering her onto her back, Phoenix hovered over her, sealing his mouth with hers, tasting her sweetness, her eagerness. Her hands wrapped around him, pulling him to her, and he gave her what she wanted. When he lifted his mouth from hers, Tarik picked up where he'd left off, drawing a soft moan from Mia as she maneuvered until she had one arm around Tarik and one around Phoenix.

Phoenix moved his lips to her neck, then lower. He pushed her sweatshirt up, revealing the silky smooth skin beneath. He kissed and licked her while Tarik devoured her mouth. Their make-out session lasted until the three of them were naked and on Mia's bed.

"I need to feel you," Mia whispered against Phoenix's lips. "I want to feel both of you inside me."

Phoenix's cock jumped. He had no idea what Mia was referring to, but his mind instantly came up with several ideas, one of which was something he'd dreamed about for weeks now.

"We don't want to hurt you," Tarik told her, sucking her nipple into his mouth.

"You won't," she said breathlessly, bowing her back and urging them both to give her breasts attention. "I trust you."

"We need lube," Tarik said, lifting his head and meeting her gaze.

"In the nightstand drawer," she said with a smile, her eyes shifting toward one of the tables beside the bed.

Phoenix had to wonder whether she knew what Tarik was insinuating. Based on her heated expression, she knew, but Phoenix wanted to hear her say it.

"Do you know what you're asking for?" Phoenix questioned, lowering his lips to hers gently.

"Yes."

"Tell us," Phoenix demanded. "What is it that you want?"

"I want to feel you both inside me," she said, reaching down and gripping his cock with her soft, cool fingers. "I want to have you both inside me. At the same time."

Phoenix growled, fusing his mouth with hers as his body responded to her words. Her fingernails clawed at his back, grinding her hips up toward him. Phoenix flipped their positions, pulling her on top of him and settling her above his cock.

Hissing in a breath, Phoenix closed his eyes when Tarik sheathed him with a condom, rolling it down slowly, grazing his balls more than was necessary.

"Are you sure?" Phoenix asked Mia as she guided him into her, her warm, wet pussy clasping him and pulling him deep.

"Oh, yeah," she moaned.

Phoenix gritted his teeth, the pleasure consuming him. She was hot and wet and so fucking tight.

"Ride me, Mia," he instructed when he spotted Tarik retrieving the lube and rolling a condom over his thick, heavy cock.

Mia began rocking her hips, moaning as she did, her breasts swaying above his head.

"So good," he said, encouraging her to continue. Gripping her thighs to keep her still, he pulled his hips forward, pushing his cock deep.

The bed shifted when Tarik joined them, moving up between Phoenix's legs. Phoenix pulled Mia down, crushing her breasts against his chest while he melded his mouth to hers once again. He couldn't see what Tarik was doing, but he swallowed Mia's moans and mewls as he continued to rock his hips, thrusting into her gently, causing enough friction to make his mind go blank.

They continued like that for long minutes, until Mia broke the kiss, trying to push her hips back.

"That's it, baby. Fuck my fingers," Tarik urged.

"Does it feel good?" Phoenix asked her. "Do you like when Tarik fucks your ass while my cock is buried in your tight pussy?"

"Yes," she said, the word coming out in a barely there whisper.

More movement on the bed, and then Mia's body went rigid.

"Relax for us," Phoenix crooned, sucking her earlobe into his mouth. "Let Tarik slide his cock into your ass. Feel us both filling you at the same time."

Tarik took his time, and Phoenix continued to talk to Mia until she relaxed enough to take Tarik inside her. Then they were both filling her. Phoenix could feel the hard ridge of Tarik's cock pressing against his own inside Mia. It was an exquisite, erotic feeling. They'd done this before, but never, not one single fucking time, had it felt this good.

"Oh, God. It's too much," Mia cried, her pussy tightening around his cock.

"Relax, baby. Let us fuck you. Let us make you feel good."

Mia nodded, but he could see the pain etched on her face. He cupped her head, pulling her mouth to his as Tarik began to retreat before sliding inside her once again. Phoenix didn't have to move; Tarik was doing all the work, sending shards of pleasure coursing through Phoenix's balls as he slowly penetrated Mia over and over, burying his cock in her ass while sliding against him inside her body.

Phoenix worked his hands down to her hips and gripped her firmly, lifting her so that he could ease his cock up into her before pulling back. Tarik picked up on his rhythm, and they began fucking her slowly, alternating thrusts so that only one of them filled her at a time. Phoenix kept his eyes locked on her face, watching the pain morph into pleasure until she was panting and moaning, trying to take them deeper.

"Oh, God, Mia," Tarik groaned. "You feel so good, baby. So tight."

"That's it," Phoenix urged. "Let it feel good, baby. Let us fuck you. I want to feel you come on my cock."

Mia cried out and her pussy clenched around his cock. She was close.

"I want you to come at the same time we do," Phoenix told her, his eyes drifting up to Tarik's. "Close?"

"Yeah. Fuck yeah," Tarik said, his hips still bucking forward as he fucked her ass, continuing to do most of the work, rocking Mia along Phoenix's dick.

"Make me come. Please make me come," Mia begged.

Phoenix doubled his thrusts, driving into her as hard as he could with the two of them above him while Tarik matched his rhythm, their cocks rubbing together inside her as they impaled her at the same time. It was so fucking good. Better than good. Probably the most exquisite thing he'd ever felt.

"Oh… Oh, fuck… Phoenix! Tarik!" Mia screamed, more garbled words following as her body tightened, her climax gripping her, milking Phoenix's release from him as he stilled beneath her.

Tarik thrust into her twice more before his body went rigid, his cock pulsing against Phoenix's as he filled her ass.

It was, by far, the most intense thing Phoenix had ever known.

Chapter Thirty

SUNDAY MORNING, MIA woke up in an empty bed. She rolled over, fully expecting a pounding throb in her temples only to find there was none. A quick glance at the nightstand explained why. A glass of water and a bottle of aspirin, along with a note, greeted her. Someone had been thoughtful enough to make sure she'd taken pain reliever before she went to bed.

Smiling, she reached for the note and rolled onto her back, blinking in the bright morning light as her eyes tried to focus on the scribble in front of her.

Morning, sunshine. We'll be back to take you to lunch, so don't go anywhere. And if you're in this bed when we get back, you won't be leaving for a while. Just a warning. ~P

When her stomach rumbled, Mia's grin widened. She was starving, and she needed to shower, although the idea of a replay from last night certainly didn't make it easy to move.

Her mind drifted back to the events of the night, specifically those that had taken place in her very bed.

Does it feel good? Do you like when Tarik fucks your ass while my cock is buried in your tight pussy?

Phoenix's words echoed in her head, making her body heat instantly. Tarik's fingers had been fucking her ass. The feeling hadn't been exactly pleasant at first, but it had quickly morphed into an overwhelming pleasure, making her want more. The thought of them both filling her at the same time had overridden any fear of pain.

Relax for us. Let Tarik slide his cock into your ass. Feel us both filling you at the same time.

The next thing she'd known, Tarik's thick cock had filled her ass, stretching her. A blinding pain had caused her to still, her brain telling her to stop him. However, between the alcohol that had relaxed her body and Phoenix's tongue as he kissed her, Mia had ignored the warnings until nothing else had mattered but Tarik and Phoenix inside her at the same time.

That's it. Let it feel good, baby. Let us fuck you. I want to feel you come on my cock.

Heat swamped her now at the memory, the way Phoenix's erotic words had sent her soaring while they had fucked her so divinely.

Yep, she was definitely in the market for a replay of last night.

But not right now. Right now, she needed to focus on getting ready.

Forcing herself out of bed, she walked gingerly to the bathroom, gauging the soreness in her body. Not too bad, actually. Last night had been … incredible, and the tenderness was merely a reminder of how wonderful she had felt crushed between the two of them. Unlike anything she'd ever imagined, but it had brought her to an entirely different level.

One that she realized was quickly and easily tightening the chain that bonded her to Phoenix and Tarik. She wasn't sure whether that was a good thing or not, but she couldn't bring herself to care. After yesterday, having to deal with Damien's nonsense, she didn't want to think about it right then.

Hurrying into the shower, she took care of every little detail, and when she climbed out, she realized she was still smiling. So much that her cheeks hurt.

Quickly dressing, Mia hoped to surprise them, but she knew that was impossible. Not both of them at the same time, anyway. She would have to call someone in order to get up to the penthouse since she didn't know the code to get up there. She decided to reach out to Tarik because she didn't think he'd mind. Another ten minutes and she was pulling up his number on her cell phone, listening to it ring on the other end.

"Mornin'," he greeted in that rough, gravelly tone that made her heart skip a beat.

"Hi," she said softly.

"I take it you're out of bed?"

"Yes," she answered. "Why do you sound so disappointed?"

She was met with a throaty chuckle, and she remembered what Phoenix's note had said. "Well, there'll be plenty of time for that later. Right now, I need to be fed, but I was hoping to surprise you both. Since that's not an option, I figured maybe we could surprise Phoenix. Could you by chance let me up there?"

"I can. I'll be down in two minutes."

"Okay." Mia hit the end button and then paced her living room as she waited. She was eager to see them both. She knew they needed to talk about Damien's article because they probably had questions the same as she did, but after last night, seeing them was her main priority.

Deciding she couldn't take the waiting, Mia grabbed her key and headed for the hall at the same time the elevator dinged to announce the car's arrival. Tarik stepped out, looking sinfully delicious in a pair of jeans and a long-sleeve black T-shirt that accentuated the hard planes of his chest.

His eyes were trained on her as he approached. Mia laughed when she realized he was backing her up against the wall. He placed his hands on each side of her head, palms against the wall before pressing his mouth to hers. She breathed him in, soothed by the delicious scent that was unique to him.

"That's the way to greet a woman in the morning," she said breathlessly when he pulled back.

"I intended to, but you were sleeping so soundly."

"Well, maybe tomorrow morning then," Mia replied before she realized what she'd said.

Tarik didn't respond, but his golden eyes glittered, and the corner of his mouth lifted in a cocky half smirk.

"Come on. Let's get Phoenix and grab some food."

Mia took his hand when he offered, and they waited for the elevator together. He held her close, wrapping his arms around her while she stood in front of him. The fact that he wanted to touch her made her insides sing. As had been the case since the first time he'd touched her, Tarik made her feel safe in ways she'd never known before. As though he would fend off all of the demons that chased her, slay all the dragons. She wasn't sure what it was about him, but she craved the security he brought to her. Even though she realized there was still so much about him that she didn't know.

The elevator arrived and they climbed in. Tarik made her watch how he entered the code so she would know in the future. "I'm not sure Phoenix wants me to know that," she told him.

"Oh, trust me, love. He does."

They were stepping into Phoenix's condo less than a minute later, and Mia heard voices. One belonged to Phoenix and the other belonged to a woman. She didn't sound happy.

"Shit," Tarik muttered.

"Tarik, is that you?"

Mia glanced up at Tarik, wondering whether or not they should flee while they still had the chance. She felt an odd sense of impending doom wash over her at the thought of another woman being in Phoenix's penthouse.

"It's me," Tarik called out, meeting her gaze. "Hope you're ready for this."

Mia wanted to tell him that she wasn't ready for anything, but Tarik linked his fingers with hers and pulled her along behind him. When they stepped into the vast room that made up most of the condo's entertainment area, Mia came face-to-face with … a woman who looked a lot like Phoenix, only prettier and much, much smaller.

She met the hard-set green eyes and wondered what she was supposed to say, but those same eyes instantly softened, and a smile formed on the woman's lovely face. The woman glanced at Phoenix and then back at her, not saying anything.

"Hey," Phoenix greeted her, drawing her gaze to him. His smile seemed forced, but he looked happy to see her. She figured whatever conversation had been taking place before they'd arrived had contributed to his mood.

"Mother, this is Mia Cantrell. Mia, this is my mother, Ellen Pierce."

"And you must be Phoenix's girlfriend?" Ellen asked directly, her voice soft yet holding an authoritative edge, similar to Phoenix's tone.

Mia glanced at Phoenix, then down at Tarik's hand still holding hers.

Well, this was certainly awkward.

"It's so nice to meet you," Ellen said, turning her attention back to Phoenix after her gaze darted down to Mia's hand still warmly ensconced in Tarik's. "You might have some explaining to do, but I'm ready to listen when you're prepared to talk."

Phoenix didn't respond, merely sipped his coffee and watched the three of them as they stood there, amusement now reflected on his attractive face. Mia didn't know what to say or do. Suddenly her desire to surprise him didn't seem like such a good idea.

"Are you hungry?" Phoenix asked Mia after several painfully long seconds.

"I am," Mia replied softly. "But no rush. We can … sit down and talk if you'd like."

Phoenix's smirk told her that she probably shouldn't have said that.

"That's an excellent idea," Ellen said cheerfully, looking back at Mia. "Come. Sit."

Tarik released her hand, and Mia felt the loss of his protection instantly. Not that she felt Ellen Pierce was a threat, but for some reason, having him next to her made her feel less under the microscope.

That feeling of security disintegrated entirely when she joined Ellen on the sofa.

The same sofa where she and Tarik and Phoenix had…

Mia's face heated as the memory swamped her.

"Do you live around here, Mia?" Ellen asked, retrieving her coffee cup that was sitting on the glass table.

The same glass table where Phoenix had…

Oh, God.

This wasn't good.

Phoenix cleared his throat, and Mia's eyes darted up to his. He was laughing at her.

"Would you like some coffee?" he asked politely.

"Yes," she said. *So I can pour it on you.* She kept that part to herself. No need getting his mother defensive.

Phoenix and Tarik both disappeared into the kitchen, and Mia wondered since when did it take two of them to make coffee.

"I've read the papers, so I have to say I probably know a little more about you than you know about me."

Mia nodded. "I hope you don't believe everything you read."

"Of course not," Ellen said, setting her coffee cup down and twisting to face Mia.

The woman was strikingly beautiful. If Mia had to guess, she was close to sixty, maybe a few years younger. Her ebony hair didn't show a hint of gray, but she knew how that worked. A good stylist could easily take care of that. But the fact that her face was smooth and flawless spoke of either good genes or a really good plastic surgeon. She didn't know which it was, but whatever had contributed to Ellen Pierce's looks, she'd taken advantage.

"You're a student?"

"Yes," Mia replied. "I'm majoring in psychology at UT."

"Interesting choice. The human psyche is quite interesting, so I can see why you've chosen that field."

Mia didn't know what to say to that, but she had a feeling that Ellen knew more about what was happening between her and Tarik and Phoenix than she was letting on. Mia had no idea what Phoenix had told her, if anything, but she certainly wasn't going to be the one to provide her with the details.

Ellen leaned over and patted Mia's hand. "Don't worry," she said softly. "I don't bite. No matter what my son tells you. I'm actually quite happy to meet you. I knew that someone was putting a rather rare smile on his face these days, and I didn't think that it was only Tarik."

Swallowing hard, Mia tried not to choke as the realization set in. Yes, Ellen was a very perceptive woman. She had evidently caught on to the attraction between Tarik and Phoenix, yet Mia had to wonder whether Phoenix knew that she knew.

"Coffee," Phoenix said from behind her.

Mia smiled at Ellen and then turned to retrieve the cup.

"Well, I really should be going," Ellen said happily as she got to her feet. Smoothing her hand over the silk pantsuit she wore, she smiled at Mia once more. "It was a pleasure to meet you. One of these days, you'll have to come to dinner. My son is gone quite a bit; maybe we'll have a chance to talk while he's gone. I could show you pictures of him as a little boy."

Phoenix grumbled and Tarik laughed, although he covered it with a cough.

"That would be wonderful," Mia said, glaring up at Phoenix. "I'd love to see pictures of him." And she would do it, too, as payback for him putting her on the spot now.

"Wonderful. Well, I'll leave the three of you to it then. Phoenix, I fully intend to resume our conversation. Soon."

"Bye, Mother," Phoenix said, Ellen's heels clicking on the hardwood as she headed for the door.

When the door closed behind her, Phoenix let out a sigh of relief, and Tarik chuckled.

"I'm going to hurt you," Mia told him, putting her cup on the table and getting to her feet. "How dare you put me on the spot like that!"

Phoenix didn't answer. At least not with words. He stalked toward her, cupping her face in his big, warm hands before planting his mouth on hers in a kiss so hungry, so fierce, she forgot everything that had happened during the last few minutes.

»»»»»» ♥ «««««

"PLEASE TELL ME y'all are hungry, 'cause I'm starving," Mia said when he reluctantly released her mouth.

"Starving," Phoenix muttered, his eyes still on her lips.

Mia slapped his arm lightly. "That's not what I meant and you know it. I wanted to surprise you. Then I hoped we could eat lunch."

She'd surprised him, all right. Showing up at his penthouse in time to meet his mother probably wasn't her idea of a surprise, though.

"I could eat," Phoenix told her.

"Thank God." Mia pulled away from him, her eyes settling on Tarik. "Please tell me you like pizza."

"One of the basic food groups, right?" Tarik asked, leaning against the wall closest to Mia.

"In *my* food pyramid, it is," Mia replied as she reached into her back pocket, retrieving her cell phone.

"What are you doing?" Phoenix asked, taking another step toward her, eliminating the gap she'd intentionally put there.

"Calling for pizza."

"Sorry, but we can't do delivery," Tarik inserted, coming to stand in front of Mia, both of them crowding her.

"No? Then what do you suggest?"

"We'll show you," Phoenix said. "But first, I think I need a little incentive."

"Incentive?" Mia's thin, silky blonde eyebrows lifted toward her hairline. She looked so damn cute with her hair pulled back in a ponytail, a pair of jeans hugging her phenomenal ass and sexy legs and another one of those body-hugging, long-sleeve T-shirts making Phoenix's mouth water.

Cupping her face in one hand, Phoenix nudged his body against hers and then lowered his mouth until he reached the smooth contours of her lips once again. This time he aimed for gentle and sweet, but Mia clearly had other plans. She gripped the back of his head, pulled him to her, and then thrust her tongue into his mouth, practically devouring him whole as she clung to him, her breasts crushing against him.

"Holy fuck," he muttered when she released him.

"That's what I'm thinkin'," Tarik said, elbowing him out of the way before grabbing Mia and lifting her easily. She wrapped her legs around his waist and kissed him with as much fervor as she had Phoenix.

"Shit, woman, I thought you said you were hungry," Tarik muttered when they broke apart.

"I am."

"Then you shouldn't kiss a man like that," Tarik teased huskily. "I'm tempted to take you to the bedroom and strip you naked. I could do without food and just feast on you for a while."

"What if I said there was more where that came from *after* we eat?"

Tarik started toward the front door, still carrying Mia. She laughed, the sweetest sound Phoenix had heard in a while, and his answering smile was proof that just being in her presence had already made his day better.

"You coming?" she asked, looking back at him.

"Something like that," he mumbled.

Tarik lowered her to the floor, and she met Phoenix's gaze, a twinkle of humor mixed with heat reflected in the crystal blue. Yeah. His day was certainly looking up.

Chapter Thirty-One

MIA PRACTICALLY SKIPPED into the restaurant when they arrived twenty minutes later. It'd been a short walk to the pizzeria that she hadn't even known existed until now. She felt light, as though all her stresses had been obliterated and she was left with clouds filling her insides.

Truth was, she had missed Tarik and Phoenix over the course of the last week. Last night had been the first time she'd seen them since Sunday morning when she'd woken up in Phoenix's bed, crushed warmly between their big, hard bodies.

As each day had passed, she'd wanted nothing more than to go back to the penthouse and spend every waking minute with them, but she had forced herself to come up with an excuse. It helped that they'd been out of town some of the time. The separation had given her time to think. Having promised herself after marrying Damien that she would never make an impulsive decision again when it came to her heart, she had feared that if she spent too much time in their company, she would want something more from them than either was willing to give her.

The sex was off the charts, as far as she was concerned, but she also knew that there was something going on between Tarik and Phoenix, and sometimes Mia wasn't sure she fit in there. She wanted to, but she wasn't sure whether it was a possibility or not, so she had convinced herself to back off a little. Give it time.

Then, of course, her conversation with Alex yesterday had redirected her priorities. Alex had somehow managed to convince her that she was worrying too much. Mia hadn't been able to argue. Especially after reading the article about Damien, she hadn't been able to do much other than worry.

Only Phoenix and Tarik had shown up last night, picked her up and taken her home, and then made her feel as though she was the most important thing in the world to them. She couldn't deny the anticipation that was building inside her again. She wanted more. From both of them.

"How's school?" Phoenix asked when they sat down at a table after ordering their pizza at the counter.

"Good, actually. I'm taking psychology this semester, and it's extremely interesting."

Phoenix's brow lifted slightly. "How so?"

"I've always been a little curious about human behavior."

"Is that why you questioned our bisexuality?" Tarik asked casually, as though it was a common topic of conversation.

Mia felt her face flame, remembering back to the conversation when she'd been the one to bring it up. Luckily she hadn't been taking a drink or she'd probably have spit it all over Phoenix, who was sitting across from her and Tarik this time.

Phoenix's lips tilted, but he was trying to hide his smile; she could see it in the way the skin by his eyes crinkled. God, he was beautiful. And he seemed so much more at ease with the situation, almost as though he'd come to accept it as much as she and Tarik had.

"Partly," she said when she managed to swallow past the nervous lump in her throat. "Let's just say I'm not exactly … up to speed on certain things. I was a virgin when I met Damien."

She noticed the way Phoenix's gaze shifted to Tarik's and lingered there for a moment.

The feeling that something was different about them returned. It'd first come up when she'd seen the two of them together in Phoenix's penthouse. Almost as though they were having a silent conversation between the two of them. Possibly a memory they shared?

Last night, she'd been intoxicated and hadn't spent much time paying attention to anything more than the pleasure they'd bestowed upon her. But now, as she watched them, she sensed something *had* changed between them. Something major. Looking at Tarik and then back at Phoenix, Mia smiled. "Did something happen between the two of you that I don't know about?"

An implacable mask fell over Phoenix's face.

"It's not an accusation," she clarified, leaning forward and resting her forearms on the table. "It's just… Something's different. The way you're looking at each other…"

Tarik leaned close to her ear and lowered his voice so that no one else could hear. "Are you asking whether I had my wicked way with him?"

Heat erupted in Mia's insides, radiating outward slowly, sinfully. It was a delicious feeling, combined with the warmth of Tarik's breath against her ear. A sudden chill raced down her spine. "If I was?" she taunted.

"If that's what you want to know, then I'd tell you. But, little girl, you've got to learn to ask the question if you want to hear the answer."

Mia studied Phoenix, noting he was still trying to appear detached from the discussion, which was all the more telling. She doubted he had any regrets if something had happened. No, what she saw there was uncertainty. He wasn't sure how she would handle the news, maybe?

"Did you?" she asked, keeping her eyes locked with Phoenix's but directing the question to Tarik. Clearing her throat, she spit out the full question. "*Did* you have your wicked way with him?"

"I did," Tarik whispered, then nipped her earlobe, making her nipples tighten painfully and her sex clench. "Maybe later I'll tell you exactly what happened."

"I'd like that," she replied, noticing that only when those words were out of her mouth did Phoenix's expression soften somewhat.

"Does it bother you?" Phoenix asked directly.

"Does *what* bother me?"

"That we had sex without you there."

Mia considered that for a moment. Was she upset? She didn't think so, which was interesting in its own right. "We never agreed to be exclusive," she said, although that was a weak argument, because as far as casual sex went, this was her first time, and there was absolutely nothing casual about the way she felt about these men.

"Maybe not," Phoenix said, leaning forward, his hands clasped together on the table. "But as far as I'm concerned, we are."

As though reiterating the intensity in Phoenix's eyes, Tarik once again spoke directly in her ear. "No other man will touch you, Mia. You understand that? No one."

Mia leaned forward, mirroring Phoenix's posture and Tarik's no-nonsense tone. "And no other woman will touch either of you." She said the words, initially meaning them as a joke but quickly realizing she wasn't kidding. As far as the two of them together, that was different. Why, she still didn't understand, but it seemed a natural occurrence that there would be instances where two of them would be together while the other wasn't.

"Just keep in mind, I plan to have you to myself some of the time," Phoenix stated as though reading her mind.

"Ditto," she said, smiling.

"You'll have to run it by me so I can check your calendar. As luck would have it, she'll probably be alone with me when you want her. Sorry for your loss," Tarik said with a smirk.

Mia watched Tarik's mouth move as the words sank in. She couldn't help the laugh that bubbled up from within. The idea of these two men fighting for time alone with her did crazy things to her. Crazier than normal.

And then just like that, the tension between them once again cracked and fell away.

"With that settled," Tarik added, "I say we get this pizza to go and head back up to your condo."

Mia laughed at Tarik's joke. At least she assumed it was a joke. Based on the glimmer in his bright brown eyes, she had to wonder.

»»»»»» ♥ «««««

LUNCH DIDN'T TAKE long to devour, which they did at the restaurant, not back at the condo as he'd suggested. All three of them decided they were too hungry to wait. And when they were finished, Tarik wasn't ready to go back to the condo yet, so he mentioned taking a walk.

He didn't know why, but he needed to get out, enjoy the sunshine for a little while. January had proven to be milder than usual, except for the few storms they'd had. No predictions of snow, and the wind was even absent today. A perfect day to head down to the lake and walk. He figured Phoenix probably needed a little fresh air to keep him from thinking too much about the shit that would be waiting for him tomorrow morning when the real world once more interfered with this crazy ride they seemed to be on.

"What is it with you two and exercise?" Mia asked as the three of them strolled slowly past the few joggers and bike riders who were trying to take advantage of the warmer midday temperatures.

"This isn't exercise," Tarik told her. "But I can think of something that'll get your heart racing."

"I'm sure you can."

The three of them were silent for a few minutes, and then when Tarik thought Phoenix was going to say something, Mia spoke up.

"So, when is someone going to enlighten me?"

"About?" Phoenix asked.

Tarik glanced down at Mia. She was between them, her hands in her pockets as she kicked small rocks on the path every so often. At first he thought she was referring to Tarik's claim of having had his wicked way with Phoenix. Unfortunately, that wasn't what came out of her mouth.

"I read Damien's article. I know what he said about you. And me."

Phoenix stopped, causing Tarik and Mia to do the same.

"I don't believe it," Mia said quickly, noticing the anger that contorted Phoenix's once-relaxed countenance. "Really."

The hard lines of Phoenix's mouth softened. "It's bullshit."

414

"I know that," she said decisively, taking Phoenix's hand and pulling him along with her as she started walking again. Tarik put one foot in front of the other and kept up with them. "I think someone told me once that they preferred to hear things rather than read them. Was I mistaken?"

"No, you aren't mistaken," Phoenix confirmed.

Tarik hadn't been privy to that conversation, obviously, but he understood her meaning.

"Once I got over the shock of his lies, I actually found it amusing. My mother, however, didn't."

"Your mother knows about us?" Phoenix exclaimed, once again coming to a jarring halt.

"My mother knows everything. If I had to guess, she's got Google alerts set up for my name and probably gets an email notification, so I figured I'd get in front of it. I went to see her yesterday. We talked. She asked about you."

"Shit."

"It's fine," Mia said. "Quit stopping. We'll never get back to the condo if you don't keep moving."

"What did she say?" Phoenix questioned.

"She's worried. She doesn't like Damien, but she doesn't trust anyone else, either. Especially guys who own hockey teams."

Tarik couldn't help but laugh when Phoenix stopped yet again. Tarik had heard the humor in Mia's tone, but clearly Phoenix was too worried to notice. Granted, Tarik knew nothing about Mia's mother, but he couldn't imagine that she wasn't at least bothered a little by the article.

"I'm kidding. Good grief. I told her it was all a bunch of crap," Mia said, yanking on Phoenix's arm again.

"Did she believe you?" Phoenix asked, once more falling into step with them.

"Probably not," Mia said, chuckling. "But I managed to turn the tables on her. I found out she has a boyfriend, and I exploited that to throw her off. I figured there really wasn't anything to tell. I don't know about Damien's business, or yours." Mia glanced at Phoenix. "I'm nothing in the grand scheme of things, just a tool for Damien to use to get his way."

Tarik was the one to stop. He'd heard something in her tone that he didn't appreciate. "The article might be bullshit, Mia, but you don't give yourself nearly enough credit. Damien's an asshole. He never deserved you in the first place."

Phoenix moved to stand behind her as people continued to pass them on the trail.

Sliding a stray piece of hair that had fallen from her ponytail behind her ear, Tarik used that as an excuse to keep touching her. Mia looked away.

He figured that showing her would mean more than words, so Tarik took her hand and began walking. Phoenix did the same, and he was proud when she ignored the people who looked at them, confusion on their faces.

"I will tell you this," Phoenix began, "whatever Landry's up to, we'll get it figured out."

"What is he really after?" Mia asked, looking over at Phoenix.

"Money. My father's not here to defend himself, and if Damien has proof that my father backed out of the deal as he claims he does, then I'll have to pay out something. He's tacking on more pain and suffering to increase the dollar amount."

"Oh, God." Mia sighed but didn't stop moving. "He's using me to extort money from you?"

"No," Phoenix stated adamantly. "However, I do think he believes he's got leverage. And using you is going to be the way he gets to me."

"Why would he think that I even matter?"

"Did you *see* the pictures in the article?" Tarik asked. He had, and they certainly depicted the three of them in a very different light. They'd reflected an intimacy that was hard to capture. And if he had to guess, that was something Damien wasn't used to seeing. Ex-wife or not, the bastard was selfish, and if he thought another man was after her, his territorial side was going to come out.

Unfortunately, the bastard hadn't considered Phoenix's territorial side, never mind Tarik's. As far as Tarik knew, no one was insinuating they were all three in a relationship. At least not together. The article had danced around the picture of the three of them holding hands and had briefly mentioned him and Phoenix together, although he knew more of that nonsense was probably coming. But he didn't give a shit about what people said or thought about him. He'd given up on that years ago. His parents had been bad enough, ensuring he knew that no one actually cared about him. Tarik had carried that with him, and the don't-give-a-shit attitude had rooted deep in his soul.

"What now?" Mia asked as they made their way back to the street that would lead to the condos.

"I'm thinking a movie sounds just about perfect right now," Phoenix stated. "At my place."

"As long as you have popcorn, I'll follow you anywhere," Mia said happily.

Tarik liked her resilience. She truly did have an optimistic outlook, which was refreshing. He just hoped they could keep her out of the line of fire in the coming days. Knowing what Damien Landry was capable of, Tarik figured it was going to get worse before it got better.

Chapter Thirty-Two

MIA WOULD'VE BEEN content to spend the rest of the evening right there, reclining on the black leather sofa in Phoenix's living room, watching the sun as it slowly slid behind the buildings, listening to Imagine Dragons drifting through the speakers that were hidden somewhere that she'd yet to find.

After they'd returned to Phoenix's condo, he'd excused himself when his phone had rung, which had disappointed her somewhat, but after hearing the frustration in his tone, she'd known he was talking business. So, instead of worrying about him, she'd sat down, and shortly thereafter, Tarik had joined her, pulling her against him until they were lying down. They had foregone the movie in lieu of watching the day pass minute by minute. At some point, she must've fallen asleep because the room wasn't nearly as bright as it had been earlier, and that was when she realized Tarik was still there, his eyes closed, his breaths slow and even. She assumed he was asleep, so she tried not to move.

When the song changed, switching over to "Sleep To Dream Her" by Dave Matthews Band, Mia listened closely, trying to see if Phoenix was still there. She didn't hear him, but that didn't mean he wasn't somewhere close.

"He went down to talk to his mother," Tarik muttered quietly, a sleepy rasp to his voice.

So he wasn't asleep.

"Everything okay?" she questioned, hoping nothing had happened.

"Yeah. She's just worried about this shit with Landry. He's trying to calm her down."

Mia pushed up onto her arm. She was wedged between Tarik's body and the cushions on the back of the sofa, her leg strewn across Tarik's, her hand resting on his chest. She'd been comfortable like that, but her muscles were starting to tighten, a suggestion that she should move.

Tarik obviously realized what she was doing, because he shifted to his side, facing her and pulling her so that she was on her back, his body partly covering her.

"You slept for a while," he said.

"How long?"

"About three hours."

"Really?" she hadn't realized she'd been that tired. Then again, she did enjoy a nice Sunday afternoon nap from time to time.

"Did *you* sleep?" she asked, her gaze slowly sliding down to his mouth.

Mia wondered if he would kiss her. She *hoped* he would kiss her.

"For a little while." His golden eyes darkened slightly, and she felt the insistent press of his erection against her hip.

"You should've woken me up," she whispered, her stomach tightening when his hand slid up to it, slipping beneath her shirt.

"I thought about it. I thought about a lot of things while you slept."

"Like?" Her inner temperature began a steady climb as his hand roamed over her skin, the gentle abrasion making her nerve endings spark and sizzle.

"Like what it's like to bury myself inside you. So deep." The rough rasp of his tone made the hair on the back of her neck stand up, chills working their way down her spine.

"What's it like?" she asked, lifting her arms up over her head when he pushed her shirt up higher, exposing her black bra to his hungry gaze.

"Heaven," he muttered as he leaned down and pressed his lips to her chest, licking downward between her breasts.

Mia pushed her chest up, trying to get closer to him. The hand he had on her stomach remained there, holding her in place. His other hand gripped her wrists, holding them above her head as he continued to lick her. She could feel the heat of his mouth through the thin, silky material of her bra.

"Tarik. Oh, God." She wasn't sure what she was trying to say, but the words spilled out as he used his mouth to torment her.

"We should get you naked," he said, lifting his head and snagging her gaze.

"We should," she agreed, getting lost in the heat in his eyes. The intensity she felt there ignited a blaze inside her, one that quickly started burning brighter and hotter.

If she hadn't known better, she would've thought their clothes had just dissolved. Tarik stripped them both quickly, wasting no time. He was even prepared, donning a condom that he retrieved from his wallet before joining her on the sofa once more, this time kneeling between her thighs.

"You're just lucky I got your clothes off first," he mumbled against her lips, clearly reading her mind.

"I'm glad you did," she said, wrapping her arms around him and pulling him closer, feeling the strength in his powerful body, the heat that caressed her from chest to knee. Digging her nails into his back, she pulled him to her, her mouth reaching for his.

Their tongues skimmed as his fingers slid into her already slick folds. She moaned against his mouth, pushing her hips up to meet his exploring hands, desperate to feel him inside her. Luckily, he didn't make her wait before his thick length was pressing against her entrance.

"Oh, God," she moaned softly. "Oh, yes." He felt so good as he made his way inside her. He stretched her so deliciously, her body ready for him as he eased in deep, his hips stilling, leaving her aching for more.

"Mia," he breathed against her mouth. "Love."

Mia forced her eyes open to look up at him. What she saw on his face had her heart wrenching in her chest. There was so much emotion right there for her to see, she wanted to throw out a net and capture it, to pull it into her so she could hold on to it forever.

His hips began a leisurely grind as his lips brushed hers softly. Slow and deep, Tarik made love to her in a way she hadn't known possible. She felt him so deep she was sure he had penetrated her soul. Her hands slid up and down his back as she scrambled to hold on, to ground herself, because she was quickly losing herself to this man, losing herself in his gaze, the way he searched her face as though looking for the same thing he was offering.

She wasn't sure if he saw it, but she knew it was there. Right there in that moment, Mia felt some of the remnants of her once-shattered heart mend, pulling together and intertwining with pieces of him.

"Oh, Mia," Tarik said quietly, his hand cradling her head, his nose brushing hers as his hips dipped and retreated, driving him deeper into her.

"Tarik." His name came out on a strangled moan as her body began to float, every cell, every nerve ending tingling as her climax grabbed hold.

"That's it, baby." Tarik's thumb brushed her cheek as his hips thrust forward. "That's it. Come for me."

His words were but a whisper in the darkened room.

Mia pressed upward to meet each delicious thrust as he increased the pace. He was driving deeper, an exquisite plunge of his hips causing him to hit her G-spot, making it impossible to hold on.

"Mia. Baby, I'm gonna come." He breathed against her lips as her body hummed, her muscles tightening, the tingling igniting into an inferno inside her as it began to trickle outward, making the hair on her arms stand up.

"Tarik," she whispered, not wanting him to let her go, because she knew she was about to shatter, and she wasn't sure, when this was over, that she was going to be the same person she had been before. It felt... "Oh, God, Tarik."

A strangled cry escaped her as she thrust her head back, her body bowing as her orgasm ripped through her.

Tarik's hips pressed forward, retreated, then again and again before he erupted, a muffled roar escaping him as he pressed his mouth against her neck.

Mia didn't move, didn't breathe as she tried to take stock of herself. She wasn't sure she was still in one piece. But what surprised her most was that it didn't scare her.

Not yet, anyway.

»»»»»»♥«««««

TARIK SOMEHOW MANAGED to get them both cleaned up and dressed and back on the couch even though his head was still reeling from what just happened.

Now, he wasn't some sort of fucking pussy who had sex with a woman and thought he saw stars and shit, but something had just happened. Something that had never happened to him before. Not with a man or a woman. What had transpired between him and Mia in those few minutes was ... earth-shattering. So completely different from anything he'd known, including his time with Phoenix — although that had altered his life in an entirely different way.

The fact of the matter was that Tarik felt something for both of them. Although it was equally strong, it was still different. In a good way. Just like they were different from one another in so many ways.

"You okay?" Mia asked as they lay on the sofa once more in the same position they'd been in before he'd found himself buried to the hilt inside her, losing a part of himself.

"Never better," he told her as he stared up at the ceiling. He watched the large circle of golden light from the small lamp beside his head that shone some twenty feet above them, but he didn't really see anything.

"Can I ask you something?"

"Sure." Tarik knew Mia well enough to know that what was about to come out of her mouth was going to be a question that would make him uncomfortable. He braced himself.

"What happened between your mother and father?"

He wasn't surprised by her curiosity. He'd already told her that his father had killed his mother, so he'd expected her to want to know what had happened. And it wasn't that he didn't want to talk about it, to share with her, he just didn't know how.

"It's okay if you don't want to," Mia said, and Tarik realized he hadn't bothered to say anything for a minute or two.

"My parents met in high school," he began, not knowing where else to start. "My dad was a senior, my mother a sophomore. From the bits and pieces of conversations I overheard, neither of them were popular, both from relatively poor families. She was the nerdy type, he was the bad boy. Typical high school crush. One thing led to another, and they had me. She was sixteen when I was born, and her father threw her out."

"Where did the name Tarik come from?" Mia questioned.

"My father was part Egyptian," he explained. "My mother picked out the name, originally intrigued by his heritage. He, of course, hadn't given a shit. Anyway, for whatever reason, my father decided to marry her, probably more out of guilt than anything. He graduated, but my mother dropped out of high school before I was born.

"They hated each other. Detested the mere sight of one another. Always fighting. And I don't mean a screaming match. They were violent with one another and with me. Throwing things, hitting each other, tearing shit up. We moved so much, always evicted. If it wasn't for not paying the rent, they were thrown out for vandalism. I think I changed schools every year through grade school. I guess one day things went too far."

Tarik remembered the day he'd come home from school to find his mother on the kitchen floor, her head at an odd angle, blood pooling beneath her, the fireplace poker lying beside her.

"Honestly, I was surprised it had taken that long before one of them was killed. I was a freshman in high school. We lived in Houston, and we'd just moved into a shitty-ass apartment in another crappy neighborhood. I came home from school one day and found my mother in a pool of blood on the kitchen floor, my father sitting in the living room, his head in his hands as he stared at the floor. I don't think he was shocked, either. Cause of death was blunt trauma to the head. He'd hit her with a fireplace tool."

"Oh, my God, Tarik," Mia whispered, the top of her head burrowing closer to his neck, her cheek on his chest.

He allowed her warmth to seep into him as he fought the chill that still lived inside him. There was a hollow spot encasing the memories of his parents. He didn't have any feelings for them one way or another. He wasn't sure he ever had.

"It was eerily calm as I dialed 911, then gave the operator the address, explaining what I saw. My father never budged from his chair until the police arrived. He went willingly, never saying a word."

"Do you see him?" she asked.

"No. I've never visited him in prison, didn't go to the hearings. I didn't care. Still don't. They might've fulfilled their parental obligation of feeding and clothing me, making sure I had a bed to sleep in, which was usually just a blanket on the floor, but I never felt any love from them."

"What about your grandparents? Did they take you in?"

"No. My parents had severed ties with both their families and not on good terms. I think they figured I was more of a nuisance than anything. I didn't know any of them at that point."

Tarik wrapped his arm around Mia when she sobbed against him. He'd never cried for his parents. Not once. Without any family to take him in, Tarik had been taken by the state and placed in foster care. He'd gone through the motions from there, never getting close enough to one family to worry about having feelings for them. When he was old enough, he'd moved to Austin, wanting to get away from the reminders of them, wanting to start anew.

Until Phoenix, Tarik hadn't even been sure he was capable of having feelings for anyone. Then again, until Phoenix, no one had ever made him feel like he mattered.

Brushing his hand over Mia's hair, Tarik inhaled deeply.

"I didn't mean to make you cry," he said softly, keeping her close.

Mia nuzzled closer, her breath warm against his skin.

"Can I tell you something?" she asked, her words so soft he wouldn't have heard her if she hadn't been close to his ear.

"Sure," he said just as quietly.

"I love you, Tarik."

For the first time in his entire life, Tarik was pretty sure those three words were going to pull tears from him. He was just grateful that it was dark.

»»»»»» ♥ «««««

WHEN PHOENIX MADE it back to the penthouse after spending nearly three hours talking to his mother, he was emotionally wrung out and exhausted. What had started out as a conversation about the Arrows, the lawsuit, and the direction the team was headed had turned into a trip down memory lane, and Phoenix hadn't been able to leave. He'd helped his mother cook, and they'd eaten together while talking about his father, the pain still fresh for both of them.

Finding Mia and Tarik asleep on the couch curled up around one another in the dark, Phoenix had pondered what to do. He hated to wake them, but he didn't want to spend the night alone in his bed, so he'd managed to nudge Tarik awake enough to get him moving. Phoenix had lifted Mia and carried her into his bedroom. He didn't bother removing her clothes, just tucked her in, then stripped down to his boxers and joined her. To his surprise, Tarik climbed in beside him, lying on his back as they both stared up at the ceiling in the darkened room.

"You okay?" Tarik asked, breaking the silence.

"I will be."

"Me, too."

Phoenix turned his head to look at Tarik, only making out his profile in the light shining in through the floor-to-ceiling windows. "Something happen?"

"She asked about my parents."

Something compelled him to find Tarik's hand with his own, linking their fingers as they lay there. "Did she cry?" Phoenix asked. He'd heard the story, knew it was heart wrenching. Having grown up with two parents who had doted on him and one another, Phoenix couldn't relate to the hell Tarik had lived through. He knew Tarik carried scars with him that would never fade, both physical and emotional. He also knew that Tarik was a much stronger man than he was.

"Yeah."

The silence lingered between them for a few minutes before Tarik spoke up again.

"I made love to her."

"I figured," Phoenix replied. "There's the distinct scent of sex in the living room. Incredible, huh?"

"That doesn't even begin to describe it," Tarik admitted, and Phoenix heard something he'd never heard in Tarik's voice.

Phoenix knew what Tarik was feeling. He'd felt it himself when he'd been with Mia. He'd known from the beginning that there was something about her, something unique. She captivated him, pulled him in, and as every day passed, the strings that tethered him to her only strengthened. The same way those that held him to Tarik continued to be reinforced. Proof was in the way Tarik held his hand, the three of them in his bed.

"This is real, huh?" Phoenix finally asked.

"It's real."

"Good." And with that, Phoenix gave in to sleep.

Chapter Thirty-Three

"DAMN IT," PHOENIX growled, tempted to punch a hole in the kitchen wall. After what had turned out to be an incredibly relaxing Sunday spent with Mia and Tarik doing little to nothing and a decidedly uneventful Monday, it was now Tuesday, and he was ready to go back to a simpler fucking time.

His mother had bombarded him with questions the moment he'd gotten back from his run that morning, apparently having gotten a few more details from Phil. The details that Phoenix had purposely kept from her for that very reason. He had enough to deal with without her getting worked up. And to make matters worse, his phone hadn't stopped ringing, his email was overrun with bullshit messages, and on top of that, he had a fucking headache.

Not enough coffee, that was the problem.

Before he got the chance to enjoy his second cup, the one he had just poured, the doorbell rang, and he spun around so fast he nearly spilled his coffee all over himself.

His initial thought was that Mia was there, but he couldn't picture her coming up without calling him first. She'd paid him a surprise visit once, and he remembered how that had gone.

So, what the fuck was someone doing ringing his doorbell? And how the fuck had they gotten up there in the first place? No one was permitted on the penthouse floor without the code to get there. Not even the doormen or the concierge were allowed to give out that information.

Glancing down the hallway toward Tarik's office, he expected to see him emerge, but he didn't. Where the hell was he? Another chime from the damn doorbell had Phoenix moving. He could easily handle whoever had made it to his front door; he just wasn't sure they were going to be walking without a limp when he got through with them. It wasn't his mother, either, he knew that much. She had a key and wouldn't bother with the doorbell.

Stalking through the entryway, Phoenix grabbed the knob and yanked it open. Hell, it hadn't even been locked.

"Teresa?" Phoenix was stunned to see her standing there, raking her fingers through her hair. "How the hell did you get up here?"

"Good morning to you, too," she said sweetly, clearly ignoring him as she flashed a toothy smile his way.

"I asked you a question," he snarled.

Her devious smirk was enough of an answer. She'd somehow figured out his code, probably having watched him enter it back when he'd brought her to his condo. He was a dumbass. And he needed to remember to have Tarik change the code.

"Are you going to invite me in?" she asked.

"I'd rather not," he said honestly at the same time Tarik came to stand behind him, the warmth of his body relatively close to Phoenix.

"What's going on?" Tarik asked, glancing past him. He was holding his phone to his ear as he peered over Phoenix's shoulder, close enough that Phoenix could smell him. He smelled good.

Shaking off the distraction, Phoenix looked back at Teresa.

"No fucking clue," Phoenix retorted and then turned away. He didn't have time for this shit. Whatever she wanted, she could just turn right back around and go elsewhere. He had nothing to say to her.

"I thought I'd make a surprise visit," Teresa said loud enough for him to hear as he headed for the kitchen. "Damien had some unfinished business to attend to with one of your tenants. I thought I'd stop by to chat while I waited."

Phoenix stopped in his tracks and slowly turned around to see Tarik had allowed her to step into the foyer. "Who?"

"Huh?" Teresa asked, looking around as though she were trying to see if anything was different from the last time she was there, which had been more than eight months ago.

"Who did Landry come to see?"

"His ex-wife. You know her, right? Mia something or other." Teresa's snotty attitude flashed like a beacon in those words, her distaste for Mia evident.

"What does he want with her?" Tarik asked, the growl in his voice causing Teresa to take a step back. She would expect Phoenix to be aggressive, to not put up with her shit, but Tarik had never so much as talked to her. According to him, she was a snake, and he hadn't wanted anything to do with her since the first time Phoenix had introduced them.

"We saw that she was in the news this morning. He felt the need to check on her," Teresa said. She was far too calm, far too easy-going about her *fiancé* supposedly wanting to chat it up with his ex-wife. Teresa had always been the jealous type, which was why Phoenix hadn't pursued even a casual relationship with her, nothing more than a couple of nights of fucking.

"Enough with the bullshit, Teresa," Phoenix snapped as he thrust his hands into his pockets. He wasn't about to let her know that he had no fucking idea what she was talking about. He'd been so caught up in the shit storm that had erupted that morning that he hadn't seen any new articles about her. "That still doesn't explain why you're here."

Phoenix shot a glare at Tarik but was met with a shrug. Obviously Tarik didn't know what was going on, either. That couldn't be good.

"Can't I just stop by to say hello? Don't tell me that you've developed some sort of feelings for the timid woman, Phoenix. I mean, seriously, Damien's told me how shitty she is in bed. You forget I know you better than that."

"You don't fucking know me at all," he argued, ignoring the comment about Mia.

"I'm going to check on her," Tarik stated.

Phoenix nodded at him.

When Teresa reached for Tarik, Phoenix knew she was up to no good. No one touched Tarik. No one. Not unless he invited them to, and he'd always kept a safe distance between himself and Teresa.

Tarik glared at the spot where her hand touched his arm.

"I'd highly encourage you to move your hand," Tarik growled.

She pulled her hand back as though she'd been burned. "I don't think they want to be interrupted. Damien called her before he decided to go by. She sounded upset."

Phoenix didn't believe a word she said, but he didn't know for certain. He hadn't had a chance to speak to Mia yet.

"Go check on her," he instructed Tarik, ignoring Teresa's nonsense. "I'll take care of this."

Tarik nodded and moved passed Teresa, forcing her to shift out of his path.

"I'm so glad you—"

"I don't want to hear it," Phoenix said. "Not another word from you until he gets back."

And with that, Phoenix headed back to the kitchen for his coffee.

»»»»»» ♥ ««««««

"MIA, I'M TELLING you. I didn't see it coming. I was blindsided by it just as much as you were. Sure, I'd been working with his father on the sale of the team when he was having financial troubles, and it's all just snowballed since Sid passed away."

"His father died ten months ago, Damien." Mia couldn't hide the incredulity in her tone. She couldn't believe Damien was using that as his argument.

"It saddened me when he passed. We'd become … well, I'd like to say we'd become friends at the time. I'd talked to him about you a few times. I…" Damien looked away as though he was ashamed of what he was about to say. "I was asking his advice. Our marriage was having problems."

Mia started to say something but clamped her lips shut. Ten months ago was the same time she'd asked for a divorce. Right about the time Damien had made her aware that he'd been cheating. She couldn't help but wonder whether the two were related as the article had mentioned, only not in his version of history.

"Our marriage was only having problems because you were cheating," Mia huffed out, unable to keep looking at him. Although that wasn't necessarily true. Mia had begun falling out of love with Damien long before that, but she'd been intent on making things work. Right up to the point when he'd slept with another woman.

"It was a setup, Mia. That's what I've been trying to tell you."

God, was there no end to his lies? Mia pushed away from the table, wanting to get as far from him as possible, but Damien grabbed her wrist to keep her in place. He wasn't hurting her, but she didn't want his slimy hands on her.

Glancing down at the spot where he touched her, she waited until he pulled his hand back. He finally released her slowly, making sure to rake his thumb over the back of her hand once. She had the urge to stab his fingers with a fork.

"Hear me out, Mia."

"Why? So you can make up more lies? What the hell is going on with you, Damien?"

Mia couldn't believe her ears. For the last fifteen minutes, Damien had been sitting at her small kitchen table, pleading his heart out — or so he claimed — trying to convince her that he'd been taken advantage of during this supposed business deal. Something about Sid wanting to sell and Phoenix trying to put a stop to it. He was trying to convince her that Phoenix was actually the one who had set him up, convincing Teresa Somerhaus to seduce Damien. He apparently would go to the ends of the earth to try to convince her that he still loved her and that he'd been wrong.

Well, he'd been wrong, she would agree there. But the rest was… It was bullshit was what it was.

She was torn between laughing in his face and shoving him out the front door. How stupid did he really think she was? Truthfully, she didn't want to know the answer to that question or the others she'd asked him. Damien thought she was clueless, lacking a single brain cell in her entire head. That was one of the reasons he'd married her. And yes, he'd been inclined to share that revelation with her at one point during one of their many arguments.

Meeting his gaze, Mia swallowed hard. "You lied and said that *I* was cheating on *you*."

"Mia... I... God, it's been so hard on me. Losing you... It—"

"You. Lied," she exclaimed.

"I don't know that..." Damien looked at the table. "I don't know that it's a lie. I've seen the pictures, Mia." He met her stare once more. "I've seen them. You two look mighty damn in love for two people who don't know each other."

"I've known them for a month," she declared, realizing instantly that she'd referred to both of them. Damien didn't seem to notice. "How long do you think it takes to get to know someone?"

Damien looked at her skeptically.

Oh, Lord. He was losing his mind. "Look, Damien," Mia said, trying to regain her composure. He was the one worked up, and the guilt glittered in his eyes because of it. There was no reason for her to try to defend herself. He was the liar. Not her.

"No, Mia, hear me out."

"I thought that's what I'd been doing, but you don't seem to have anything to say," she snapped. "Everything that's come out of your mouth has been a lie."

Hell, at one point, he'd tried to convince her that, although he'd been unfaithful, it hadn't been his fault. Teresa had tricked him because Phoenix had put her up to it. Something about Phoenix wanting to get to her so that he'd have leverage against Damien and the lawsuit. Not that Mia understood how any of it would've worked, but okay.

A knock on her front door had her looking over Damien's head.

"Don't answer that. We need to finish talking first."

They *were* finished, but she didn't bother to tell him that. Mia placed her hands on the table and pushed to her feet, staring at her ex-husband as she did. "I'll be right back."

Leaving Damien behind in the kitchen, Mia escaped down the narrow hall that led to the door. She glanced in the security hole to see Tarik standing in the outer hallway. Instantly opening the door, she hoped he saw the relief in her eyes. "What are you doing here?" she whispered.

"Are you okay?" he asked directly, looking past her into her condo.

"I'm…" Glancing over her shoulder, she shook her head before meeting his gaze once more. "As good as can be expected, I guess."

"Landry's here?"

"Yeah." Mia stepped out into the hall and shut her front door behind her so they could talk in private. She didn't particularly like leaving Damien alone in her condo, but she didn't have much of a choice. She needed a breather, and he clearly wasn't planning to leave. "Wait. How did you know he was here?"

"His *fiancée* stopped by for a visit," he said, rolling his eyes.

"Really?" What the hell was Teresa doing there?

"Just showed up a little while ago. Mentioned Landry was down here talking to you."

"Well, he's talking, all right. He's not saying anything, but his lips keep moving. Honestly, I think he's got a screw loose." Mia smiled, refusing to think about Teresa talking to Tarik and Phoenix alone upstairs.

"Yeah, well, I think there might be a few *missing*, too," Tarik replied.

Tarik automatically pulled her into his arms and hugged her. Without releasing her, he slid his hands into her hair and pulled, tilting her head back so that she was forced to look up at him. She had to crane her neck to meet his gaze, but she didn't mind. And she certainly didn't have any issues when he leaned in and placed his mouth on hers. God, she'd missed him. Both of them. After spending most of the weekend with them, being alone in her bed last night had been hell. And with everything Phoenix was dealing with, she hadn't been sure she was going to get the chance to see them today, either. Tarik's arrival was certainly a nice surprise.

"So what does Teresa want?" Mia asked when Tarik released her lips and her hair, allowing her to take a step back so she could see him better.

"Don't know for sure, but I know they're up to something. She mentioned Landry was down here paying you a visit because you were upset."

Mia noticed the way Tarik continued to stare at the front door as though he had x-ray vision and could see through it. If that were the case, Damien would probably be burned to a crisp at the moment.

She suddenly wished superpowers were real.

"Yeah, well, he's talking nonsense, and if I'm upset, it's only because he's here," Mia explained.

"Speaking of nonsense," Tarik muttered, and a cold chill raced down Mia's spine. "His lawyer hasn't been able to produce anything yet, so I still think he's lying, but he claims Sid actually moved forward with the sale. The question is why wait till now?"

"Lying is second nature to him," she said. "But I'm with you. This seems farfetched, even for Damien. What he's really after, I don't know."

"Just whatever you do, don't let him get you talking about Phoenix."

Nodding her head, she didn't know what to say to that.

Tarik cupped her face in his big, warm hands. "Do you trust us, Mia?"

"Yes," she said, surprising herself by the truth in that single word. She did trust them, even though everything that Damien had said about Phoenix so far should've made her think otherwise. Then again, she'd have to dig through the blatant lies to possibly decipher even an ounce of truth.

Just as Tarik opened his mouth to say something more, Mia's front door opened, and Damien loomed over her. Turning to face him, Mia welcomed the warmth of Tarik's arms when he pulled her in against him.

"What are you doing here?" Damien asked Tarik as though he had every right to question her visitors.

"He came to see me," Mia responded. "I'll be inside in a minute, Damien."

Her ex-husband nodded but didn't hurry to close the door. He continued to watch Tarik. A strange expression crossed his face, but Mia couldn't place it.

Once the door closed, she turned back to Tarik.

"Do you want me to come in?" he asked.

"No. I need to handle this on my own," she explained.

"Call me when you're finished," Tarik told her.

"I will." Mia took a deep breath and turned back to her front door. Looking back with her hand on the knob, she said, "Oh, and do me a favor, would you?"

"Anything," Tarik said.

"Get Teresa Somerhaus away from Phoenix. I don't want her near either one of you."

The knowing smirk that tilted his lips said he approved of her possessiveness, and that made Mia feel good.

The feeling didn't last long when she pushed open the door. She didn't want to talk to Damien any longer. She knew what he was trying to do, but she didn't see any way to avoid it aside from not going back home. And that wasn't an option.

The moment she stepped inside, Damien was right there, reaching for her.

Mia had to jerk away to keep him from touching her. "What are you doing?" she asked, suspicious.

"Are you okay? He didn't hurt you, did he?"

"What the hell are you talking about?" she asked. She wanted to ask him whether he was taking any new medication, something that could possibly throw off his brain function, because he was certainly acting strange.

"I just wanted to make sure. It's just like Phoenix to send his lackey to do his dirty work."

"He's not Phoenix's lackey," she snapped.

Damien stared down at her for a minute before he finally spoke. "I thought you were seeing Phoenix. Are you…" Damien glanced over her head toward the front door before he continued, "You're not seeing *him*, are you?"

Mia sighed heavily. She did not have any intention of going into details about her personal life with him. He'd given up all right to ask her questions when he'd started sleeping with other women. The best thing to do was to get him out the door. It was that or scratch his eyes out. He was obviously doing his best to upset her. "Damien, it's not gonna work."

His blond eyebrows lifted in question.

"I'm not interested in telling you anything more. And I'm done listening. Now, if you don't mind, I really do have things to do today." Motioning toward the door, Mia prayed that he would leave.

"I came to tell you that I'm sorry, Mia. I'm so sorry for hurting you. Is there any possibility that you'll give me another chance? Give *us* another chance?"

Mia's eyebrows furrowed. "*Us?* Are you serious? Don't you have a fiancée waiting for you upstairs in Phoenix's penthouse?"

The guilt returned to Damien's eyes, something she was all too familiar with. She waited for him to lie, to tell her some other bullshit story about how he'd been duped into something he didn't want. There had been a time in her life when she might've believed him, but not today. Not ever again.

The first thing she'd done when she'd woken up, the same as she'd done since she'd stumbled upon the last article that had mentioned her name, was check the Internet.

She'd become a pawn for Damien, and based on what she'd read that morning, he wasn't relenting, even though he pretended to want to make amends. What she'd found online had surprised her. Damien's name, as well as Phoenix's, was everywhere. Everyone was talking about both of them at the moment, and she'd been curious as to what had spurred the sudden intense interest. A lawsuit alone wouldn't incite the press that much.

What she'd found hadn't been surprising. Someone was trying to dig up dirt on Phoenix. It always worked that way, and since she'd been hounded by a couple of reporters on her way home from school last week — something she hadn't bothered to tell Tarik or Phoenix because they had enough to worry about — she'd been expecting it.

Of all the things the media could've said, Mia probably would've believed anything other than Phoenix was after her to get Damien off his back. It sort of negated all of the other nonsense. First of all, she knew Phoenix hadn't been hurting for female companionship when she had met him. She'd read more than her fair share of articles from his past about the women he'd been seen with. He'd been with some incredibly beautiful women. She was nothing compared to them. Phoenix didn't need to use her. She truly believed that.

The fact of the matter was, someone was trying to use *her* to get to Phoenix. The question was why.

"Look, I've got things to do, so if you don't mind," Mia repeated. Holding out her arm, she reached for the doorknob.

"Mia, please."

"I know what you're doing, Damien. And it's not gonna work."

And just like that, the pleading tone and the sad eyes were gone, and in their place was the crude businessman she knew so well. The one who didn't do anything for anyone other than himself. Whatever he was up to, Mia knew she needed to be cautious. He was looking for something. Likely details on Phoenix, as Tarik had suggested, although she truly didn't understand why. Or why he thought she would give him any information.

It was a little ridiculous, even for Damien. Not to mention, he was rich in his own right, and his business was thriving, so why was he putting so much effort into getting money from Phoenix?

Making a mental note to do a little digging, Mia turned her attention back to Damien and opened the door. Just as she did, the elevator in the hall dinged, and the doors slid open. Out walked Phoenix, looking incredibly handsome in a pair of jeans and a navy polo. His hair was haphazardly sexy, a look she wasn't used to seeing on him. He was usually so well put together, his hair generally styled to perfection. She decided she liked this look on him. Immensely.

Teresa was beside him, glaring at her, and Tarik followed behind them.

"I think this belongs to you," Phoenix told Damien as he nudged Teresa toward him.

The couple glanced at one another, a scheming look passing between them. What the hell were they really up to?

Phoenix moved to her side just inside her condo while Tarik moved past and came to stop behind her. She had no idea what Damien was thinking as he looked at the three of them, and quite frankly, she didn't care.

"Thanks for stopping by," Tarik said gruffly before taking a step back and gently urging Mia to move so he could close the door.

Damien didn't say another word, but the look on his face would likely be something that would haunt Mia for days to come.

She didn't know what he was after, but she'd somehow been trapped in his crosshairs yet again, and that was really beginning to piss her off.

Chapter Thirty-Four

"THAT WENT WAY too well," Mia said offhandedly as the door closed behind her and she leaned against it to stare at Tarik and Phoenix.

On one hand, at least Mia was calm. On the other, Tarik wasn't so sure whether that was a good thing or a bad thing.

However, Tarik knew just what she was saying. According to what the most recent article had said — Landry's story shifting from Sid being the one to back out of the deal to basically Phoenix setting up the entire thing in order to bring Damien to his knees, which was horseshit all on its own — and knowing the shit that was going down with the legal team for the Austin Arrows … that *had been* far too easy. There was no doubt that Damien Landry was only there to stir up more shit. He probably wanted more attention than he was getting.

"What're you thinking?" Mia asked Phoenix as he turned and walked into Mia's living room. She shot Tarik a concerned glance before following.

Tarik took a minute to look around. The last time he'd been there, he hadn't spent much time checking things out. Other than noting how bright the space was and how it suited Mia perfectly, he hadn't paid much attention to the little things. He'd been more interested in *other* things. Now that it looked like they might be there for a little while, he took the time to admire what she'd done to the place.

It felt like her in every way. Light and airy, lots of color and life. It felt like a home.

Tarik knew his own condo would not make the pages of any designer magazines. He had little to nothing in his place, just enough to get by. Not that Tarik minded the extremely masculine decor of Phoenix's place, either, which was where he spent most of his time. It'd been that way since the first time Tarik had been there. Not much had changed, other than a trinket or two here and there — added by Ellen because Phoenix wasn't one for knickknacks and shit. It still made his place look like a room with walls and little else.

Even with the lack of color and furniture and knickknacks, it was a far cry from where Tarik had grown up. His parents had never owned a house, but they had rented plenty, usually skipping out without paying more than a couple months at a time. If that. Just as he'd told Mia, Tarik had changed schools more times than he could count, never settling into one place for too long. Grades had been the only thing he had focused on, and it wasn't until he was a freshman in high school that he didn't move around anymore.

His parents had had an unstable relationship from the get-go; neither of them had ever tried to deny that. In fact, there were plenty of nights he'd gone to sleep wondering why they were even together. They had hated each other, and the verbal and physical abuse — doled out by both of them — had been brutal. But then one day it had all stopped.

And so had the moving, but it wasn't until he'd graduated from high school that he'd gotten his own bedroom. College hadn't been an option, because Tarik had been tossed into the system without any family to take him in after they'd carted his father off. And maybe that was the real reason he was grateful for the security he felt with Phoenix. The lack of change didn't bother him in the least.

Unlike the bright, cheery room Mia slept in, Tarik's bedroom was just as monochromatic as the rest of his place, with black furniture, black sheets, and a black-and-gray comforter. Nothing fancy, just a place to sleep at night. A place he'd hoped to be sleeping less after the first night he'd spent with Phoenix and Mia, but as of yet, little had changed. He'd suspected Phoenix had needed space afterward, and that was exactly what he'd given him.

He was quickly growing tired of the space between them. All three of them. He wanted to eliminate it permanently, although he wasn't about to tell Mia or Phoenix that.

"Can I get you something to drink?" Mia offered as Phoenix took a seat on the cream-colored sofa with the brightly colored pillows.

"It's too early for what I'm thinking," Phoenix muttered as he rested his head in his hands while propping his elbows on his knees.

"Not if we put it in coffee," Mia teased. "Then it's fine."

Phoenix looked up at her to see if she was serious, and a smile tilted his lips for the first time since Tarik had walked out of Phoenix's office to find Teresa Somerhaus decorating the entryway with her too-fake appearance and her overabundance of perfume.

"Want to tell me what's going on?" Mia asked. "And yes, I've read all of the articles, I've watched the news, and I've listened to Damien's crap. For the record, I'm not buying any of it. It just doesn't make sense to me."

"It's all bullshit," Tarik assured her, glancing over at Phoenix to see if he was going to explain. He didn't look in any mood to talk, so Tarik continued. "No matter what Landry claims, Sid did not back out of any deal. There *wasn't* a deal. Ever. The man died nearly ten months ago, and this is way too fucking convenient. The question is why Landry is pulling this shit now. What prompted him to bring it up and try to push it?"

"It just seems too coincidental," Mia mentioned. "My marriage fell apart about the same time that your father passed," Mia told Phoenix. "Well, that's not coincidental. I think what happened with Damien and me is, though. He came home one night smelling like cheap perfume knowing that I would smell him. That was it for me. And now this. It just seems like he had a hand in moving things forward, so to speak. Did he set it up on purpose? Or is he using me? Or hell, is it *because* of me?"

Her questions were riddled with the same confusion Tarik felt when he tried to wrap his mind around what Landry was after.

"I don't know what he's after, but I know that it isn't *because* of you," Phoenix inserted. "Regardless, I'm not worried about it. He wants money. And if I have a say in the matter, he's not going to get a fucking penny from me."

Mia perched on the arm of the sofa and glanced between the two of them. "Do you know when Damien claims to have made this agreement with your father?"

"He hasn't been specific. I've heard a couple of months before my father died."

"So, again, it's convenient. Your father isn't here to deny Damien's claim."

"Correct. Landry's a fucking moron," Phoenix snapped as he got to his feet. "Even before my father died, I was a minority shareholder. I would've had a say in the matter. My father would've told me."

"So I don't understand what he could possibly think he can get out of this." Mia looked just as confused as Tarik felt.

"Do you think he's looking to get Mia back?" Tarik asked, sliding his hands into his pockets as he leaned against the wall, keeping his eye on the two of them. Mia was right, it was too coincidental. When Tarik and Damien had come face-to-face at the charity ball when he'd been dancing with Mia, the shit storm had begun.

"Why would he?" Mia questioned. "Honest to God, he's the one who wanted the divorce. Well, technically, I'm the one who filed, but I'd told him in the beginning that I didn't tolerate cheating. He cheated; he had to have seen it coming."

"If you don't mind me asking," Tarik said to Mia, "were things good before you found out he was cheating?"

"No," she said sadly. "Things started deteriorating long before that. We hardly spoke to one another. He would stay away on business, probably so he didn't have to see me."

Tarik frowned at Mia's admission. He hated that Damien would've treated her that way. If she belonged to him, Tarik would make sure she knew just how much she was wanted. Every damn day.

"I just don't understand what's spurring this," Phoenix commented. "Is he hurting for money?"

"That's a good question," Mia stated, causing them to both look her way. "Maybe he is. And I'm just speculating here. Damien never allowed me to know anything about his business. He claimed I didn't have the wherewithal to understand it, and I didn't argue with him. It was pointless. So, I honestly don't know, but it seems logical."

Tarik didn't know what seemed logical anymore. It was all fucked up, and he couldn't wrap his head around it.

"You know what?" Phoenix said, pacing toward them. "I just want to forget this even happened. For a little while."

"What'd you have in mind?" Mia asked, watching Phoenix as he moved closer.

Tarik didn't take his eyes off Phoenix as Phoenix stalked toward Mia, a determined expression on his face.

"Something that involves you naked."

Tarik's eyes darted to Mia to see her reaction. The sharp intake of breath was telling. She was probably thinking about what had happened between them a few nights ago, starting in this very room, and based on that expression, a replay wasn't a bad idea. Tarik had wanted a replay on Sunday, but with Phoenix gone, one thing had led to another and then... Tarik wouldn't trade that night for anything in the world.

Pushing off the wall, Tarik moved toward them.

"You're not gonna buy me lunch first?" Mia asked, breathless and not moving from her spot.

"If that's what it'll take," Phoenix said, grinning.

Mia shook her head. "I'm suddenly not hungry. Not for food, anyway."

455

Phoenix lowered himself to the couch and pulled Mia to him. She tumbled on top of him, straddling his hips as their mouths met. Tarik could see the pent-up energy that Phoenix was working to hold back as his eager hands slid beneath her shirt, caressing the smooth expanse of her back. Phoenix might claim he wasn't worried about Landry, but the proof was in the way he was holding himself.

And Tarik knew just what to do to take his mind off of it.

»»»»»♥«««««

PHOENIX COULD FEEL the tension coursing just beneath his skin. Touching Mia was about the only thing that had come close to calming him in the last hour, but even then, it was a different type of calm. He wasn't sure he could be gentle with Mia, but he damn sure was willing to try. If he didn't find a way to release some of the frustration that the morning's events had brought on, he was going to implode.

"Quit thinking," Mia said, cupping his face and pulling her lips from his. She stared back at him, studying him.

"I'm trying," he said honestly. He didn't want to think. At the moment, he just wanted to feel.

"I need to take care of something," Tarik said, drawing Phoenix's gaze to him.

Mia twisted to look at him as well.

"What?"

"Don't worry. I'll be back. You two have fun." With that, Tarik leaned over and kissed Mia. It wasn't just an innocent peck on the lips, either, but Tarik didn't linger for too long.

Meeting Tarik's hard gaze, Phoenix tried to figure out what his angle was but then gave up. He didn't have the brainpower at the moment, and if Tarik wanted to excuse himself and leave Mia all for Phoenix, then so be it.

Tarik left without another word, leaving Phoenix alone with Mia, something he'd been longing for. After he'd learned that Mia and Tarik had made love on his sofa on Sunday evening while he'd been occupied conversing with his mother, he'd been anxious to get Mia alone. Not because he was jealous but because he wanted to have her all to himself for a little while. Something had changed in Tarik since that night, and Phoenix wanted to know why.

Secretly, he wanted a little piece of it for himself.

"Why are you looking at me like that?" Mia asked, her voice soft and sweet.

"Because you're so easy to look at," he told her sincerely.

Her cheeks turned a soft rosy color before she leaned forward and pressed her lips to his. Phoenix got lost in her kiss, the gentle way she moved against him, the urgent feel of her tongue against his. And then it dawned on him as he pulled back, cradling Mia's face in his hands and staring back at her ... Tarik had left them alone on purpose.

Phoenix would have to thank him for that.

"Now where were we?" Phoenix cupped the back of Mia's head, bringing her lips to his once more. She opened for him easily, a slow, gentle glide of her tongue against his. He lingered there, sliding his fingers through the cool silk of her hair, brushing his thumb over her jaw, tasting the sweetness of her mouth. He felt a calm wash over him, but that didn't last long when Mia inched closer, rubbing the heat of her pussy against the rigid length of his cock.

Without asking questions, Phoenix let his hands slide down her chest, easing between them, pushing his hand into the stretchy material of her yoga pants. God bless spandex. He needed to feel her slick heat against his fingers, his mouth, his cock. He wanted to spend the next hour making her beg and plead for him to let her come.

A heavy exhale escaped her when his fingers dipped into her pants, finding her warm and wet and ready for him.

"I think we need more room," he muttered against her mouth as he inched toward the edge of the couch and then used his legs to lift them both. Mia's legs wrapped around his hips as he carried her to her bedroom.

Making his way to the bed, Phoenix lowered her to the mattress, but he didn't join her immediately, taking a minute to admire the space. The last time he'd been there, it had been dark, and when he and Tarik had left that next morning, he hadn't wanted to linger, so that he didn't wake Mia.

White bedding accented with neon-green-trimmed pillows, and matching curtains offset the dark wood furniture and hardwood floors. Just as bright and cheery as the rest of her place, and she looked so at ease as she stared back at him from her bed.

When she held out her hand for him, he shook his head, grinning. "Lie down," he instructed.

She leaned back on her elbows, her legs dangling over the edge of the bed as she stared at him, a sexy grin tugging at her mouth.

Knowing there was only one way to get to where he wanted to be, Phoenix made quick work of stripping them both, but he still didn't join her on the bed once they were naked. Instead, he tossed a condom from his wallet onto the bedspread and, after admiring her for a minute longer, knelt on the floor between her legs, pushing her thighs apart as he let his gaze linger on her face, then slowly travel down her body to the glistening pink folds of her sex.

"Phoenix."

"Yes?" he asked as he leaned in and blew warm air against her folds, using his fingers to separate the glistening lips of her bare pussy, exposing the little bundle of nerves that he was aiming for. Using the tip of his tongue, he slid over her clit slowly, his eyes still locked with hers.

"You're a tease," she whispered, her feet coming to rest on his shoulders, her knees falling to the side, opening her fully to his gaze and his tongue.

"Such a pretty pussy," he said, admiring the soft pink flesh before looking back up at her. Her eyes dilated as he spoke, the musky scent of her arousal flooding his senses, making him punch-drunk on desire. "I've been dying to taste you again."

And that's what he did, but he didn't rush, didn't try to send her flying over the edge yet. He wanted to savor her, to listen to her sweet moans and urgent cries for more. He continued to eat her while inserting one finger into her slickness, teasing her at first before pushing in deep.

"Phoenix. Oh, God, I need more," she groaned, clearly not happy with his torment.

He gave her more, suckling her clit while he added another finger, fucking her slowly as she began rocking her hips toward him, trying to urge him deeper. Controlling the depth and the pace, Phoenix continued to watch her as she remained propped up, her hooded gaze intently focused on where his lips pressed against her heated sex.

"It's not enough," she whispered. "Not nearly enough."

Relenting, Phoenix thrust two fingers into her while he suckled her clit, flicking it with the end of his tongue, over and over until she was writhing on the bed, her fingers digging into the comforter, her feet pushing against his shoulders as he brought her dangerously close to the precipice. He considered making her wait, but the urgency in her cries had him pushing her higher and higher until she screamed his name as her climax tore through her, her pussy gripping his fingers as she came.

Getting to his feet slowly, admiring the way she looked sated and sexy lying against the white comforter, Phoenix had intended to climb on the bed with her, wanting to taste every inch of her, but Mia somehow managed to head him off before he got there. She sat up quickly, reaching for his cock and bringing her lips to the head before he knew what she was doing.

She took him in her mouth, teasing the tip. When she pulled back, he placed his fingers on her lips. "Suck them. I want you to taste yourself," he ordered. Mia took his fingers into her mouth, her tongue darting over them, licking them. She looked so fucking sexy as she cleaned him. "Now take my dick in your mouth again."

Mia released his fingers and then pressed her lips against the sensitive head of his cock, her fingers wrapped around the base as she sucked him into the blazing hot depths of her mouth. He loved the way her tongue laved the tip, sliding under the crest, as though she were trying to memorize the feel of him in her mouth.

"Mia," he hissed, sliding his fingers into her hair. He was already hard and aching, desperately wanting to give her as much pleasure before he took his buried in the hot depths of her pussy, but the way she sucked him into her mouth wasn't helping his cause. His head began to spin as the pleasure rocked him, her persistent tongue sliding over his shaft, her smooth fingers cupping his balls as she continued to lick him.

"Mmmm."

Her soft hum had his balls tightening. He'd been waiting for this moment — being alone with her — dreaming about it, and now she was going to push him over the edge before he was ready.

Realizing he had better regain control or they were going to be done far too soon, Phoenix gripped her hair harder and pulled her head back, freeing his cock from the heaven of her mouth.

Her eyes slid up to meet his, a mischievous gleam in them.

"Naughty girl," he said. "It's still your turn."

"I was taking my turn."

Crushing his mouth to hers, he crowded her as he crawled up onto the bed, forcing her down until she was on her back and he was settling between her legs. He kept his mouth fused with hers, letting her taste herself on his lips as he positioned himself above her.

When he pulled back, Phoenix smirked as he knelt between her spread thighs, propping his upper body above her on one hand resting beside her head, the other sliding between her thighs, teasing her folds. He flicked her clit with his finger before sliding lower and then pushing two fingers into her.

Mia's eyes closed, her head digging into the mattress as her hips came forward, meeting the thrust of his hand.

"You like that?" he asked.

"Yes."

"Do you want my cock inside you, Mia? Fucking you slowly?"

She didn't answer, just another groan.

"Or do you want it hard and fast?"

"Hard," she cried out as he began finger fucking her faster, deeper.

Phoenix saw the hunger in her eyes as she stared back at him, and he couldn't resist. Ripping open the condom and rolling it over himself, he flipped Mia onto her stomach, drawing a surprised squeal from her. He pulled her hips up, forcing her onto her knees, and then guided himself into her without so much as a warning.

She was so wet, so hot, he bit his lip as her pussy sheathed him like a silk glove.

"Fuck," he groaned, leaning over her as he paused, still pushing into the tight recesses of her body.

"Don't stop," Mia begged, trying to push back against him. He was surrounding her small body, his arms bracketing her head, his hips pressed against her ass, his abdomen pressed against the warmth of her back. She wasn't in control. Much.

"I don't plan to, baby." That was only a partial lie. He did plan to continue, just as soon as he caught his breath. Driving his hips forward, he pushed into her, going deeper, the tight clasp of her pussy gripping him.

Once he was balls deep inside her, Phoenix gripped her shoulder with one hand to hold her where he wanted her, his other keeping him propped above her as he began to thrust. He'd wanted to be gentle with her, but the overwhelming need to possess her took over. He began driving into her, the bed rocking with every punishing thrust of his hips against her sweet ass.

"Oh, God, yes," she cried out, her hand lying atop his where he held her shoulder, that small connection making his balls draw up against his body. "Harder, Phoenix."

He gave her what she asked for, pummeling her over and over, faster and faster until the motion was a blur. The pleasure was generating a heat so intense, so powerful, sweat beaded on his forehead.

"So fucking tight." Pressing her shoulder blades down to the bed, Phoenix gripped her hips and changed the angle, her cunt strangling his dick in the most exquisite way. He didn't stop, continuing to pound into her, his cock tunneling through her tight, wet depths until he was blinded by the pleasure.

"I'm coming, Phoenix!" Her orgasm gripped her before he was ready, her muscles locking on him, milking him until he couldn't stop his own climax.

He roared his release, still pounding into her until his legs felt like liquid and he fell to the bed, careful not to crush her as he did.

"Holy crap," she mumbled as she snuggled up against him, breathing hard. "That was … amazing."

A smile tipped his lips. "You can say that again."

»»»»»♥«««««

MIA WAS BONELESS and sated and… God, she couldn't even begin to describe the incredible feeling that had washed over her after that … whatever *that* was. It was just as she'd said: amazing.

So maybe her sexual history was limited to one man before Tarik and Phoenix, but even then, she hadn't realized sex could be that liberating. It wasn't the same as making love to Tarik, which had transcended anything she'd ever known, but in a different way. This had been freeing in a way that she hadn't expected. Phoenix had given her exactly what she'd asked for, not being gentle about it, either. She'd needed that from him, needed to know that he didn't want to wrap her in velvet and keep her safely ensconced there.

"You all right?" Phoenix asked.

"Mmm hmm." Mia drew circles over the hard planes of Phoenix's smooth chest as she smiled to herself.

Something had clicked in her, and she felt … what it was exactly, she couldn't pinpoint, but it was definitely something. Even after having sex with Phoenix and Tarik together, it hadn't made her feel that sense of empowerment that she'd felt this time.

They'd needed this — her and Phoenix. The alone time. The same as she'd needed it with Tarik. There was a deeper connection that formed between the three of them. At least as far as she was concerned.

Mia admired Phoenix's lean body as she listened to the rapid thump of his heart beneath her ear. The only thing she knew for a fact was that she was beginning to crave the way Tarik and Phoenix made her feel. For the first time in her life, she felt as though she was finally in control of her own life, her own decisions.

And above all else, she was in control of her heart.

Chapter Thirty-Five

TARIK FOLLOWED PHOENIX into Pierce Industries' main office the following morning just after eight o'clock. After dropping Mia at school, they'd driven in silence, Phoenix spending most of his time tapping the screen on his cell phone, probably checking the millions of emails he was riddled with on a daily basis.

Whatever it took to keep him calm, that was all Tarik really cared about.

They were heading into the office to meet with Damien Landry. According to Phil, Landry and his lawyer wanted to have a discussion about options, since it was clear Phoenix wasn't giving an inch on Damien's demands.

The whole thing reeked of desperation on Landry's part. None of it made sense, and when Tarik had talked to Phil on the phone yesterday, trying to come up with a time for the meeting, the lawyer pretty much said it was all nonsense and a complete waste of time. There was still no proof, which meant Damien was stalling. And lying.

Tarik agreed, but there was something Landry wasn't telling anyone, which was the only reason he had convinced Phoenix to listen to what the man had to say. He wanted a little more time to dig into the details. He'd started yesterday, and he was pretty sure he'd stumbled upon something interesting. Something telling.

Pulling into the parking garage, Tarik parked in the designated parking spot and wasted no time climbing out and following Phoenix into the building. A few minutes later, they stepped out of the elevator on the fifth floor, passing the empty conference room where the meeting would take place in about half an hour. Without saying a word, Tarik headed into his office while Phoenix disappeared into his own.

He hadn't been at his desk for more than five minutes when his cell phone rang. He snapped it off his hip and glanced at the screen, only a little concerned when he saw Mia's phone number.

"Hey, love," he greeted her, trying not to reflect his worry in his tone.

"Do you have a minute?" she asked.

"Sure. What's up?" Tarik glanced up at his open office door and considered closing it but didn't want Phoenix to question him.

"I did some thinking last night. After y'all left. So I called a guy who used to work for Damien. His name's Harrison Abbott. He's an accountant. He and Damien had a falling out less than a year ago, right about the time everything seemed to start."

An accountant? Interesting.

"Was he willing to talk?" Tarik asked.

"He wouldn't say much over the phone, so I didn't push it last night. Well, I couldn't let it go, so I called him a few minutes ago to see if he'd be willing to go to lunch. I'm meeting him at eleven thirty."

"Today?" Tarik sat up straight.

"Yeah."

"Mia, do you know this guy?"

"Yes," she said, but he heard the uncertainty in her tone. "We're not exactly friends, but I have spoken to him a number of times. I'll meet him at a public place, I promise. I just want to ask him a few questions about Damien's company finances. It seems logical that money is at the root of this."

Tarik hated for Mia to do this, but after the information he'd pulled yesterday, he had to believe he might know just where she needed to look. "Okay, Mia, but here's what I need you to ask him."

Twenty minutes later, without a minute to spare, Tarik hung up the phone with Mia, got Phoenix a cup of coffee, and met him in the conference room. Phil was already there, but Landry and his lawyer had yet to show up.

"We good?" Phoenix asked Phil.

Phil nodded. "This is just to get a better understanding of what Landry is really after. To bring you both up to speed, he hasn't produced documentation yet, probably because it doesn't exist. But once he can tell us what he wants, we can decide where to go from there."

"I really need to give the press an update," Tarik informed them. "Hoping we can agree on something when we're finished here."

Phoenix nodded as Tarik watched him. Phoenix was acting strange. As though he'd withdrawn into himself, not ready to deal with all the shit that was going on. It bothered him, but not as his bodyguard or as his assistant or anything else business-related. It bothered him as Phoenix's lover, as the man who cared about him, the man who…

God, he wasn't even sure he knew how it all worked, but Tarik had a feeling that he *loved* him.

Tarik wanted to beat Landry to a bloody pulp just to relieve some of the stress Phoenix was having to deal with. He knew that the pain of losing his father was still fresh, still raw. It pissed him off that Landry was using that as his bargaining chip.

A sudden knock on the door had Tarik glancing up. He pushed off the wall where he'd been standing and opened the door, allowing Landry inside. He was with three other men. None of them looked familiar to Tarik.

Phil stood, his eyes slowly assessing the three men.

Landry introduced them. "This is Bill, Ed, and Steve, my legal team."

The whole *team* had to join him today? Landry certainly couldn't do things the easy way.

Phoenix didn't bother looking up as the four men took their seats around the table. Tarik moved to stand behind Phoenix once more, off to the right side enough that he could see Phoenix's face, Phil sitting to Phoenix's left.

"Phoenix," Landry prompted.

Phoenix's head barely lifted. "You can address Phil about anything you need."

Without hesitation, Phoenix returned his gaze to the phone in his hand.

"This is bullshit," Landry declared. "We need to get this settled. I'm tired of the reporters camping out in front of my office looking for a statement. I'm sick of them bringing to my attention the fact that my wife is currently in bed with you."

The last statement had Phoenix's head snapping up, his body going rigid. "First of all, she's your *ex*-wife. Second, you shouldn't have sicced them on us if you didn't want to deal with the fucking reporters."

"Look," Phil began, his tone calm as he addressed Landry. "I don't think we're going to get anywhere until we understand what it is that you're looking for. You originally claimed that Sid verbally agreed to sell, and now you've stated that Sid Pierce agreed to sell the Austin Arrows to you on paper and then backed out of the deal, yet you haven't produced any documentation substantiating your claim. On top of that, even if you had, the sale didn't finalize; therefore, Phoenix has made it clear he has no intention of selling."

"I think it's in the best interest of both parties to come to a final decision on how to handle this. Mr. Landry isn't looking to purchase the team anymore. He's interested in a settlement for his time, along with pain and suffering," Bill-Ed-Steve said.

Tarik had no idea who was who, but the one in the middle spoke kindly, yet he didn't make eye contact with Phil or Phoenix. "Sid Pierce obviously was interested in selling at some point. We feel that honoring his wishes would be beneficial to both parties, and settling with Mr. Landry is pertinent."

Tarik didn't have to be looking at Phoenix to see the fury that resonated in his eyes. He could sense it in the way his breathing changed, in the way his muscles tensed. Phoenix pushed to his feet slowly, a deadly calm coming over him. "If you know what's best for you, or your client, you'll stand up, turn around, and walk out of my office right now. Don't think on it too long, because I assure you that you won't like what happens next."

Not surprisingly, Bill-Ed-Steve all three got to their feet instantly. The only jackass who didn't move was Landry. Tarik moved to stand closer to Phoenix, directly behind Phil, making sure Landry knew he was there.

Bill-Ed-Steve disappeared out the door as Landry was getting to his feet. The man obviously had balls of steel, because he leaned forward and lowered his voice as he said, "We can do this the easy way or the hard way, Pierce. Your choice."

"Humor me," Phoenix said, his voice hard as steel. "What's your version of the easy way?"

"First, you agree to my settlement request. I'll even return to my original requested amount of five million. Second, you leave Mia alone."

Phoenix leaned in slowly. "Looks like you're gonna get the hard way then, doesn't it? Now get the fuck out of my office."

Landry had the good sense to back up as Phoenix's voice rose, the anger in his tone echoing off the walls.

Once Landry was out the door, Tarik urged Phil to follow, asking him to close the door behind him. Tarik moved across the room and flipped the lock, ensuring they had a few minutes of privacy. Only then did he take a seat and give Phoenix a minute to burn off some of the pressure that was weighing down on him.

»»»»»»♥«««««««

"WHERE'S MIA?" PHOENIX asked Tarik when the rage that boiled inside him managed to cool to a simmer. It was a testament to his sheer determination that Landry wasn't dead on the floor in the conference room.

"She's meeting with an accountant for lunch," Tarik said.

It wasn't *what* he said but *how* he said it that had Phoenix looking at him, trying to read between the lines.

"Care to elaborate?" Phoenix encouraged when he couldn't figure out the riddle.

"Harrison Abbott," Tarik explained. "Used to work for Landry. According to Mia, Abbott and Landry had a falling out about ten months ago, when all this started. She's going to see if she can get any information from him that might be beneficial to us."

Phoenix knew that look on Tarik's face. He wasn't telling him something. Taking a deep breath, Phoenix lowered himself into the chair opposite Tarik and glared at him. "What the hell's going on?"

Tarik didn't bother trying to pretend he didn't know what Phoenix was talking about. Instead, he rested his forearms on the table and stared back at Phoenix. "Yesterday, when I left you and Mia alone, I did some digging. I started looking at all the business deals Landry's been involved in for the past year. Something had to spur Landry to make this claim, for whatever reason. I think he's hurting for money, so I figured that was a good start. I found something interesting."

Phoenix cocked an eyebrow, waiting.

"Landry invested in a casino opportunity in Vegas," Tarik said, watching Phoenix.

Clearly the other man wanted Phoenix to put two and two together, but he was having a hard time. He had no idea what he was talking about. Phoenix's real estate investments were limited to Texas by his own choice, not to mention, he had no desire to invest in the gambling industry, so of course, he wasn't up to speed on any Vegas opportunities. "And? Is that supposed to mean something to me?"

"It made the news about ten months ago. The group behind the investment went bankrupt before the casino even broke ground," Tarik informed him. "My guess is that Landry got caught up in that. Probably lost a pretty penny."

"And Mia's talking to the accountant about this?"

"I explained my suspicions to her and told her to bring it up. See if Abbott knows anything."

"Fuck." Phoenix thrust his hands through his hair. "And why the fuck did you think that was a good idea?"

"This was her idea. I don't control what she does," Tarik said, defensively. "She at least called to let me know."

There was that. Although it didn't make Phoenix feel any better. At all.

Leaning closer to Tarik, Phoenix met his unwavering gaze. "I want this shit buried. Got it? And I don't want Mia dragged into it anymore."

Tarik nodded affirmatively, his eyes hard, his expression harder. Phoenix knew he didn't have to tell Phoenix that Mia was the most important thing here. Whatever Landry wanted, he wasn't above using Mia to get it. Unfortunately for Landry, he was going to have to come up with another plan, because that was the last damn thing Phoenix was going to allow to happen.

This shit had gone on long enough.

"Find out where she is," Phoenix said, getting to his feet. "And let's go talk to Abbott ourselves."

Phoenix made it to the door, his hand on the knob when Tarik met him, crowding him. Before he knew what was happening, Tarik's entire hand was gripping his chin firmly and his mouth was claiming his. Not caring where they were, Phoenix gave in, pressing his mouth to Tarik's, kissing him back, thrusting his tongue into his mouth. Calm washed over him, as it always did when Tarik took the reins.

"We'll figure this out," Tarik said softly when he pulled back, releasing Phoenix. "One way or the other."

Phoenix nodded and adjusted his suit jacket before turning the knob and leaving Tarik behind.

»»»»»❤«««««

"THANKS FOR MEETING me," Mia told Harrison when they were seated at a small table at the back of the café. The place was busy with the lunch crowd descending, but they'd managed to get a table.

"Sure," Harrison said, looking around as though someone might be watching him.

That was quite possible, although Mia doubted they were watching Harrison. She'd felt eyes on her ever since she'd left campus to meet Harrison. She wasn't sure the reporters were lurking, either. However, she had brushed off the notion that someone would be following her and made her way to the café where Harrison had agreed to meet.

"What can I get you to drink?" the harried waitress asked as she came to an abrupt stop beside their table, a pad and pencil in her hand.

"I'll take iced tea," Mia said, glancing over at Harrison.

"Water's fine," he mumbled.

"Be right back," the woman declared as she headed off as fast as she'd come.

"So what did you want to talk about?" Harrison questioned when they were once again alone.

Mia could tell he was nervous. She wanted to assure him that everything would be fine, but she didn't have a clue what she was getting herself into. "How are you?" she asked, hoping to ease into it.

Harrison looked around once before his weary brown eyes met hers. "Mia, I know you didn't just come to check on my well-being."

"Why would you think that?" she asked.

His eyebrow quirked.

"Okay, fine," she muttered, looking down at the table. "Do you know who Phoenix Pierce is?"

Harrison's eyes widened, but he didn't answer her.

"I take that as a yes. Well, it seems that Damien has an issue with him."

"The lawsuit," Harrison muttered.

"Yeah," Mia stated, watching Harrison closely. Clearly he was familiar with what was going on. At least from a news perspective. "I don't know exactly what Damien's after, or why, but … well … let's just say he's been stirring up shit, and he's dragged me into the middle of it. I don't know if it's relevant or not, but I thought maybe you could enlighten me on what happened between you and Damien."

Harrison immediately shook his head. "Nothing happened. We just had a disagreement, and I decided to go my own way."

"Right," she said, not believing him for a second. "Look. You don't have to talk to me if you don't want to, Harrison, but I'd appreciate if you didn't lie to me. We can sit right here and have a nice lunch just like friends. Or you can help me out, and maybe, just maybe, you'll get some closure on whatever happened between you and Damien."

The waitress came by with their drinks and then asked for their order. Mia rattled off hers and Harrison followed. When she walked away, they sat staring at one another once again, neither of them saying anything. The normal busy sounds of the café rang loudly around them, the clank of silverware against glass and the drone of voices as everyone spoke at once. Every now and then, a loud voice would call out an order from the kitchen, causing the racket to dim slightly before it resumed once again.

Mia took a sip of her tea, wondering if Harrison really was going to avoid her question. But then, with his hands wrapped around his water glass, he met her gaze.

"About a year ago, Damien came to me to talk about an investment opportunity. A casino in Vegas. He was excited, wanted to pursue it sight unseen."

Looked like Tarik was on the right track. Mia nodded, encouraging him to continue.

"He asked me to go with him to Vegas. Invited my wife, as well. We made a weekend of it just to check it out. We met with a group who claimed to be leading the charge. Damien's excitement intensified."

Mia tried to remember when Damien had gone to Las Vegas. He'd gone on plenty of trips, but never had he mentioned he was going to Vegas. "He was interested?" Mia asked.

"Highly. I told him to give me a little time. I wanted to have someone look into the company's background, check out their financials. All normal stuff. He insisted that he'd already done that and this was a gold mine. He wanted to get in on the ground floor, aiming to take a larger share. He even mentioned moving to Vegas, resuming his business there."

Mia wondered if Damien had gotten caught up in the glitz and glamor associated with Sin City.

"I got very little research done. While we were still in Vegas, I reached out to a couple of people on my staff, had them do some number crunching to see if this was even a possibility for Damien. At the time, Damien's company was showing a continued profit, but when I was reviewing some of the reports, I noticed something strange. What we thought was continued growth actually wasn't correct. There was a glaring error in the numbers that I looked at. Turned out, DL Properties had a trending loss for a few months."

"Damien was losing money?"

"Yeah," Harrison confirmed, taking a sip of his water. Mia noticed that he didn't meet her eyes when he continued.

"The falling out happened while we were in Vegas…" Harrison glanced up toward the door, his eyes widening. Mia turned to see what he was looking at, and that was when she noticed two incredibly attractive, albeit extremely determined-looking, men stalking toward them.

Good grief. If Harrison hadn't been on edge before, he certainly would be now. Hell, just looking at Phoenix made her nervous. He did not appear happy that she was having lunch with Harrison.

Neither man bothered to introduce himself as they took seats at the table, their attention fully directed toward her.

"Hi," she said hesitantly, glancing back and forth between Tarik and Phoenix.

"You forgot to invite us to lunch," Phoenix said sternly. Only then did his eyes move to Harrison. "Phoenix Pierce. You must be Harrison."

Harrison nodded.

"Please continue; we didn't mean to interrupt."

Mia laughed. "You didn't mean to interrupt, huh? Then why are you sitting here?" she asked, trying to keep her voice down. She'd just been getting somewhere with Harrison. She doubted he would continue with Tarik and Phoenix now glaring at him.

"Harrison, I'd like you to meet Phoenix and Tarik. They're…" She didn't know how to finish that sentence.

"Her boyfriends," Phoenix inserted, surprising Mia to the roots of her hair. Had he really just said that?

Harrison's eyes widened, proof that she hadn't been hearing things.

The table was silent for a moment, and Mia knew she had better do something or Harrison was going to bolt. As it was, he looked incredibly uncomfortable.

"Harrison was explaining how he and Damien had a falling out."

Tarik turned his hardened gaze on her at that point, and Mia nodded, letting him know that his original suspicions had been accurate.

"We aren't here to make things difficult for you," Tarik said, his tone even, although it held a dangerous edge to it. "As you can imagine, we're a little concerned about Mia's … safety. Please, do continue."

The waitress interrupted once more, bringing their food and taking an order from Phoenix and Tarik as though this were a normal lunch date for the four of them. Mia wasn't hungry, but she did want Harrison to continue, so she started eating, trying to keep things casual. As casual as possible, considering.

"Harrison," she said softly, "I really would like to hear what you have to say."

Harrison nodded, his eyes dropping to his plate as he opened his mouth, closed it. He took a deep breath and then cleared his throat. "We were having dinner in Vegas. My wife was there with me and…" Harrison looked up then, hesitantly casting a look at Phoenix, then Tarik. "Damien was there with Teresa Somerhaus."

Mia's harsh intake of breath had all three men looking at her.

"I'm sorry, Mia. I should've told you."

"Yes, you should have," Tarik growled.

"It's just… Things weren't that simple." Harrison looked at her again, remorse in his dark brown eyes, and continued, "It was that night that I told Damien to hold off on pursuing the casino investment and gave him a few details about my suspicions on *his* financials. I hadn't even had a chance to look into the group backing the casino. He got pissed, told me I didn't know what I was talking about. It was very volatile. Turned out, Damien had already moved forward without the consent of those who worked for him. It was an emotional decision. That I was certain of."

"Damien invested in the casino without having all of the details? Or the money?" Mia asked, surprised. Damien had always been so level-headed.

"Yes. I tried to encourage him to wait. I even informed him in detail about the problem, not in so many words. Teresa was paying close attention to everything I said. Oddly, Damien told me not to worry about it. Told me mistakes happened and it wasn't a big deal. He was sure that it could be fixed. I knew immediately that something was off. First of all, a mistake of that nature should've been grounds for termination. Since I was ultimately responsible for missing the error, it should've been my head on the chopping block.

"Needing my job, I dismissed Damien's nonchalant response. He quickly changed the subject that night. I was already suspicious, but I let it go."

"So Damien *was* having financial problems before then?" Phoenix inquired, sitting back in his chair, looking as though he didn't have a care in the world. Mia knew better. He was hanging on Harrison's every word.

481

"Looked that way," Harrison confirmed, hardening his gaze as he looked at Phoenix. "But I quickly learned, the following week, that Damien already knew that, which was how he ended up in bed, so to speak, with Teresa. He was looking to partner with her father."

"Because he lacked the funds?" Tarik questioned.

Harrison nodded. "Someone was trying to cover it up. He called me into his office that week and asked for my honest opinion on the Vegas deal. I told him that it wasn't a financially sound decision at the moment, considering the errors I'd found. This time he got really pissed. Told me this was unacceptable, that he was working with Teresa's father on the Vegas investment; they were both moving forward. Informed me that I needed to find a way to fix the problem immediately. Basically, he asked me to make it go away. Things got tense at that point."

"Make it go away? How is that possible? It's not like you can just summon money from the sky. If he didn't have it, he didn't have it," Mia stated. "I don't understand."

"Neither did I."

Chapter Thirty-Six

TARIK SAT BACK and watched the interaction between Harrison and Mia. Although he and Phoenix had crashed their little lunch date, he was doing his best to pretend he was invisible. More for Harrison's sake. The man clearly had some secrets, and he wasn't above sharing them with Mia. It was just a damn good thing the man looked remorseful or Tarik would've punched him in the fucking face at this point.

The bastard had known that Damien was cheating on Mia from the beginning. He would've been her proof, netting her the additional ten mil that the prenup had declared was hers in the event Landry was unfaithful. Mia didn't seem concerned about the money, though, and that had him paying close attention to her. No, she seemed more concerned about getting information that would help Phoenix, although the man she was talking to had known the fate of her marriage long before she had.

He wondered if Phoenix noticed. Likely, since the guy was pretty damn perceptive. However, Phoenix was being equally silent, allowing Harrison to spill his guts.

"So is that why you no longer work for him?" Mia questioned.

"Damien became obsessed with the Vegas property. He went off on tangents that this could be the biggest deal of his lifetime."

"How did my father play into this?" Phoenix asked.

Harrison turned his attention back to Phoenix. "I don't know exactly. I do know that Damien mentioned running into Sid at one of the Arrows games. Before the Vegas deal, he'd had an obsession with hockey. Wanted to own a team. He went on and on that he'd had a conversation with the Arrows owner. I joked that he should offer to buy the Arrows and then he wouldn't need the Vegas investment."

Phoenix's gaze hardened. "Did he or did he not make a deal with my father?"

Tarik already knew the answer to that question, as did Phoenix. Evidently Phoenix was looking for confirmation.

"I have no idea, honestly. Damien's obsessions multiplied, and for the next few weeks, while I was still employed, he mentioned wanting to own the team once again. Said it would be a solid investment. I laughed it off, considering he'd said the same thing about the Vegas opportunity, but he seemed serious. Then" — Harrison looked back at Mia — "Mia asked for a divorce, and all hell broke loose."

"But you said Damien was already out of control," Phoenix mentioned.

"He was, but when Mia left him, he became someone different. Someone I'd never seen before. Within a few days, he fired me."

Tarik noticed the sadness reflected on Harrison's face. He only questioned the look because he couldn't imagine that he was upset that Damien had let him go after all the hell he'd been put through. "Did something else happen?" Tarik asked.

"Yes," Harrison said, looking up, his eyes hard. "My wife informed me that she'd cheated. With Damien."

Mia gasped and Tarik automatically reached for her hand.

"After Mia left him?" Phoenix asked, his tone serious.

"No. She … had apparently been sleeping with him for a while. According to her."

If it hadn't been for the fact that he was holding Mia's hand, he would've balled up his fist. Not only had Harrison known about Damien and Teresa, but he'd also known his own wife had had an affair with Damien. "I take it the two of you weren't really friends." Tarik nodded between Harrison and Mia. "If you were, I'd like to think he would've shared this information with you. Before now," Tarik said snidely, his eyes locked on Harrison.

"I confronted Damien about it. Not only did he fire me but he'd been knowingly screwing my wife," Harrison retorted angrily. "Damien threatened to announce that I'd intentionally made the accounting error," Harrison added quickly. "He informed me that if I said one word about what had gone down in Vegas, or that he'd been cheating, I'd lose my CPA license."

Mia was silent, as was Phoenix, but Tarik could see that he was fuming. He was probably trying to keep himself in check the same way Tarik was.

"Is there anything else I can get you?" the waitress asked as she made a drive-by.

"The check," Phoenix said harshly.

The woman nodded warily, pulling a pad of paper out of her pocket. When she went to hand it to Phoenix, he pointed to Harrison. "He'll be picking up the tab today."

Harrison didn't bother to argue. If Tarik had to guess, the guy felt bad about what he'd done to Mia; however, that still didn't make it right, in his opinion.

"Thank you for the information," Phoenix said, taking Mia's hand and helping her up. She went willingly, her expression sad.

Tarik allowed them to move away from the table before he leaned in to Harrison. "I'm sure you're a nice guy, but you're damn lucky I haven't laid you out flat on that floor for what you did to Mia. It's in your best interest to find a way to make amends." Tarik got to his feet. "And I suggest you fucking do it soon."

Harrison nodded his head as Tarik turned and walked away.

»»»»»» ♥ «««««

FORTY FIVE MINUTES later, the three of them were walking into Phoenix's condo. It would've taken less time, but the stupid elevator had taken its own sweet fucking time. Apparently, the damn thing wasn't on the same timeline Phoenix was. Ever since Harrison's admissions, he'd been hard-pressed not to punch the fucking wall. His anger was at a boiling point. He could attribute his ability to maintain his composure to the fact that Mia was there, seemingly still processing all that Harrison had told her at lunch.

"Don't sit down," Tarik commanded when Phoenix headed right for the sofa in the living room. He turned and looked at his lover, trying to figure out just what he had in mind. He couldn't quite pinpoint what Tarik was going to do, but right there in those glittering gold eyes was just what Phoenix needed. There was no softness there. There wasn't any fear of hurting Tarik the way he worried with Mia.

With a minimum amount of hesitation, knowing his control was about to be stripped from him and there wasn't a damn thing he could do about it, Phoenix remained on his feet, but he didn't do anything more.

"Lose the jacket, shirt, and tie," Tarik instructed, followed by, "Mia, come here, love."

Phoenix shrugged out of his jacket, loosened his tie, and then unbuttoned his shirt as he watched Tarik. When he rid himself of the shirt, he tossed it onto the arm of the sofa with his jacket and then placed his arms down at his sides.

Mia came to stand in front of Tarik, both of them facing him, Tarik behind her.

"For the next few minutes, I want you to forget everything that Harrison told you. Understand?" Tarik asked Mia, his voice soft as he spoke close to her ear.

Mia nodded, her eyes locked with Phoenix's.

Tarik's hands moved around to Mia's chest, plucking one button on her white blouse from its mooring. He continued down her chest, moving slowly as he looked down at her. Phoenix couldn't do anything other than watch the show. When she leaned against Tarik, raising her arms to wrap around behind his neck, causing the shirt to open, the creamy skin of her stomach coming into view, he found himself transfixed on her.

Once all the buttons were released, Tarik easily lifted the cotton up and off her arms, tossing it away while Mia returned her hands to his neck, still facing Phoenix.

"Do you see the way he's looking at you, Mia?" Tarik asked her.

Mia nodded.

"That's the look of a man who would give anything to be with you."

Phoenix instantly realized what Tarik was doing. He was reinforcing for Mia just how much she was wanted. Just how much they needed her. "I want you more than my next breath," Phoenix admitted, his voice coming out laced with the emotion he felt for her.

Phoenix wanted to lean forward and place his mouth on her breasts, suck her nipples between his lips through the sheer white bra that still covered her. He wanted to wrap her in his arms and never fucking let her go.

All of the shit he'd listened to from Harrison had reinforced Phoenix's hatred for Landry. How the bastard had ever managed to be with Mia was beyond him. Landry didn't deserve her, never deserved her.

Tarik's big hands slid down her chest, stopping to gently knead the glorious mounds before continuing lower until he reached the button on her jeans. He quickly flipped it free and then lowered the zipper, pushing the denim down her hips. Mia wiggled, causing her jeans to slide down her legs and pool at her feet. She toed off her shoes and then stepped out of them, kicking them in the direction of her shirt. Her eyes locked with Phoenix's as she stood there, nearly naked and on display for him. He wanted to touch her, but he wasn't sure he could get his hands to move. He was lost in her beauty.

Tarik pressed his mouth to Mia's neck as he spoke once more. "I dream about this, Mia. Dream about touching you, tasting you. Feeling your soft skin against my fingers."

Tarik cupped Mia's breasts, hefting them in his hands while Phoenix was helpless to watch.

"I dream about watching you take Phoenix's cock inside you while you ride him. I crave seeing the pleasure on both of your faces. It's all I want, all I need. Do you understand what I'm telling you, Mia?"

Mia nodded. "I've never felt this before," she admitted, and the words pierced Phoenix's heart as he continued to hold her gaze. "I've never wanted anything in my life more than I want the two of you."

Phoenix swallowed hard, her words making him feel things he hadn't ever felt before.

"Kick off your shoes," Tarik said, interrupting his thoughts, his eyes meeting Phoenix's once more.

He did as he was told.

"Now remove your slacks and socks. Leave your boxers on."

A few seconds later, Phoenix was mostly naked, save for his boxers, while Tarik was still completely dressed.

Tarik must've read Phoenix's mind, because he instructed Mia to face him. While he proceeded to have her undress him, one article of clothing at a time, starting with his suit jacket, Phoenix watched, admiring her cute little heart-shaped ass bisected by the white thong she wore.

"Put your mouth on me, Mia," Tarik instructed, cupping Mia's head in both of his hands and pulling her forward. Her lips pressed against the hard planes of Tarik's chest. "I want to feel you, Mia."

Mia kissed Tarik's chest while Tarik held her head in his hands, his golden eyes meeting Phoenix's. Without a single touch, Phoenix could feel Tarik's need like a physical caress. He was proving to them both just what this was. It was more than any of them had anticipated.

While Phoenix watched Mia, his mouth watered to taste her. He wanted to drop to his knees and kiss her soft skin, starting with the backs of her thighs and moving higher. She was so fucking beautiful.

By the time Tarik had Mia turning back around to face Phoenix, Tarik was down to a pair of black boxer briefs that did little to hide the massive erection straining to get free.

"Now what?" Phoenix asked, the words barely spoken past his dry throat, his anxiety level ratcheting up a notch.

"Be patient," Tarik said, his eyes narrowing as though warning Phoenix not to cross that line.

Biting his tongue to keep from lashing out, to keep from begging for something, anything, Phoenix managed to remain silent.

Tarik leaned down and pressed his lips to Mia's ear. Phoenix could hear the muffled sound of words, but he couldn't make them out this time. It must've been more instructions, because she moved over to the chair and sat down, primly pulling her legs up beneath her as though she was about to watch a show.

"Come here," Tarik stated firmly.

Phoenix moved forward, closing the gap between them in two steps. His muscles were tense, his hands beginning to shake as the adrenaline and need barreled through him. There was a time for patience, and then there was now. Tarik was pushing him to his limits, and he was close to snapping.

Tarik's hand came up to cup the back of Phoenix's head, his fingers twining into his hair and pulling roughly, holding him still.

"I'm in charge," Tarik leaned in and whispered against Phoenix's ear, his voice too low for Mia to hear. "If you have a problem with that, let me know now."

Phoenix considered that for a moment. He wasn't sure how far Tarik would go. He wasn't sure how far he wanted Tarik to go. But he knew he wasn't going to find out unless he gave in. "I'm in," Phoenix answered just as quietly.

"You're at my mercy, you know that, right?"

Phoenix nodded, but no words came out, because Tarik chose that moment to slam his mouth over Phoenix's, his tongue driving into his mouth in a kiss so hot, so fierce, Phoenix was lightheaded. He grabbed for Tarik, his arms going around him, his fingers digging into the rigid muscles of Tarik's back as he kissed him with all the hunger, all the fury that raged inside him.

The next thing Phoenix knew, Tarik was forcing him toward his bedroom, tugging Mia behind him. Her soft laughter made something loosen in Phoenix's chest, and when she came over to him, he kissed her, trying to be gentle. She took his control from him instantly with the way she captured his mouth, her hands cradling his head.

Tarik stripped her completely while her mouth was locked with Phoenix's.

"On the bed," Tarik growled.

Mia smiled against Phoenix's lips, pulling him with her as she settled onto the mattress. "He's awfully bossy, isn't he?" she said in a mock whisper.

Phoenix grinned but resumed kissing her, delving into her mouth, letting her consume him with her sweetness, her eagerness. He wanted to be inside her, and he didn't want to wait.

Letting his fingers trail down between her legs, he teased her gently. "You're ready for me."

"Always," she answered, her hands sliding to his hips and forcing his boxers down.

Tarik assisted, pulling his boxers off, and the next thing Phoenix knew, he was sliding into Mia's warm, wet heat.

"Fuck," he growled, realizing instantly that he wasn't wearing a condom. "Oh, fuck, Mia. Baby, we need a condom."

Mia didn't seem to hear him. That or she was ignoring him completely. He didn't know. He wasn't sure he cared, except he wanted to make sure she was okay with this before he proceeded.

"It's okay," she told him. "I'm on the pill."

Phoenix met her gaze. There was more to it than just the risk of pregnancy, but he could see in her eyes that she trusted them. The same as they trusted her. Nodding, he pressed his mouth to hers and closed his eyes as he pushed inside her.

Holy fucking shit. Without the latex barrier, the sensations were intense, blasting him from all directions.

"Don't move," Tarik instructed from somewhere behind him.

Phoenix tore his mouth from Mia's. "What?"

"You heard me," Tarik replied with a rasping laugh. "Stay right there."

Mia's smile distracted him momentarily, but Phoenix focused on the shift of the bed behind him, on Tarik's rough hands sliding over his ass, separating him.

"Motherfucker," Phoenix growled as the most exquisite pleasure, aside from the feel of Mia's smooth cunt sheathing him, ripped through him.

Tarik was... *Oh, fuck.*

Tarik's tongue was rimming his asshole, awakening nerve endings that had never been awakened before. It was... "Oh, God. Don't stop." Phoenix wasn't above begging. He wasn't above anything if that pleasure would remain. He managed to hold himself above Mia, his cock buried inside her, skin to skin, her legs wrapped around his hips as Tarik fucked his ass with his tongue.

"Do you like that?" Mia asked, her voice as soft as her hands when they caressed his jaw.

Phoenix momentarily wondered how she knew what Tarik was doing, but then he looked over, seeing Tarik's reflection in the mirror above the dresser. Mia would have a perfect view of all that Tarik was doing to him.

"Yes," he groaned. "Oh, fuck."

Mia's pussy clenched around his cock as he retreated and then pushed into her, trying to force Tarik where he wanted him.

Mia moaned.

Phoenix growled.

Tarik's mouth disappeared, and his hand came to rest on Phoenix's back. He found himself sandwiched between Mia and Tarik as cool liquid dribbled over his ass moments before Tarik... "Oh, fuck, yes."

Tarik pressed the head of his cock against Phoenix's hole. He wasn't gentle, but Phoenix didn't need gentle. As it was, his cock was pulsing, his balls drawing up against his body. He was going to come without even moving, with the phenomenal heat of Mia's pussy hugging him tightly.

"Let me do the work," Tarik whispered against his ear as he pushed into him.

Mia shifted, forcing her hips upward, changing the angle as Tarik began fucking Phoenix's ass. He fought the urge to move at first, allowing Tarik to control the pace, forcing him into Mia, deeper, deeper still, until he couldn't hold back. He began pumping his hips, fucking Mia with shallow strokes while Tarik fucked his ass.

"It's too much," Phoenix said. "I can't... Shit. I'm gonna come."

Tarik's thrusts increased in speed and intensity until Phoenix was pounding into Mia, then driving back to meet Tarik's cock.

Mia cried out, and Phoenix let go, letting Tarik finish them off until all movement stopped, Tarik's fingers digging into his hips as he came with a rush, filling Phoenix's ass. It was then that he realized Tarik hadn't worn a condom, either, which explained the exquisite sensations that had ripped through him.

They'd taken the next step. A step Phoenix had been wanting but not sure how to ask for. Now he didn't have to, and the only thing he could think about was how they got to the next step from here. And the one after that. Whatever that might be.

No matter what, Phoenix knew without a doubt that this was it for him. These two were his future.

And he damn sure wasn't going to let anyone take them from him.

Chapter Thirty-Seven

ON THE FOLLOWING Monday, Mia rapped her knuckles on the front door, a nervous flutter coursing through her as she realized just what she was doing. She had accepted the invite without question, not wanting to spend the evening alone while Tarik and Phoenix were both out of town for a round of away games. They had tried to convince her to come along, but after missing two of her classes last week when having lunch with Harrison, she knew she couldn't miss any more. It was a tempting invitation, but she had declined, only to accept this one. Dinner with Ellen Pierce on a Monday night.

"Mia." Ellen greeted her kindly as she opened the front door.

The woman looked as elegantly put together as she always did. Her hair was glossy and straight, her makeup subtle yet perfect, her green eyes keen and bright. There was no denying the fact that she was Phoenix's mother. They looked so much alike, yet so different at the same time.

"Thank you for inviting me," Mia said as she made her way inside Ellen's condo.

It looked similar to her own in layout, however the decor was vastly different than what she'd expected. It was very … homey. For some reason, she'd expected something significantly different, something that reflected Ellen's all-business personality.

"I'm so glad you could make it. Dinner's almost ready."

Mia followed Ellen into the living room, noting the pictures that sat on every available surface. There were dozens of Phoenix now, even more of a young boy she assumed was also him.

The pictures told a story over time as Phoenix grew up. There were pictures of him in school — from grade school to what she assumed was his college graduation. There were even pictures of Tarik and Phoenix together.

"They've been close for a while, huh?" Mia asked, referring to one of the images of Tarik and Phoenix together.

"It's never been solely a working relationship between those two. They met when Phoenix was working with a local boy's club, creating a hockey program. Tarik was the volunteer who took over the program. They'd become friends somewhere at that point."

Mia thought about Tarik volunteering at a boy's home, and her heart turned over. The man seemed so unsure about his feelings, yet … he did things such as volunteer, which only proved how incredible he was. And that was a trait at his core, obviously not something he'd learned.

Her heart swelled with even more love for him.

Moving to another picture, Mia's eyes instantly watered at the sight of Phoenix with his father. They were at a hockey game, and based on the way Phoenix appeared, it hadn't been that long ago.

"That's Phoenix's father, Sid," Ellen said, coming to stand beside Mia when she moved in to get a closer look.

"Wow. And I thought Phoenix looked like you," Mia said absently. They had the same black hair, the same prominent nose. The only difference was Sid's eyes were green, although not nearly as dark as Phoenix's.

Ellen chuckled. "He's the spitting image of his father when he was Phoenix's age. Take your time looking around. I'll be in the kitchen finishing up."

Mia nodded, unable to look away from all the pictures. They were everywhere. Not only on surfaces; they also decorated the walls of the hallways. They were likely Ellen's daily reminder of the two men she'd built her life around. Mia felt a pang in her heart as she thought about what Ellen had gone through losing her husband.

"They're quite handsome, don't you think?" Ellen asked when Mia joined her in the kitchen.

"I think that's an understatement," Mia said honestly. "Can I help you with something?"

"You can set the table if you'd like."

Mia busied herself setting the table while Ellen pulled something out of the oven and then moved on to stir a pot on the stove. A few minutes later, they were sitting at the table, a delicious aroma surrounding them.

"This is one of Phoenix's favorites, although he'll claim he doesn't have one. Homemade shepherd's pie. Peas, carrots, ground beef, and mashed potatoes. Simple. So very unlike him," Ellen explained.

Mia laughed. "He certainly is rather complex," she agreed. "This looks wonderful."

Once Ellen served herself, Mia did the same, hoping she didn't look as nervous as she felt. Sitting down to dinner with Ellen was … unexpected. Dating Phoenix and Tarik was one thing; spending time with their parents was something else.

"I informed Phoenix that I stole you for the evening," Ellen informed her as they ate.

Mia smiled. "What did he say?"

"He told me to go easy on you."

"Is that right?"

"He's always worried, that one. I think he spends so much time worrying about everyone else that he forgets to think about himself sometimes."

Mia understood what Ellen was saying. From the day she'd met him, Phoenix had been worried about one thing or another. He wasn't just complex, he was intense. Although he did know how to have a good time, it seemed to take quite a bit of work to get his mind to clear. It seemed to her that she and Tarik balanced him out well.

"At least the Arrows are doing well this season," Ellen said. "That should be one less worry he has."

"I've heard they may make the playoffs," Mia said. "For the record, I don't know anything about hockey. I've been to one game in my life, and that was with Phoenix and Tarik."

"Phoenix's entire life has been about hockey. His father got him into it when he was very young. Oh, he was so good. That's ultimately how Sid ended up going down the path he was on, purchasing the Arrows. It kept the two of them close."

Mia remembered the conversation she'd had with Phoenix about the same subject. "Could he have played professionally?"

"Absolutely. But he didn't want to. His mind has always been on business. He's a lot like his grandfather — Sid's father — was in that sense. We never discouraged him from doing what he wanted to do. When he decided he wanted to be part of the team from a business perspective, Sid was delighted. They made a good team."

Mia noticed the sadness that distorted Ellen's features. Reaching across the table, Mia touched her hand softly. "I'm so sorry for your loss. That'll never make it better, I know."

Ellen smiled, but it was sad. "Thank you. I miss him every day. It pains me all that Phoenix has had to deal with since Sid died. He hasn't had much time to grieve himself."

Mia nodded. "You're referring to the lawsuit," Mia said, swallowing hard. She was suddenly no longer hungry. Thinking about what Damien was doing to Phoenix made her blood boil. The idea that Damien was using her to get at Phoenix made her chest hurt and her stomach churn.

"Don't you dare take that on yourself, young lady," Ellen stated firmly, shocking Mia with the authority in her tone. "I see your mind working in that pretty little head of yours. This isn't your fault. I know that. Phoenix and Tarik know that. They'll fix this. I know they will."

"I hope so," Mia said. She wanted it all to go away. Things were going so well between her and Tarik and Phoenix, she didn't want anything to interfere, certainly not Damien.

"It will. The three of you need to keep doing what you're doing. Lean on one another. That's all anyone can ask for."

Mia couldn't hide the surprise on her face as her eyes rose to meet Ellen's. Phoenix's mother answered with a laugh.

"Honey, if you think I don't see everything that goes on, you're just as oblivious as my son."

Mia didn't know what to say to that. She took a sip of her water, hoping not to choke. "So you know about…"

"About Tarik and Phoenix? Or about the three of you? I see more than he gives me credit for. I've known for a very long time how Tarik feels about Phoenix. I also know that Phoenix has been confused a long time, too. Until you."

"Until me?" Mia was confused.

"I don't know what it is about you, but when you came along, Phoenix changed. And don't take that the wrong way. It's definitely a good thing. It's like his guard came down. He let you in. He let Tarik in. He's evolving. I thought for a while he was going to regress. He's always been … adventurous," Ellen stated, smiling. "This little triad you have going with them isn't the norm, but … it seems to be working. I hope you aren't questioning that."

Mia couldn't believe that Ellen was freely telling her that she approved of their "triad," as she had called it. Mia hadn't even considered how her own mother would react when she found out — which no doubt she would. Eventually.

"That's probably the only thing I'm *not* questioning," Mia said softly.

"That's good," Ellen said. "There are some things in life you fight for, and there are some things in life you don't fight against. This is one of those times that you do both." Ellen pointed at Mia's plate with her fork. "Now, finish eating. We've got a game to watch."

»»»»»»♥«««««

"IT'S A DAMN good thing the team wasn't depending on you for that W tonight," Tarik joked as he and Phoenix made their way into their hotel room after the game. The room they were sharing this time — something they'd never done before.

503

He'd been preoccupied with so many things, one of which was the fact that his girlfriend was having dinner with this mother. As soon as the game was over, Phoenix had texted Mia to check in. She'd congratulated him on the win and assured him that dinner had been fantastic. He'd breathed a little easier at that point.

Phoenix glared back at him but didn't say a word. It was the truth; he couldn't deny that. He'd been so preoccupied with his thoughts, his team could've put on fucking tutus and danced around the ice for all he knew.

"Where're you at?" Tarik asked, his tone softer, the teasing tone absent. "You're lost in your own head."

Taking off his suit coat, Phoenix folded it and laid it over the back of the chair before dropping to the bed. He proceeded to remove his shoes, socks, tie, belt. All while watching Tarik watching him. When he started to unbutton his shirt, he saw the glimmer of heat that sparked in Tarik's eyes. It was something Phoenix had seen more often than not these last few weeks. For the longest time, he'd pretended not to notice Tarik, pretended he wasn't drawn to him in ways he'd never imagined. He couldn't deny any of that anymore.

After removing his cuff links on his shirt, Phoenix crooked his finger at Tarik, loving how the big man moved closer without a word being spoken. It was empowering to know the sort of control he had over Tarik. But it wasn't a power trip. There was something deeper, more complex than anything Phoenix had ever known.

Phoenix reached for Tarik's belt, unhooking it while he kept his eyes locked with Tarik's as Tarik stood above him. Without a word, he proceeded to undress Tarik until he was standing in front of him, his erection bobbing out from between his thighs. Leaning forward, Phoenix sucked Tarik into his mouth, tearing his eyes away from Tarik's so he could focus.

"Fuck yes," Tarik groaned softly, his fingers sliding into Phoenix's hair. "God, that's good. Your mouth... So fucking good."

Phoenix swept his tongue along Tarik's thick shaft, curling around the head, swiping over the tip, tasting him. He took his time, savoring the salty taste, the musky scent, the way Tarik groaned when Phoenix focused on the vein that ran the length of Tarik's cock.

When Tarik pulled his hair, effectively dislodging his cock from Phoenix's mouth, Phoenix didn't complain. He looked up as Tarik moved over him, pushing him to the bed as their mouths met, their tongues dueled. No words were necessary as they came together. Phoenix knew what Tarik would give him. Security, peace of mind... It was all there. And he craved it like a fucking drug.

Tarik's lips left his mouth but trailed down his neck, his chest, his nipple. While Tarik pleasured him with his lips, tongue, and teeth, he worked to remove the rest of Phoenix's clothes, and Phoenix did his best to help him. When they were both naked, Tarik reached for something in one of the bags on the chair and returned with a bottle of lubricant.

Phoenix reached for it. It was his turn this time. His turn to claim Tarik.

"On your back," Phoenix instructed as he squirted lube into his hand, coating his cock as he watched Tarik's impressive body sprawl out on the bed before him.

With Tarik propped up on the pillows, Phoenix knelt between his thighs, adding more lube to his hand, then working two fingers into Tarik's asshole.

Tarik's eyes closed, and his head tilted back, his corded neck too much of a temptation for Phoenix to resist. He sucked on Tarik's skin while he finger fucked him, working him open, getting him ready for him. When Tarik began rocking on the bed, Phoenix removed his fingers and replaced them with the head of his cock. He grabbed Tarik's right leg and bent it, forcing Tarik's knee up near his chest as he pushed his way in, his eyes locked on Tarik's face.

"Fuck yes," Tarik moaned. "Deeper. I want to feel you all the way inside me."

Phoenix pushed in farther, until his pelvis rested against Tarik's ass. He didn't want to wait, didn't have reason to ease into him, so he began pumping his hips, fucking Tarik slow and easy, keeping a steady rhythm while Tarik's ass stretched around his cock.

Tarik's hand came up, wrapping behind Phoenix's neck, and he leaned down until their mouths were just a breath apart.

"Fuck me, Phoenix," Tarik commanded. "Fuck me hard."

Phoenix met his gaze, studying him as so many thoughts swamped his head. Thoughts of doing this forever, having Tarik and Mia all to himself for the rest of his life. It was enough to make his cock jump eagerly.

"I own you," Phoenix told Tarik roughly. "And I don't mean just right now."

Tarik nodded as Phoenix began to drive his hips forward, pulling them back and then driving them forward again. He began pounding into him, Tarik's ass clenching around his dick, the pleasure driving every thought from his brain.

"Always, Tarik. I own you, always." Phoenix couldn't stop the words. Tarik's hand tightened behind Phoenix's neck, their foreheads touching, their breaths rushing between them as Phoenix fucked him harder. "Say it, Tarik. Tell me you understand."

"You own me," Tarik said on a primal growl. "The same as I own you. Fuck! Coming!"

Phoenix's hips stilled as his release shot from him, filling Tarik's ass at the same time his words pierced his heart. Tarik was right. Tarik owned him the same way Mia owned him.

Chapter Thirty-Eight

GETTING BACK HOME to Mia had been the only thing on Tarik's mind since he'd woken up that morning. The last few days away from her had been hell, and he was beginning to wonder how they were going to keep doing it. If he had his way, she'd be traveling with them, but with her classes, he knew that wasn't an option.

For most of the time they'd been gone, Phoenix had been preoccupied, with the exception of when they went to bed. And then they were too busy undoing one another for anything else to intrude. Except when they were finished, they would talk about Mia, about getting back to her.

When she'd called Phoenix to tell him she was having dinner with Ellen, Tarik had thought Phoenix's head was going to explode. Her assurance afterward that things had gone well was the only thing that had saved him. Tarik found it all amusing, which Phoenix hadn't found at all funny.

Now, as he drove to the condos from the private airport where Phoenix kept his company jet, Tarik's anxiety level was rising. They had both received a text from Mia that morning, informing them that she needed to talk to them as soon as possible. And not by phone, which had filled him with an overwhelming sense of dread.

"Did she answer your text?" Tarik asked, referring to the fact that Phoenix had texted Mia as soon as the plane had landed. As he drove, he tossed a glance at Phoenix, who was typing something into his phone.

"No. Not yet. I'm just gonna call her."

Phoenix put the phone to his ear, and Tarik returned his attention to the road.

"Mia? Hey. Where are you?"

Tarik couldn't hear Mia talking on the other end of the line, and he desperately wanted to know what she was saying. After the text they'd both received that morning, he knew whatever she had to tell them wasn't going to be good.

"Okay, baby. We'll be there in a few."

"Where is she?"

"At her condo. Alex and Johnathan are there with her."

Tarik darted another look at Phoenix.

"So is my mother," Phoenix added, his face grim.

"Did she tell you what the hell is going on?" Tarik asked, his voice rough.

"No. So pay attention to the road and fucking drive."

Tarik knew Phoenix was feeling the same dread he was, so he brushed off the harsh words and focused on the road.

Twenty minutes later, Tarik was knocking on Mia's front door, Phoenix standing beside him. When the door opened, Ellen greeted them, her face lined with worry.

"What's going on?" Phoenix demanded as he pushed past Tarik and Ellen on his way to find Mia.

The second she saw them, Mia was off the couch and rushing toward them. She walked right into Phoenix's arms first but then released him and headed for Tarik. He was surprised that she stayed in his arms a little longer. The feel of her against him soothed that restless energy that had been pulsing since her text.

"Someone really needs to tell me what the fuck is going on," Phoenix demanded.

Mia pulled away from Tarik and turned to face Phoenix.

"I was served with papers this morning. Apparently, Damien is suing me for three million dollars."

"What?" Phoenix roared. "He's lost his fucking mind."

"No, he's hard up for money," Alex said softly. "I mean *really* hard up."

"Damien's in the process of suing Mia for the three million he paid her in the divorce. He claims that she was the one cheating on him; therefore, she shouldn't have received the money," Johnathan explained.

"That's not all," Ellen said.

Tarik, along with everyone else in the room, turned his attention to Phoenix's mother. She was sitting on the edge of the chair, her hands clasped together in her lap. "Phil asked me to provide some of your father's handwriting samples. He had some, but he wanted a few more. Damien's lawyers told Phil that they would be sending him the document showing that Sid did make a deal to sell the Arrows."

"I've got to sit down," Phoenix said, sounding defeated.

Ellen stood, then went to him, easing down beside him when he dropped to the sofa. Tarik watched the scene before him for a moment.

Tarik leaned down to Mia's ear. "I'll be back in a few minutes. Don't go anywhere."

She nodded, and with that, Tarik walked out the door. It was time to put a stop to this shit once and for fucking all.

»»»»»»♥«««««

"I'M SO SORRY, Phoenix," Mia said when the door closed behind Tarik. She had no idea where he was going, and she didn't have the good sense to ask, either. She was too focused on Phoenix. He looked as though he was going to lose it any second now, and she didn't know what to do.

"You're sorry?" Phoenix asked, disbelief in his tone, his turbulent green eyes lifting to meet hers. "Come here."

Mia made her way across the living room, fear making her move slowly, carefully. She hated that Damien was doing this, and she couldn't help but think this was all her fault.

Phoenix took her hand and tugged her down beside him, placing his arm over her shoulder and pulling her against him as he leaned back against the cushions. His lips brushed her hair, but he didn't say anything.

The room was silent, and Mia felt all eyes on her. For the last couple of hours, ever since the man had shown up at her door with papers that she'd had to sign for, she'd been shaking. Damien was suing her, insisting that she was the one who had cheated. With Phoenix, at that. He claimed he had proof.

She hadn't known what to do, so she had texted Tarik and Phoenix, knowing they were in flight back home. Then she'd called Alex but had to leave a voice mail. She had considered calling her mother, but didn't want her to worry until Mia knew what she was going to do, so she'd done the only thing she could think of. She'd gone up to Ellen's condo and knocked on the door.

After explaining to her what had happened, they had sat at Ellen's kitchen table. That was when Ellen had received the phone call from Phoenix's lawyer, Phil, asking about handwriting samples. The bottom had dropped out of Mia's stomach at that point. Everything had snowballed from there. When Alex called her back, Mia and Ellen had returned to Mia's condo to meet them.

And here they all were. Mia had no idea what to do or what to say. She wanted to fix this, but she didn't know what that entailed.

Confusion wracked her, made her thoughts mushy, her head ache.

Phoenix lifted his head and glanced around the room while Mia curled up against him, inhaling him, drinking him in. She never wanted to let him go. She felt safe in his arms, although she knew that things were still falling apart around them.

"Where'd Tarik go?" Phoenix demanded, sitting upright instantly, obviously just realizing he'd left.

"He said he'd be back in a few minutes," Mia told him, forced to sit up, too.

"Why didn't Phil call me?"

Mia realized Phoenix was talking to his mother.

"He said he tried," Ellen said calmly, that authoritative tone once again in place. "I assume you were on the plane."

Phoenix turned to Mia, cupping her face in his hands before pressing his lips to her mouth. "I need to find Tarik. I don't want you to worry about any of this."

Mia cocked an eyebrow. Right. Like that was even possible at this point.

"I'm serious, Mia. We'll get it taken care of. I'll be back in a few minutes."

Mia nodded and pressed her lips to Phoenix's when he kissed her gently. When he withdrew his lips, he pulled her head to his shoulder and pressed his lips to her ear. "I love you, Mia. You have nothing to worry about."

Her heart stopped beating. It actually stopped in her chest for a moment before it resumed, kicking harder than she'd thought possible. Phoenix pulled back and looked at her before pressing his lips to hers once more.

"I love you, too," she whispered, forcing her eyes not to water. She wasn't going to cry. This was a good thing.

Phoenix smiled.

And then he was gone.

She stared after him, wondering if she'd heard him correctly. Her heart claimed she had, the too-hard beat making her chest hurt. Her stomach swirled with a mixture of hope and love and everything she'd kept bottled inside for the past few weeks. She'd told Tarik that she loved him and she'd meant it. Although the opportunity hadn't presented itself — until now, apparently — Mia had been trying to find a way to tell Phoenix how she felt. Now that she had, she wasn't sure what to do.

"Are you okay?" Alex asked, coming to sit beside her, taking her hand.

"I will be," she said, conviction backing up her words.

Mia met Ellen's eyes, and she noticed the older woman was smiling. She'd heard what Phoenix had said.

»»»»»♥«««««

PHOENIX DIDN'T BOTHER going to his penthouse when he left Mia's. He went straight to Tarik's, needing to find out what the man was up to. When he walked in, he wasn't surprised to find Tarik on the phone, speaking gruffly to whomever was on the other end.

Pushing his hands into his pockets, he stood in the living room, watching Tarik.

"This is your chance to make things right," Tarik said. The ruthless tone he used had the hair on the back of Phoenix's neck standing on end. "Technically, you owe her, and I assure you, you'll never be able to repay her for what she's been through. Never."

Phoenix watched as Tarik listened to whomever was on the other end. He turned and met Phoenix's eyes as he said, "Good. I'll meet with you first thing Monday morning." Tarik paused for a moment. "Yes. Pierce Industries. I'll have her lawyer there."

Tarik disconnected the call.

"Who was that?"

"Harrison Abbott. Looks like the guy is up for a good deed."

Phoenix smirked. He knew that Harrison probably had had a little helping hand in coming to that conclusion. Tarik could be quite persuasive when he wanted to be.

"So what do we do now?" Phoenix asked, curious as to what Tarik had in mind.

"We schedule a meeting with Landry and his lawyers for Monday afternoon. And then we wait."

Chapter Thirty-Nine

MIA HAD THOUGHT she would be nervous, had even wondered whether or not she was going to be sick when she had considered the meeting she would be attending on Monday afternoon.

The meeting she was sitting in now.

Tarik and Phoenix had driven her to Pierce Industries early that morning to meet with Phil, the lawyer who was currently managing her side of the lawsuit that Damien had instigated just last week. They had settled into a conference room, and she'd answered a number of questions. Shortly thereafter, Phoenix and Tarik had taken her to lunch, and now they had returned. Same conference room, only this time, they were seated beside her. One on each side, and the three of them were waiting for Damien and his legal team to arrive so they could discuss options.

No, she wasn't nervous, but her stomach was churning. It wasn't from the cheeseburger she'd scarfed down at lunch, either. This was from anger and hurt. It had erupted in her belly as soon as she had returned to the room, realizing that she would have to face Damien today.

A knock on the door had Mia looking up. Phoenix took one of her hands in his beneath the table while Tarik took the other, both reassuring her that things were going to be fine. She had no reason not to believe them, and that was what it all boiled down to. She trusted them.

A little ironic that she had to face a man who had destroyed her trust with his deceit only to find herself being consoled by the two men who'd proven to her that not everyone was like Damien.

Three men in suits came into the room, none of them saying a word as they took a chair on the other side of the table. Damien followed behind them, his gaze moving from one person to the next, a cocky smile forming on his lips.

"Are we all here?" Damien asked as though he were the one directing the meeting.

"Take a seat, Landry," Phoenix commanded.

Damien glared at Phoenix but took a chair between two of the suits across from her. Mia made a point not to meet his gaze. She didn't want to look at him.

"Well, you called this meeting," Damien said. "Might as well get down to business. I assume you aren't just wasting my time here."

Phoenix's hand tightened on Mia's, but he kept silent.

Phil cleared his throat. "I want to start out by listing what Mr. Landry is currently seeking with the multiple lawsuits, to ensure we are on the same page. His original suit for five million in damages from Mr. Pierce has been amended to the amount of ten million. Is this correct?"

"That's correct," one of the suits across the table said.

"And then there is the matter of the lawsuit against Mia Cantrell in the amount of three million. The grounds are that Mia was awarded three million in her divorce settlement for the three years she spent with Mr. Landry. According to the lawsuit, Mia did not deserve this money due to the fact that she was unfaithful during the marriage. Is this correct?"

"That's correct," the same suit said.

Mia continued to stare at the lawyers, refusing to look at Damien.

"It has been advised that there was a legally binding contract signed by Sidney Pierce and Damien Landry, executing the sale of the majority share of the Austin Arrows franchise back in March of this year."

"That is correct," Damien said firmly. "This is all information we already know. I'm not sure the reason to rehash it here and now."

"It's important to establish the authenticity of the document signed by Sidney Pierce," Phil continued as though Damien hadn't spoken. "We are requesting a copy of this to compare signatures against those on file. We've hired a third party handwriting expert to handle this for us."

Mia's gaze did slip to Damien's, and the way his brow furrowed told her he wasn't as confident that his paper was going to hold up in court.

"I'm not sure why this is necessary," Damien said, although it lacked the heat it should have, in her opinion. For a man who'd walked in there so self-assured, he seemed to be retreating somewhat.

"It's justifiable," one of the suits told Damien. "If they ask for it in court, the judge will allow it, considering Sidney Pierce is deceased."

"The longer this takes, the more I'm going to ask for," Damien said snidely.

"If I may ask, what proof do you have that Ms. Cantrell was unfaithful during the marriage?" Phil asked, the question directed at the lawyers.

"We have people who are willing to state that they saw Ms. Cantrell with Phoenix during the marriage."

Phil nodded, jotting something down on the paper. "And I assume they are willing to testify in court, correct?"

"Yes, that is correct."

"Do you have the names of these witnesses?" Phil asked.

"That's not important at this time," one of the lawyers said.

Phil had already informed Mia that they would say that. They did not have to disclose them until it was necessary.

Phil wrote something else on the paper.

As was planned, Tarik lifted their clasped hands and rested them on the table, effectively pulling Mia slightly closer to his side. Phoenix continued to hold her hand beneath the table.

Damien's eyes instantly went to their joined hands, confusion marring his expression. Mia fought the urge to smile.

Phil addressed the lawyers directly. "As I mentioned on the phone earlier, I wanted to inform you of the conclusion we've come to."

Damien's gaze slid to Phil's, his interest apparent.

"We are in the process of filing a countersuit on behalf of Ms. Cantrell. She's countersuing Mr. Landry for an additional ten million dollars, which, according to the prenup, she would've been awarded in the event that Mr. Landry was unfaithful." Phil paused as the door opened.

Damien twisted in his seat as all eyes turned to the two newcomers. Harrison Abbott and his ex-wife, Michelle, made their way into the room, both of them taking a seat at the end of the table.

"What the hell is this?" Damien grumbled.

"Thank you for joining us. It'll be just a minute," Phil told Harrison and Michelle before turning his attention back to Damien's lawyers. "In addition to the ten million, Ms. Cantrell is seeking three million in damages."

"Under what claim?" one of the lawyers asked, sternly meeting Phil's stare.

"Defamation of character. Mr. Landry accused Ms. Cantrell of being unfaithful during the marriage, and we also have witnesses to back her claim. At the same time" — Phil motioned to Harrison and Michelle — "we have witnesses who will testify in a court of law that Mr. Landry was unfaithful when he had an affair with Harrison Abbott's wife."

"*Ex*-wife," Harrison noted.

Mia smiled to herself.

Phil sorted the papers in front of him, pulling another page to the top. "As for Mr. Pierce, we will also be filing a countersuit in the amount of five million dollars for damages."

"Five million?" Damien snarled.

"I didn't want to be greedy," Phoenix said roughly, a smirk drawing up the corners of his mouth.

Mia squeezed his hand beneath the table.

"Is this what you really want?" Damien asked, his question directed at Phoenix.

"No," Phoenix said, sitting up and pulling Mia's other hand, still clasped with his, onto the table. "*She* is what I want, but if I recall correctly, you informed me we could do this the easy way or the hard way. I've never taken the easy way out of anything. I certainly don't intend to start now."

The door opened, and in walked several more men wearing suits, along with Ellen Pierce, Alex, and Johnathan, as well as Teresa Somerhaus's father, Charles. They eased into the room and came to stand behind them. Damien's eyes roamed from one face to another.

"Welcome to the hard way," Mia told him. "We didn't feel the need to hold out. We'd like to introduce you to our legal team. As well as the upstanding citizens who are willing to testify on our behalf. Now, if you'll excuse us, we've got some things to take care of."

"Did I mention we'll be asking for legal fees?" Phoenix added, glancing behind him before meeting Damien's bewildered gaze. "And *this* is going to cost you."

Mia pushed her chair back and got to her feet, Phoenix and Tarik standing with her. Mia didn't bother looking at Damien as they walked out. The last thing she heard was one of Damien's lawyers asking if they could have a few minutes alone with Phil.

»»»»»» ♥ «««««

TARIK FOLLOWED MIA and Phoenix out of the room. He only released her hand so that she could move in front of him as they exited.

"You did well," Phoenix told Mia when they went into Phoenix's office.

Tarik closed the door, effectively shutting out everyone else who was now filing from the conference room behind them. He knew some of them would want to talk, but for now, he wanted a moment alone with her and Phoenix. They had agreed to wait for Phil, knowing that he would finish up the meeting with the lawyers regardless of the outcome, otherwise Tarik would've suggested they go back to the condos.

"Do you think he's going to drop everything?" Mia asked as Phoenix led her over to his desk.

Stepping behind her, Tarik placed his hands on her shoulders and urged her to lean back against him. He suddenly needed to feel her.

"I don't think he's going to have a choice. Damien Landry is a bully. His first mistake was thinking that I wouldn't come back with something. Proof that he doesn't know me very well. Nor did he know my father."

"Sidney would've buried Damien in debt if he were alive," Tarik informed Mia. "Not that Landry hasn't done a good job of that already."

Phoenix perched on the edge of his desk, holding one of Mia's hands. "Now, I will say that according to Phil, there is a good chance you could win a countersuit against him for the ten million," Phoenix informed her. "Even if he does drop all of it, we can still go after that."

"No," Mia said adamantly. "I just want him to go away. I didn't want his money when I asked for the divorce, and I don't want it now. I want to move on with the rest of my life."

Tarik really liked the sound of that. Although he wasn't quite sure just what that entailed, he had a few ideas.

A knock sounded on the door, and before he could move, Phoenix called out that it was unlocked.

Phil stuck his head in the door. "Can I talk to you a minute?" he asked Phoenix.

"I'll be right back," Phoenix told them both before following Phil out into the hallway and once again closing the door.

Tarik turned Mia in his arms and pulled her against him, resting his chin on the top of her head.

"Thank you," she said, her voice muffled as she buried her face against his jacket.

"I'm not sure what you're thanking me for," he said, pulling back and tilting her head so he could meet her eyes.

"I know you did this. I know you're the one who called Harrison, and you're the one who convinced Phoenix to file a countersuit if Damien was going to keep moving forward. So, thank you."

"I don't need any thanks, Mia," Tarik told her.

"I know why you did it," she said softly, her small hands coming up to cup his cheeks. He leaned into her touch, his eyes locked with hers.

"Why's that?"

"Because you love us."

Tarik shifted his gaze away from her, unsure what to say to that.

"Look at me," she said, her tone just as soft but much more commanding than before. "You can pretend that's not the case, but—"

"I'm not pretending, Mia," he told her sadly.

"Maybe not, but I'm here to tell you that this" — her hand slid down to rest just over his heart — "this feeling you get when the three of us are together, that's love."

He swallowed hard.

"You might think it's a foreign emotion, but it's not. You feel it just the same as we do. You didn't grow up with someone showing you what it was to love someone or even how to do it, but you figured it out on your own. You're a good man, a strong man. And you feel from *here*." Mia patted his chest again. "You might not understand it, but that's love."

"I…" Tarik had no idea what to say to her.

"You love me," she said, a smile forming on her pretty pink lips. "That's all there is to it. You love me and you love Phoenix. You might as well admit it now, because I won't rest until you do."

An answering smile formed on his lips because he couldn't help it. This woman, she had found a spot inside him, and she'd burrowed there, filling him with that unnamed emotion that, yes, might be love. She *and* Phoenix had made him feel things he didn't understand.

Mia's face turned serious once more. "I know what it's like to have your heart shattered in a million tiny pieces, Tarik. It sucks big-time. But what I didn't know, until you and Phoenix, was that those tiny pieces could be pulled back together. Only when they do, the bond is stronger, more solid. That's what I feel for you and Phoenix. I love you both. With my whole heart. Every single one of the million tiny pieces that it once was. It's whole again. Stronger than ever."

Tarik rested his forehead against Mia's, closing his eyes. If she could tell him all that, her heart in her beautiful eyes, then he knew he could tell her just the same.

"You're right, Mia. I do love you. And I love Phoenix. But it *is* foreign. It's not something I'm familiar with, but I can promise you that I'm working toward it. Getting comfortable with it. I want to get there, to be able to express it in words—"

"You don't have much of a choice," Mia countered. "Because I plan to spend the rest of my life making sure you tell me how much you love me. After all, I have every intention of telling you how much I love you. Every single day."

The door opened once more, and Tarik reluctantly pulled away from Mia. He turned to see Phoenix standing there, a solemn expression on his face. The door closed behind him, and Tarik noticed that Phoenix turned the lock on the knob.

"What's the matter?" Mia asked.

"It's done."

"What's done?" she inquired, her voice rising slightly.

"Damien's dropped all of the lawsuits. Phil is putting together paperwork for him to sign stating he won't pursue this in the future."

"So why do you look upset?" Mia questioned him.

"I'm just trying to figure something out."

Tarik's brow furrowed as he attempted to follow where Phoenix was going with this. If it was all over, they shouldn't have anything else to figure out.

Phoenix thrust his hands into his pockets, glancing down at the floor as he headed toward them.

"Why is it that you," Phoenix said to Tarik, his face grim as he lifted his head, "told her that you loved me. *Before* you told me?"

Silence followed Phoenix's question, and then it sank in for both him and Mia. She laughed, slapping Phoenix on the arm, probably for making her worry.

"Because I didn't know *until* her?" Tarik suggested.

"She's good like that," Phoenix stated, glancing down at her. "But I already knew that."

Mia moved into Phoenix's arms, snuggling up to him the same way she was still holding Tarik, and then Phoenix reached up, cupping his hand on the back of Tarik's neck, pulling him closer. Their mouths were just a hairsbreadth away when he said, "I love you. But you already knew that, too."

"Doesn't mean I don't want to hear it," Tarik said, the honesty in his statement surprising even him.

"And I've already told you."

"No, you haven't," Tarik countered, hating himself for arguing.

Phoenix's mouth touched his. "You own me, Tarik. I've told you that already. In my eyes, it means the same thing."

"So let me get this straight," Mia said, taking a step back and forcing Tarik and Phoenix apart.

"You own him. He owns you. I love you. I love him. You love me. He loves me. Did I get it right?"

Phoenix grabbed Mia, lifting her up and planting her on his desk before his lips met hers. "That's the gist of it. Now what do you say we do what you said you wanted to do earlier?"

"Which was?" Mia asked, glancing between them.

"Move on with the rest of your life."

"And how do we do that?" Mia asked.

Phoenix glanced down at his watch. "Well, we've got a plane to catch in just under two hours."

"That's not much time," Mia replied.

"Agreed," Tarik said, looking at them both. "So what do you say we start the rest of our lives by joining the Mile-High Club?"

The pretty pink blush that spread up Mia's neck to her cheeks told Tarik just what he wanted to know.

She was game.

"But first," Mia said, her smile widening. "We have to go talk to my mother."

Phoenix's face went pale, and Tarik felt his stomach drop to his feet. Talk to her mother?

"You didn't think we'd move forward without telling her, did you?"

Well, it had crossed his mind.

Chapter Forty

"MOM! WHERE ARE you?" Mia called out as soon as the three of them stepped inside the elegant home that she said her mother lived in.

Phoenix's heart was pounding a mile a minute, his palms sweating and his ears ringing. The last time he'd met a girl's parents... Well, shit. The last time would've been in high school. Yet here he was, and he felt like that same bumbling teenage boy all over again.

"You're still pale," Tarik told him, chuckling.

"Shut up. So are you."

"You wish," Tarik retorted, following Mia as she disappeared down the wide, tiled entryway.

Phoenix remained where he was, taking a look around, doing his best to calm his nerves. It was a little ironic that he could stand up to grown men, both on the rink and off the rink, without blinking, but he was having heart palpitations because he was about to meet Mia's mother.

"Phoenix? Are you coming?"

Phoenix looked up to see Mia smiling back at him from down the hall. She was obviously waiting for him, so he put one foot in front of the other, stopping only when he reached her.

"Don't worry. We surprised her, and her boyfriend's here. I haven't met him yet, so I'm sure she's just as nervous as you are."

Right. Like he was buying that for a minute.

Mia took his hand, and Phoenix followed her into the kitchen, where he saw Mia's mother, the woman who looked so much like Mia, sitting at the kitchen table with an older man, both of them drinking coffee.

"Mom, this is Phoenix Pierce and Tarik Marx. Phoenix, Tarik, this is my mother, Clarice Cantrell."

Clarice stood and offered her hand. Phoenix could see the blush that was creeping into her cheeks as she looked at them both. "It's a pleasure to meet you," Phoenix said.

"This is … uh…" Clarice glanced over at the older man still sitting at the table.

"Her boyfriend, Al," Mia supplied. "I'm sorry to be the one to introduce you, but it seems my mother has misplaced her manners."

Al grinned behind his coffee cup as he watched Clarice's face redden.

"Very nice to meet you, Al," Mia said cheerfully. "I just wanted to stop by, introduce you. We're going to be out of town for a few days. Phoenix owns the Austin Arrows, and they're playing tonight in Buffalo, New York."

"Against the Sabres," Al mentioned.

"That's right," Mia said quickly.

It was obvious to Phoenix that she was hurrying through the introduction, probably as eager to get out of there as he was before Clarice began asking questions. He was all for answering them, but he needed a little time to prepare. Like, maybe a year. Possibly two.

"Well, we'll be on our way. Our flight leaves in an hour, so we have to head to the airport. It was so nice to meet you, Al. Maybe the five of us can plan to have dinner sometime in the near future."

"The five of us?" Clarice asked.

Mia's face turned as red as her mother's. Phoenix didn't move. He couldn't. He flipped his gaze over to see Tarik standing stone still watching the entire thing as it played out in front of him.

"Yes, Mom. The five of us. We really should be going."

Mia moved quickly, herding them both toward the door. Phoenix's feet didn't argue as he moved with her. He'd seen the millions of questions that were forming in Clarice's mind as they flittered across her face, and he really didn't want to stick around to answer them. Not today, anyway.

"Mia!" Clarice called when they made it to the front porch.

"Give me a minute," Mia whispered, pushing them down the steps. "I'll meet you in the car."

Tarik turned back and said, "It was very nice to meet you, Clarice."

"You ... uh ... you, too."

Phoenix laughed, but it was strained. He didn't know what to say. Wasn't even sure his voice would work, so he kept going, offering her a wave as he climbed into the passenger seat of the Escalade. Tarik joined him, and they sat there watching Mia have a conversation with her mother.

He had no idea what they were saying, but when Clarice's eyes widened, her gaze landing on the Escalade, he had an idea.

"Oh, shit," Tarik muttered.

"Exactly."

Neither of them said anything more until Mia joined them a few minutes later.

"Well, that went better than I thought it would."

Tarik's laughter bellowed through the car as he reversed out of the driveway.

"Oh, and we'll be having dinner with them next Wednesday. I'll let one of you pick the restaurant."

Oh, hell.

»»»»»»♥«««««

"YOU SERIOUSLY HAVE a bed back there?" Mia asked, glancing over her shoulder toward the back of the private jet that Tarik and Phoenix had steered her onto a few minutes before. After leaving her mother's house, they'd stopped by her condo and given her a few minutes to pack. When she'd started searching through her closet, Tarik had offered a helping hand, while Phoenix had chuckled at her after she'd started picking out clothes that obviously weren't even remotely warm enough for New York — his words. When she'd questioned what they would be wearing, she'd been informed that their things were already on the waiting plane.

She'd thought they were kidding.

Evidently they weren't, because when she'd walked into the cabin, she'd noticed their coats, which they hadn't brought with them, were being hung up by a man who'd been introduced to her as William. When she had questioned her own outerwear at that point, Phoenix had gifted her with a new coat and gloves, which were so beautiful she'd nearly sobbed as she'd thanked them. Tarik had assured her it was their pleasure, not to mention necessary since what she had wasn't going to cut it.

And now, here they were, sitting in the plush cabin of Phoenix's private plane, buckled in and ready for takeoff. William, the flight attendant — at least that's what she assumed he was — even came by and offered them drinks while the pilots finished with their procedures. After downing a vodka and Sprite, she was feeling a tad more relaxed than she had since that morning.

But her interest continued to be drawn to a door at the back of the plane.

"Relax," Tarik told her, placing his hand over hers. "I promise, once we're in the air, we'll make sure you get very acquainted with that room."

Heat pooled in her core at his words. Swallowing, she sat back in her seat and tried to relax. She was strung tight, a nervous energy pulsing through her. So much had happened, and the day wasn't even over yet. Now they were about to take a flight to New York, of all places, so they could go to a hockey game. It seemed surreal.

The captain's voice came over the speaker, and he introduced himself and the co-pilot. He rattled off something about the temperature and the flight time, but Mia blocked it all out as she closed her eyes and willed the plane to get in the air.

She wasn't nervous about flying.

That wasn't it.

No, she was anxious to… Well, she was anxious to join the Mile-High Club, as Tarik had put it.

Twenty minutes passed before the captain's voice came back on, informing them that they were free to move around the cabin.

"Ready?" Phoenix asked, leaning over her and unbuckling her seat belt.

She hadn't even seen him stand up.

Mia slid her hand into his, her nerves rioting as she followed him to the back of the plane. She shot a look over her shoulder to see that Tarik was behind her, a sexy smirk fixed on his sinfully delicious mouth.

Once inside the room, Mia looked around.

Well, there was a bed. That was about all that fit in there, but it was definitely big enough to fit the three of them, and that was all that mattered. Despite being on the cramped side, the room was nicely decorated. Very similar to Phoenix's condo with its black-and-chrome theme. There was a giant television on the wall.

"Did you want to watch TV?" Tarik asked, pressing up against her back.

Mia shook her head. Television was the last thing on her mind.

Phoenix had climbed onto the bed, fully dressed. He looked as though he didn't plan to remove his clothes.

"I want you naked," Phoenix told her. "Then I want you to crawl up here and sit on my face so I can taste your sweet little pussy."

A rush of heat flooded her, and Mia was pretty sure her panties were now wet.

Tarik confirmed that fact a moment later when he managed to rid her of her clothes. As her panties slid down her legs, his fingers eased between her thighs.

"So wet," he mumbled against her ear. "I can't wait to slide into your pussy and feel your juices coat my cock."

Mia outwardly shivered.

Phoenix crooked his finger at her, and Mia complied, crawling up on the bed. She allowed her hands to roam over him as she went. It didn't matter that he was fully clothed; she could still see the outline of his rigid erection beneath his black slacks. She wanted to unzip them and feel the silky hardness of him against her hand, but he had other ideas.

"Sit on my face."

Mia continued crawling up the length of his body until she was perched above his head. There wasn't a headboard to hold on to, so she braced herself against the wall. Good thing, too. When Phoenix's tongue grazed her slit, she jerked, the sensation sending chills racing down her spine. He moaned and the vibrations lit her up.

"Ride his face," Tarik instructed.

Mia realized he was behind her, also fully clothed. He was straddling Phoenix's chest, his hands sliding up to cup her breasts while he pressed against her back, his mouth to her ear.

"Do you like when Phoenix licks your pussy?"

"Yes," she said on a moan.

"If he's like me, he dreams about it, craves it," Tarik told her.

"Oh, God," Mia cried out, grinding down on Phoenix's mouth, trying to get him where she wanted him. He was teasing her, flicking her clit, sliding his tongue into her, but never enough of either.

The next thing she knew, Mia was on her back, both men kneeling on the bed, staring at her.

"What'd you do that for?" she asked Phoenix.

Phoenix smiled. "You had too much control. I want to play with you for a while."

Mia groaned, but that was quickly replaced with a sigh when Phoenix used his fingers to spread her swollen lips. She watched as Tarik leaned down and speared her with his tongue.

They ganged up on her, alternating, driving her mad as they licked her clit, teased her with their fingers, their tongues, their teeth. "Please," she begged. "Please make me come."

"She's so sweet when she begs," Phoenix said. "And because you asked so nicely…"

Phoenix inched up the bed, and Mia grabbed his head, pulling him to her and thrusting her tongue into his mouth. Her body bucked when Tarik sucked her clit into his mouth, tormenting her as he thrust two fingers into her. And then…

"Oh, God, yes!" Mia screamed, not caring whether the flight attendant could hear her. Her orgasm sent shockwaves of pleasure vibrating through her entire being, leaving her breathless and sated.

"Oh, we're not finished with you yet," Phoenix said as he shifted on the bed.

"Well, you're gonna have to do all the work," she told him sleepily.

"We plan to, baby."

Mia felt herself being lifted, and the next thing she knew, she was lying on top of Phoenix. He was still mostly clothed, which she found oddly sexy, but he'd unzipped his slacks and lowered them enough that his impressive erection sprang free. The fact that she was naked and they weren't... It was crazy hot.

"Put my cock inside you," Phoenix instructed.

Mia reached between them and guided Phoenix to her entrance.

"Slide down on me."

Mia did as instructed, her body stretching to take him inside. She couldn't keep her eyes open as the exquisite pleasure resurfaced, flooding her as he filled her.

"Are you ready?" Phoenix asked.

She had no idea what he was asking, but she nodded anyway.

Phoenix gripped her hips as he fucked her. His strokes were slow and deep.

But then he pulled out completely. Mia was about to ask what he was doing when she felt more hands on her hips and then Tarik was filling her.

"Tarik." She moaned his name as he began sliding in and retreating, keeping his rhythm as slow as Phoenix's had been.

And then they switched again, keeping her hanging on the precipice. She had no idea how long they continued to fuck her, taking turns filling her, but her body began to hum, and she knew she needed more.

"Fuck me. Please!" she demanded.

Tarik was the one to grant her wish, gripping her hips and pounding into her, crushing her against Phoenix as he did, her body molded to them both.

"Oh ... yes ... please ... more..." She managed one word after every punishing thrust until she cried out one final time, her muscles locking as her orgasm gripped her, this one more powerful than the last.

Tarik's fingers dug into her flesh, and she felt him pulse as he came inside her.

The bed shifted and then Phoenix groaned. Mia could barely register what was happening; her body was liquid.

"Fuck yes, Tarik. Suck my cock. Make me come in your mouth."

Phoenix's words echoed through the bedroom, followed by grunts and groans of pure pleasure. Mia found his hands, held them flat to the bed as she rested atop him and let Tarik send him over the edge with his mouth.

When they were done, Mia didn't bother to move. She wasn't sure she would ever move again.

Chapter Forty-One

TARIK STARED UP at the hotel room ceiling, listening to Mia breathe softly beside him. They'd worn her out, and he figured she would likely sleep half the day away tomorrow. As for him, he couldn't even get his eyes to close. He wasn't sure he wanted to go to sleep.

He was too content. For the first time in… Possibly for the first time in his entire life, he felt whole.

They'd gone to the game, and although the Arrows hadn't won, the night had been one of the best of his life. All because the Kiss-Cam had landed on them and Mia had done something so shocking he was sure he would never in his life forget it. The stadium had gone wild afterward, and he could still see the replay in his head. When Phoenix had told her what she was supposed to do, she hadn't hesitated, planting a kiss on Phoenix's lips that had half the crowd going crazy. But then, she'd held up one finger — the universal signal for wait a minute — and then she'd turned to Tarik. When her lips had met his, everything in his world had come together in that moment.

Perfection.

She was perfection.

After the game, they'd grabbed a burger before heading back to the hotel, where she'd proceeded to rock both their worlds.

And now, as he lay in the dark, he couldn't sleep although his body was completely sated, his mind more at ease than ever even as Mia's words from earlier echoed in his head.

I know what it's like to have your heart shattered in a million tiny pieces, Tarik. It sucks big-time. But what I didn't know, until you and Phoenix, was that those tiny pieces could be pulled back together. Only when they do, the bond is stronger, more solid. That's what I feel for you and Phoenix. I love you both. With my whole heart. Every single one of the million tiny pieces that it once was. It's whole again. Stronger than ever.

Those words had resonated with him throughout the evening, and he realized how true they were. Growing up, he hadn't known what love was. His parents had hated each other, and they'd merely tolerated him. But he'd never let that define him, and he hadn't even realized it until Mia had pointed it out. He hadn't wanted to end up like them.

And now, he had more love than he knew what to do with.

"I love you," Mia whispered as she curled up against him, her head on his chest, her hand over his heart.

"I love you, too, love," Tarik said, the words coming easily this time.

"What am I? Chopped liver?" Phoenix asked, his voice rough with sleep. The bed shifted, and Phoenix's hand came to rest on Tarik's stomach.

"I love you, too," Mia told him.

"I love you, too, baby."

Tarik found Phoenix's hand and placed his atop it. "You own me, Tarik."

Tarik's heart swelled at the words. "You own me, too."

He smiled into the darkness. For whatever reason, he liked that they had their own term for how they felt about one another. It was still love; he knew that much. But it was more than that. Stronger, more resilient. The way Mia had described it.

"Just remember, I own you both. Now and forever," Mia whispered, followed by a little laugh that sent a jolt right through him. "Now go to sleep."

Epilogue

I RECENTLY HAD the honor of sitting down for an exclusive interview with the owner of the Austin Arrows, Phoenix Pierce. You might remember that just a year ago, Mr. Pierce moved into the role as full owner of the Arrows franchise after his father, Sidney Pierce, died of a heart attack.

Of course, I hadn't anticipated quite as exciting an interview as the one I received when I was originally contacted by the Arrows spokesman, Tarik Marx. Not only did I get to congratulate Phoenix on his team making it to the playoffs for the first time in six years, but I also got to congratulate him on something even more impressive. At least on a personal level, anyway.

Although we don't know which team will walk away with the coveted Stanley Cup just yet, the Arrows certainly have earned their chance. But I can tell you that Phoenix has already walked away a winner. It has officially been announced that Phoenix will be tying the knot in just a few hours.

But get this… Not only will Phoenix be marrying the lovely Mia Cantrell, he will also be sharing his vows with Mr. Marx as well. Yes, you heard me correctly, this threesome has taken the world by storm with their nontraditional relationship, and just as we are with the Austin Arrows, we'll be rooting for them all the way.

Stay tuned for my full interview with Phoenix tonight at ten.

As Tarik made his way into the room, Phoenix hit the button on the remote to turn off the television. Looking up, he smiled. "Is it bad luck to see the groom before the wedding?" Phoenix asked.

"Maybe," Tarik said, handing him a beer. "I figure as long as we don't see Mia, we're doing good."

"Between my mother and her mother, there's not a chance of that happening." They'd both been warned within an inch of their lives to stay away. Now, as they sat waiting in Johnathan Henry's man cave to be told when and where they were needed, Phoenix couldn't keep the smile from his face.

"Don't forget Alex. She's a bulldog when she wants to be."

"I wouldn't let her hear you say that," Phoenix said with a smirk.

"Trust me, I won't."

Phoenix nodded as Tarik dropped down onto the arm of the sofa. Tarik turned slightly and lifted his beer bottle up. "This is it. The first day of the rest of our lives."

"That it is," Phoenix said, clanking his bottle against Tarik's. "And what an amazing fucking way to kick it off."

Acknowledgments

My daughter recently brought it to my attention that I've written 26 books, at this point, 24 of those have been published. A little over 2 million words down (holy crap, 2 million!) and millions more to go. And with every single word comes a world of support from so many people. Although being a writer can be a solitary endeavor at times, it certainly isn't done in a vacuum.

I have to thank my family first, for putting up with my craziness. From my sudden outbursts when I think of something that needs to be added or when I question why one of the characters did what they did, to the strange hours that I keep and the days on end when I'm MIA because I'm under deadline or just engrossed in a story... Y'all are incredibly tolerant of me and for that, I am forever grateful. I love you with all that I am.

My street team – The Naughty & Nice Posse. Ladies, your daily pimping and support fills my heart with so much love. You are a blessing to me, each and every one of you.

My beta readers, Chancy and Denise. Ladies, I'm not sure thanks will ever be enough. However, not only are you the ones who catch the weird things and ask the bigger questions, you've both become my friends and you keep me going.

My copyeditor, Amy. Punctuation and grammar... well, that's not my strong suit. But it is yours and you are truly remarkable at what you do. You simply amaze me and I am so glad that I found you.

My agent, Mark. It's been a bumpy ride, I know. I'm not the easiest person to work with (just ask my husband), but we've made progress over the last year. Thank you for allowing me to be candid with you on what I want.

Blackstone Audio for investing in me and putting my books in audio.

My lawyer, Steve. Yes, you deserve a tremendous amount of credit. I'll be the first to say that contracts, trademarks, copyrights and the like confuse the hell out of me. If it weren't for you, I'd still be rereading all the fine print.

Jennifer at Enticing Journeys. You are incredible at what you do. The amount of work you put into making sure word gets out about my new releases allows me to celebrate with the readers.

Nicole Nation 2.0 for the constant support and love. This group of ladies has kept me going for so long, I'm not sure I'd know what to do without them.

And, of course, YOU, the reader. Your emails, messages, posts, comments, tweets... they mean more to me than you can imagine. I thrive on hearing from you, knowing that my characters and my stories have touched you in some way keeps me going. I've been known to shed a tear or two when reading an email because you simply bring so much joy to my life with your support. I thank you for that.

About Nicole Edwards

New York Times and *USA Today* bestselling author Nicole Edwards lives in Austin, Texas with her husband, their three kids, and four rambunctious dogs. When she's not writing about sexy alpha males, Nicole can often be found with her Kindle in hand or making an attempt to keep the dogs happy. You can find her hanging out on Facebook and interacting with her readers - even when she's supposed to be writing.

Website: www.NicoleEdwardsAuthor.com
Facebook:
www.facebook.com/Author.Nicole.Edwards
Twitter: www.twitter.com/NicoleEAuthor

Nicole also writes contemporary/new adult romance as Timberlyn Scott.
Website: www.TimberlynScott.com

By Nicole Edwards

The Alluring Indulgence Series
Kaleb

Zane

Travis

Holidays with the Walker Brothers

Ethan

Braydon

Sawyer

Brendon

The Club Destiny Series
Conviction

Temptation

Addicted

Seduction

Infatuation

Captivated

Devotion

Perception

Entrusted

The Devil's Bend Series
Chasing Dreams

Vanishing Dreams

The Dead Heat Ranch Series
Boots Optional

Betting on Grace

By Nicole Edwards (cont)

The Sniper 1 Security Series
Wait for Morning (coming 2015)

Stand Alone Novels
A Million Tiny Pieces

Writing as Timberlyn Scott
Unhinged
Unraveling
Chaos

18011039R00309

Made in the USA
Middletown, DE
18 February 2015